D1796881

Palgrave Studies in Nineteenth-Century Writing and Culture

General Editor: **Joseph Bristow**, Professor of English, UCLA

Editorial Advisory Board: **Hilary Fraser**, Birkbeck College, University of London; **Josephine McDonagh**, Kings College, London; **Yopie Prins**, University of Michigan; **Lindsay Smith**, University of Sussex; **Margaret D. Stetz**, University of Delaware; **Jenny Bourne Taylor**, University of Sussex

Palgrave Studies in Nineteenth-Century Writing and Culture is a new monograph series that aims to represent the most innovative research on literary works that were produced in the English-speaking world from the time of the Napoleonic Wars to the *fin de siècle*. Attentive to the historical continuities between 'Romantic' and 'Victorian', the series will feature studies that help scholarship to reassess the meaning of these terms during a century marked by diverse cultural, literary and political movements. The main aim of the series is to look at the increasing influence of types of historicism on our understanding of literary forms and genres. It reflects the shift from critical theory to cultural history that has affected not only the period 1800–1900 but also every field within the discipline of English literature. All titles in the series seek to offer fresh critical perspectives and challenging readings of both canonical and non-canonical writings of this era.

Titles include:

Eitan Bar-Yosef and Nadia Valman (*editors*)
'THE JEW' IN LATE-VICTORIAN AND EDWARDIAN CULTURE
Between the East End and East Africa

Heike Bauer
ENGLISH LITERARY SEXOLOGY
Translations of Inversions, 1860–1930

Katharina Boehm
BODIES AND THINGS IN NINETEENTH-CENTURY LITERATURE AND CULTURE

Katharina Boehm
CHARLES DICKINS AND THE SCIENCES OF CHILDHOOD
Popular Medicine, Child Health and Victorian Culture

Luisa Calè and Patrizia Di Bello (*editors*)
ILLUSTRATIONS, OPTICS AND OBJECTS IN NINETEENTH-CENTURY
LITERARY AND VISUAL CULTURES

Deirdre Coleman and Hilary Fester (*editors*)
MINDS, BODIES, MACHINES, 1770–1930

Eleanor Courtemanche
THE 'INVISIBLE HAND' AND BRITISH FICTION, 1818–1860
Adam Smith, Political Economy, and the Genre of Realism

Stefano Evangelista
BRITISH AESTHETICISM AND ANCIENT GREECE
Hellenism, Reception, Gods in Exile

Trish Ferguson (*editor*)
VICTORIAN TIME
Technologies, Standardizations, Catastrophes

Margot Finn, Michael Lobban and Jenny Bourne Taylor (*editors*)
LEGITIMACY AND ILLEGITIMACY IN NINETEENTH-CENTURY LAW,
LITERATURE AND HISTORY

F. Gray (*editor*)
WOMEN IN JOURNALISM AT THE FIN DE SIÈCLE
'Making a Name for Herself'

Jason David Hall and Alex Murray (*editors*)
DECADENT POETICS
Literature and Form at the British Fin de Siécle

Yvonne Ivory
THE HOMOSEXUAL REVIVAL OF RENAISSANCE STYLE, 1850–1930

Colin Jones, Josephine McDonagh and Jon Mee (*editors*)
CHARLES DICKENS, A TALE OF TWO CITIES AND THE FRENCH REVOLUTION

Jock Macleod
LITERATURE, JOURNALISM, AND THE VOCABULARIES OF LIBERALISM
Politics and Letters 1886–1916

Kirsten MacLeod
FICTIONS OF BRITISH DECADENCE
High Art, Popular Writing and the *Fin de Siècle*

Sean O'Toole
HABIT IN THE ENGLISH NOVEL, 1850–1900
Lived Environments, Practices of the Self

Tina O'Toole
THE IRISH NEW WOMAN

Virginia Richter
LITERATURE AFTER DARWIN
Human Beasts in Western Fiction 1859–1939

Laura Rotunno
POSTAL PLOTS IN BRITISH FICTION, 1840–1898
Readdressing Correspondence in Victorian Culture

Deborah. Shapple Spillman
BRITISH COLONIAL REALISM IN AFRICA
Inalienable Objects, Contested Domains

Laurence Talairach-Vielmas
FAIRY TALES, NATURAL HISTORY AND VICTORIAN CULTURE

Sara Thornton
ADVERTISING, SUBJECTIVITY AND THE NINETEENTH-CENTURY NOVEL
Dickens, Balzac and the Language of the Walls

Paul Young
GLOBALIZATION AND THE GREAT EXHIBITION
The Victorian New World Order

Palgrave Studies in Nineteenth-Century Writing and Culture
Series Standing Order ISBN 978–0–333–97700–2 (hardback)
(*outside North America only*)

You can receive future titles in this series as they are published by placing a standing order. Please contact your bookseller or, in case of difficulty, write to us at the address below with your name and address, the title of the series and the ISBN quoted above.

Customer Services Department, Macmillan Distribution Ltd, Houndmills, Basingstoke, Hampshire RG21 6XS, England

---

Fairy Tales, Natural History and Victorian Culture

Laurence Talairach-Vielmas

Professor of English, University of Toulouse, France

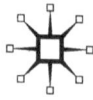

© Laurence Talairach-Vielmas 2014

All rights reserved. No reproduction, copy or transmission of this
publication may be made without written permission.

No portion of this publication may be reproduced, copied or transmitted
save with written permission or in accordance with the provisions of the
Copyright, Designs and Patents Act 1988, or under the terms of any licence
permitting limited copying issued by the Copyright Licensing Agency,
Saffron House, 6–10 Kirby Street, London EC1N 8TS.

Any person who does any unauthorized act in relation to this publication
may be liable to criminal prosecution and civil claims for damages.

The author has asserted his right to be identified as the author of this
work in accordance with the Copyright, Designs and Patents Act 1988.

First published 2014 by
PALGRAVE MACMILLAN

Palgrave Macmillan in the UK is an imprint of Macmillan Publishers Limited,
registered in England, company number 785998, of Houndmills, Basingstoke,
Hampshire RG21 6XS.

Palgrave Macmillan in the US is a division of St Martin's Press LLC,
175 Fifth Avenue, New York, NY 10010.

Palgrave Macmillan is the global academic imprint of the above companies
and has companies and representatives throughout the world.

Palgrave® and Macmillan® are registered trademarks in the United States,
the United Kingdom, Europe and other countries.

ISBN 978–1–137–34239–3

This book is printed on paper suitable for recycling and made from fully
managed and sustained forest sources. Logging, pulping and manufacturing
processes are expected to conform to the environmental regulations of the
country of origin.

A catalogue record for this book is available from the British Library.

A catalog record for this book is available from the Library of Congress.

For my little fairy, Margaux May, with love

Contents

Acknowledgements

As you enter the Natural History Museum of Toulouse, one of the first rooms when you start your journey through the Ages of the Earth welcomes you with a dark cave-like atmosphere. The circular room presents minerals that glitter in the dark, some of them illuminating the space with bright and uncanny colours. Along the wall on the right-hand side are cavities protected by glass panels. As you peer into them, all you can see at first is rock. Suddenly, one, then two, then dozens of little creatures hidden in recesses catch your attention. Children are generally the first to notice them, while the attention of their parents is focused on the minerals and gems locked up in the bigger display cases. The children, on the contrary, generally react as if the little people hidden in the geological cases belonged to the place, ready to hold their hands and embark with them upon a fantastic venture into natural history. The association of natural history exhibits and characters coming from the world of folklore or fairy tales (designed here to evoke chthonian divinities) is one of the many intriguing and fascinating details the visit holds in store.

My starting with the example of the Toulouse Natural History Museum is not coincidental. In 2008 the Museum welcomed a project – EXPLORA – that aimed to develop interdisciplinary research through a collaboration with the centre for English studies of the University of Toulouse (CAS – EA 801)/UTM). EXPLORA has since organized many events gathering scholars from different disciplines so as to examine the relationships between the sciences and the arts. From study days on the popularization of natural history in nineteenth-century children's literature and colloquia on Darwin and literature to international conferences on entomology ('Insects and Texts: Spinning Webs of Wonder', 4–5 May 2010), palæontology ('Lost and Found: In Search of Extinct Species', 31 March–2 April 2011) and oceanography ('Into the Deep: Monstrous Creatures, Alien Worlds', 14–15 June 2012), EXPLORA has shown not only how enriching looking at the interactions between science and the arts could be but also how crucial it is to look at objects and themes through multiple lenses.

As director of EXPLORA, having seen the project grow to a surprising size and attract more and more scholars from all over the world, and having learned so much from the meeting with other researchers, curators and all the people working behind the scenes, such as taxidermists, I would like to take the opportunity to thank all the people involved in the project, whether directly or peripherally. This book is the result of five years of collaboration with the Natural History Museum of Toulouse, a collaboration which has taught me about natural history, its objects and their display, its popularization and its audiences. Naturally, as a Victorianist, my research was done in libraries on the other side of the Channel. But I owe the place the inspiration for this book, which developed over the years, as I discovered fields and specimens unknown to me and learned to pronounce names that had sounded Greek until then.

Parts of Chapters 1, 2 and 7 started as papers presented at the Toulouse Natural History Museum ('From Margaret Gatty to Arabella Buckley: Victorian Women Popularisers of Science and Evolutionary Theory' (Darwin, 'Multiple States', 24 March 2009); 'Victorian Women Popularisers of Science and Ecology' ('Children's Literature and Environmental History', 2 April 2009); 'Extinct Creatures in Nesbit's Fiction' ('Lost and Found: In Search of Extinct Species', 31 March–2 April 2011); 'Bringing the Sea to the City: The Craze for Aquaria and the Popularisation of Marine Life in Victorian England' ('Into the Deep: Monstrous Creatures, Alien Worlds', 14–15 June 2012). 'From the Wonders of Nature to the Wonders of Evolution: Charles Kingsley's and Arabella Buckley's Nursery Fairies' appeared in Laurence Talairach-Vielmas (ed.), *Science in the Nursery: The Popularisation of Science in Britain and France, 1761–1901* (Newcastle: Cambridge Scholars Publishers, 2011), pp. 108–39. Shorter versions were also presented in the UK at conferences on women and science or on children's literature and ecology ('"How are we to enter the fairy-land of science?" The Wonders of the Natural World in Arabella Buckley's Popular Science Works for Children' ('Women and Science in the Nineteenth Century: Science Fiction and Science Education', Leeds Trinity and All Saints College, 27–8 June 2011); 'Victorian Children's Literature and the Natural World: Parables, Fairy Tales and the Construction of "Moral Ecology"' (International Conference IBBY (International Board of Books for Young People)/NCRCL (National Centre for Research in Children's Literature); 'Deep into Nature: Ecology,

Environment and Children's Literature' (Roehampton University, 15 November 2008), published in Jennifer Harding, Elizabeth Thiel Alison Waller (eds), *Deep into Nature: Ecology, Environment and Children's Literature* (Lichfield: Pied Piper Publishing, 2009), pp. 222–47. A shorter and earlier version of Chapter 6 also appeared in an essay, 'Rewriting *Little Red Riding-Hood*: Victorian Fairy Tales and Mass Visual Culture' (*Lion and the Unicorn* 33.3 (2009), pp. 259–81). I am grateful to Pied Piper Publishing, Cambridge Scholars Publishers and the editor of the *Lion and the Unicorn* for permission to use the material here.

Because all this work on Victorian natural history, its representations and its popularization would never have come into existence without EXPLORA, my deepest thanks go to the director of the Museum, Francis Duranthon, who believed in the project from the start, actively participated in all the events, and encouraged me to expand the research programme further. Moreover, the discoveries he enabled me to make in storage rooms, such as some lost specimens, in search of a story, spurred my reflections on natural history, literature and culture. I am also grateful to all the participants who contributed many fruitful discussions on science and literature and helped develop reflections on science and culture more generally.

Needless to say, there are many colleagues and friends who provided help, support and guidance as the project was evolving and the idea of this book blossoming. I am particularly indebted to two of them: Jack Zipes and John Pickstone, the former for encouraging me to work on Victorian fairy tales and always providing excellent advice, the latter for his interest in the crossings between science and literature and for making me think about science differently. Both, with their wide knowledge, immense wit and irresistible sense of humour, have been influential in my reflections and choice of material, and this book would have been different had my path never crossed theirs. Above all, both have always managed to galvanize me when I needed it most.

Over the five years of its writing, this book was also shaped by many of the discussions I had with MA students in class, some of them rediscovering fairy tales they had long forgotten, and whose intellectual curiosity informed my own reflections. As ever, I am very happy to thank some of my unflagging readers, Ellen Levy, Meg Ducassé and Carolyn Malden, who regularly and patiently read chapters, always providing very helpful comments and suggestions. It has also been a genuine pleasure to work on this book with the staff at Palgrave Macmillan, and I wish to thank the series editor, Joe Bristow, for his comments on the manuscript. Finally, I am also fortunate to have very dear friends who regularly remind me that there is a life outside academic life, more especially some with whom I share the same office. If I see them all less often than I would like, I would like to thank them sincerely – for the wonderful evenings, meals, books and laughter we share, in addition to the office.

This book is dedicated to my daughter, who has a passion for museums, natural history and fairy tales, and who is the greatest of gifts.

Introduction

That natural history fascinated the Victorians is a truism. Natural history was a fashionable activity and significantly participated in the construction of a bourgeois ethic: practising natural history implied healthy outdoor activity combined with intellectual engagement. The Victorians' taste for natural history launched more or less short-lived fads, collecting bugs, seaweed or shells, adding aquaria or butterfly cabinets to the middle-class drawing-room's heavy collection of pieces of furniture, while books by Philip Henry Gosse were on display in bookcases.[1] The same may be said concerning fairies. As the seminal works of Carole G. Silver (*Strange and Secret Peoples: Fairies and Victorian Consciousness*, 1999) and Nicola Bown (*Fairies in Nineteenth-Century Art and Literature*, 2001) have shown, fairies were part and parcel of the Victorian age, and the Victorians were experts in fairies and fairy lore far more than their predecessors or followers. Both studies highlight how fairies made up for the Victorians' own disenchanted world, giving them back 'the wonder and mystery modernity had taken away from the world';[2] they also show how fairies helped the Victorians voice social and political issues, in particular concerning the nature of woman and her legal status; they demonstrate how understanding the Victorians' relation with fairies is central to understanding 'their emotional responses to their own world'.[3] Moreover, as Silver and Bown have pointed out, the Victorians used, exhibited and delighted in giants and dwarfs, freaks and monstrous creatures extracted from the bowels of the earth, or microscopic animalcules – natural wonders which typified nature's marvellous potential, just like fairies, creatures which were part of the yet unelucidated mysteries of the earth, awaiting to be caught by the naturalist to be pinned and exhibited among other specimens.

This book deals with the way in which natural history was connected to the world of fairies, at a time when fairies changed faces,
some of them playfully wearing different masks. Indeed, the aim
of this book is to develop further Silver's and Bown's discussions
on fairies in the Victorian period so as to probe the links between
Victorian constructions of the natural world as enchanting and
enchanted, new definitions of the natural world brought about by
developments in natural history and the literary fairy tale, a genre
which, whether it featured fairies or not, was the object of many
experiments in the second half of the nineteenth century. In the
1860s, as fairies permeated Victorian culture, appearing in works of
art, scientific essays and even advertising, the publication of fairy
tales exploded. Fairy tales were revised in manifold different ways,
ultimately becoming as difficult to classify as the folk and fairy tales
anthropologists were striving to collect and order at the very same
time. In his last collection of tales, the folklorist Andrew Lang (1844–
1912) complained about the number of published fairy tales[4] which
targeted children more and more and, as a result, were gradually severing their connections with the (sometimes evil) fairies of folklore.
Writers such as George MacDonald (1824–1905), Mary Augusta de
Morgan (1850–1907), Dinah Mulock Craik (1818–87), Anne Isabella
Thackeray Ritchie (1837–1919), Juliana Horatia Ewing (1841–85),
Mary Louisa Molesworth (1839–1921) or Edith Nesbit (1858–1924)
became typically associated with fairy stories and fantasies playing
upon magic and fairy godmothers. More strikingly perhaps, Lewis
Carroll's *Alice* books epitomized Victorian fairy-tale experimentation.
Today, anthologies of Victorian fairy tales systematically include tales
by Ritchie, Ewing, Molesworth and Nesbit, especially when they seek
to bring to light the feminist discourses that these women writers'
revisions of literary fairy tales conveyed.[5] The latter often feature
fairies that are poles apart from the domesticated fairies that could
be seen in Victorian advertising – the toy-like or angel-like fairies
which served as purveyors of bourgeois discourse. Victorian experiments with the literary fairy tale also show that, although fairies
offered journeys away from the Victorians' own disenchanted world,
they were intricately linked to many aspects of modernity, be it
technological advances,[6] scientific ideas, or even socio and political
issues. However, such anthologies do not pay homage to the ways in
which these literary fairy tales are informed with natural historical

knowledge – a connection with natural history which suggested how the fairy tale became a relevant literary material to negotiate tensions at a time when nature became a much debated word. The idea behind this book, therefore, is that fairies encapsulated many different discourses which were running in parallel and sometimes overlapping, most especially whenever fairies and fairy tales touched upon the issue of nature. In other words, borrowing John Pickstone's terms, we might say that as the dominant 'natural historical way of knowing' the world attempted to 'record[–] variety and change',[7] the literary scene, generating many varieties of fairies and fairy tales, showed how nature and society were ruled by the same laws, often driven by the emergent sciences of life.

Pickstone's stress on the nineteenth-century 'natural historical way of knowing' and his focus on the significance of contemporary methods of science and the systems of meaning and values they produced lies at the basis of this study of Victorian fairy tales. Whether they were used to disseminate a discourse on natural history, to describe the natural world or to deal, say, with the nature of woman, fairies and fairy tales carried new ways of thinking about nature, conveying and/or developing the knowledge structures that were characteristic of the period. The works of Lyn Barber (*The Heyday of Natural History: 1820–1870*, 1980) and Lynn L. Merrill (*The Romance of Victorian Natural History*, 1989) have significantly underlined that the development of natural history in the Victorian period made it difficult to assign a fixed meaning to the term 'nature'. Nature could represent God's work or the British countryside, be peacefully observed in one's garden, dramatized in Romantic poetry, or be completely redefined by new theorizations on the earth and the origin of life.[8] Others, such as Barbara T. Gates (*Kindred Nature: Victorian and Edwardian Women Embrace the Living World*, 1998), have highlighted the part that women played in the development of natural history and their limitations as well, imposed upon them by Victorian gender constructions. For Gates, indeed, '[w]hat women said about nature was...determined in part by what men said about nature and by what men said about women; what women said about nature was predicated in part upon the ways in which they themselves were constructed *as* nature'.[9]

The very close relations between women and nature or women and natural history appear both in Victorian literary fairy tales and popular science books, publishing spheres in which women often played a key part. Tellingly, many of them were both writers of fairy tales and naturalists, active participants in both the literary and scientific fields, such as Juliana Horatia Ewing, for instance. This is the reason why this book aims to explore the ways in which natural knowledge was shaped and disseminated in Victorian culture through exploring the interaction between the scientific and literary fields. Indeed, as this book will show, not only did fairies and fairy tales help naturalists and scientists frame new visions of the natural world but also shifts in the understanding of natural history, especially after 1859, had a significant impact on fairy stories and Victorian experiments with the literary fairy tale. This idea is obvious in Victorian art, as Bown and Silver have argued: Victorian art uses fairies and fairy lands in order to offer viewers an escape into romantic natural worlds. The paintings bring home Victorian romanticism: on the canvasses fairies merge with the natural world, hide in trees or behind mushrooms. But Victorian fairy painting, as exemplified by the works by John Anster Fitzgerald (1819?–1906), Joseph Noel Paton (1821–1901), John George Naish (1824–1905) or Richard Dadd (1817–86), is above all characterized by an attempt at combining fairy art with 'truth to nature',[10] reconciling reality and fantasy in detailed descriptions of fairies in a natural environment. In so doing, Victorian fairy art testifies to the period's association of fairy lands with natural wonders. On the canvasses, the wonderful is often evoked through plays on different scales, especially as fairies share their land with other animals and insects, from birds and squirrels to snails, beetles and butterflies. But if Victorian art disseminated and was influenced by developments in natural history, what about the literary fairy tale? It is partly to answer this question that this book aims to prolong discussions started in or developed in ground-breaking studies of Victorian fairies and Victorian natural history, in order to explore cultural practices through which new representations of nature and the natural world were popularized – an exploration which requires an investigation of narratives beyond genre categories and even disciplinary divides. To do so, this book will bring together narratives dealing with natural history, in particular popular science works aimed at (women and) children and literary fairy tales. Building upon Silver and Bown's focus on materials for adults, I will examine the fruitful dialogue between natural history and literature which marked the Victorian period, showing how the rhetorical strategies of works of popularization borrow from fairy tales, just as how Victorian fairy tales borrow from natural history to illustrate modern wonders and talk about nature. As I will highlight, the interpenetration of the scientific field and literary and artistic culture can be grasped through following the circulation of images and metaphors between these fields. While natural history was redefining the term 'nature' and permeating culture in the second half of the nineteenth century, a series of motifs borrowed from literary culture helped naturalists form a language that could convey emerging theories about nature. The circulation of such images, metaphors and motifs used to define or redefine nature and give shape to new representations of knowledge, I argue, could best be gauged through tracing references or allusions to fairies and motifs associated with the fairy tale. The blend of fictional and non-fictional narratives that this book examines should provide a survey of nature in the second half of the nineteenth century and make explicit how natural history, through its study of nature, highlighted questions related to gender and, more generally even, human identity – an issue which permeates many a Victorian fairy tale. By analysing the intersections between different types of narratives and different discourses and by looking at both types of texts from a literary point of view, therefore, I aim to show how they all shared a cultural background.

The sources I have selected were all addressed to a middle-class readership and most of them aimed at a child audience.[11] The successful reception of books by writers like Charles Kingsley (1819–75), in the field of science popularization, or the strong association of figures like Mary Augusta de Morgan, Anne Isabella Thackeray Ritchie, Mary Louisa Molesworth or Edith Nesbit with the literary fairy tale, all of them known for their collections of fairy tales, explains why their narratives are investigated here. Others, perhaps less celebrated or remembered today, such as Harriet Childe-Pemberton, are studied because their fairy tales were overt adaptations of classical fairy tales to the Victorian modern world. Other famous children's writers only appear marginally, as figures such as Margaret Gatty (1809–73), the founder of one of the most famous Victorian middle-class children's magazines for girls, *Aunt Judy's Magazine*, also known for her popularization of natural history (best illustrated by her (anti-Darwinian)

Parables from Nature (1855–71)), have not much in common with the modern rewritings that de Morgan, Ritchie or Molesworth proposed and which typified Victorian experiments with literary fairy tales. Still, many references to Victorian popularizers of natural history and children's writers will be found throughout the book so as to offer an overview of the type of literary material that the Victorians and their children could read and which touched upon contemporary discourses on the natural world.

Furthermore, as this book will point out, Victorian fairies and fairy tales were strongly connected to the theory of evolution, and the disappearance of fairies at the end of the nineteenth century – or the nostalgia which fairies conjured up at the turn of the century – increasingly shaped fairies and fairy tales as extinct creatures. As the victims of massive industrialism and of the destruction of natural ecosystems, they illustrated and encapsulated the growing awareness of the world as an ecosystem – Darwin's vision of a cruel environment where the weakest could not survive. Fairies were therefore at the heart of cultural preoccupations; fairies and fairy stories were part of the debate on the origin of the earth and of humans on earth, and the constant revision and revamping of fairies and fairy tales throughout the period can help us understand the Victorians' responses to a daily imperilled natural world. As I will show, the changing definitions of the word 'nature', following the metamorphosis of the face of England and the view of the world more generally, climaxed with the publication of Charles Darwin's *On the Origin of Species by Means of Natural Selection, or the Preservation of Favoured Races in the Struggle for Life* in 1859. The naturalist and collector's book gave to the wonders of the natural world new meanings which the Victorians tried to grasp and appropriate. Like the worlds of fairies, moreover, evolutionary theory could not be visualized, casting empirical science away to favour a radically different scientific method. Though epitomizing science's materialism, Darwin's vision of nature, as Gillian Beer and George Levine have underlined, 'radical[ly] *re*-enchant[ed]'[12] the natural world. This notion of *re*-enchantment is crucial, because it encapsulates how Darwin, inspired by other thinkers, such as Charles Lyell, for instance, developed a new scientific method which gave some room to the invisible or the impossible – opening up the world of nature to a new type of marvellous, possibly inhabited by fairies, as popularizers of natural history suggested. Therefore, though '[n]ature had to be objectified'[13] and even if the Victorians were progressively moving away from a romantic perception of nature, science nonetheless pointed out the natural world's marvels.

In addition, nineteenth-century natural history, and the natural sciences more generally, strongly impacted contemporary definitions of and attempts at framing human nature. Darwin's work suggested that humans were part of the natural world. Thus, as the Victorians classified, represented or defined a nature that they sought to understand and control (whether nature meant the natural environment or *human* nature), they re-evaluated themselves in the process. Indeed, the theory of evolution spurred anxieties related to humans' place within the ecosystem. As a result, Bown contends, 'to look at the natural world was also to see the human there'.[14] Human nature had to be envisaged as belonging to the animal kingdom, endowing the term 'nature' with new meanings and ambiguities. Thus, not only was humans' supremacy over the natural world slightly jeopardized but also humans became as well subjected to scientific analysis. As this book contends, fairies and fairy tales particularly brought to the fore these new definitions of nature, either by showing how fairies were miniature versions of humans or by enabling insights into the construction of human nature – and most especially *woman* nature.

This study will start with an exploration of popular science works on natural history so as to underline how conceptions of nature and of the natural world fused with the marvellous or the fantastic. As Chapter 1 shows, natural history, as a scientific discipline, stands at the crossroads between science and literature: it deals with facts but is loaded with affect, and natural history books were often 'motley in content and tone',[15] appealing to the rhetoric of wonder and invoking fairies and the marvellous from the cover on, as suggested by such titles as *Wonders of the Sea Shore* (1847) or *Marvels of Pond Life* (1861).[16] This particular rhetoric recalls, of course, the audience these books aimed at, mainly children and women – readers to whom fairy tales were also at the time generally addressed. Allusions to fairies and marvels ensured the narrative's attractiveness and promised a mix of instruction and entertainment which fitted well with Victorian theories of education. But, as the first two chapters suggest, moreover, the way in which Victorian fairies often managed to reconcile the supernatural and the natural, or the invisible and the visible, could serve other causes.

My starting with the Reverend Charles Kingsley, famous for his popular science books and children's fiction, is not unmotivated, for his books typify the shift from a romantic perception of the natural world to a more 'Victorian' construction of nature. With the Evangelical Revival, the Victorians' interest in or fascination with the natural world was accompanied by a new ethical code which stressed morality and emphasized natural theological perceptions of nature, as defined by William Paley (1743–1805).[17] Significantly (or, perhaps, surprisingly), this view of nature charged with religiosity was even more highlighted in popular science books which followed the publication of Darwin's *On the Origin of Species*, fairies and the fairy-like playing, in fact, subtle parts to reconcile the findings of material science with the tenets of Evangelicalism. As Chapter 1 shows, therefore, Charles Kingsley's writings typify the difficulties that popularizers encountered in the years that preceded and followed the advent of evolutionary theory. The chapter examines some of Kingsley's most famous popular science works as well as his well-known fairy tale, *The Water-Babies: A Fairy Tale for a Land Baby* (1863), the tale standing out as a good illustration of how developments in natural history informed the literary scene. The analysis brings to light similarities in Kingsley's treatment of fairies and his representation of new ways of shaping the natural world through images and tropes which permeate many fairy tales of the 1860s, as I show throughout the following chapters. The way in which nature was aestheticized in Victorian popular science books is examined further in Chapter 2, which deals with later examples of popular science works for children and focuses on Arabella Buckley's use of fairies and fairy tales. Arabella Buckley's popular science works (*The Fairy-Land of Science* (1879), *Life and Her Children* (1880) and *Winners in Life's Race, or the Great Backboned Family* (1883)) recurrently use fairies to mediate science, her works particularly stressing the role of imagination and bringing to light the 'narrative quality of science'.[18] As I explain, Buckley's use of the visual to mediate evolutionary theory is revealing of contemporary scientific methods. Like Charles Kingsley, Buckley attempted to deal with the mid-nineteenth-century redefinition of nature caused by the advent of evolutionary theory and to reconcile science with religion. While Kingsley used the wonders of nature to trope a divinely ordered nature in children's imagination, however, Buckley hinged her scientific method on natural theology to illustrate evolutionary theory. As I underline, in both Kingsley's and Buckley's writings, the world of nature is filled with wonderful creatures still unknown to humans, and the images and tropes they use show how wonder and religion are not only compatible with science but also essential to the scientific method.

If the first two chapters recall stereotypes of Victorian fairies inhabiting a pastoral and romantic natural world, they also highlight the extent to which fairies and fairy tales expressed fears and anxieties related to the changing world and changing conceptions of the natural world. Because, as already argued, Victorian fairies were more often than not urban creatures linked with industrial power and scientific progress, the following three chapters take us into urban communities, where fairies are invited to represent the marvels of technological advances and the visual rhetoric informing new scientific methods. Indeed, in Victorian art fairies merge with the natural world; they sit on flowers and lie in birds' nests; and Fairyland seems miles away from the noisy, polluted and bustling modern urban world. In the literary field, however, though water sprites sometimes haunt rivers and fairies dance in fairy rings,[19] many mid- and late Victorian literary fairy tales are rooted in a modern world the better to question contemporary issues, whether social, political or cultural. For, even though Victorian revisions of classical fairy tales often reflected the Victorians' own dreams of better worlds,[20] they were also meant to denounce industrialization, utilitarianism and materialism, from John Ruskin's *The King of the Golden River, or the Black Brothers* (1841) to Oscar Wilde's 'The Happy Prince' (1888) at the end of the century. In fact, industrial England, which discreetly looms in the background of a few fairy paintings,[21] is frequently prominent in Victorian fairy tales, acting as a backdrop to these tales' social and political discourse. Many of the fairy tales aimed at children, moreover, make explicit that scientific materialism and scientists' construction of nature and humans have divorced humans from nature. Their discourse, as the following chapters explain, is informed with contemporary ways of knowing, ordering and analysing the world, showing an obsession with the categorization of humans and animals or the classification of species.

Thus, the three Victorian fairy tales I examine next engage with natural history through showing heroines trying to understand, survey or control nature. Whether they are faced with a body framed by natural sciences and defined as mechanical or animal, or whether they are themselves amateur naturalists, the Victorian princesses, Cinderellas or Little Red Riding Hoods illustrate the influence of natural history on the literary fairy tale. The fairy tales all typify how new definitions of the natural world impacted gender constructions: women, in particular, the fairy tales suggest, seem to embody the forces of nature, rendering uncannily ambiguous the images of the light and asexual domestic fairies extolled in Victorian culture. Indeed, the fairy-tale revisions that Chapters 3, 4 and 5 explore compare nature and the development of humans' control over nature through technology and science with *woman's* nature. They show how fairy tales frequently bring to the fore the issue of woman's relationship with nature, a relationship which led women in the nineteenth century to be more and more constructed '*as* nature', to borrow Barbara T. Gates's words again. The tales record the heroines' initiatory journeys, mapping out young girls' growth and transformation into women. In doing so, the writers constantly question the passage from nature to culture. As Chapters 3, 4 and 5 emphasize, the rewriting of traditional fairy tales proved to be a new approach to the study of nature for a few Victorian women writers. In Chapter 3, Mary de Morgan uses the fairy tale to examine the clash between nature and humans' environment which the development of industrialism entailed. In 'A Toy Princess' the world of magic, dreams, wish fulfilments, pleasure and feelings, on the one hand, and the world of modernity and civilization, on the other, are clearly set apart from each other. The civilized world is a highly repressive land where women die of consumption. With the help of her fairy godmother, the princess is sent by the sea and replaced by a manufactured toy princess. But the automaton, admired and praised by the Court, is not just a means of deriding the Victorian feminine ideal. By drawing upon the transformations related to mechanistic science, humans' obsessive control of nature ultimately turning humans themselves into machines, standardized and moved by regular laws, the fairy tale also points out how dangerous scientific and technological advances may be. To do so, it plays with the clichéd link between women and nature the better to enhance the widening gap between humans and the natural world, using woman, most especially associated with the forces of nature in the second half of the nineteenth century, to convey de Morgan's discourse on mankind's changing relationship with nature and with the powers of nature.

Furthermore, if in the period of mass transparency glass played a key part in the construction of bourgeois identity, metaphorizing purity and lack of secrecy and particularly defining ideal femininity,[22] glass was also involved in the Victorians' relationship with nature, most especially at a time when the greater availability of glass enabled the urban middle classes, exiled from nature, to transport nature within their homes. In the following chapter, fairies and fairy-tale motifs blend the marvels of nature with those of industry. Chapter 4, develops further the Victorians' merging of discourses on femininity with discourses on nature by using the Crystal Palace as a giant glasshouse in which the young fairy-tale heroine is artificially grown. As a matter of fact, if the Crystal Palace triggered natural history curiosity the building of the Palace itself was also related to nature and nature's wonderful metamorphoses: the project resulted, indeed, from the engineer and gardener Joseph Paxton's experiments with glasshouses to host his 'hothouse lily', or *Victoria regia*, which led him to imagine a building inspired by the ribbed undersides of the flower's giant leaf-pads. In Anne Isabella Thackeray Ritchie's 1868 rewriting of Charles Perrault's classical fairy tale, not only is Cinderella an amateur naturalist but also the tale compares the modern woman to exotic flowers artificially grown in glasshouses, glass mediating the transformation of woman from nature to culture. As the chapter shows, as the rewriting plays upon the blurring of the distinctions between the organic and the inorganic, or between the vegetable, the animal and the human, associating magic powers with greenhouse cultivation, it lays bare contemporary constructions of women as a potentially dangerous species – an idea patent as well in Hans Christian Andersen's fairy tale, 'The Dryad', published at the same time, and which also plays upon the glass motif the better to align woman with natural specimens, as shall be seen.

The Victorians' obsession with the control of nature is explored as well in Chapter 5. 'Little Red Riding Hood', a classical fairy tale which figures a little girl who trusts her own nature and indulges in sensual pleasures, is perhaps one of the fairy tales which best encapsulates woman's relationship with nature. Perrault's version

highlights the restraining of natural instincts, since a little girl is punished for indulging in sensuality and must learn to discipline herself
and to suppress her instincts. Anne Isabella Thackeray Ritchie's 'Little Red Riding Hood' (1868) and Harriet Louisa Childe-Pemberton's
'All My Doing; or Red Riding-Hood Over Again' (1882) rewrite
Perrault's tale, underlining in so doing the links between classical
fairy tales' stress on nature and humans' control over nature and the
Victorian modern world. In Childe-Pemberton's tale, the forest has
been replaced by a train journey. The train epitomized, perhaps more
than any other machine, the Victorians' changing environment.
Through the motif of the train and its links with the metamorphosis
of nature, the tale parallels the speed of travel with the young girl's
maturation into a woman. But Childe-Pemberton's revision also uses
the motif of the train as an image of the conquest of nature the better to associate it with her revamped wolf who conceals his wildness
beneath manners and clothes – visual codes typifying the gentleman,
which counteract any physiognomical reading of his character. This
effacement of 'nature', I argue, is revealing of changing definitions of
bestiality and of mankind's attempts at controlling natural forces in
the second half of the nineteenth century.

The beastly nature of man/humans and humans' potential to
endanger nature lies at the heart of the last two chapters, which
turn towards late Victorian and early Edwardian discourses on the
protection of nature. Chapter 6 deals with a late Victorian fantasy
which borrows from the conventions of natural history books and
illustrations and connects fairies with a pre-industrial world. By playing on the storyteller's link with the natural world, on the one
hand, and on the relationship between women and nature in classical fairy tales, such as the Brothers Grimm's, for instance, on the
other hand, Mary Louisa Molesworth's fantasy *Christmas-Tree Land*
(1884) draws a sharp line between the civilized and cruel world and a
natural environment which invites children to protect nature. Moreover, Molesworth's merging of contemporary constructions of nature
and physiological definitions of women's nature develops further
the feminist messages underlined in Chapters 3, 4 and 5. In fact,
Mrs Molesworth's fantasy emphasizes women's closeness to nature
to teach the children of the fantasy how to deal with their own
'nature' – metaphorized throughout the fantasy through the wild
territory of their imagination.

As argued in most of the chapters, the technological developments of the nineteenth century and the change from a rural way
of life to an urban world peopled with factories and iron buildings
explain why fairies, as natural forces, were threatened by extinction.
The development of technology in the nineteenth century seemed,
indeed, to be to blame for the fairies' departure, as the geologist
and folklorist Hugh Miller argued in *The Old Red Sandstone* (1841),[23]
a popular science book on geology. For Nicola Bown, the vision
of Fairyland as 'an Arcadia for the industrial age'[24] resulted from
England's massive urbanization and transformation of rural landscapes. The Industrial Revolution, leading to a widespread exploitation and destruction of nature, had radically altered humans' relation
to nature, and such examples of fairies becoming extinct and leaving
England, found both in fiction and in popular science works, revealed
how fairies helped the Victorians illustrate and voice human disre-
gard for ecology and the environment.[25] Chapter 7 on Edith Nesbit's
Five Children and It (1902) offers an ultimate look at the relationship
between fairies, fairy tales and nature at the close of the Victorian
period. Nesbit hinges her tale on a fairy as a natural creature likely to
be collected by the children as an unknown specimen. Nesbit's fairy –
a Psammead, or 'sand fairy' – is an endangered specimen which the
children dig out of a quarry. Nesbit's hint at natural history amateurs and collectors, going on excursions in search of shells, ferns or
other collectibles, works in tandem with allusions to the evolution
of the earth, its changes and the reality of extinction. In fact, *Five
Children and It* plays on 'Otherness' and the mapping of the imperial
expansion, pointing out fears related to the collections of specimens
regarded as uncivilized and primitive. In so doing, Nesbit aligns freaks
of nature and primitive people with children, suggesting that the
Psammead is a survival of the distant past. As the chapter shows,
as a primitive being endowed with supernatural powers, Nesbit's
Psammead is prototypical of post-Darwinian literature, and exemplifies how magic and transformation were used to negotiate new views
of the natural world.

Through the analysis of the relationship between fairies, the fairy
tale and natural history, this book reveals how fairies and fairy tales
alike pointed out new ways of *thinking* about nature and the natural
world. The narratives under study, be they fiction or non-fiction, all
unite fairies with the search for a language to express a new reality – a

modern world which to many Victorians often looked stranger than fiction. It is this language that this book, by looking beyond genre categories, tries to uncover, tracing, in so doing, a part of the history of the mediation of knowledge about nature in the second half of the nineteenth century, and showing how the mediation of this new knowledge about nature and the circulation of knowledge structures ultimately contributed to the Victorians' awareness of environmental issues.

1
From the Wonders of Nature to the Wonders of Evolution: Charles Kingsley's Nursery Fairies

The romance of natural history

> The charm lay here, that it was *unknown*: the imagination can people the unexplored with whatever forms of beauty or interest it pleases...One of the greatest pleasures of the out-of-door naturalist depends upon this principle. There is so great variety in the objects which he pursues, and so much uncertainty in their presence at any given time and place, that hope is ever on the stretch. He makes his excursions not knowing what he may meet with; and, if disappointed of what he had pictured to himself, he is pretty sure to be surprised with something or other of interest that he had not anticipated. And much more does the romance of the unknown prevail to the natural history collector in a new and unexplored country.[1]

As Philip Henry Gosse highlights, surprise, wonder and expectation partake of the Victorian naturalist's work as he discovers *terra incognita* and unknown species – even in England. The naturalist's quest, close to that of the knight of romance, seems to inhabit a fantastic world where magical spells may be cast at any time. Gosse's *Romance of Natural History* (1860) makes explicit how, as unknown natural specimens were discovered in England, brought back from foreign countries, or even revealed by the microscope, nature constantly flirted with the impossible and the marvellous. His popular science book epitomizes how naturalists and natural history writings emphasized the endless possibilities and bizarre forms of nature, clothing the natural world with wonderful and fanciful garbs paradoxically as naturalists and scientists unveiled its secrets. As this book will underline, the rhetoric and images of Victorian natural history permeated Victorian culture, and Philip Henry Gosse's *Romance of Natural History* is a significant case in point to start our survey of the narratives that popularizers of natural history were offering readers at the time. The title of Gosse's book makes explicit how natural history was seen as fraught with imaginative potential, nature looking like 'the enchanted imaginings of an author in a medieval romance', in Lynn Merrill's terms.[2] This imaginative way of looking and defining the natural world, I argue, paved the way for powerful connections between natural history and fairy stories which particularly developed in the second half of the nineteenth century, even if they had long been part of discourses on nature and had especially been used by popularizers and children's educators in the early nineteenth century. In his preface, Gosse contrasts several ways of studying natural history: learning facts, 'statistics as harsh and dry as the skins and bones in the museum where it is studied', in Dr. Dryasdust's way, observing nature, 'statistics as fresh and bright as the forest or meadow where there are gathered in the dewy morning', or looking at nature through an aesthetic glass, 'with the emotions of the human mind, – surprise, wonder, terror, revulsion, admiration, love, desire, and so forth'.[3] Choosing the aesthetic lens, Gosse proposes to his readers a journey as romantic as a poem by Wordsworth.[4] Nature becomes animated, vibrant with a mysterious energy. Gosse's description of nature teems with personifications: the newts 'have donned their vernal attire, and appear veritable holiday beaux, arrayed in the pomp of ruffled shirt and scarlet waistcoat'; creatures are 'willing', 'cheerful',[5] or 'lovely' and have 'laughing blue eyes',[6] like the germander speedwell.

Gosse's sensational style is a significant instance of the ways in which science popularizers attempted to make the world of nature more appealing. His narrative transforms a natural history lesson into an expedition into unknown lands, following in the footsteps of famous entomologists such as William Kirby (1759–1850), travel writers like Thomas Witlam Atkinson (1799–1861), naturalists like Alfred Russel Wallace (1823–1913) and Charles Darwin (1809–82), or explorers, such as David Livingstone (1813–73). Homely England becomes an exotic land hosting natural mysteries and rare species where the amateur naturalist can assert his national pride through capturing, say, a swallow-tail moth:

> We come back from scenes so gorgeous, to quiet, homely England. How pleasant to the schoolboy, just infected with the entomological mania, is an evening hour in June devoted to 'mothing!' An hour before sunset he had been seen mysteriously to leave him, carrying a cup filled with a mixture of beer and treacle. With this he had bent his steps to the edge of a wood, and with a painter's brush had bedaubed the trunks of several large trees, much to the bewilderment of the woodman and his dog. Now the sun is going down like a glowing coal behind the hill, and the youthful savant again seeks the scene of his labours, armed with insect-net, pill-boxes, and a bull's-eye lantern. He pauses in the high-hedged lane, for the bats are evidently playing a successful game here, and the tiny gray moths are fluttering in and out of the hedge by scores. Watchfully now he holds the net; there is one whose hue betokens a prize. Dash! – Yes! it is in the muslin bag; and, on holding it up against the western sky, he sees he has got one of the most beautiful small moths – the 'butterfly emerald'. Yonder is a white form dancing backward and forward with regular oscillation in the space of a yard, close over the herbage. That must be the 'ghost-moth', surely! – the very same; and this is secured. Presently there comes rushing down the lane, with headlong speed, one far larger than the common set, and visible from afar by its whiteness. Prepare! Now strike! This prize, too, is won – the 'swallow-tail moth', a cream-coloured species, the noblest and most elegant of its tribe Britain can boast.[7]

Suspense, exclamations, imperative forms give pace to the prose, keeping the reader alert – or on the watch. We follow the naturalist through his expedition into the natural world; we vicariously experience his excitement; we discover the creatures as he notices them. The strange-looking insects become exotic specimens which must yield to the Western amateur scientist, as the reader experiences Wallace's 'delight' and the 'blood rush[ing] to [his] head',[8] for instance, when he encounters a grand new *Ornithoptera* in one of the isles on the eastern part of the Malay Archipelago.

Gosse's writing, at times violent and gothic, is 'atmospheric'.[9] Indeed, the prose becomes even darker when the narrator encounters a hyena, an 'obscene monster' whose 'demon[iac]' laugh – 'an unearthly sound' – rises above 'the gaunt heaps of stone'. Another soon appears, bearing in its jaws a human skull, and cracking and grinding the bones in its teeth.[10] In contrast, the romantic experience of Mr Thomas, the Bird-keeper at the Surrey Zoological Gardens, looks more like a fairy tale:

> By sunset he found himself many miles from London, in a field in which the newmade hay was ready for carrying. No human being was near, and so he threw two of the haycocks into one, at the edge of a wood, and 'mole-like, burrowed into the middle of the hay', just leaving his head exposed for a little fresh air, and free for any observations he might make under the light of the unclouded moon. In such a soft, warm, and fragrant bed, sleep soon overcame him, till he awoke with a confused idea of elves, sprites, fairies and pixies, holding their midnight dances around him.

It is the pastoral and romantic vision of nature here that conjures up the little people. Thomas's observation of the fern-owls, 'suddenly appear[ing] close to [him], as if by magic, and then shoot[ing] off, like meteors passing through the air', furthers the parallels with the fairy tale:

> The spectral and owl-like appearance, the noiseless wheeling flight of the birds as they darted by, would almost persuade one that he was on enchanted ground. Spell-bound, whilst witnessing the grotesque gambols of this singular bird, there only wanted Puck, with his elfin crew, attendant fairies, &c., in connexion with the aerial flights of the fern-owl, to have made it, as it was to me, a tolerably complete 'Midsummer Night's Dream', especially as my night-haunted imagination had not yet vanished. As it was, I was delighted with my nocturnal and beautiful scene from nature, and I wished at the time that some of our museum naturalists had been with me, to have shared the pleasure that I felt.[11]

The naturalist frames the natural world; his 'scene from nature' becomes a *tableau vivant* arousing the man's senses and turning him into a spectator the better to dramatize the landscape and its inhabitants. The reference to Shakespearian fairies is typically romantic and is strongly reminiscent of fairy painting, from Henry Fuseli's *Titania and Bottom* (*c*.1788–90) and William Blake's *Oberon, Titania and Puck with Fairies Dancing* (*c*.1786), to Victorian paintings, such as John Anster Fitzgerald's *Titania and Bottom* and Daniel Maclise's *Priscilla Horton as Ariel* (1838–9).[12] Moreover, Gosse's attempt at drawing parallels between humans' feelings and nature, as when sadness is experienced at the sight of autumn, 'in the decrepitude of age, and...verging towards death',[13] or hope in spring, strengthens a romantic construction of the natural world directly inspired by Blake's, Percy Bysshe Shelley's or Samuel Taylor Coleridge's Queen Mabs and pixies.[14] As shall be seen, however, with the advent of evolutionary theory, such a romantic construction of the natural world was remorphed little by little, popularizers using fairies not just to foregound the wonders of nature but also to tone down tensions and present to their audiences new scientific methods. The microscopic world of fairies that Victorian fairy painters and poets offered their readers,[15] the very same world that Gosse resurrects through his romantic prose, gradually turned into an invisible world that demanded imaginary reconstruction. Although the rhetoric of natural history remained loaded with affect and its language colourful, constantly aestheticizing or even sometimes sensationalizing nature, fairies came to embody polyvalent meanings, as we shall see.

Indeed, if fairies and fairy tales were frequently used throughout the Victorian period to focus on the wonders of nature or of science, they also aimed to express doubt and anxieties related to the implications of scientific knowledge. Before the publication of Charles Darwin's *On the Origin of Species*, the issue of extinction sometimes informed popular science books, a practice that often pointed to the popularizers' difficulties in explaining natural history without undermining revealed religion. With the publication of *On the Origin of Species* in 1859, the idea that the theory of evolution was something impossible to see, demanding therefore to be conceived through the use of the imagination and certainly not empirically verifiable, made the task of popularizers even more difficult. In the second half of the nineteenth century, fairies, connoting both 'the marvels and difficulties of science',[16] in Nicola Bown's terms, were often to be found whenever popularizers aimed to introduce their readers to the latest scientific developments and conceptions of the natural world. Because the latest scientific discoveries – and especially, of course, evolutionary theory – touched on the foundations of religious belief, their implications were to permeate Victorian culture, and were refracted in such popular science works. If science appeared to disenchant the world, scientists increasingly explaining away the mysteries of natural phenomena,[17] Victorian popularizers played a key part in presenting the natural world as enchanting and entrancing: although the wonders of science could account for the mysteries of nature, nature nonetheless remained a fairyland, and the explanatory power of (evolutionary) science, suggesting, for instance, that transformations of all kinds were always possible, could appear magical. Thus, beneath this contradictory construction of fairies and Fairyland one may discern not just the Victorians' ambivalence towards science but also the way science seemed to desecrate the world, robbing religion of its aura – or, worse, undermining religious faith itself.

As this chapter and the following underline, fairies entered popular science works, particularly in the second half of the nineteenth century,[18] as a substitute for God, recalling that, although scientists may attempt to explain nature away, nature retained some of its mysteries. In fact, throughout the nineteenth century fairies typically inhabited science books for women and children (both groups being audiences for which elementary science books were destined). In most of these books the magic and wonders of Fairyland rewrote the wonders of creation. Early science books for children had already called attention to the wonders of the natural world and highlighted its magical dimensions. Samuel Clark's *Peter Parley's Wonders of Earth, Sea, and Sky* (1837) or A. L. O. E.'s [C. M. Tucker's] *Fairy Know-A-Bit, or a Nutshell of Knowledge* (1866)) are significant examples. *Peter Parley's Wonders of Earth, Sea, and Sky* is punctuated with natural wonders or wonderful natural mechanisms and uses fairies and the marvellous in order to give a divine dimension to natural creations. The world of fancy is repressed through the presence of rational explanations for mysterious processes or appearances, however, as in the explanation of Aurora borealis, Ignes Fatui (Will-o'-the-Wisps), the 'spectre of the Brocken' and Fata Morgana (or *Fairy Illusion*).[19] In the last case, only, does the narrator equate the natural phenomenon with a fairy tale: 'The scene must look as wonderful as any thing you have read about in a fairy tale.'[20] Peter Parley merely deals with facts, making explicit that science is poles apart from the supernatural, the marvellous or the world of fancy, as when he describes Mary Anning's recent palæontological discoveries and advises his readers to visit the British Museum to see such specimens:

> I will show you a picture of what creatures were once living where the town of Lyme Regis, in Dorsetshire, now stands, and tell you something about their structure and their habits. You may perhaps be ready to think that a great deal of what we profess to know concerning them, is the work of fancy, but I can assure you that it is not, and by and by I will endeavour to convince you that there is reason enough for you to believe what I tell you.[21]

In fact, as we will see throughout this book, the meaning of fairies and Fairyland changed as anthropology started to examine folklore through an evolutionary lens: fairies increasingly fuelled scientific discourse as vehicles of a much more ambivalent discourse.[22] Books such as Rev. J. G. Wood's *Common Objects of the Country* (1858), the Kirby Sisters' works or Annie Carey's *The Wonders of Common Things* (1880) all draw parallels between the natural world and Fairyland: 'the moth [is] the epitome of every fragile, fairy-like beauty, and seems fitter for fairy tale, "once upon a time", than for this nineteenth century'.[23] Yet, the romantic language of wonder which informed such works, thus bridging the gap between science and religion and showing that 'the claims of science and salvation would be perfectly complementary',[24] gradually opened up new metaphoric possibilities. Indeed, in the decades that followed the publication of Darwin's *On the Origin of Species*, the marvellous came to represent contemporary scientific methods. This trend was particularly underlined in works of popularization aimed at children. For instance, John Cargill Brough's *The Fairy Tales of Science: A Book for Youth* (1859), just like Rev. H. N. Hutchinson's *The Autobiography of the Earth* (1890) and *Extinct Monsters: A Popular Account of Some of the Larger Forms of Ancient Animal History* (1892), laid emphasis on the proximity of myth and science to stimulate the readers' imagination as a means of developing their rational faculties.

Charles Kingsley (1819–75), and a few years later Arabella Buckley (1840–1929), were Victorian popularizers of science who offered their readers a highly aesthetic view of nature. Both constructed the natural world in terms fairly reminiscent of Gosse's *Romance of Natural History*, and their emphasis on the marvels of the natural world aimed to elicit an aesthetic response in their readers. Of course, their mid-century fairies may be understood as attempts to play with scale in order to adapt to the diminutive world of the child and to that of childhood more generally, through nursery motifs and tamed fairies. Indeed, Kingsley's fairies' diminutive world matches Susan Stewart's analysis of the miniature. As she contends, miniature books have been books destined for children since the fifteenth century and the miniature is a recurring device in children's literature. Because

> the child is in some physical sense a miniature of the adult, but also because the world of childhood, limited in physical scope yet fantastic in its content, presents in some ways a miniature and fictive chapter in each life history... We imagine childhood as if it were at the other end of a tunnel – distanced, diminutive, and clearly framed.[25]

As I shall demonstrate, however, Kingsley's, and later Buckley's, appeal to wonder through the motifs and characters of the literary fairy tale constitutes more than just a reduction of scale. Unlike Gosse's approach to nature in his *Romance of Natural History*, their use of fairies and fairy-tale motifs to enhance the beauty and wonders of the natural world is also, I will argue, a means of dealing with tensions, in particular those related to the crisis of faith which followed the publication of Darwin's *On the Origin of Species*. As John Cargill Brough writes in his *Fairy Tales of Science*, his intention is 'to divest the different subjects treated in it of hard and dry technicalities, and to clothe them in the more attractive garb of fairy tales – a task by no means easy'.[26] As we shall see, the Fairyland that Brough describes in his work, with its metamorphoses, invisible beings and extinct species seems magical not so much because it transposes scientific phenomena through the fairy-tale mode but because the use of the fairy tale mediates between magic and evolution, thus bringing to the fore new scientific methods resulting from the advent of Darwinism.

'A Mere Advertiser of Nature's Wonders':[27] fairy tales and children's education in Victorian England

It has been well remarked by a clever author, that bees are *geo-metricians*. The cells are so constructed as, with the least quantity of material, to have the largest sized spaces and the least possible interstices. The mole is a *meteorologist*. The bird called the nine-killer is an *arithmetician*, also the crow, the wild turkey, and some other birds. The torpedo, the ray, and the electric eel are *electricians*. The nautilus is a *navigator*. He raises and lowers his sails, casts and weighs anchor, and performs nautical feats. Whole tribes of birds are *musicians*. The beaver is an *architect, builder*, and *wood-cutter*. He cuts down trees and erects houses and dams. The marmot is a *civil engineer*. He does not only build houses, but constructs aqueducts, and drains to keep them dry. The ant maintains a regular standing army. Wasps are *paper manufacturers*. Caterpillars are *silk-spinners*. The squirrel is a *ferryman*. With a chip or a piece of bark for a boat, and his tail for a sail, he crosses a stream. Dogs, wolves, jackals, and many others, are *hunters*. The black bear, and heron are fishermen. The ants are *daylabourers*. The monkey is a *rope dancer*. Shall it, then, be said that any boy possessing the Godlike attributes of Mind and Thought with Freewill can only eat, drink, sleep, and play, and is therefore lower in the scale of usefulness than these poor birds, beasts, fishes, and insects? No! no! Let 'Young England' enjoy his manly sports and pastimes, but let him not forget the mental race he has to run with the educated of his own and of other nations; let him nourish the desire for the aquisition of 'scientific knowledge', not as a mere school lesson, but as a treasure, a useful ally which may some day help him in a greater or lesser degree to fight 'The Battle of Life'.[28]

My dear BOYS AND GIRLS, – When I was your age there were no such children's books as there are now. Those which we had were few and dull, and the pictures in them ugly and mean, while you have your choice of books without number, clever, amusing, and pretty, as well as really instructive, on subjects which were only talked of fifty years ago by a few learned men, and very little understood even by them.[29]

Natural history and scientific subjects more generally were not studied at school in the Victorian period. They belonged to the world
of the nursery, a realm of women instructors.[30] The association of
natural history with the nursery space or domestic hearth gives us an
idea as to why it was frequently linked with the fairy tale. In Britain,
however, fairy tales were not deemed worthy of interest, especially
as regards children, before the beginning of the nineteenth century. Unlike in France and in Germany, the pervasive influence and
strength of puritanism, with its emphasis on reason and morality,
kept literary fairy tales out of the nursery. Imagination and civilization were poles apart – just like amusement and education. Before the
eighteenth century, the one category of fiction which was generally
accepted in the nursery were tales in the vein of Aesop's *Fables* (first
translated into English in 1484).[31] Throughout the eighteenth century, children's literature was designed to purvey religious lessons,
and the children's book industry was mostly limited to such books
as conformed to prevailing moral standards. Though more and more
chapbooks (popular pamphlets aimed at the masses) suggested that
literature for children could be entertaining, books such as Isaac
Watts's *Divine Songs, Attempted in Easie Language for the Use of Children*
(1715) still prominently figured on the bookshelves of the nursery.[32]
Nurtured by didactic stories in the vein of Maria Edgeworth's narratives and sermons,[33] children were protected from the dangers
of imagination and trained into becoming industrious and respon-
sible citizens. When middle-class children were actually read fairy
tales, the latter were more instructive than imaginative works, while
fairy tales appeared as chapbooks and pennybooks for the lower
classes rather than as proper reading for children of the higher social
classes.

It is certainly when the publisher John Newbery started to merge
amusement and instruction in his publications for children that the
market for children's literature was launched. Though his *Lilliputian
Magazine* (1751–2) was a failed commercial venture and was not as
successful as Madame Leprince de Beaumont's *The Young Misses Magazine*, the English translation of her *Magasin des enfans* in 1757 – which
reproduced the format of dialogues between a governess and her
pupils that Sarah Fielding had imagined in *The Governess, or, The Little Female Academy* (1749)[34] – many of his books sold well, illustrating
the expansion of the market of children's literature.[35] At the end of

the eighteenth century, entertaining tales appeared more and more alongside moral stories. Anna Laetitia Barbauld's writings for children increased the importance of amusement, adding folk or fairy-tale touches to her stories, as her six-volume collection *Evenings at Home; or, the Juvenile Budget Opened* (1792–6), co-written with her brother John Aikin, exemplifies. Though still very much instructive and didactic and highly repressing fancy, her method was, however, disapproved of by Sarah Trimmer, who strictly condemned fairy stories and whose own writings closely tied science to revealed religion, seeking less to develop rational faculties in children's minds.[36] It was not before the beginning of the nineteenth century, when the booksellers Benjamin Tabart and John Harris (successor of Newbery) started publishing Perrault's tales for children, that the literary fairy tale for children appeared. Avoiding didacticism, the animal tales published by Harris (such as Sarah Catherine Martin's *The Comic Adventures of Old Mother Hubbard and Her Dog* (1805), William Roscoe's *The Butterfly's Ball* (1807) or Catherine Dorset's *Peacock 'At Home'* (1807)) typified the new view of children's literature as highly visual and entertaining rather than instructive. The tales, figuring animals, birds or insects, anthropomorphized them humorously, offering fantasies poles apart from earlier dry didacticism.

Among the Victorian writers who attempted to explain natural history to children, Charles Kingsley, Arabella Buckley, Margaret Gatty (1809–73) and Charlotte Yonge (1823–1901) are the most significant. Kingsley's *Madam How and Lady Why* (1870) celebrates in the preface John Aikin and Anna Laetitia Barbauld's *Evenings at Home*, a collection of narratives combining natural history and more 'scientific' topics, such as chemistry or astronomy, with poetry and moral stories. More particularly, Kingsley praises the story called 'Eyes and No Eyes' – a story which is also alluded to by Arabella Buckley in her *Eyes and No Eyes* (1903)[37] – suggesting that his method will not entirely be grounded upon the empirical and what is visible to the naked eye.

In fact, in his lecture on 'How to Study Natural History',[38] Kingsley praises imagination as an essential faculty that must be developed in children from an early age. Though under the influence of the Franklin and Edgeworth school of education imagination was 'at a discount', it has now become 'glorif[ied]', Kingsley claims, to the point of 'aton[ing] for every error of false taste, bad English, carelessness for truth; and even for coarseness, blasphemy, and want of common morality'. Kingsley clearly separates imagination from 'fancy' (uncontrolled and unchecked), his lecture aiming to show that the study of natural history must become a means of developing the child's imaginative faculties 'without heating the brain or exciting the passions':

> The fact is, that youth will always be the period of imagination; and the business of a good education will always be to prevent that imagination from being thrown inward ... To turn the imagination not inwards, but outwards; to give it a class of objects which may excite wonder, reverence, the love of novelty and of discovering, without heating the brain or exciting the passions – this is one of the great problems of education; and I believe from experience that the study of natural history supplies in great part what we want.[39]

The 'class of [natural] objects' – natural history – plays a key part in the child's education and the development of his mental faculties. So does the fairy tale. For Kingsley, bees, flowers, pebbles, just like swamps or tufts of heather are so many 'fairy tale[s] of which [he] could but decipher here and there a line or two, and yet [find] them more interesting than all the books, save one, which was ever written upon earth'.[40] The wonders of this natural fairy tale lie in the mystery of the natural world, leading the naturalist and the amateur to investigate the 'form of plants, shells, and animalcules, on each of which a whole volume might be written'.[41] It is most especially the 'tiniest' natural details which make the naturalist 'fancy a fairy-land'.[42] Kingsley's transformation of nature into a text and, moreover, a fairy tale is revealing of the ways in which natural history writings aestheticized nature in order to elicit emotional responses in their readers. Kingsley's emphasis on the role of imagination in children's education also shows how fairies and fairy tales were given a didactic role to convey scientific lessons: for Kingsley, it was imagination which 'raise[d] man above the brutes'[43] – morphing imagination into a sign of humans' evolution.[44] Moving away from John Locke's *Essay Concerning Human Understanding* (1689), Kingsley thus places reason and imagination on the same level, suggesting thereby that the scientific method must include imagination and never reject art.

Kingsley's *Glaucus; or, the wonders of the shore* (1855) was published at a time when children's education in natural history benefited from several factors. The Kay-Shuttleworth reforms in the 1850s gave a spur to education, with more government expenditure on schools.[45] The children's weeklies and monthlies boomed in the 1850s as lower costs of production and distribution opened the market of juvenile literature even further. From Samuel Beeton's *Boy's Own Magazine* (founded 1855), W. H. G. Kingston's *Magazine for Boys* (founded 1859) and the *Boy's Own Paper* (founded 1879) to Margaret Gatty's *Aunt Judy's Magazine* (founded 1866), more exclusively aimed at girls, children's magazines toned down religious material to entertain children with a mix of fiction and secular instruction, not unfrequently using nature studies or featuring explorers and scientists as a means of merging instruction and entertainment.[46] Richly illustrated, these publications testified to the increasing dependence on pictures in multiple forms of popularization. But the use of visual images in such publications, as in books, were to transform modes of representation. At a time when science itself was becoming increasingly material, there was a corresponding urge to make science more visible and tangible. These visual images went hand in hand with rhetorical images, nineteenth-century scientific discourse being frequently interwoven with figurative language, creating narratives increasingly poised between science and literature, between the real and the fantastic.

Moreover, reading was also boosted by the development of railway travel, which saw the opening of railway bookstalls – with natural history publishing boasting good sales figures, as typified by the Rev. John George Wood's *Common Objects of the Country* which sold 100,000 copies in one week.[47] At the opening of Kingsley's *Glaucus*, the narrator imagines his reader travelling by railway to some watering place along the coast and making the most of his journey by observing the natural world unscrolling before his eyes. The allusion to railway travel recurs frequently in Kingsley's popular science works. In *Madam How and Lady Why* (1870)[48] Kingsley compares the scenery behind the window to a picture in a book. Recalling how the digging of railways had revealed the fossil remains of extinct creatures, the framed scenery magically juxtaposes scenes from the past with those of the present:

To me the longest railroad journey, instead of being stupid, is like continually turning over the leaves of a wonderful book, or looking at wonderful pictures of old worlds which were made and unmade thousands of years ago. For I keep looking, not only at the railway cuttings, where the bones of the old worlds are laid bare, but at the surface of the ground; at the plains and downs, banks and knolls, hills and mountains; and continually asking Mrs. How what gave them each its shape: and I will soon teach you to do the same.[49]

In *Glaucus*, the railway motif spurs the narrative's construction of nature as a book to be read and, what is more, as a fairy tale. The vignette quoted above also recalls how the expansion of railroads, enabling the discovery of new sights (and unknown territories, like new lands discovered by British explorers), was accompanied by the fad for sea-side studies, from shell collecting to fern cultivation, inviting people to explore (and plunder) littoral zones.

Glaucus was originally an article reviewing recently published books on sea life, including Philip Henry Gosse's *A Naturalist's Rambles on the Devonshire Coast* (1853) and *The Aquarium* (1854), which was published in the *North British Review* in 1854 and expanded into a book the following year. It sold well, with four editions within four years of its first publication and a fifth in 1873.[50] The aim of Kingsley's work was to differentiate itself from the usual association with 'light' literature: 'to feed the [children's] imagination with wholesome food', enabling them to set themselves apart from 'the ignoble army of idlers, who saunter about the cliffs, and sands, and quays'. Kingsley deplores as well 'French novels, and that sugared slough of sentimental poetry, in comparison with which the old fairy-tales and ballads were manful and rational.'[51] *Glaucus* is divided into three main parts. The first one defines natural history and the ideal naturalist, strengthening the moral aspects of scientific activity; the second one introduces the reader to marine creatures; while the third one explains the principles of the aquarium, mentioning the tanks at the Zoological Gardens and the Crystal Palace and giving directions on how to form an aquarium.

The book is a significant example of the popularity of marine natural history, triggered by John Ellis's first collections of seaweeds in 1751 and subsequent collections. Greville's *Algae Britannicae* (1830),

Mrs Mary Wyatt's *Algae Danmonienses* (1833), Isabella Gifford's *The Marine Botanist* (1840) or W. H. Harvey's *Manual of British Algae* (1841) constitute so many examples of the interest shown in marine life in the early decades of the nineteenth century. Interestingly, the boom in marine natural history in the 1820s was linked to the development of the compound microscope, and we will see below how Kingsley's sea world invites readers to wonder at the minute and the minuscule.[52] Indeed, the microscope revealed unsuspected beauty: new forms and colours suddenly appeared to the amateur naturalists – a world close to Fairyland appearing as if by magic under the lens of the optical instrument.

Kingsley's popular science narrative is in keeping with the didactic and moralistic natural history books of the period 1840–70, most of them aimed at children.[53] His natural theology highlights the wonders of nature as those of the creator: *Glaucus* teaches its young readers 'to find wonder in every insect, sublimity in every hedgerow, the records of past worlds in every pebble, and boundless fertility upon the barren shore'.[54] Wonder is thus religiously charged, Kingsley recommending that his readers look at the minuscule, receding into smaller and smaller worlds and remember that 'there is nothing wonderful in the world outside you but has its counterpart of something just as wonderful, and perhaps more wonderful, inside you'.[55] Kingsley thus insists on the optical instruments as significant means to access unsuspected minute worlds that manifest the creator's power: 'Look at it through the field-glass; for it is truly wonderful'.[56] Like many natural history books, Kingsley's popular science books recurrently stress the minute and the invisible, proposing their readers' insights into worlds of ever smaller size in order to 'push[–] the limits of human consciousness and human wonderment outward at both ends of the scale of natural size'.[57] Kingsley's microscopic vision is enhanced through the contrast between the microscopic and the gigantic, as when he compares the microscopic creatures of the sea with the extinct monsters of the Crystal Palace Park.[58] His play with scale and his hidden worlds, concealed in the dark recesses of the earth or sea, aim to align the mystery of nature with that of God. Nature's 'oddly-fashioned, suspicious-looking being[s]'[59] are revealed to the naturalist as evidence of the power of the creator, the innumerable and still undiscovered forms of life exemplifying God's mystery. Thus, the natural revelations appearing through artificial lenses or close observation bring out a sense of wonder in the young naturalist in *Madam How and Lady Why*:

> Wonder if you will. You cannot wonder too much. That you might wonder all your life long, God put you into this wondrous world, and gave you that faculty of wonder which He has not given to the brutes; which is at once the mother of sound science, and a pledge of immortality in a world more wondrous even than this. But wonder at the right thing, not at the wrong; at the real miracles and prodigies, not at the sham. Wonder not at the world of man. Waste not your admiration, interest, hope on it, its pretty toys, gay fashions, fine clothes, tawdry luxuries, silly amusements. Wonder at the works of God ... The theatre last night was the fairy land of man; but this is the fairy land of God.[60]

Kingsley's use of natural history to purvey religious lessons equates wonder with Christian faith. In fact, his theological perspective constantly emphasizes science's powerlessness to explain nature away. Distancing himself from contemporaneous materialistic conceptions of the natural world, Kingsley praises faith as the sole means of accessing the truth: Mother Nature will never answer the '*How*' and '*Why*'.[61] The inability of materialistic science to pierce the mysteries of nature is likewise underlined in *Madam How and Lady Why*. The power of Analysis, one of Madam How's grandsons, is limited by the scientist's lack of faith, and his study of Life as a mere analysis of 'dead things' cannot reveal the truth about matter:

> Because Analysis can only explain to you a little about dead things, like stones – inorganic things as they are called. Living things – organisms, as they are called – he cannot explain to you at all ... He has to kill his goose, or his flower, or his insect, before he can analyse it: and then it is not a goose, but only the corpse of a goose; not a flower, but only the dead stuff of the flower.[62]

Faith and natural history march hand in hand, since matter alone will only offer limited and imperfect information. Kingsley's definition of natural history is heavily moralistic: the naturalist's activity should aim to develop virtue. This idea is strengthened by the use of motifs and figures from medieval romance. Personified by the chivalrous knight, the naturalist is manly, brave and devoted to the furthering of knowledge for the benefit of others:

> [The] qualifications required for a perfect naturalist are as many and as lofty as were required, by old chivalrous writers, for the perfect knight-errant of the Middle Ages... our perfect naturalist should be strong in body... he should know how to swim for his life, to pull an oar, sail a boat, and ride the first horse which comes to hand... and, if he go far abroad, be able on occasion to fight for his life.
>
> For his moral character, he must, like a knight of old, be first of all gentle and courteous, ready and able to ingratiate himself with the poor, the ignorant, and the savage...
>
> And last, but not least, the perfect naturalist should have in him the very essence of true chivalry, namely, self-devotion; the desire to advance, not himself and his own fame or wealth, but knowledge and mankind.[63]

The healthy naturalist Kingsley describes reflects some of the anxieties of the day, in particular those related to seaside resorts which regularly saw waves of workers invading the British shores on weekends and whose swimming outfit (or lack of, thereof) often shocked the bourgeoisie.[64] The flesh and the spirit must be strengthened by the study of natural history, as Kingsley makes explicit, his popular science work advocating 'Muscular Christianity' and calling for an active lifestyle. Thus, Kingsley does not merely foreground the narrative qualities of natural history: the romance, the marvellous and the motifs associated with Fairyland enable the popularizer to blend science and religion. The use of medieval chivalry also helps Kingsley convey a popular discourse of morality in Victorian England.[65] For Kingsley's knightly faith confirms the compatibility of natural history with Christian faith: because natural history helps the practitioner reinforce submission to and belief in authority, it helps train the very faculty of faith. Kingsley therefore makes claims for the naturalist's belief in received truth, and 'reveals how natural history can train the mind to believe by emphasizing how faith in scientific authority is necessary to it'.[66] Furthermore, although Kingsley aims to train his readers' eyes so as not to 'gaze lazily around at earth and sea and sky',[67] fighting idleness as did

many other popular science books aimed at a middle-class audience, his emphasis on seeing what appears to be too minute or
invisible is highly significant. On the one hand, the naturalist's eye,
properly trained, is 'a redeemed eye' which 'sees significances, har-
monies, laws, chains of cause and effect endlessly interlinked':[68]
'*The Art of Seeing*', as can be seen in his later works, is the 'highest faculty'.[69] On the other hand, and therefore paradoxically, it
also helps Kingsley reconcile his natural theology with evolutionary
theory.

As mentioned above, the preface of *Madam How and Lady Why* celebrates John Aikin's and Anna Laetitia Barbauld's 'Eyes and No Eyes'.
The importance of seeing is constantly emphasized: 'One man walks
through the world with his eyes open, another with his eyes shut;
and upon this difference depends all the superiority of knowledge
which one man acquires over another.'[70] The stress on vision goes
hand in hand with the activity of reading: nature is God's wonderful 'picture-book'.[71] The metaphors of the two books (the Bible
and that of God's works – Nature), often found in natural theolo-
gies, help Kingsley fictionalize his narrative of nature even more.
His fairy, Madam How, 'lives here upon the moor, and indeed in
most places else, if people have but eyes to see her'.[72] Embodying
nature, the fairy enables Kingsley to represent the invisible, making explicit that knowledge of nature is accessible only through the
imagination – the mind's eye. Lady Why, in contrast, 'is another
fairy . . . whom we can hardly hope to see'. Madam How is the servant
while Lady Why is the mistress, 'though she has a Master over her
again – whose name I leave for you to guess'.[73] The issue of sight and
invisibility strengthens Kingsley's natural theology, further blending
science and religion: 'You must believe it; for in science, as in higher
matters, he who will walk surely, must "walk by faith and not by
sight".'[74]

Kingsley's emphasis on vision and imagination is of capital importance for our understanding of how the naturalist manages to pro-
mulgate Christian morality in the context of evolutionary theories.
That Kingsley advocated evolutionary theory is obvious in both his
pre- and post-Darwinian works, all underlining his rejection of literal-
ist readings of Genesis and his belief in uniformitarianism. In *Glaucus*,
for example, extinction is part of the process of evolution as well as a
sign of God's creative activity:

[A]s we know that species of animals lower than those which already existed appeared again and again during the various eras, so it is quite possible that they may be appearing now, and may appear hereafter: and that for every extinct Dodo or Moa, a new species may be created, to keep up the equilibrium of the whole. This is but a surmise: but it may be wise, perhaps, just now, to confess boldly, even to insist on, its possibility, lest any should fancy, from our unwilingness to allow it, that there would be ought in it, if proved, contrary to sound religions.

I am, I must honestly confess, more and more unable to perceive anything which an orthodox Christian may not hold, in those physical theories of 'evolution' which are gaining more and more the assent of our best zoologists and botanists.[75]

Of course, as suggested, it is obvious that Kingsley's use of romance and the fairy tale (literary genres which departed from realism (and hence from a materialistic vision of reality) and which played on belief and faith in divine (or supernatural) powers, foregrounding Christian ideals and suggesting the intangibility of some forms of life, enabled him to equate belief in the marvellous with worship, thereby reconciling science and religion: 'love of the marvellous which is inherent in man' can but 'lead the reader to more solemn and lofty trains of thought'.[76] But Kingsley's popular science writing is also highly representative of the ways in which, in the second half of the nineteenth century, science increasingly reconstructed reality from elements or clues which could not be directly apprehended.[77] The idea that knowledge was constructed through partially invisible data climaxed in Darwin's theory of natural selection. Darwin's theory, in Jonathan Smith's terms, 'violat[ing] the most basic principles of Baconian induction ... was mere speculation, the product of an individual's fertile imagination rather than a gradually ascending series of inductions grounded in observed facts'.[78] Darwin had been much influenced by Charles Lyell (1797–1875), who, in his *Principles of Geology* (1830–3), called for the necessity to use reason and imagination to 'picture' the natural world, since the geological processes of the Earth – as uniformitarianism posited – could not be visualized. Darwin's account of his journey on the HMS *Beagle* was published six years after the completion of Lyell's *Principles*, whose rhetoric presented uniformitarianism 'as simultaneously inductive and imaginative – indeed, as more imaginative than its catastrophist rivals'.[79] Lyell's theory, and later Darwin's, claimed that some hypotheses were not observable to the naked eye and could therefore not be verified. This conception of science radically altered the vision of reality, as G. H. Lewes suggests here, comparing modern science to a fantasy:

> Science is essentially an ideal construction very far removed from the abstractions expressing modes of existence which never were, and never could be, real; and are very often at variance with sensible Experience. It not only deals with data that are extra-sensible, but with data avowedly fictitious... the truth is that Science mounts on the wings of Imagination into regions of the invisible and impalpable, peopling these regions with Fictions more remote from fact than the fantasies of the Arabian Nights are from the daily occurrences in Oxford Street.[80]

James Krasner's analysis of Darwin's narrative method underlines how Darwin's abandonment of omniscience for a narrative characterized by 'misprision, illusion, and limitation' aimed to foreground 'the optical illusions and visual failures to which the physical eye is prone, the formal instability of evolutionary nature'.[81] Darwin did not use such representations of nature to make up for the fallibility of human vision, however. The perceptual dysfunctions of the eye figured 'as the model for an imagined evolutionary nature; the abundant complexity of Darwinian vision is born out of the powerlessness and the limitation of the evolving human eye beholding nature'.[82] In addition to making the invisible visible, therefore, the 'mixture of science and fiction' expands the reader's imagination 'beyond the visually verifiable without sacrificing any scientific authority... Once we have imagined nature from the gnomish and amphibian perspectives we are able to form more scientifically accurate theories than our limited vision would otherwise allow.'[83]

Moreover, post-Darwinian science was about 'likeness and transformation, about the ways in which things resembled each other or, even, could turn into one another', in Amanda Hodgson's terms.[84] But Darwin's use of 'literary and imagistic techniques'[85] to envision evolutionary theory had an important impact on Victorian culture, and cast new perspectives upon nature and the natural world. As I argue in this book, taking further Nicola Bown's argument in *Fairies in Nineteenth-Century Art and Literature*, the Victorians clung to fairies and fairy tales as if they were the only creatures that could make sense of their changing reality, its tensions and contradictions. Fairies and fairy tales invaded the cultural scene, serving, in popular science works, I contend, to bridge the gap between old and new visions of nature and manage shifts in the understanding of natural history. This idea is manifest in many essays dealing with new scientific methods following the advent of evolutionary theory. Imagination – presented here as 'fancy', by the anthropologist and ethnologist Daniel Wilson, writing in 1873, the two terms being sometimes used interchangeably – was at the centre of the debate:

> in those stages of real or hypothetical evolution, and the transitional states of being which their assumption involves, fancy has to play its part... The comprehensive faith which his novel doctrines involve, makes ever new demands on the cultivated imaginings of the man of science; and it requires a mind of rare balance to preserve the fancy in due subordination to the actual demonstrations of scientific truth.[86]

As Hodgson contends, Daniel Wilson not only borrows from the language of religious experience to define the new scientific methods but also epitomizes how the shift towards 'imaginative methods as implication, suggestion, ambiguity and analogy'[87] are in fact the methods of fiction. Images of nature's flux and fluidity, of transformation and metamorphoses were thus as much a part of mid-Victorian scientific discourse as they were of narratives using fairies and magic – a parallel which suggests that science and literature went hand in hand, literary works perhaps not only mirroring the latest scientific discoveries but also – and more importantly – 'offering a solution to the problem of constructing a suitable language for the new science'.[88]

Interestingly, the Victorian scientists most associated with a mechanistic and materialist vision of the world, like T. H. Huxley (1825–95) and John Tyndall (1820–93), refuted the idea that science had moved away from imagination: reason and imagination must be combined. Hence Huxley's description of the new vision of science as a 'Cinderella', giving Theology and Philosophy the roles of the ugly sisters:

> In her garret, she has fairy visions out of the ken of the pair of shrews who are quarrelling downstairs. She sees the order which pervades the seeming disorder of the world; the great drama of evolution, with its full share of pity and terror, but also with abundant goodness and beauty, unrolls itself before her eyes.[89]

Huxley's Cinderella is typical of the ways in which fairies were used in the second half of the nineteenth century both to call attention to the importance of imagination and – as popular science books on natural history make clear – to quiet fears related to scientific materialism. In *Madam How and Lady Why* Kingsley's powerful fairies revamp the stereotypical 'Why and Because' or 'The Reason Why' usually found in children's natural history books. Because such books never tell the ' "Reason Why" things happen but only "the Way in which they happen" ',[90] Kingsley's fairies remain highly mysterious. They describe God's creatures, help children visualize them, but refuse to speak further. Consequently, their fairy tales, compared to which nursery stories seem dull, elicit wonder in those who listen to them:

> All those feelings in you which your nursery tales call out, – imagination, wonder, awe, pity, and I trust too, hope and love – will be called out, I believe, by the Tale of all Tales, the true 'Märchen allen Märchen,' so much more fully and strongly and purely, that you will feel that novels and story-books are scarcely worth your reading, as long as you can read the great green book, of which every bud is a letter, and every tree a page.[91]

We can see here, especially with the use of the term 'Märchen', calling to mind the German tradition of classical fairy tales, the blurring of boundaries between imagination and the realm of fairy tales. Fairy tales encapsulate the power of the imagination; they become clichéd representations of new ways of looking at the natural world in line with current scientific theories, emphasizing the image of the natural world as a book to be read – a book which does not, however, suggest that Genesis must be read literally but which nonetheless leaves room for a conciliation of science and religion. Moreover, the idea that the fairy tale helps materialize reality undergirds Kingsley's depiction of the natural world: 'a wonderful fairy tale... and every word of it true'.[92] Fairies partake of Kingsley's geological presentation of the natural world: they dwell among the banks and knolls; their music may be heard, like their jingling bells. Significantly, the most wonderful of all fairy tales is that of the evolution of the earth and of humans – '[t]he true fairy tale' – a tale so wonderful that it will 'explain to you how our forefathers got to believe in fairies, and trolls, and elves, and scratlings, and all strange little people who were said to haunt the mountains and the caves'.[93] Kingsley sets humans apart from apes, arguing that 'men can go on civilising themselves, and growing richer and more comfortable, wiser and happier, year by year' – an evolution that is 'a wonder and a prodigy and a miracle, stranger than all the most fantastic marvels you ever read in fairy tales'.[94] Such an association of humans' evolution with the fairy tale is telling, for Kingsley actually constructs fairy tales as primitive stories of mankind:

> But what has all this to do with my fairy tale? This: –
> Suppose that these people, after all, had been fairies?
> I am in earnest. Of course, I do not mean that these folk could make themselves invisible, or that they had any supernatural powers – any more, at least, than you and I have – or that they were anything but savages; but this I do think, that out of old stories of these savages grew up the stories of fairies, elves, and trolls, and scratlings, and cluricaunes, and ogres, of which you have read so many.[95]

Kingsley's narrative is informed by contemporary anthropological research on fairy tales, at a time when fairies formed part of the debates concerning the changing definitions of nature and the rise of theories of cultural evolution. As Carole Silver contends, the rise of Darwinism made the study of fairies possible because the debate on origins launched the development of theories of social, cultural and spiritual evolution.[96] In Darwin's theory as applied to culture, fairies were believed to represent 'savage' societies. The popular Thomas Crofton Croker's *Fairy Legends and Traditions of the South of Ireland* (1825–6), the Brothers Grimm's essay, 'On the Nature of the Elves'[97] or, later, Thomas Keightley's *The Fairy Mythology* (1828, revised in 1850, newly prefaced in 1860) were signs of the era's interest in fairy scholarship on the part of artists and folklorists alike.[98] The linguistic analysis, categorization and systematization initiated by such research into fairy lore were the first steps towards turning 'the quest for fairies into science', all the more so with the development of anthropology and ethnology.[99]

As a matter of fact, Kingsley further alludes to nineteenth-century research into the physical phenomena attributed to fairies, from fairy rings (produced by fungi) to elf-shots, fairy bolts or fairy pipes (prehistoric flint shards, arrows, or small pipes often found near prehistoric monuments), or even changelings (disabled children suffering from congenital diseases). The ogres found in fairy tales were in fact 'savages' – cannibals who ate human beings – exaggerated through storytelling, while other tribes, such as Esquimaux and Lapps, were so small that tales suggested they might make themselves invisible.[100] Far from distancing the readers from the subject, the use of fairies and fairy tales hence objectifies nature and the evolution of life on earth. Kingsley's reconciliation of science and religion in his popular science works seems very close to earlier Paleyan versions of natural theology. Nature remains a divine creation which humans must look at and study to develop their moral and intellectual faculties. The natural world, however, is never used to prove the existence of God. At a time when evolutionary theory was starting to be advocated by many men of science, Kingsley's theological presentation of nature shows therefore how natural theology could be interpreted differently.

Put-them-all-in-spirits: collecting impossible monsters in *The Water-Babies, a Fairy Tale for a Land Baby*

'Now I'll give *you* something to believe. I'm just one hundred and one, five months and a day.'

'I can't believe *that*!' said Alice.

'Can't you?' the Queen said in a pitiful tone. 'Try again: draw a long breath, and shut your eyes.'

Alice laughed. 'There's no use trying,' she said: 'one *can't* believe in impossible things.'

'I daresay you haven't had much practice', said the Queen. 'When I was your age, I always did it for half-an-hour a day. Why, sometimes I've believed as many as six impossible things before breakfast...[101]

If Kingsley's popular science works used fairies and fairy tales to give shape to natural phenomena and explain the natural world, his children's fiction, notably *The Water-Babies, a Fairy Tale for a Land Baby* (1863), is permeated with contemporary scientific discourse, offering us a very good illustration of the role that natural history played in the development of post-Darwinian fairy tales and the permeable boundaries between scientific and literary discourse. The fantasy, or 'fairy tale', revolves around the issue of species and species classification, while images of transformation anchor the narrative in mid-century scientic debates. Indeed, the narrative not only foregrounds species transformation but also makes clear that species which fail to evolve will inevitably become extinct, as the example of the Allalonestones, who refuse to share the attributes of lower creatures (here wings), demonstrates.

The narrative relates the story of Tom, a chimney-sweep, who runs away from his employer, Grimes. But the boy falls into a river and is transformed into a water-baby. His transformation enables him to meet all sorts of creatures. In so doing, Tom learns moral lessons. The way in which Kingsley uses natural elements or creatures to shape Tom's moral improvement turns the fantasy into a parable. The 'fairy tale for land babies', however, reads very much like a popular science book. Tom's magical transformation is as wonderful as other natural metamorphoses ('If he says that it is too strange a transformation for a land-baby to turn into a water-baby, ask him if he ever heard of the transformation of Syllis, or the Distomas, or the common jelly-fish').[102] Moreover, the narrator contrasts his story with the dry lessons learnt in the schoolroom, signalling thereby that the story will blend instruction and entertainment and match contemporary pedagogical methods especially used to popularize science. Kingsley stops from time to time to explain the etymological meaning of words, such as 'amphibious' used to define water-babies: 'Adjective, derived from two Greek words, *amphi*, a fish, and *bios*, a beast. An animal supposed by our ignorant ancestors to be compounded of a fish and a beast' (p. 83). The technical vocabulary used to define Tom ('having round the parotic region of his fauces a set of external gills (I hope you understand all the big words)' (p. 67)) reinforces the construction of a narrative poised between a fairy tale and a natural history lesson. The anthropomorphization of natural creatures, such as the sea-snails or the sunfish, which are given a voice when Tom asks them where they come from, recalls as well popular science books aimed at children. Furthermore, this idea is strengthened by frequent references to various modes of diffusion of scientific knowledge, such as when the narrator advises his readers to look at (and know) Bewick[103] and visit the Zoological Gardens to observe otters.

Tom, as an amphibious creature, becomes a sort of natural enigma – a wonder likely to intrigue naturalists. But Tom's journey as a water-baby and his encounter with many natural creatures is also presented as a discovery of unimaginable species which the natural history lesson will make readers familiar with as Tom meets them. Thus Kingsley recurrently stresses nature's wonderful garbs:

> You must not talk about 'ain't' and 'can't' when you speak of this great wonderful world round you...You must not say that this cannot be, or that that is contrary to nature. You do not know what Nature is, or what she can do; and nobody knows; not even Sir Roderick Murchison, or Professor Owen, or Professor Sedgwick, or Professor Huxley, or Mr. Darwin, or Professor Faraday, or Mr. Grove, or any other of the great men whom good boys are taught to respect. (pp. 69–70)

The mention of the famous scientists of the time helps the narrator combine the wonders of the natural world with natural history. What is 'contrary to nature' and yet exists, from the elephant and the giraffe, when first brought to Europe, 'impossible monster[s], contrary to the laws of comparative anatomy' (p. 72), to flying dragons (Pterodactyls) shows that empiricism is no longer a valid scientific method. On the contrary, the fairy tale aims to bring to light how contemporary science is contingent on scientists' belief in impossible things. Moreover, Tom's naive point-of-view enables Kingsley to define mythic creatures as constructions resulting from people's lack of knowledge, as when Tom believes deer 'to be monsters...in the habit of eating children' (p. 5).

As suggested, the fantasy resonates with contemporary scientific debates. The controversies over humankind's relationship to monkeys, particularly manifest in the quarrel over the anatomy of apes and the comparisons drawn between apes' and humans' brains, are obvious through many allusions: some to the altercation between Bishop Samuel Wilberforce (1805–73) and T. H. Huxley, at a meeting of the British Association for the Advancement of Science (BAAS) in 1860,[104] others to the clash between Huxley and Sir Richard Owen (1804–92) over the hippocampus minor, as well as references to Paul Belloni du Chaillu (1835–1903), who exhibited a collection of decapitated ape-heads in 1860 and helped to blur further the boundaries between humans and apes, giving gorillas humanoid features, as illustrated in his *Explorations and Adventures in Equatorial Africa* (1861).[105] Kingsley strongly contributed to making the hippocampus controversy known to the general public. He had attended the 1862 BAAS Cambridge meeting,[106] when Owen's anti-Darwinian stance was particularly illustrated, as shown in his papers 'On the Characters of the Aye-Aye' and 'On the Zoological Significance of the Cerebral and Pedal Characters of Man' – papers which prompted Huxley's riposte, both men attacking each other's claims and neither willing to listen to the other.[107] Following the meeting, Kingsley's 'Speech of Lord Dundreary in Section D, on Friday Last, on the Great Hippocampus Question',[108] written in reaction to the debate, was a first step in his satire of the hippocampus controversy, which he developed further in *The Water-Babies*, serialized in *Macmillan's Magazine* around the same time. In both texts the hippocampus minor becomes a 'hippopotamus major', and the connexion between the two men seeps through Kingsley's defining them as the chief authorities on nature and his frequent comparisons of the two scientists, as when he contends that a water-baby, if caught, would soon be 'cut...into two halves', one 'sent...to Professor Owen, and one to Professor Huxley, to see what they would each say about it' (p. 69). Surprisingly enough, Huxley and Owen find themselves reunited in the figure of Professor Ptthmllnsprts. The latter is a naturalist, chief professor of *Necrobioneopalæonthydrochthonanthropopithekology*. He embodies Victorian scientific materialism in the very same way as Huxley, believing 'anything to be true, but what he could see, hear, taste, or handle' (p. 153). The parallel with Huxley is reinforced when Professor Ptthmllnsprts declares at the BAAS that 'apes had hippopotamus majors in their brains just as men have' (p. 153). In addition, at another British Association meeting, the Professor presents a paper which defines '*nymphs, satyrs, fauns, inui, dwarfs, trolls, elves, gnomes, fairies, brownies, nixes, wilis, kobolds, leprechaunes, cluricaunes, banshees, will-o'-the-wisps, follets, lutins, magots, goblins, afrits, marids, jinns, ghouls, peris, deevs, angels, archangels, imps, bogies,* or worse' as 'nothing at all, and pure bosh and wind' (p. 155). He later declares, however, that the 'great hippopotamus test' (p. 154) is able to tell man apart from apes ('all important difference between you and an ape is that you have a hippopotamus major in your brain, and it has none...as Lord Dundreary and others would put it' (p. 154)). The contradiction enables Kingsley to blur the figures of Huxley and Owen, and foreshadows Professor Ptthmllnsprts's change of mind.

Setting science apart from the world of the Little People and compared with Huxley, Professor Ptthmllnsprts becomes a symbol of secular science. This idea is particularly illustrated by his obsession with collecting. Aptly named Put-them-all-in-Spirits, the Professor is, indeed, first and foremost characterized by his compulsive collecting – collected specimens becoming emblems of modern science and scientific materialism. From the beginning of Tom's journey, the discovery of and knowledge about nature works in tandem with the collection and exhibition of natural specimens. When Tom looks at the water and sees 'beetles and sticks; and straws, and worms, and addle-eggs, and wood-lice, and leeches, and odds and ends, and omnium-gatherums' (p. 111), the profusion of natural creatures instantly conjures up naturalists' collecting activities: there is 'enough to fill nine museums' (p. 111). Throughout the fantasy recurrent references to birds' eggs being taken and creatures caught in a net, to people keeping creatures in tanks and bottles, birds being shot, stuffed and 'put...into stupid museums' (p. 255) are so many allusions to the world of Victorian collecting. At the end of the fairy tale, the old giant Tom encounters, who 'has a heart, though it was considerably overgrown with brains' (p. 294), is another representation of Victorian scientists' obsession with collecting nature:

He was made principally of fish bones and parchment, put together with wire and Canada balsam; and smelt strongly of spirits, though he never drank anything but water: but spirits he used somehow there was no denying. He had a great pair of spectacles on his nose, and a butterfly-net in one hand, and a geological hammer in the other; and was hung all over with pockets, full of collecting boxes, bottles, microscopes, telescopes, barometers, ordnance maps, scalpels, forceps, photographic apparatus, and all other tackle for finding out everything about everything, and a little more too. (p. 294)

Armed with the complete naturalist's equipment, the giant incarnates the nineteenth-century 'natural historical way of knowing': he can collect and conserve, freeze nature by putting it in spirits, frame it by taking pictures, his paraphernalia facilitating his successful study of nature and ensuring his knowledge. Tom, as a water-baby, thus becomes an intriguing specimen likely to 'spoil [scientists'] theories' (p. 161), and spends his time trying to avoid getting collected and given 'two long names of which the first would have said a little about Tom, and the second all about himself' (p. 157). For Tom represents the 'wonders of nature' (p. 159) that scientific materialism denies. His flight is thus symbolical and illustrates Kingsley's critique of his material – and visual – culture. Of course, Kingsley does not condemn museums or other places of exhibition, such as the Crystal Palace (p. 277), but his fairy tale humorously bridges the gap between natural history and the constitution of natural historical knowledge and the objects representing that knowledge which his naturalists attempt to capture and bottle up. If the giant magnifies the excesses of Victorian scientific methods of analysing the world, Tom, as a water-baby, will not be caught up, objectified and exhibited in a glass full of spirits. He thus becomes a visual representation of what can be neither grasped nor represented, what can be neither measured nor gauged, what does not fit classification and yet which most people must believe in – the contrary model of the bottled specimen displayed on museum shelves. The Professor's lesson consists therefore in forcing him to believe in impossible things, as the White Queen in Lewis Carrol's *Alice* advises the eponymous little girl. As a matter of fact, it may be interesting here to compare the two narratives, both satirizing contemporary scientific debates,[109] both popularizing as well current scientific theories and typifying the impact of evolutionary theory on the literary fairy tale after the publication of Darwin's *On the Origin of Species*, both evidencing how the fairy story became a fashionable and efficient way of dealing with, presenting, or even criticizing new definitions of nature and the natural world as this book contends.

In Lewis Carroll's *Alice's Adventures in Wonderland* (1865) and *Through the Looking-Glass, and What Alice Found There* (1871), Alice's fall down the rabbit hole or passage through the glass enables the little girl to discover mysterious worlds in which her size constantly changes. Like Tom, Alice undergoes metamorphoses: she becomes as tiny as caterpillars or flowers and is terrified at the idea that she might be eaten up by a puppy or stung by a giant insect. Moreover, Alice's obsession with size throughout her journeys points to the narratives' interest in questions of scale. In *Alice's Adventures in Wonderland*, Alice first believes she is falling through the earth, reaching lands situated on the other side of the globe, and the tale recurrently calls to mind the period's urge to travel farther and to see farther, peering into unknown worlds – or even planets as the motif of the telescope intimates. The tale easily reads, indeed, as a humorous rewriting of a travel narrative, with the young naturalist entering a wild territory where codes of conduct and signs of civilization have become useless or turned upside down. Defined as a 'fairy tale' by Carroll, *Alice's Adventures in Wonderland*, like its sequel, takes us into a realm inhabited by talking animals and flowers, extinct species, mythical creatures and imaginary beings. But Carroll's tale, if aimed at children, is highly representative of the issues that concerned the Victorians: it encapsulates debates revolving around representations of nature at a time when such definitions were changing, especially with the popularization of evolutionary theory; it alludes to the development of scientific knowledge linked to a new mapping of the world and the discovery of exotic, unknown or unseen species and peoples; it tackles as well the diffusion of such knowledge, either through references to specimens exhibited at the time in museums (like the Dodo in the Oxford University Museum) or to popular science works. Furthermore, the little girl's experience of natural selection and struggles for life in Wonderland, just like Tom's constant sense of danger and his flight to escape his pursuers, recall the journeys that writers of natural history books proposed at the time, inviting their readers to travel into unknown territories in order to discover new species and constantly triggering wonder and curiosity. Both Kingsley's and Carroll's narratives, moreover, inviting their readers to imagine what was hard to fancy and mentally shape what they could not visualize, and following the White Queen's advice to Alice in *Through the Looking-Glass*, do exactly what popular science works aimed at children were doing in the years that followed the publication of Darwin's book on natural selection.[110]

Ironically enough, if the Mad Hatter is no reproduction of Professor Ptthmllnsprts, the Professor's sudden belief in '*unicorns, fire-drakes, maticoras, basilisks, amphisbœnas, griffins, rocs, orcs, dog-headed men, three-headed dogs, three-bodied geryons*, and other pleasant creatures' (p. 162) nonetheless turns him into a medical case, his brain becoming a subject of investigation. Punished for collecting nature too much, for bottling and stuffing specimens, just like Tom who is punished for his cruelty to nature, Professor Ptthmllnsprts embodies the material scientists who fail to practise natural history with Christian faith. As the fantasy makes clear, if Kingsley mocks anatomy and morphology, he nevertheless merges the biological and the spiritual: extinction threatens those who are both unable to evolve physically and morally, as when Tom refrains from damaging the caddis-fly's pupa, enabling thereby its metamorphosis into a beautiful creature and his own, ultimately, into an angel. It is thus no wonder that the moral of the story exhorts young readers to protect the natural world, should the 'efts [be] nothing else but the water-babies who are stupid and dirty, and will not learn their lessons and keep themselves clean' (p. 328):

> And now, my dear little man, what should we learn from this parable?
>
> We should learn thirty-seven or thirty-nine things, I am not exactly sure which: but one thing, at least, we may learn, and that is this – when we see efts in the pond, never to throw stones at them, or catch them with crooked pins, or put them into vivariums with sticklebacks, that the sticklebacks may prick them in their poor little stomachs, and make them jump out of the glass into somebody's work-box, and so come to a bad end. (p. 328)

Transformation results from moral evolution, not from chance, and if the protected creatures amend, as Kingsley hopes, they may 'become something better once more' (p. 329). The discourse on the protection of nature interweaves mankind's evolution with humans' relation to animals and fashions the narrative into an evolutionary parable. Thus, Kingsley's conflation of scientific and religious discourses brings home anxieties regarding the ways in which children's literature could popularize contemporary scientific theories without relinquishing religious instruction. In both his popular science works and his fiction, as his characters' and readers' entry into Fairyland coincides with entry into natural worlds, the motifs of the fairy tale appear as an efficient means to map out evolutionary processes *and* instil moral lessons. As we shall now see, the wonders of nature that Kingsley attempted to popularize by offering his readers dreams as wonderful as 'Alice had when she went into Wonderland'[111] were further highlighted by Arabella Buckley, whose 'fairy tales of nature' were even more strikingly aimed at teaching children evolutionary theory. Representing the enduring wonder that the natural world offered to those who opened their eyes, Buckley's fairies stimulate enchantment and praise divine creation while remaining firmly anchored in modern Victorian science.

2

'How Are You to Enter the Fairy-Land of Science?': The Wonders of the Natural World in Arabella Buckley's Popular Science Works for Children

> Once upon a time, in a quiet sea-bay on the south shores of Great Britain, five curious little oval jelly bodies were swimming about by their jelly-lashes in the depths of the smooth water.[1]

> This idea of *unearthliness* is a great element in the Romance of Natural History. Our matter-of-fact age despises and scouts it as absurd, and those who are conscious of such impressions acknowledge that they are unreal, yet feel them none the less. The imaginative Greek peopled every wild glen, every lonely shore, every obscure cavern, every solemn grove, with the spiritual, only rarely and fitfully visible or audible. So it has been with all peoples, especially in that semi-civilized stage which is so favourable to poetic developments: the elves and fays, the sprites and fairies, the Jack-o'-lanterns, the Will-o'the-wisps, the Robin-goodfellows, and Banshees, – what are they all but the phenomena of nature, dimly discerned, and attributed by a poetic temperament to beings of unearthly races, but of earthly sympathies?[2]

As seen in the previous chapter, in the second half of the nineteenth century, fairy tales were increasingly seen as primitive stories of mankind, gnomes, elves and fays resulting from people's unscientific or uneducated reading of the natural world. The rise of folktale scholarship, moreover, manifest in the multiple attempts at collecting and classifying folk and fairy tales in the nineteenth century, from Thomas Keightley's *The Fairy Mythology: Illustrative of the Romance and Superstition of Various Countries* (1828) to Edwin Sidney Hartland's *The Science of Fairy Tales: An Inquiry into Fairy Mythology* (1891) at the end of the century, more and more constructed the fairy tale as more or less a natural material: once collected and catalogued, the tales could be observed by folklorists and anthropologists, as if with a magnifying glass or a microscope. Such works also underlined how fairy tales reflected primitive people's beliefs and interpretation of the natural world. Analyses of the fairy tale of this type influenced children's literature as well. In many mid-century children's magazines, such as Margaret Gatty's *Aunt Judy's Magazine* or Charlotte Yonge's *The Monthly Packet*, the connection between fairy tales and natural phenomena was often stressed, not simply providing children with rational explanations for natural processes that were believed to be supernatural, as seen with the example of Samuel Clark's *Peter Parley's Wonders of Earth, Sea, and Sky* (n.d.), but also explaining to children what led primitive peoples to create such fairy stories, as the following article highlights:

> Perhaps all these stories originally sprang from an allegorical way of describing the actions of nature... Of those which are most clearly what are called *nature-myths*, we may mention Thorn-rose (or, as it is often called in English, 'The Sleeping Beauty'), which simply arises from an allegory of the Spring kissing the Earth into new life.[3]

The allegorical way of reading natural phenomena developed here was revamped in the Victorian period, as Philip Henry Gosse's *The Romance of Natural History* (1860) makes explicit, popular science books inviting their readers to look at the natural world through a romantic lens and to keep faith in fairies or water-babies. As we shall see, however, fairies, even when modernized, retained their connections with folklore, encapsulating many tensions and ambiguities when they were used to point out the marvels of the natural world, natural history and certain areas of Victorian science.

As argued in the previous chapter, in the second half of the nineteenth century, science books for children reworked the popularization of natural history through entertaining storytelling. Science had become 'sensational'[4] or 'commercial'.[5] Spectacular shows and gigantic exhibitions were being staged; the London Zoo and the British Museum welcomed new specimens brought from across the Empire. As a result, popularizers often appealed to the readers' eyes, using verbal or colourful visual images and inviting their readers to observe the natural world and experience nature as explorers would. Interestingly, natural history writing was most typically feminine. Women have always been very active in the dissemination and popularization of science. For Alan Rauch, women were 'not merely [involved] as ancillary figures in the grand tradition of the history of science, but both critical and central contributors to the public's understanding of science', making 'their contributions to scientific knowledge as enduring and as influential as possible'.[6] In the late eighteenth century, nursery novels were mostly written by women, who emphasized the instructive aspects of narrative.[7] Among the most famous are Anna Laetitia Barbauld (1743–1825), Sarah Trimmer (1741–1810), Priscilla Wakefield (1751–1832) and Jane Marcet (1769–1858). For Rauch, science appealed to women writers in the late eighteenth and early nineteenth centuries because it 'was a clear entrée... into the life of the mind',[8] although this often implied merging science with religious belief and praise. In the second half of the nineteenth century, popularization became for women the only means of access to the scientific world, especially as the growing professionalization of science pushed women to the margins, excluding them from universities or scientific societies, and as evolutionary theory defined them as intellectually inferior. The natural world, in particular, seemed to appeal to women, as exemplified by the numerous works by Sarah Bowdich (1791–1856), Mary Roberts (1788–1864), Agnes Catlow, Jane Loudon (1807–58), Phebe Lankester (1825–1900), Elizabeth Twining (1805–89), or Elizabeth (1823–73) and Mary (1817–93) Kirby. Their works, such as those of the naturalist and children's writer Margaret Gatty (1809–73), whose *British Sea-Weeds* (1863), with its colourful illustrations, typified the significance of visual culture for popular science,[9] illustrate their adaptation to a competitive market.[10] As we shall now see, Arabella Buckley is another case in point: for Barbara T. Gates, Buckley 'strove to present science as visually apprehensible'.[11] Buckley is a good instance of the way in which women popularized modern science and its changing attitudes towards nature without dismissing religion. In so doing, Buckley followed in the footsteps of late eighteenth-century women popularizers. But her presentation of evolutionary theory went beyond the mid-Victorian conflict between science and religion, showing on the contrary the need to reconcile them in order to understand the natural world.

Once upon a time: picturing the invisible

Arabella Buckley remains famous today for *The Fairy-Land of Science* (1879), a work on physics which brings home the magic of science. Buckley's use of fairies to introduce children to the marvels of the natural world and natural phenomena goes further than simply showing the wonder-working forces at stake in the natural world. Drawing upon a Christian tradition of popular science works, Buckley's fairies constantly tone down the clash between natural theology and scientific naturalism by suggesting that nature and natural selection are ruled by supernatural forces which children must learn to imagine. In so doing, Buckley reconciles two visions of the natural world, illustrating how fairies and fairy tales could be used to reveal the fears and anxieties of the second half of the nineteenth century. Indeed, in *The Fairy-Land of Science* Buckley's aim is primarily to show that fairy tales were a means not only of capturing the readers' attention but also of inviting them to embark upon a fanciful voyage in the natural world:

> Let us see for a moment what kind of tales science has to tell, and how far they are equal to the old fairy tales we all know so well. Who does not remember the tale of the 'Sleepy Beauty in the Wood', and how under the spell of the angry fairy the maiden pricked herself with the spindle and slept a hundred years? ...
>
> Can science bring any tale to match this?
>
> Tell me, is there anything in this world more busy and active than water, as it rushes along in the swift brook, or dashes over the stones, or spouts up in the fountain, or trickles down from the roof, or shakes itself into ripples on the surface of the pond as the wind blows over it? But have you never seen this water spell-bound and motionless? ...
>
> All this water was yesterday flowing busily, or falling drop by drop, or floating invisibly in the air; now it is all caught and spell-bound – by whom? By the enchantments of the frost-giant who holds it fast in his grip and will not let it go.

But wait awhile, the deliverer is coming. In a few weeks or days, or it may be in a few hours, the brave sun will shine down; the dull-gray, leaden sky will melt before him, as the hedge gave way before the prince in the fairy tale, and when the sunbeam kisses the frozen water it will be set free. Then the brook will flow rippling on again; the frost-drops will be shaken down from the trees, the icicles fall from the roof, the moisture trickle down the window-pane, and in the bright, warm sunshine all will be alive again.

Is not this a fairy tale of nature? and such as these it is which science tells...

In fairy-land, flowers blow, houses spring up like Aladdin's palace in a single night, and people are carried hundreds of miles in an instant by the touch of a fairy wand.

And...this land is not some distant country to which *we* can never hope to travel. It is here in the midst of us, only our eyes must be opened or we cannot see it.[12]

The image of water frozen by a giant and delivered by a courageous sun and the multiple personifications are common narrative techniques found in popular science works which we have already examined. Moreover, in keeping with the many Victorian attempts at connecting fairy tales with natural phenomena, this imaginary journey amid giants and charming princes mirrors the scientific context of the time. But Buckley does not merely propose allegories of nature. Her narrative technique aims to train children to visualize her 'fairy-land'. As Kate Flint contends,

The functioning of the metaphor to explain the operations of the invisible was necessarily crucial to the figuration and popularization of many further developments in Victorian science, particularly those concerning molecular laws, the workings of electricity, magnetism and wave theory.[13]

Thus Buckley's fairies and fairy tales take an active part in a contemporary search for a language able to give shape to invisible physical phenomena, as in the following example where she lays bare her method:

Can you see in your imagination fairy *Cohesion* ever ready to lock atoms together when they draw very near to each other: or fairy

Gravitation dragging rain-drops down to the earth: or the fairy of *Crystallization* building up the snow-flakes in the clouds? Can you picture tiny sunbeam-waves of light and heat traveling from the sun to the earth?[14]

It is well to know that when a piece of potassium is thrown on water the change which takes place is expressed by the formula $K + H^2O = KHO + H$. But it is better still to have a mental picture of the tiny atoms clasping each other, and mingling so as to make a new substance, and to feel how wonderful are the many changing forms of nature... No one can love dry facts; we must clothe them with real meaning and love the truths they tell, if we wish to enjoy science.[15]

The stress on mental pictures, on the need to picture physical actions through animated fairies, is typical of Buckley's popular science work. Her fairies push dry facts and chemical formulas away to make room for a fantastic realm where abstract physical phenomena can take shape. Of course, the use of fairies to metaphorize physical phenomena was not rare in the Victorian period, and such new conceptions of the scientific method could best be felt in works directed to children. But Buckley explores the metaphoric possibilities of literary genres associated with children's literature in order to combat scientific materialism. Indeed, in the presentation of her narrative method, we see how the invisible forces which her fairies represent enable her not only to merge science and literature but also to revamp natural theology:

I have promised to introduce you to-day to the fairyland of science – a somewhat bold promise, seeing that most of you probably look upon science as a bundle of dry facts, while fairyland is all that is beautiful, and full of poetry and imagination. But I thoroughly believe myself, and hope to prove to you, that science is full of beautiful pictures, of real poetry, and of wonder-working fairies; and what is more, I promise you that they shall be true fairies, whom you will love just as much when you are old and grayheaded as when you are young; for you will be able to call them up whenever you wander by land or by sea, through meadow or through wood, through water or through air; and though they themselves will always remain invisible, yet you will see their wonderful poet at work everywhere around you.[16]

The sight of nature triggers emotions and feelings, its 'poetry' bearing the stamp of the creator. In such a 'fairyland of science', ice is conceived as spellbound water and is compared to Sleeping Beauty, while Catskin's walnut containing three beautiful dresses pales in comparison with the shell palaces of many minute living creatures. Buckley's narrative strategies are more than just a means of attracting her readers' attention: as she borrows from older natural theology narratives aimed at children, she simultaneously opens her readers' eyes to new scientific methods which include the imagination in order to shape hypotheses and make deductions. Just as you must believe in fairy tales to see fairies, you must believe in nature's marvels if you want to see invisible phenomena. Like Charles Kingsley's parallel between natural history and Christian faith, science and belief go hand in hand:

> The peasant falls asleep some evening in a wood, and his eyes are opened by a fairy wand, so that he sees the little goblins and imps dancing round him on the green sward, sitting on mushrooms, or in the heads of the flowers, drinking out of acorn-cups, fighting with blades of grass, and riding on grasshoppers.
>
> So, too, the gallant knight, riding to save some poor oppressed maiden, dashes across the foaming torrent; and just in the middle, as he is being swept away, his eyes are opened, and he sees fairy water-nymphs soothing his terrified horse and guiding him gently to the opposite shore. They are close at hand, these sprites, to the simple peasant or the gallant knight, or to anyone who has the gift of the fairies and can see them. But the man who scoffs at them, and does not believe in them or care for them, he *never* sees them...
>
> Now, exactly, all this which is true of the fairies of our childhood is true too of the fairies of science. There are *forces* around us, and among us, which I shall ask you to allow me to call *fairies*, and these are ten thousand times more wonderful, more magical, and more beautiful in their work, than those of the old fairy tales. They, too, are invisible, and many people live and die without ever seeing them or caring to see them. These people go about

with their eyes shut, either because they will not open them, or because no one has taught them how to see. They fret and worry over their own little work and their own petty troubles, and do not know how to rest and refresh themselves, by letting the fairies open their eyes and show them the calm sweet pictures of nature.[17]

The passage draws upon stereotypical images of fairies dancing in the moonlight in fairy rings, sitting on mushrooms or riding insects, in the vein of Richard Doyle's fairy pictures, for example,[18] and seemingly match late Victorian representations of tamed fairies typically associated with the world of childhood and children's literature.[19] Buckley capitalizes, indeed, on 'the fairies of [the children's] childhood' to develop her narrative and build up links. But if fairies are used to materialize invisible physical phenomena they also reflect new scientific methods which conceive hypotheses without relying solely on physical observation. In fact, the imagination is the only means to visualize and understand heat, cohesion, gravitation, chemical attraction or electricity, as so many fairies inhabiting nature to picture 'something quite as invisible as the Emperor's new clothes in Andersen's fairy-tale':[20]

There is only one gift we must have before we can learn to know them – we must have *imagination*. I do not mean mere fancy, which creates unreal images and impossible monsters, but imagination, the power of making pictures or *images* in our mind, of that which *is*, though it is invisible to us.[21]

Buckey's stress on and definition of imagination, as opposed to fancy – unchecked – lies at the root of her lesson and is as important as the physical phenomena described throughout the book. For the fairy-tale discourse in Buckley's *The Fairy-Land of Science* particularly brings to the fore the extent to which the use of fairy-tale motifs aims to help the reader overcome the limitations of the human eye. Buckley had probably been influenced by Charles Lyell's highly visual work.[22] Moreover, Buckley wrote at the time evolutionary theory was being popularized, and the way she stresses imagination and the human mind's power to 'correct for the human eye, [showing] how the two function together in shaping a view of the world'[23] is strongly reminiscent of Darwin's attempts at dealing with the impossibility of visualizing evolutionary theory. Indeed, it is in Buckley's refusal to separate science from the imagination that her advocation of Darwinian theory is mostly illustrated. As a matter of fact, the use of fancy in Buckley's *The Fairy-Land of Science* was meant to teach her readers 'how to *think* science'.[24] As the following passage suggests, the 'fairy wand of imagination' aligns the (amateur) scientist with fairy-tale characters, presenting science as a method hinged upon inner vision:

> How are you to enter the fairy-land of science?
>
> There is but one way. Like the knight or peasant in the fairy tales, you must open your eyes. There is no lack of objects: everything around you will tell some history if touched with the fairy wand of imagination.[25]

It is noteworthy that Buckley's narrative is quite reminiscent of John Tyndall's 1870 lecture, 'Scientific Use of the Imagination', as she draws upon Tyndall's theory to underline the fallibility of human sight. For Tyndall (1820–93), imagination is essential for the scientist. In 'Scientific Use of the Imagination', Tyndall explains how light and ether are related to the mechanisms of optical action. Light, like life, 'lies entirely without the domain of the senses'.[26] Hence the necessity to 'lighten the darkness which surrounds the world of the senses' through the power of the imagination. Tyndall's stress on imagination as 'the mightiest instrument of the physical discoverer'[27] advocates post-Darwinian science: imagination is what lies at the root of the 'science which is now binding the parts of nature to an organic whole'.[28] Though checked by reason, humans' speculative faculty enables them to imagine and discover ever smaller and unsuspected worlds, as in the case of microscopy, leading them, perhaps, to understand the origins of life: 'Life was present potentially in matter when in the nebulous form, and was unfolded from it by the way of natural development.'[29] This idea, he argues, is not alien to Christianity, for it 'leaves in fact [the] mystery [of the universe] untouched'[30] and merely posits the origins of life a few millions years before Genesis.

Tyndall's emphasis on the mystery of the universe enables him to promote new views of the natural world without totally dismissing religion. The idea that, though science was trying to explain the mechanisms of life, life retained its mysteries, permeated Victorian popular science works that were attempting to present to a middle-class public the findings of modern science. In an article published in the *Cornhill Magazine* in 1862, James Hinton praises contemporary science yet manages to make room for a religious vision of the natural world through rewriting material facts as *forces*. The forces, energies or powers at stake in the natural world shape a fairy-tale realm which humans can look at and which yet remains unfathomable:

> Dwelling on this idea of unalterable power, we begin to feel ourselves in a new world of fascinating interest and mysterious awe... All things put forth universal relations, and assume a weird and mystical character. The world becomes doubled to us: it is one world of things perceived; one unperceivable. The objects which surround us lose their substantiality when we think of them as forms under which something which is not they, nor essentially connected with them, is presented to us; something which has met us under forms the most unlike before, and may meet us under other forms again. In short, all nature grows like an enchanted garden; a fairy world in which unknown existences lurk under familiar shapes, and every object seems ready, at the shaking of a wand, to take on the strangest transformation.[31]

Both Tyndall's and Hinton's essays highlight how scientists recurrently stressed 'how profound a mystery hides itself behind all that they can teach us',[32] nature constantly reflecting a 'higher meaning', 'a mightier presence' which triggers awe, suggesting 'a profound Unity unreached by that natural apprehension to which the varying forms are all'. Thus, what looks like an unfathomable mystery can only be understood through fusing science and religion and reading a 'spiritual significance in all material things'.[33] We can see here that, instead of underlining the material aspects of modern science and its reading of the natural world, Hinton calls for a reconciliation of matter and spirit as the sole means of accessing knowledge. The emotions that he claims nature arouses in humans result therefore from the divine which modern science reveals daily to untrained eyes. As Nicola Bown explains, for Hinton, the universe is animated by forces that even when envisaged in materialistic terms nonetheless reveal divine power – a force one can feel through intuition and which 'gives science its transcendental meaning'.[34] The significance of an intuitive approach to nature tones down materialistic definitions of the universe and insufflates the spiritual, the sacred and some enchantment into reality.

Bown's conclusion that Hinton's attitude to science is revealing of mid-Victorian anxieties, particularly illustrated by the comparison of science with the world of fairies, which stands both for the wonders of science and fears related to the implications of scientific knowledge, is significant to this discussion.[35] If Hinton's concern with the nature of 'life force' or the relations between matter and spirit result from his training, as physiologist and physicist, it nevertheless permeated the reflections of the most materialistic scientists, such as T. H. Huxley (1825–95), and it is therefore no wonder that popular science works aimed at children should capitalize on the fairy-tale mode to negotiate fears related to the secularization of the natural world. As a matter of fact, Buckley contends in her work that she owes a lot to contemporary popular science works and recurrently cites Sir John Herschel (1792–1871), Charles Lyell (1797–1875), John Tyndall, Louis Agassiz (1807–73), T. H. Huxley or Ernst Haeckel (1834–1919). Moreover, Sir John Herschel's belief that pursuing material laws 'open out vista after vista, which seem to lead onward to the point where the material blends and is lost in the spiritual and intellectual', mentioned in Hinton's article,[36] informs Buckley's *Fairy-Land of Science*. Buckley's representation of forces, in particular sun beams, borrows from Herschel's experiments with light. As a result, Buckley's invisible fairy messengers, illustrating forces or waves unseen to the naked eye, enable her to offer an enchanting vision of the natural world that both suits the commercial needs of her popular science work and simultaneously combines the marvels and doubts of scientific knowledge:

> But perhaps you will ask, if no one has ever seen these waves nor the ether in which they are made, what right have we to say they are there? Strange as it may seem, though we cannot see them we have measured them and know how large they are, and how many can go into an inch of space...
>
> I promised you would find in science things as wonderful as in fairy tales. Are not these tiny invisible messengers coming

incessantly from the sun as wonderful as any fairies? and still more so when ... they are doing nearly all the work of our world.[37]

Buckley's evolutionary epic: from the fairy messengers to the natural ecosystem

As suggested above, Buckley's stress on the link between modern science and the importance of the imagination is closely related to her attempt to present evolutionary theory to middle-class audiences in a non-threatening way. One of the new narrative formats that Victorian popularizers increasingly used in the second half of the nineteenth century was what Bernard Lightman termed the 'evolutionary epic'.[38] Arabella Buckley, who was Charles Lyell's secretary between 1864 and 1875 and who knew the leading scientists of the time, from Alfred Russel Wallace (1823–1913) to Darwin and T. H. Huxley, was one of the most significant exponents of this genre, capitalizing on the narrative qualities of natural history. Buckley's use of fairy-tale motifs in *Life and Her Children* (1880) and *Winners in Life's Race* (1883), popular science works aimed at explaining evolution to children, is in keeping with what we have seen so far. The motifs associated with the world of the fairy tale evoke the wonders of the natural world: the world is peopled by 'wondrous little beings', 'wonderful things', 'fairy structure[s]', 'sylph-like creatures whose histories are more like fairy poems', 'beautiful fairy jelly-bells', sea-urchins, like the 'goblins of fairy tales', 'fairy-like' insects or 'fairy-shrimps', and even 'fairy cradles' for spiders.[39] What is striking, however, is her use of fairies and motifs associated with the fairy tale to illustrate evolutionary theory. In fact, her creatures are significantly marvellous because of their adaptation and 'gradual rise in power'.[40] The sponges are 'wonderful' because of their development of 'weapons of defence'. The 'wonderful and deadly' instruments are the 'wonderful defensive weapons' that are developed by species as they adapt and climb up the evolutionary scale: they are all 'examples of the tricks which life has taught to her children for protection and attack'.[41] Likewise, the ecosystem she describes, showing how devourers are in turn devoured, is rendered in terms associated with the marvellous: 'the wonderful rapidity with which the living matter is devoured'.[42] While earlier science popularizers had highlighted the cruelty of nature, Buckley's evolutionary epic, in which species fight in a hostile environment, sensationalizes Darwin's theories. The 'struggle for life' or the 'battle of existence'[43] demands that species adapt to their hostile environment by growing weapons to survive: 'in many places the battle is fierce, and each one must fight remorselessly for himself and his little ones'.[44] Of course, the idea that the devouring of one animal by another is necessary for the balance of species may be traced back to William Paley's natural theology and nature's population check. Nevertheless, Buckley manages to draw upon Paleyan clichés the better to advocate a vision of natural selection which does not dismiss religion.

Indeed, if Buckley and other popularizers who used the narrative format of the evolutionary epic were closer to evolutionary naturalists than the women popularizers or Anglican clergymen who advocated natural theology, they did not merely uncritically reproduce, simplify or fictionalize science. On the contrary, as Lightman argues, David Page and Buckley, in particular, adapted the evolutionary epic in order to 'subvert the secularising goals of Huxley and his allies'.[45] Not only does Buckley's prose teem with descriptive detail when she depicts species' appearance, focusing on their shape, colour or texture, but her use of similes is also strikingly visual. Her language is both concrete and metaphorical, even to the point of personifying the species she describes. Lynn Merrill contends that Buckley's use of sensory words which imply an aesthetic judgment highlights her wish to engage the reader with highly emotive prose.[46] I would argue that Buckley's use of an emotional and subjective language is not just meant to evoke 'a deep sense of religious awe',[47] as is the case of much moralizing Victorian nature writing. Rather, like Charles Kingsley, Buckley's use of the marvellous and fairy-tale metaphors signals more than mere aesthetic judgement: it underlines Buckley's attempt, in the course of popularizing evolutionary theory, to negotiate the tensions between science and religion – hence her rapturous depiction of struggles and fights.

In order to achieve this, Buckley constantly intermingles the scientific and literary or artistic worlds. For instance, she inserts literary quotes into her development, alludes to romantic poetry to aestheticize the world, describes the natural world in terms of pictures and paintings, some creatures' bodies looking like 'a painter's easel' or pleasing the eye 'more than gaudy pictures', and her works employ illustrations in which natural elements and letters are merged.[48]

The resulting visual unity, combining science and the arts, is fundamental to her definition of nature which aims at uniting matter and spirit. Moreover, Buckley's reference to Tyndall, who attempted to demonstrate the compatibility of evolutionary science with religion, explains why Buckley felt safe to popularize Tyndall's ideas and use them to promote natural selection. As a matter of fact, Buckley stressed the spiritual dimension of evolution. Her 'spiritual evolutionism'[49] is foregrounded at the opening of *Life and Her Children* when she aligns nature's invisible mother, whose law is that 'all living beings [must] "increase, multiply, and replenish the world"' with 'the great Creator'.[50] In both *Life and Her Children* and *Winners in Life's Race*, Buckley draws more and more on the idea of life as 'a superproductive mother nature ... balanced against the notion of struggle'.[51] In fact, Buckley makes explicit the idea that evolution marches hand in hand with the development of 'maternal care' and 'sympathy'.[52] Because of the vertebrates' 'higher feelings', the notion of the ' "struggle for existence" ' inculcates a sense of 'higher devotion of mother to child, and friend to friend, which ends in a tender love for every living being, since it recognizes that mutual help and sympathy are among the most wonderful weapons, as they are also certainly the most noble incentives, which can be employed in fighting the battle for life'.[53]

Buckley's advocacy of Darwin's idea of the transmutation of species, though germane to the theology of nature praised by Margaret Gatty and many other women popularizers, nonetheless emphasizes the view of the universe as an organic whole in which organisms are interrelated and interdependent. In *Life and Her Children*, Buckley describes nature through 'the family bond uniting all *living* beings'.[54] Hence Buckley's conclusion to *Winners in Life's Race*, which foregrounds the idea of love transcending the struggle for life. Mutual affection results precisely from the laws of evolution:

> [O]ne of the laws of life which is strong, if not stronger, than the law of force and selfishness, is that of mutual help and dependence. Many good people have shrunk from the idea that we owe the beautiful diversity of animal life on our earth to the struggle for existence, or to the necessity that the best fitted should live, and the feeblest and least protected must die. They have felt that this makes life a cruelty, and the world a battlefield. This is true to

a certain extent, for who will deny that in every life there is pain and suffering and struggle? But with this there is also love and gentleness, devotion and sacrifice for others, tender motherly and fatherly affection, true friendship, and a pleasure which consists in making others happy ... after all, the struggle is not entirely one of cruelty or ferocity ... the highest and most successful education which Life has given her children to fit them for winning the race is that 'unity is strength'; while the law of love and duty beginning with parent and child and the ties of home life, and developing into the mutual affection of social animals, has been throughout a golden thread, strengthened by constant use in contending with the fiercer and more lawless instincts ... Thus we arrive at the greatest and most important lesson that the study of nature affords us ... that amidst toil and suffering, struggle and death, the supreme law of life is the law of SELF-DEVOTION AND LOVE.[55]

The end of her narrative discards images of life as a battlefield ruled by the struggle for existence – the very same images the whole book (and its illustrations) has dwelled upon and praised in dramatic terms – so as to make room for love and devotion, placed at the top of the evolutionary tree. Buckley's works on evolution are good examples of her refusal to advocate Darwin's materialistic vision of mankind. For Buckley, contemporary scientific authorities misread Darwin if they believed evolutionary science robbed humans of their conscience and reduced them to matter. This idea is particularly foregrounded in her article 'The Soul, and the Theory of Evolution', while the spiritual dimension of evolution that she preached appears most clearly in 'Darwinism and Religion' (1871) and *Moral Teachings of Science*. In the latter, Buckley deplores the waning of religion and suggests how the study of science might become a means of instilling moral principles. Buckley's interpretation of natural selection posits that the world is a tangled bank, an ecosystem in which 'life is not a mere selfish warfare ... mutual help and service are among the very laws of existence, and ... the truly fittest to survive are those who, in working for self-preservation, promote the good of others'.[56] The examples of plants affording shelter and food for ants in order to protect themselves from their attack, just like the need to render service in return for not bringing about an attack, are so many examples proving that 'those [who] succeed best ... in fulfilling their own life, also compass the good of other beings'.[57] As a consequence, 'in the struggle for existence, self-preservation and mutual help work hand in hand'; 'self-devotion and self-sacrifice for the good of all' will ensure the survival of the fittest.[58]

As Barbara Gates contends, Buckley was a pioneer in realizing 'the tentativeness in Darwin's thought on the development of moral qualities in the animal kingdom, set out in his discussion of "social instincts" in *The Descent of Man*'.[59] For Buckley, the moral is a highly evolved sense. Thus, her popularization of natural history and Darwinism attempts to go beyond tensions, and her fairies successfully mediate between scientific and religious discourses. In fact, Buckley's interest in spiritualism (and even her belief that she might be a medium herself)[60] reinforces the idea that the fairies and 'spirits' with whom she peoples her works really encapsulate the union of science and religion. For Lightman,

> Although the analogy she draws between invisible natural forces and fairies in [*The Fairy-Land of Science*] can be interpreted as a device to entice children to become interested in the wondrous world of nature while retaining a naturalist perspective, it could also reflect her fascination with spiritualism.[61]

Lightman's contention is quite relevant, because late Victorian scientific approaches to fairy tales sometimes read fairy tales as primitive forms of spirituality and reflections of the belief in humans' immortal souls. For instance, in 1891 Edwin Sidney Hartland defined fairy tales as traditional narratives of 'the lower races ... to account for the phenomena of nature, or their own history and organization',[62] and his construction of the 'doctrine of Spirits' shows how such scientific approaches to fairy tales in the last decades of the nineteenth century drew upon materialist science: folklorists and anthropologists reproduced Darwinian conjectural methods, while pseudo-scientific discourses recuperated scientists' analyses of light, space and etheric undulations to justify the invisible world of spirits. Hartland's evolutionary vision of fairy tales as narratives representing how '[t]he different stages of [mankind's] progress have everywhere left their mark on the tales and songs, the sayings and superstitions, the social, religious and political institutions'[63] also strongly relies on the inductive method. For him, 'reasoning by induction'[64] is central to being able to grasp the origins of fairy tales – just as it is central to understanding the origins of life on earth and of mankind.

Hartland's scientific construction and definition of fairy tales suggests that fairies and fairy tales could touch upon mystical as much as magical phenomena and it is enlightening to study Buckley's use of motifs associated with Fairyland. For Buckley's fairies and her stress on the imagination, backed up by Tyndall's views on science, reveal perhaps more occult preoccupations in keeping with her interest in spiritualism. As Srdjan Smajic argues, if Tyndall's use of the word occult 'has mystical resonances' so 'does *imagination*, a word that most scientists avoid, Tyndall observes, "because of its ultra-scientific connotations"'.[65] Consequently, Buckley's almost metaphysical description of material reality, showing her refusal to view humans as soul-less creatures aligned with animals, illustrates the polyvalence of the imagination and how multi-faceted invisible beings, such as fairies, could be. Indeed, as Carole G. Silver's study of the Little People illuminates, the belief that fairies were life-forms developed on a separate branch of evolution was sustained by evolutionary scientists, such as Alfred Russel Wallace, for instance, for whom there existed 'preter-human discarnate beings'.[66] Fairies were redefined as nature spirits that occultists and clairvoyants firmly believed in, creatures that were invisible because posited outside the human colour spectrum.[67] Thus, Buckley, who was a close friend of Wallace's, and who shared an interest in spiritualism with him,[68] may well have fashioned fairies that enabled her to unite matter and spirit so as to promote spiritualism.

Perhaps more significantly, however, her emphasis on parenting and mutuality in her reading of natural selection gradually shaped a 'moral ecology',[69] as her visionary call for the protection of the environment suggests: 'This world is not one in which, by chance or by solicitation, we can escape the consequences of our acts, or reap that which neither we nor our ancestors have sown.'[70] Thus, the fairies that inhabit her works may also hint at the potential disappearance of natural marvels. Consequently, at a time when scientists, amateur naturalists and collectors started being concerned with endangered flora and fauna and the pollution and destruction of natural sites, as highlighted for instance by Edmund Gosse in *The Naturalist of the Sea-shore, The Life of Philip Henry Gosse* (1890),[71] Buckley's popularization of natural history and evolutionary theory provides a good instance of popularizers' attempts at making children aware of their responsibility on earth as thinking and moral beings.

Indeed, at the time when Buckley was writing children's fiction and magazines aimed at middle-class audiences, such as *Aunt Judy's Magazine*, particularly aimed at girls, used the natural world to teach children lessons about Christian faith and duties, mixing fiction and natural history lessons. But their publications gradually evolved towards a concern with the degradation of the natural world caused by scientific and technological developments. The parables and fairy tales published by such magazines, as those by its editor, the naturalist Margaret Gatty, or her daughter, Juliana Horatia Ewing (1841–85), proposed allegories of nature that more and more denounced Britain's massive industrialization and urbanization.[72] As we shall now see, many literary fairy tales of the same period warned children and adult audiences alike of the dangers of technological advances and the implications of scientific knowledge. On the literary scene, writers capitalized on the metaphorical potential of fairies and fairy-tale motifs and drew on images that were informed by current scientific theories. Because it was based upon literary images and techniques, the language that scientists and popularizers of science used to make science more tangible and represent new definitions of nature infused Victorian literary narratives. The fairy tale, more especially, offered writers a means to look at Victorian reality through the looking-glass. Its motifs and images, both rooted in a literary tradition and conveying a much more modern approach to nature, enabled Victorian writers to play with contemporary constructions of nature and to counteract, in so doing, a materialistic science that increasingly turned individuals into machines or defined them as a series of visual ciphers. In the fairy tales of the 1860s and 1870s we will now examine, the tales more and more denounce contemporary definitions of femininity shaped by scientific discourse. Women, as fairies or readers, are at the centre of the narratives, their bodies often used to mediate knowledge about nature.

3
The Mechanization of Feelings: Mary de Morgan's 'A Toy Princess'

It is the Age of Machinery, in every outward and inward sense of that word.[1]

The world is growing too clever for the fairies, I fear, unless perhaps, unseen and unsuspected, they are still behind the scenes in some of the marvels and inventions all around us. Who can say?[2]

As argued in the Introduction, as early as in ancient times the term 'nature' was polyvalent, indifferently used to define the natural world and human nature alike. In the nineteenth century, the 'natural historical way of knowing', to draw upon John Pickstone's phrase again, implied the breaking down into pieces of natural specimens and humans alike, as naturalists, scientists or medical professionals looked for 'regularities',[3] recurrently comparing humans to machines to understand function. Moreover, because of the old and enduring association of women and nature, with the onset of the Scientific Revolution the mechanization of the world-view and the attendant increase in mechanistic models aimed at explaining nature saw women as disorderly beings that needed to be controlled, restructuring them in a way as machines. The reordering of the world through the machine metaphor – as an image of the power of humans and technology to control nature and human life – redefined reality. As Carolyn Merchant argues, '[r]ational control over nature, society, and the self was achieved by redefining reality itself through the new machine metaphor'.[4] Since bodies were seen as marvellous machines made up of different pieces, the Scientific Revolution saw the making and popularization of automata, contraptions often defined as wonderful, all the more so because many of them came from the East.[5] Not only were automata emblems of scientific and technological progress but also represented humans' achievement in duplicating nature. Poised between the world of science and the realm of wonders, they were aligned with clocks and mathematical instruments in eighteenth-century cabinets of wonder,[6] advertised at travelling fairs, shown at Madame Tussaud's and Bartholomew Fair or used in ventriloquism shows at the end of the nineteenth century,[7] fascinating artists precisely for their capacity to counterfeit nature. It was often in the gap between the natural and the artificial that fairies appeared in mid-Victorian experiments with automata. For instance, in an article published in *All the Year Round* in 1870 reviewing several automata from the past and the present, the deceptive nature of automata seemed to march hand in hand with the release of fairy creatures: in the case of the Invisible Girl, which made the audience suppose an invisible girl was suspended in mid-air in a small globe, visitors were led to believe that the lady was 'a very young and diminutive being indeed – a fairy, an invisible girl'.[8] These blatant illustrations of humans' superiority over nature heralded the death of human nature, however, as the writings of several Victorian writers seem to suggest.

Mary Augusta de Morgan, women and the scientific world

Mary Augusta de Morgan (1850–1907) was the daughter of Augustus de Morgan (1806–71), Professor of Mathematics at University College, London. Her mother was Sophia Elizabeth (1809–92), who had a thirst for knowledge and was particularly interested in phrenology and even published a book on spiritualism, *From Matter to Spirit* (1863). Sophia Elizabeth de Morgan also fought for social improvement and the higher education of women, supported Elizabeth Fry's campaign for prison and workhouse reform, promoted Bedford College for women and was an early advocate of women's suffrage.[9] As the sister of William de Morgan, well known as an artist involved in the arts and craft movement and novelist, Mary de Morgan was close to many Victorian artists, such as Dante Gabriel Rossetti (1828–82), William Morris (1834–96), Edward Burne-Jones (1833–98) and Rudyard Kipling (1865–1936), especially as she shared a house with her brother when her father died in 1871 and told tales to Jenny and May Morris, Phil and Margaret Burne-Jones (to whom *The Windfairies* is dedicated) and Rudyard and 'Trix' Kipling.[10] She wrote three volumes of fairy tales: *On a Pincushion and Other Fairy Tales* (1877), *The Necklace of Princess Fiorimonde* (1880) and *The Windfairies* (1900), before she moved to Egypt when her health began to fail, and looked after a reformatory for children in Cairo until her death in 1907.

Her fairy tales are difficult to classify. Some of them follow in the footsteps of Hans Christian Andersen's tales, as the characters are severely punished for their sins and the tales often close on death. But her fairy tales also frequently seem to rewrite uncanny or supernatural tales as though to domesticate them. Echoes from E. T. A Hoffmann resonate in 'The Story of Vain Lamorna', since Lamorma's stolen reflection recalls Hoffmann's 'A New Year's Eve Adventure'; the children's eyes stolen by the owl in 'Siegried and Handa' hint at the sandman's children, sitting in the nest with their hooked beaks like owls waiting to be fed with children's eyes, while in 'A Toy Princess' (1877)[11] the toy princess is another automaton in the vein of Hoffmann's stupid though beautifully formed wooden doll Olimpia who can only say 'Ah' or 'Goodnight, dear'.

'A Toy Princess' combines a concern for the feminine ideal reminiscent of the perfect housewives praised in classical fairy tales with an awareness of the way in which modern science and technology sever humans from their own nature. On the one hand, de Morgan's fairy tales frequently show a fascination with woman's beauty and the construction of femininity: the fairy princesses are often too vain, as in 'Vain Kesta',[12] or in 'The Story of Vain Lamorna',[13] in which the heroine is punished by being scarred. In 'The Ploughman and the Gnome', the gnome, who grants the ploughman everything he wants if he can always get the best, is an ugly little black woman who eventually wants to cut off the ploughman's wife's face with her knife to be beautiful.[14] In 'The Hair Tree', the Queen becomes bald and tries all remedies for her hair to grow again on her head.[15] On the other hand, de Morgan's tales also bring to the fore her knowledge of educational works for children, such as her collection of tales, *On a Pincushion and Other Fairy Tales*, the title of which is reminiscent of an early book for children blending instruction and amusement,

Mary Ann Kilner's *The Adventures of the Pincushion designed chiefly for the use of young ladies* (1788).[16] In de Morgan's collection of tales, a pebble Brooch, a jet Shawl-pin and a common Pin tell each other stories. From time to time the stories are permeated with scientific phenomena. In 'The Story of Vain Lamorna' elves steal the reflection of Lamorna who spends her time looking at herself, and explain what reflection is.[17] In 'The Story of the Opal' the description of sunbeams and moonbeams recalls popular science works for children playing on fairy-tale motifs to represent natural phenomena.[18] The tale offers lessons in astronomy: Sunbeam and Moonbeam are in love with each other but unable to be together at the same time. The definition of the Opal, heralded by the title of the tale, is given when they shelter in a stone from which shoot up bright, beautiful rays of light, silver and gold. The explanation reinforces the connection between de Morgan's tales and nineteenth-century didactic literature.[19] Similarly, in 'The Hair Tree', an embedded animal-bridegroom tale relates the story of Trevina, who is stolen by the king of the tortoises when she searches among the rocks for strange animals and seaweed like an amateur naturalist.[20] Another instance might be 'Through the Fire', which plays on water-fairies, wind-fairies and fire-fairies serving as tropes for physical phenomena to explain how water puts out fire: Princess Pyra wants to marry the water King's son, Prince Fluvius, but they are afraid of touching each other lest he should be dried up or she put out.[21] As 'The Wise Princess' suggests, however, with a princess whose thirst for knowledge is eventually fatal, de Morgan's narratives also satirize children's education, an idea which de Morgan develops further in 'A Toy Princess' through the denunciation of the civilizing process.[22]

'A Toy Princess' blends de Morgan's interest in femininity and science through the figure of the automaton. The fairy tale, designed for children, popularizes British technological advances, the automaton epitomizing progress. But de Morgan's satirical view of society also denounces contemporary politics. The fairy tale thus groups together science and politics, showing the implications of the mechanization of feelings. In so doing, I argue, de Morgan illustrates how characteristic structures of knowledge inform society and permeate other discourses: in her fairy tale, new conceptions of nature defined by scientists eventually determine power structures. Doomed to die in the kingdom which represses citizens and forbids them to express their emotions, a princess is rescued by her fairy godmother who takes her to the seaside to be brought up by a family of fishermen. To replace her at the court, the godmother buys a toy princess who appears the spitting image of the princess but only says 'If you please', 'No, thank you', 'Certainly' and 'Just so'. Because the king is about to abdicate in favour of his daughter, however, the godmother reveals the plot by striking the toy princess on the head with her wand: the head rolls on the floor, showing the princess as 'an empty shell'.[23] Just as the magic wand does not enable the godmother to perform magic feats and sensational metamorphoses, the court is a disenchanted and dangerous society ruled by utilitarian philosophy. The toy princess is placed in a cupboard until the mystery of the 'real' princess is solved. But when the flesh-and-blood princess, now grown up into a young woman, appears in court, she is dismissed, mainly because of her uninhibited feelings and lack of restraint, and the government is left in the hands of the toy princess.

The replacement of the female body by an automaton not only illustrates the power of technology over nature but also derides the ideal Victorian woman generally extolled in fairy tales. By turning the traditional representation of ideal femininity on its head and disrupting expectations, de Morgan highlights gender ideologies and undermines contemporary definitions of woman. Moreover, through the figure of the automaton, de Morgan's changes in the formula condemn stereotypical princesses, whose sole qualities lie in beauty, politeness and self-abnegation. The tale *does* point to such living-dead and passive princesses, from Snow White, locked up in her glass coffin, to Sleeping Beauty, patiently awaiting the coming of the prince. It is also reminiscent of many of the Brothers Grimm's fairy tales, featuring dumb or silent heroines, who please kings and become queens precisely because of their voicelessness.[24] Indeed, as the fairy tale makes clear, the princesses in classical fairy tales, just like the ideal Victorian woman, are constructs – doll-like women generated by bourgeois norms. The transformation of fairy-tale motifs and stock characters therefore enables de Morgan to explore the fairy tale's potential to defamiliarize the real in order to reveal ideologies of domesticity.

The idea that mores and norms are sterile and deadly is not only illustrated by the deaths of the princesses but also by the turning of creation into reproduction: instead of visualizing the fairy godmother's magical powers and creations, she is shown purchasing an artefact which results from mechanical reproduction. Thus mechanized and dehumanized, reproduction is sterile and dangerous. In classical fairy tales, the death of the princess's mother at the opening of the tale indicates that the time is now ripe for the princess to evolve and become a woman in her turn. Hence, death signals rebirth, highlighting the cycles of a woman's life. However, in de Morgan's tale, death does not prefigure renewal. Politeness and repression, epitomizing *civilité*, are not signs of evolution and rebirth: 'it was thought to be the rudest thing in the world for any one to say they liked or disliked, or loved or hated, or were happy or miserable' (p. 165). Hence the princess's mother's unsuitability: just like her people, she shows what she feels, cries and laughs. Furthermore, as the princess grows quieter, her face becomes thinner and paler, matching more and more the stereotype of the Victorian wasting woman who refuses to eat.[25] Repression is, moreover, figured as a literal imprisonment: just as Ursula can neither cry nor sigh nor speak, she is isolated in her bedroom, compelled to look at the outside world through the window (she later escapes with her godmother through the very same window). The birds flying in the sky are contrasted with the feminine ideal whose clipped wings condemn her to remain indoors. The depiction of Ursula's education further foregrounds ideologies of control and the repressive aspect of the civilizing process. The lack of toys and dolls in Ursula's bedroom and her exclusion from any kind of entertainment aim to suppress any form of imagination. In a country where people do not speak more than 'quite necessary' (p. 165), utilitarianism reigns supreme.

Obviously, the fairy-tale mode is used by de Morgan to underline the divide between civilization, and its related technological progress, and humans. It becomes a means of questioning the severing of humans' connection with nature and the natural world as well as with their own nature. Indeed, de Morgan sets the world of nature, dreams, wish-fulfilments, pleasure and feelings and the world of the court and civilization apart from each other. The seaside inhabited by fishermen where the fairy godmother takes the princess becomes a fairy land – constructing the natural environment as a realm where humans live happily ever after. The replacement of the real princess by a mechanical one becomes a means of voicing protest. In order to rebel against the ideal of the mute feminine ideal, which emblematizes the civilizing process, Taboret attempts to show the gap which separates the ideal from the real and the impossibility of matching up to society's expectations. The toy princess is an automaton which, if it bespeaks its society's manners and modes, also epitomizes human control over nature and brings to light the conflict between nature and civilization, between the organic and the mechanistic. In so doing, it counteracts contemporary constructions of science as marvellous and fairy like. The tale's critique of the civilizing process – the unnaturalness of civilized life – bears an uncanny resemblance to Hoffmann's 'The Sandman'. Indeed, in 'The Sandman', Olimpia is a wax-doll beauty who is seen as soulless and seems to be dependent upon some wound-up clockwork. She can say a few words, play, sing or dance *like* a living creature but is only an automaton – a wooden doll – with good manners introduced into high society circles. Once the plot is revealed, Olimpia's artificial and soulless good manners have raised so much doubt about ideal women that yawning and sneezing – the expression of physiological needs – become keywords for women not to pass for automata.

Scientific progress and the reinvention of nature:[26] the wonders of automata

David Brewster's *Letters on Natural Magic, Addressed to Sir Walter Scott, Bart.* (1832) were written at a time when the blurring between science and magic made it difficult to distinguish between scientific and technological advances and hoaxes. For Brewster, automatic toys were seen as both reflectors of the wonders of science and emblems of progress and civilization:

> Those mechanical wonders which one century enriched only the conjuror who used them, contributed in another to augment the wealth of the nation. Those automatic toys which once amused the vulgar, are now employed in extending the power and promoting the civilization of our species.[27]

Though Brewster was the first to suspect that the Hungarian Wolfgang von Kempelen's chess player[28] concealed a dwarf in the machinery,[29] his comparison of automata with wonders and magical spells shows how close the world of science and technology was to the realm of fairy tales.[30] A few decades later, however, as de Morgan's 'A Toy Princess' highlights, fairy godmothers no longer create magical aids – they buy them from a shop in Fairyland. Spells and charms are sold, and so are toy princesses. Although de Morgan seems to suggest here that automata are magical products from Fairyland, their mechanized production recalling British industry and technological advances, Fairyland is nevertheless disenchanted. Not only does de Morgan give the benevolent godmother a witch-like appearance (she wears a red cloak, has bright black eyes, a hooked nose and a long chin), blurring the figures of the godmother and the witch, but the merging of the two figures enhances even more the female character's loss of power. Though she can make herself invisible and uses her wand to fly through the air or to stick the severed head on the Toy Princess at the end of the narrative, Taboret, the godmother, must indeed systematically visit a shop in Fairyland to buy her magic aids (she is 'a good customer' there (pp. 166–7)). The shop turns the fairy-tale world into a distorted version of Victorian capitalist society: offering as it does 'every sort of spell or charm' (p. 166), the shop sells, in fact, illusions, as the toy princess illustrates. Indeed, the 'Princess' Taboret is looking for in the shop is a product of consumer society: Taboret can choose its size from among those 'in stock' (p. 167) and discuss its price, which may 'come rather expensive' or 'to a good deal' (p. 167). Taboret's bargaining with the seller serves to emphasize the displacement of the marvellous onto the market economy: ' "It is too much"…She did not really think it dear, but she always made a point of trying to beat tradesmen down…"I consider the price very high" ' (p. 167). The fear that the mechanical doll might be flawed and Taboret's inspection of the 'piece of work' furthers the tale's critique of industrialization, interestingly conflating the suppression of magic with the booming industrial society and the world of mass production. Moreover, the monetary exchange remains invisible (Taboret must pay with 'four cats' footfalls, two fishes' screams, and two swans' songs' (p. 167)). The invisibility and immateriality of money encapsulates the tale's play on the dehumanization of the feminine ideal: the perfect woman, as image or construct is as immaterial as money is invisible – just as society speculates, woman is a product of capitalism and its illusions, commercialized in shops. In addition, the toy princess is a spitting image of the 'real' princess: 'a little girl so like the Princess Ursula that no one could have told them apart' (p. 167). The mechanical creation is therefore a reproduction of the model, thereby intimating that the feminine ideal is a construct modelled by society's mores and norms just as the doll is fashioned by machinery. The toy princess scarcely ever speaks and exhibits 'the most elegant manners in the country' (p. 169), though she is, in fact, 'only a *sham*' (p. 172), recalling Dickens's ghostlike Miss Havisham in *Great Expectations* (1861), especially because, as we will see further on, Dickens's heartless woman in white is linked with clocks, the mechanisms of which she has stopped, and compared with waxworks at the fair.

Moreover, in de Morgan's tale, the court is a world where civilization has turned men into insensitive machines. By contrast, the place to which Taboret takes the princess to save her is a fairyland. The princess, who wants to go and live on the moon, ends up by the sea. The natural world, represented by the moon or the sea, is thus associated with typically feminine symbols; it is a place where people can express their desires and feelings. Ursula is, in addition, 'sucking her thumb' (p. 168), suggesting a newborn. De Morgan's romantic construction of childhood as innocent and uninhibited is highly reminiscent of fairy tales in which disobedient princesses are sent on difficult journeys away from their kingdoms and come back as well-behaved ladies and properly educated housewives. At the beginning, the princess is 'naughty' (p. 168), refuses to eat and to go to bed and even lets tears rise to her eyes. Her journey away from the court, however, is a journey from which there is no return. As the fairy godmother makes explicit, the Court must change – not the princess. The tale's emphasis on growth suggests how education and civilization involve a change in woman's relationship to nature. After her marriage, the princess's mother '[grows] thinner and thinner' (p. 165), losing corporeality. Similarly, as the princess '[grows] older, her eyes [grow] less and less merry and bright, and her fat little face [grows] thin and pale' (p. 166). Education is aligned with repression, turning women into living-dead creatures. This is why the automaton '[grows] to be a great favourite' (p. 169) by remaining quiet, with a pale face and 'only a very slight tint in her cheeks' (p. 171). Like people at the Court, who 'never changed but were always the same just as stiff and quiet', the toy princess's arrested development is morbid. At the same time, at the seaside Ursula '[grows] tall and straight as an alder, and merry and light-hearted as a bird' (p. 170). Once again, the rhetoric and its playful comparisons relating woman to the natural world mirror the sea as a metaphor for renewal and life.

Through the figure of the automaton, moreover, the tale exploits the ambiguous status of such mechanized objects. Simultaneously meaning 'mechanisms with concealed motive powers, and persons behaving mechanically without active intelligence', automata are 'mechanical dissembler[s]...appearing to possess that which, by definition, [they] cannot – autonomy'.[31] Thus, as a mechanical reproduction of the ideal living-dead woman, de Morgan's automaton articulates anxieties related to the collapse of the boundary between the machine and the human. Interestingly, in the Victorian period automata were popular because they offered an insight into their inner workings: it was 'the mechanics themselves that generated interest rather than the usefulness of the objects'.[32] In fact, automata mirrored physiologists' attempts at explaining human physiology and their mechanistic vision of mankind. The link between automata and human physiology can be traced back to Julien Offray La Mettrie's *Man A Machine* (1748), which aligned humans with the model of the machine. For Orford, furthermore, '[t]he root of La Mettrie's work is a focus on functionality, and it touches upon the same fears voiced by critics of the widespread industrialisation of the nineteenth century'.[33] It is, indeed, the increasing mechanistic vision of mankind which led to the making of automata,[34] and it is therefore tempting to envisage automata as reflecting the implications of materialistic science for human nature.

That the impact of the Industrial Revolution and its technological developments changed the vision of the body is a truism, and the emergence of science fiction on the literary scene at the very same time highlighted the need to redefine the body in an age of technology. As factories were making mechanical subjects, medical science was also reducing humans to no more than organic machines whose levers could, perhaps, be manipulated. Automata thus stood at the heart of the debate concerning human nature, foregrounding the divide between the machine and the organic yet offering a vision of humans *as* organic machines. As a matter of fact, with the advent of physiology, scientists began to investigate the nature of the will and the relationship between body and mind, redefining humans through voluntary or involuntary movements and actions. The dissemination of such knowledge in Victorian culture, as automata informed the reflections of physicians, engineers or even mesmerizers who seemed to turn rational humans into automata,[35] may explain why children's literature could become a significant material to mediate modern constructions of human nature.

In fact, the fairy tale, as a genre generally associated with women readers, may have been particularly efficient to diffuse ideas about contemporary associations between women and nature. Unlike women, men were 'not automatons or mindless parts of the social machinery but self-willed individuals'.[36] The figure of the automaton thus easily emblematized woman's subjection to the forces of her body. For Sally Shuttleworth, from the late eighteenth century onward, 'the traditional, rather undefined, associations between woman and the body [were] strengthened, particularized and codified in medical science'.[37] So, throughout the Victorian period, this 'shift to a taxonomy of gender'[38] was mostly reflected in the development of medical science: the increasingly mechanistic vision of female physiology constantly underlined the necessity for medical professionals to control the forces to which women seemed subjected. This may be the reason why the model of the perfect machine is often female.[39] Villiers de l'Isle-Adam's *L'Eve future* (1886), staging a perfect mechanical woman, is a case in point, underlining the links between the machine and the feminine ideal. Tellingly, in the novel the dissection of the master scientist Thomas Edison's creation, Hadaly, is permeated with terms linked to the marvellous, as if what was most fairy-like about artificial femininity was man's control over the woman's body. Programmed, the woman's body is regulated by the scientist.

Such connections between automata, female physiology and the feminine ideal are highly representative of mid-Victorian definitions of femininity. An article entitled 'Dolls' published in *Household Words* in 1853 deals with the booming manufacturing and commerce of dolls. However, the reviewer quickly draws parallels between the toys and anatomical models. Indeed, as he explains, the crafts required in doll-making involve several professions or artists, from the perruquier to the dolls'-eye-maker. The making of a doll, therefore, implying that 'one component part [derives] from one artist, one from a second, one from a third; while the master-hand puts together all the little bits which others have made for him', constructs the doll as a 'watch'.[40] The 'mathematical' precision that enables the doll to 'ris[e]

into existence',[41] together with the watch metaphor not only compares the doll to automata but also draws parallels between the toys
and contemporary mechanical conceptions of human physiology.
The dolls are 'humanised', their eyes are 'made by the same persons as those who manufacture eyes for human creatures' so as to
'bear a resemblance to nature' and their hair is often human hair.[42]
All in all, their 'like-like truthfulness'[43] constructs them as doubles
of the little girls who will play with them. More significantly still,
the article shifts from the manufacturing of dolls to waxdolls – such
as Madame Napoleon Montanari's waxdolls exhibited at the Great
Exhibition and displaying the different stages of femininity. The parallel between dolls and girls growing into women is furthered when
the reviewer proceeds to explain the links between wax modelling
and anatomical models. Dr. Auzoux's papier-maché life-sized models,
showing the workings of the human body in all its minute details,[44]
leads the reviewer to connect the medical models to the outstanding
technology of automata: 'The triumph of genius in doll-making is to
produce a doll which will speak',[45] saying 'papa' and 'mamma'[46] – a
rare species that is only made by one person.[47]

Speaking automata magnified, in fact, the way in which the
development of technology inevitably upset the divide between the
natural and the artificial. The debate on what was 'human' was
particularly encapsulated by automata which seemed more and more
able to take the place of humans, as underlined by another article of the mid-century, 'The Euphonia, or Speaking Automaton',
which marvels at another piece of mechanism just arrived in England
(the Viennese Prof. Faber's Speaking Automaton) able to articulate
sounds. Describing how the 'chief organs of articulation are formed
of caoutchouc, and a pair of bellows is substituted for the lungs', the
writer explains that the inventor was 'seven years in getting the figure
to pronounce the vowel E correctly': 'We repeat that this exhibition
is most wonderful'. Able to speak several languages, to whisper, laugh
or sing, the automaton can be seen breathing ('The breath is felt coming from the lips; and, by compressing the nostrils, it speaks with a
nasal accent immediately').[48] Furthermore, the issue of intelligence
was often at stake, as in the case of Kempelen's chess player who
fascinated audiences.

Throughout the article on the doll-making industry, the increasing parallel between dolls and 'miniature women of doll-loving

juvenility'[49] brings to light the way in which such examples of technological progress uncannily hinted at woman's physiology and revealed a desire to control woman's nature. Almost a century before, Madame Tussaud exhibited her 'breathing' waxwork, the 'Sleeping Beauty', sculpted in 1763, and the Swiss watchmaker Pierre Jaquet-Droz's (1721–90) 'Musical Lady' was brought to London and exhibited in 1776, her eyes moving and her bosom heaving. As Simon Schaffer contends, 'seduction was an indispensable accompaniment of the trade in automata'.[50] Moreover, such automata played strongly upon the 'mechaniz[ation] [of] the passions, especially those of women', the 'neat connection between passion, exoticism, mechanism and money permeat[ing] the showrooms'.[51] Another famous automaton was the naked silver dancer, built for the East India Company. Though never exhibited at Week's Museum, which closed in 1834, it was bought at auction and restored by engineer and entrepreneur Charles Babbage (1791–1871). It is noteworthy that Babbage was a friend of Augustus de Morgan, Mary de Morgan's father, and the link between automata and calculating engines in Babbage's projects, as well as the connotations of desire associated with the automata, suggest that Mary de Morgan may have heard more about automata at home than through the press or popular exhibitions.

Consequently, by figuring a toy princess, de Morgan follows in the footsteps of many other Victorian writers capitalizing on the popularity of automata, such as Charles Dickens,[52] and many other narratives where the machine metaphor served as a trope for the human condition in society. Jean Ingelow's *Mopsa the Fairy* (1869), for instance, is another case in which the hero visits a country in which women are fashioned like clocks. They have holes at the back of their heads designed to wind them up while their pulses have been replaced by a ticking noise – a hint at Jaquet-Droz's animated dolls. The women's mechanized bodies, thus reified, signal their powerlessness: since they are incapable of turning the keys at the back of their own heads to stay alive they are unable to handle time. Like Ingelow's, de Morgan's fairy tale underlines women's lack of agency and propensity to become object-like, but de Morgan goes a step further. By hinting both at civilizing practices and the socio-economic and cultural context, de Morgan connects the mechanization of feelings with industrial society, ultimately conveying a political

discourse. The Court, where people revere possessions more than people and where the manners and mores have dehumanized people and
changed them into mechanical toys, calls to mind other Victorian
fairy tales which also denounced industrialization and capitalism,
from John Ruskin's *The King of the Golden River, or the Black Brothers* (1841) to Oscar Wilde's 'The Happy Prince' (1888) at the end
of the century. But by playing upon the boundary between natural
and artificial humans, de Morgan conjures up older links between
the development of industrial technology and the early automata,
such as Vaucanson's, which seemed to 'announc[e] the modern factory, the central site where man-as-machine, worker-as-automaton,
is produced'.[53] Becoming the 'worker's mechanical doppelgänger',[54]
the automaton epitomized the impact and danger of industrialization for the human. It embodied the industrial ideal, and the image
of humans as machines was often used to voice criticisms against
industrialism. For Shuttleworth, '[c]ritics and apologists of industrialism alike proposed a similar model of man as automaton, a model
seemingly confirmed on the factory floor with its endless subdivision
of manual tasks and the subordination of human labor to the require-
ments of machinery'.[55] Tellingly, automata emerged at a time when
governmental controls were rising, setting side by side the 'rational-
ization of administration and of the natural order'.[56] This explains
why automata were more often than not used to emblematize social
or political conflicts, illustrating in so doing the pervasive influence
of knowledge structures.

This is the case in de Morgan's fairy tale. By placing her princess at
the heart of political discussion, since the automaton is ultimately
elected as queen, de Morgan also sets side by side the narrative's
emphasis on humans' lack of agency in industrial society and the
issue of despotic rulers. Ironically, the princess's fall down the social
ladder is not followed by the revelation of her royal identity and
her marriage to the prince: Ursula ends up marrying a fisherman's
son and lives 'happily ever after', thereby dismissing class and capital
as necessary to happiness. In de Morgan's utopian vision of society,
wonders and marvels are poles apart from technology and progress,
as suggested by many of her princesses, all closely linked to the natural world, such as Lucilla, in 'The Windfairies', who is taught how
to dance by the windfairies,[57] or the heroine of 'The Rain Maiden',
who loves water and rain.[58] Thus, de Morgan's use of the fairy tale

and her construction of princesses as toys offer a sharp political comment by miniaturizing the world, its institutions and inhabitants. By showing humans as programmed, dwarfed citizens who have lost all autonomy, and cancelling magic from the narrative, de Morgan's bleak picture of modern England, where science and technology have suppressed feelings and the supernatural has, in a way, been naturalized, conveys discourses fairly similar to those generally found in science fiction.[59] Moreover, by illustrating the impact of scientific advances and the pervasive influence of knowledge structures on society, de Morgan's mechanical princess offers a significant instance of the ways in which fairies and the fairy tale could illustrate the relationship between science and culture, the fairy tale and its wonders appearing as a language able to express the effects of scientific thought and definitions of nature on the nation – and on humans.

4
Nature under Glass: Victorian Cinderellas, Magic and Metamorphosis

The magic realm of world exhibitions

> Conceive a Crystal Palace, (for mere difference in size, as both the naturalist and the metaphysician know, has nothing to do with the wonder) whereof each separate joist, girder, and pane grows continually without altering the shape of the whole; and you have conceived only one of the miracles embodied in that little sea-egg, which the Creator has, as it were, to justify to man His own immutability, furnished with a shell capable of enduring fossil for countless ages, that we may confess Him to have been as great when first His Spirit brooded on the deep, as He is now and will be through all worlds to come.[1]

Charles Kingsley's comparison of nature's creatures to the glass-and-iron building which hosted the 1851 Great Exhibition in London ironically suggests that the study of natural history was not that far from the Victorian world of engineering and technological advances. The simile, if perhaps surprising, is in fact not coincidental. Indeed, fairies were recurrently used to represent the wonders of the world of industry in the Victorian period, and were even part and parcel of the Crystal Palace experience: when Queen Victoria, who was privately dubbed 'the Faery' by her favourite Prime Minister, Disraeli,[2] entered the Crystal Palace for the first time in 1851, the place, she claimed, 'had quite the effect of fairyland',[3] all the more so because a tableau of fairies representing 'Art, Science, Concord, Progress, Peace, Wealth, Health, Success, Happiness, Industry and Plenty' appeared at the entrance.[4] Likewise, a contemporary description of the Crystal Palace compared the venue to Fairyland:

> The magician is right; but as Beauty's chamber was guarded by griffins, and all enchanted castles are defended by dragons, so is Fairyland guarded by gnomes; blue, and uncompromising. One occupies the little crypt on either side of the door by which visitors are admitted to Fairyland in crystal. To judge from the costumes of these gnomes you would take them to be plain constables of the Metropolitan Police; but, my word for it, they have all the gnomical etceteras beneath their uniform and oilskin. The entrance to Fairyland is not effected by rubbing a lamp, or clapping the hands three times, or by exclaiming 'Open Sesame'; but, as a concession to the non-magical tendencies of some of the visitors, a commutation is accepted in the shape of five shillings current money of the realm.[5]

Of course, the jarring contrast between the world of fairies and the industrial world aims to shed light here on the disenchanting experience of modernity and progress, miles away from enchanted Fairyland. But many writings were much more ambiguous than this essay: as Nicola Bown contends, fairies and Fairyland were both a retreat for Victorians striving to cope with humans' increasing power over nature *and* images of themselves – their tiny size and fragile-looking appearance illustrating humans' bodies, dwarfed by the height and power of factories and machines.[6]

Moreover, Kingsley's simile reveals as well how the history of natural history has particularly been linked to the history of glass. After the repeal of the duty on glass in 1845, scientific equipment made of glass became cheaper, and the craze for natural history, visible in Victorian collections of insects, ferns or seaweeds, boomed in the 1860s, spurred by the development of aquaria, vivaria or Warden sealed cases – equipment enabling amateur naturalists to keep their finds alive under glass.[7] At the very same time, the glass-and-iron Crystal Palace, which attracted millions of visitors, was also a site which triggered natural history curiosity. When it was relocated at Sydenham, some writers and naturalists, such as Charles Kingsley, in *Glaucus* (1855)[8] and Juliana Horatia Ewing, in *Aunt Judy's Magazine*,[9] advised children to visit the aquarium to cast a glance at nature's marvels. The building, just like its exhibits during the exhibition, looked like Fairyland, most especially at a time when popularizers of science were foregrounding the wonders of nature, like the naturalist Philip Henry Gosse, who presented the giant water lily as a 'vegetable wonder!'[10]

In order to understand the impact that this glass building, first erected in Hyde Park, could have on the Victorians, it is useful to look at the significance of glass itself in Victorian culture and its multiple meanings. For Isobel Armstrong, Victorian culture may be defined as a 'glass culture', the term 'crystal' encapsulating nineteenth-century modernism.[11] Yet crystal is also 'a derivation of rock, a growth of the geological world, a product of vapour, minerals, and subterranean action', constantly underlining 'crystal's apparent nearness to the natural world of cave and grotto'.[12] This affiliation of glass with the natural world may explain why glass motifs recur in Victorian fiction, art and culture to mediate the tensions of the age and deal with the divide between modern urban life and nature. In fact, the history of the building of the Crystal Palace is closely related to natural history and the understanding of nature's metamorphoses. If Joseph Paxton remains famous today for his Crystal Palace, few people know that the head gardener to the sixth Duke of Devonshire at Chatsworth in Derbyshire was the first man in England to bring the 'hothouse lily' (the Amazonian water lily) into flower in November 1849. Designed by Paxton to house and protect his *Victoria amazonica* (also known as *Victoria regia*), the glasshouse was first a lily house, and it was his observation of the strong, ribbed undersides of the giant leaf-pads of the lily that inspired the structure of the Crystal Palace, with its iron-ribbed design. In addition, the hothouse lily that Paxton nurtured until it grew with surprising vigour to unmanageable size came to epitomize a force which both 'reminded England of nature's potential capacity to overwhelm all human enterprise'[13] and was also – paradoxically – linked to femininity. *Victoria regia*, vulnerable yet bearing the name of the mighty Empress, symbolized, at one and the same time, power and technology *and* feminine delicacy. While serving to further the association of genteel femininity with flowers, it also represented the 'mysteries of nature, and probably also masculine anxiety about woman's reproductive power and the need to control it'.[14] The wonders the glass-and-iron building held and enclosed were thus hard to frame, for the Crystal Palace was both a world of artificially grown marvels and a greenhouse filled with potentially uncontrollable species.

As this chapter will highlight, some Victorian fairy tales used the Crystal Palace as a significant site to represent the transformation of young maidens into marriageable women and mediate their passage from nature to culture. As significant examples, Anne Isabella Thackeray Ritchie's 'Cinderella' (1868) and Hans Christian Andersen's 'The Dryad' (1868) use glass buildings and Great Exhibitions as signs of humans' industrial and technological processes. The tales align young maiden's social ascension with their growth into women, both using glass as a structural motif bound to the magical transformation of the female characters, as in the classical fairy tale. But, in so doing, the fairy tales also construct their female characters as natural specimens and trace their maturation as natural historians would follow the growth of their species. The comparison of women with natural species, as we will see, reveals anxieties related to the 'nature' of women in the light of evolutionary theory, highlighting issues such as women's desire or women's reproductive power. Indeed, 'The Dryad', which plays on a wood nymph's wish to see the 1867 Paris Great Exhibition, as well as Anne Isabella Thackeray Ritchie's 'Cinderella', in which Cinderella meets Prince Charming at the Crystal Palace, use fairy-tale motifs and patterns to rework the city as a place of desire, phantasmagoria and transcience – a magic world typically linked to modernity. As a result, the discourse on the marvels of science remains ambivalent, epitomizing the Victorians' mixed feelings with regard to science, progress and humans' capacity to control nature.

Anne Isabella Thackeray Ritchie's Cinderella – collector and consumer

In a review of London entertainments published in *All the Year Round* in 1865, the author describes the pleasure-seeking holiday makers waiting for the train to the Crystal Palace in the following terms:

> Proceeeding through the streets to my railway (which goes everywhere), and seeing the servant-maids, dressed in all their best,

emerging from the front door, and tripping gaily upon the pavement, I have thought of cage doors opening, and long impris-oned birds fluttering out into the free air...At the station of my railway which goes everywhere, I find the escaped birds assembled in a great flock. They are chiefly of the feminine gender, and few of them have been happy in hitting the convenient dimensions for a crinoline, as appears by the tendency of those articles of attire to emulate the restive disposition of Old Joe for kicking up behind and before. I notice that on the down platform convenient for the trains which run towards Richmond and Kew, and, by some mar-vellous junction arrangement, the Crystal Palace, there is a much larger flock of birds than on the up platform...

I begin to understand at last. I perceive that pleasure is being centralised. The great mass of the holiday-makers are at the Crys-tal Palace...if I turn to the amusements at the Crystal Palace, I find that, in addition to the normal attractions of the place, the courts, the statues, the works of art, and the flowers, the public are offered, for the small charge of one shilling, a great variety of entertain-ments...On Easter Monday the Crystal Palace opened with extra attractions – the Wizard of the North, the Alabam Minstrels, and a pantomimic ballet in the theatre. On the same day the South Kensington Museum was open free, and thousands thronged it all day long, preserving their appetite for wonders to the last, and coming away still hungry.[15]

As ironically presented by the reviewer, the wonders offered to the female customers are poles apart from the wonders of natural his-tory exhibited at the South Kensington Museum: the natural history specimens cannot compete with the Crystal Palace, now located at Sydenham, a place of sheer entertainment which attracts thousands of bird-like women. The 'escaped birds', donning the latest fash-ionable accessories, willingly fly to the palace whose glass structure encases its visitors like so many exhibits. The writer's construction of the glass building as a site which encapsulates female desire is not exceptional[16] and may explain why Great Exhibitions were not only seen as fairy lands but also tightly linked to women and to issues related to femininity.

This idea is particularly illustrated in Anne Isabella Thackeray Ritchie's 'Cinderella'. Anne Isabella Thackeray Ritchie (1837–1919) was an essayist, novelist and biographer.[17] Most of her essays were initially published in the *Cornhill Magazine*, first edited by her father, as were her novels, short stories and fairy tales, later collected in *Five Old Friends and a Young Prince* (1867) and *Bluebeard's Keys and Other Stories* (1874). The *Cornhill* targeted all sorts of readers. For W. M. Thackeray, the magazine should both 'amuse and interest', keeping in mind that 'ladies and children [were] always present'.[18] Ritchie's 'Cinderella' reworks the classical fairy tale to engage with nineteenth-century 'glass consciousness' and 'environment of mass transparency'.[19] As Isobel Armstrong contends, the numerous revisions of 'Cinderella' throughout the second half of the nineteenth century constantly foreground a 'culture of excess',[20] whether they deal with addiction or consumption.[21] In fact, Victorian revisions of the classical fairy tale enabled writers to tackle new constructions of the 'real' resulting from the rise of capitalism, its illusions and its phantasmagoria. These constructions were mostly crystallized by the heroine of the tale and her glass slipper, which functioned as an epitome of the Victorian glass culture.

Perrault introduced glass into the story in 1697, a mistranslation of 'vair' (fur) which Iona and Peter Opie believe to have been intentional.[22] This reading is validated by Jack Zipes's analysis of the revisions of fairy tales through the seventeenth, eighteenth and nineteenth centuries. As he argues, if Cinderella is not a vain coquette, she is nonetheless 'clothed in a baroque manner' and wears a – necessarily – fragile and delicate glass slipper, which securely confines her in a passive role by limiting her freedom of action.[23] As a matter of fact, the role that clothes play in the adaptation and rewriting of folktales into literary fairy tales is revealing of the way in which bourgeois mores and norms redefined the feminine ideal according to the demands of patriarchal ideology.[24] The desire to supply young women with glass slippers, and thus to use glass to mediate the transformation of a young woman from servant to princess, was even more significant in the Victorian period. The rise of consumer culture and the building of department stores in the Victorian period turned women into consumers, obsessionally fashioning an artificial appearance. Charles Dickens's rewriting of 'Cinderella' in his 'Fraud on the Fairies' in 1853 (written in reaction to George Cruikshank's revisions of traditional fairy tales) lays emphasis on the relationship between Cinderella's transformation, the world of fashion and the repeal of the excise tax:

> Upon which the old lady touched her with her wand, her rags disappeared, and she was beautifully dressed. Not in the present costume of the female sex, which has been proved to be at once grossly immodest and absurdly inconvenient, but in rich sky-blue satin pantaloons gathered at the ankle, a puce-colored satin pelisse sprinkled with silver flowers, and a very broad leghorn hat. The hat was chastely ornamented with a rainbow-coloured ribbon hanging in two bell-pulls down the back; the pantaloons were ornamented with a golden stripe; and the effect of the whole was unspeakably sensible, feminine, and reviving. Lastly the old lady put on Cinderella's feet a pair of shoes made of glass: observing that but for the abolition of the duty on that article, it never could have been devoted to such a purpose; the effect of all such taxes being to cramp invention, and embarrass the producer, to the manifest injury of the consumer. When the old lady had made these wise remarks, she dismissed Cinderella to the feast and speeches, charging her by no means to remain after twelve o'clock at night.[25]

Obviously, as Dickens makes explicit, glass mediated the artificially constructed Victorian woman and marked woman's metamorphosis into a cultural artefact. Interestingly, glass itself results from transformation. Made from sand, glass is 'pure transparent matter derived from waste matter, artificial matter derived from primary matter, confirm[ing] the magic of a transition from nature to culture'.[26] This may be one of the reasons why the motifs and plot patterns of 'Cinderella' appealed to Victorian writers who wished to deal with and symbolize a young woman's mysterious and marvellous transformation. This metamorphosis, moreover, was not far from the experiments carried out in glasshouses in which artificially grown exotic flowers, like Paxton's lily, could grow to amazing size. Furthermore, 'Cinderella', staging as it does the transformation of a pumpkin into a coach, mice into horses and rats and lizards into coachmen and footmen, seemed to blur the boundaries of the human, animal and vegetative worlds. Such a play on boundaries was all the more revealing in a period marked by 'taxonomical panic' and anxieties of hybridity, as shall be seen.[27]

Ritchie's 'Cinderella' maps out the fairy-tale heroine's journey from a 'little green plant stringing up through the mild spring rains and the summer sunshine'[28] to a married woman whose meeting with Prince Charming takes place at the Crystal Palace. Ritchie readapts the classical fairy tale to the Victorian modern world, using consumerism as the new magic wand capable of turning working-class girls into upper-class ladies. The magic of capitalism, represented as able to change social identity through just a change of clothes, is enhanced by the use of fairy-tale motifs. The classical fairy tale, illustrating as it does a young woman's ascension of the social ladder, was, indeed, often used to deal with class relations in the second half of the nineteenth century.[29] In Ritchie's tale, the fairy godmother's magical powers are bestowed on her by her social identity: maids appear 'as if by magic' (p. 116) because Lady Peppercorne's servants fly at her commands, and her servants' transformation from workhouse boys – 'as thin and starved as church mice' (p. 116) – into pages is merely social.

The blending of the physical and economic transformation of the pages paves the way for the maturation of Cinderella into a marriageable woman. Ritchie's rewriting uses the marvellous to constantly confront nature and culture, whether nature is safely encased in glass and exhibited as a specimen or poses a threat to the onlooker. For Ritchie foregrounds modern anxieties relating to the nature of woman and woman's sexuality, the classical fairy tale enabling her to deal with anxieties related to evolutionary theory, such as Darwin's survival of the fittest. Ella is first a 'wild' (p. 108) young woman. She is compared to birds and dances like a fairy ('she was all in white. She'd no hat, or anything; she bounded six foot into the air. You never saw anything like it' (p. 109)). Her association with the natural world is poles apart from the civilized woman, who can only dance at balls and must 'put[–] a curb on the life and vitality which is in [her]' (p. 109). In addition, the heroine collects 'sea-anemones in a glass, gaping with their horrid mouths', 'strings of birds' eggs' (p. 110), and keeps a bird in a cage, a dog and a squirrel – the latter being, we may suppose, a piece of taxidermy. The reshaping of Cinderella as an amateur naturalist partakes, of course, of her construction as a well-educated middle-class young maiden who follows such manuals of domestic advice and natural history guidebooks and journals that would tell young women 'how to preserve curious insects, collect and lay out seaweed, make skeleton leaves, preserve fungi, take leaf impressions, model wax flowers and prepare birds' eggs for cabinets'.[30] As shall be seen, however, the sea anemones in the tank also connote the young maiden's dangerously budding sexuality, the glass motif mediating the tale's discourse on (woman's) nature and enlightening the significance of the Crystal Palace as the site where the prince and the princess meet.

Indeed, the motif of the sea anemones, though hinting at Victorian amateur naturalists and the development of natural history, also reverberates with images of sexual predation, suggesting the power of glass technology to reveal what lies on the other side of the looking-glass. Ella's metamorphosis thus aims to change the 'natural' woman into one of the saleable commodities displayed at the Crystal Palace. Nature must be tamed, seasons merely punctuating the time that young women spend in the capital in search of the right suitor. Unlike Ella, her stepmother and stepsisters are commodified ladies, 'laced and dressed and adorned and scented and powdered ... always posing' (p. 106). The two stepsisters grow up into 'two fashionable bouncing young ladies', 'pierc[e] their ears, turn[-] up their pigtails, and dress[-] very elegantly' (p. 111), 'say[-] nothing, taking it all in' (p. 110). Moreover, the stepmother's silk gowns, 'rippl[ing], and wav[ing], and flow[ing] away as she came and went' (p. 106), illustrate the way in which nature has been turned into objects of social use, as highlighted by women's fashions at the time. One of the step-sisters, Lisette, wears a 'bird-of-paradise' (p. 120); Ella owns a 'coral necklace' (p. 111).

As a matter of fact, in the years following the publication of Darwin's *On the Origin of Species* (1859), women's fashion increasingly included parts of animals, whether peacock feathers, fish scales or wasp wings. Susan David Bernstein's analysis of the connections between evolutionary anxieties and the world of fashion is relevant to this discussion. Bernstein gives two significant examples, bringing the world of fashion into alignment with the process of evolution in nature and the issue of taxonomy: one visual (Edward Linley Sambourne's 1867 *Punch* caricatures, entitled 'Designs after Nature' and showing animal-fashioned women) and one textual (an essay published in 1862 in the *Cornhill Magazine*, a few years before Ritchie's 'Cinderella').[31] The 'vestimentary excesses' donned by women, especially in the 1860s, Bernstein argues, suggested 'a vision of sexual selection', reversing Darwin's account of sexual selection (according to which males are arrayed ostentatiously to compete for the attention of females).[32] The way in which natural history and new theorizations on nature, as well as Darwinian anxieties, undergirded the fashion industry explains why Ritchie's tale uses 'Cinderella' – a fairy tale whose quintessential motifs (the glass slipper and the magic pumpkin) are linked to glass and nature's metamorphoses or transformations – to map out a young woman's maturation and deal with contemporary perceptions on female sexuality. The tale recurrently lays stress upon fashionable accessories – *'bouillon'* (puff), *'ruches'* (ruche), *'choux'* (rosette) and *'jardinière'* (p. 107) – which interweave the world of fashion and the natural world (insects and vegetables), correlating nature and culture further and suggesting even more the proximity between humans and animals. The ephemerality and variations of fashion, just like Darwin's theory of evolution through continuous change, could explain why design provided 'a linchpin for exploring a cultural uneasiness around boundaries'.[33] For Bernstein, the focus on 'constant modifications in women's fashion [in the 1860s] is similar to the process of evolution in nature',[34] an argument illustrated by Ritchie's tale, which blends discourses of fashion and romance. For instance, the intermingling of the conversation on fashionable outfits with the romance between Cinderella's father and Mrs Garnier ends up associating the latest fashionable accessory Madame de Girouette has just been describing with the husband all women need to reach happiness: 'Everybody wants one' (p. 108). As a result, marriage becomes an artificially manufactured accessory, interestingly underlining the link between 'natural laws of reproduction and economic laws of production'.[35] In addition, Ritchie's Prince Charming does not need to be the 'handsomest man in the county' (p. 104). The 'gentleman' is a *collage* of fashionable accessories:

> What are the young princes like now-a-days? Do they wear diamond aigrettes, swords at their sides, top-boots, and little short cloaks over one shoulder? The only approach to romance that I can see, is the flower in their button-hole, and the nice little moustaches and curly beards in which they delight. (p. 117)

The multiple twists to the fairy tale here betray Ritchie's use of the genre to probe gender construction and feminine identity. The fairy tale is reduced to a marriage plot and has no magic about it: the prince is ugly; Ella does not even lose her slipper; she fails to get into the carriage in time and there is no mystery about Cinderella. Moreover, Ella's transformation into a lady results from the godmother's 'conjuring': that is, her giving Ella her own 'old pearl necklace with the diamond clasp' (p. 122). The young woman's metamorphosis is performed through a journey through shops, prefiguring Cinderella's visit to the Crystal Palace, a place in which fashion aids and products (ironically often derived from organic matter)[36] were aimed at female consumers:

> Ella in a moment found herself transformed somehow into the most magnificent lady she had seen for many a day. It was like a dream, she could hardly believe it; she saw herself move majestically, sweeping in silken robes across the very same pier-glass, where a few minutes before she had looked at the wretched little melancholy creature, crying with a dirty face, and watched the sad tears flowing... (p. 116)

The significance of the young maiden's physical appearance as a means to attract Prince Charming is revealing of Ritchie's rewriting of romance into a tale about selection and the quest for the male suitor. Ella's appearance significantly retains links with nature: she wears white azaleas as a headdress and her 'snow and sunlight dress' (p. 122) is 'frothed and frothed up to the waist, and loomed up with long grasses' (p. 122), the naturalistic metaphors suggesting the relation between the construction of an ideal femininity and the taming of nature, turned into objects of social use. Moreover, the stress on observation points out how identity is here mediated by glass; just as Ella realizes her social inferiority when she 'chance[s] to see her shabby face and frock and tear-stained cheeks in one of the tall glasses over the gilt tables' (p. 114), so glass turns her into a magnificent lady. Such hints at the regime of glass punctuate the fairy tale. When the narrator describes the modern world in the frame-narrative, the prodigious effects of the glasshouse, that enables the unseasonable maturation of fruits and flowers (even those from the tropics), thus denying time and space, are compared to magic: 'There are glasshouses where heavy dropping bunches of grapes are hanging, so that one need only open one's mouth for them to fall into it all ready cooked and sweetened' (p. 103). Interestingly, the glass-houses at the opening of the narrative and the Crystal Palace at the end of the tale shape Ella's romance, intimating the young woman's maturation. It is therefore certainly not coincidental that Ella is able to go to the Crystal Palace because her fairy godmother – Lady Jane Peppercorne – is a first-rate gardener and must attend the flower-show there:

> All sorts of delicious things, scents, colours, spring-flowers and vegetables came out of the hamper in delightful confusion. It was a hamper full of treasures – sweet, bright, delicious-tasted – asparagus, daffodillies, bluebells, salads, cauliflowers, hot-house flowers, cowslips from the fields, azaleas . . .
>
> 'Here, you John, get some bowls and trays for the vegetables, green pease, strawberries; and oh, here's a cucumber and a nice little early pumpkin. I had it forced, my dear. Your stepmother tells me she is passionately fond of pumpkins.' (p. 115)

The association of the fairy godmother's magical powers with greenhouse cultivation foregrounds the enchantment of science and technology and how the latter helped develop natural history. In her hamper, flowers and vegetables are all mixed up, and spring flowers and cauliflowers mature simultaneously, regardless of the cycles of nature and the seasons. Significantly, the pumpkin, which ensures Cinderella's transportation to the ball in the classical fairy tale, has here been manifestly artificially grown. Thus, if the Crystal Palace looks like Fairyland, it is also a realm where control prevails, framing the young woman's first steps into womanhood. As a 'descendant of panoptical technology',[37] the Crystal Palace is meant to shape humans' control over nature. At the same time, however, it epitomizes consumer culture and the customers' – more especially women's – desires. The staging of Cinderella's romance in the Crystal Palace is of capital importance to convey Ritchie's satirical view on the marriage-plot and the construction of women as commodities sold to the highest bidder. As the exemplar of the 'glass fantasia', in Isobel Armstrong's terms, the transparent glass prison also embodies 'glass's dialectic of longing and consumerism'.[38] In fact, exhibited behind the glass windows of the 'great wonderful fairy Palace' (p. 116), Ella's desire surges:

> And she was so happy: music playing, flowers blooming, the great wonderful fairy Palace flashing over her face ... She had never been so happy; she had *never* known what a wonder the Palace might be. (p. 118)

Ritchie's construction of female desire is characterized by the breakdown of boundaries as Cinderella walks with her Prince Charming through the various exotic courts teeming with glitter, perfumes, statues and Indian figures: the profusion of objects on display hints at taxonomical anarchy, all the more so because, in this meandering through the world of the exotic and the ordinary, geographical boundaries collapse, and behind the glass panels east and west are conflated. This anarchic fecundity, suggestive of new representations of the natural world at the time when glasshouses were highly in fashion, is in keeping with many of the symbolical meanings underlying 'Cinderella'. The enduring motifs of the fairy tale – the glass slipper, the pumpkin and animals whose transformation enables Cinderella's transportation to the ball – 'remythologize for *modern* experience', as Isobel Armstrong posits.[39] The glass slipper, the pumpkin and the animals, 'feeding off human debris or quietly sharing resources',[40] all cross categories through magic, disrupting the boundaries between objects and beings, the mineral, vegetable, animal or human world. In the Victorian period such transgressions were typically bound to modernity, the magic of consumerism and the marvels of industrial technology. As Thomas Richards argues, the 1851 Great Exhibition particularly ordered manufactured objects into taxonomies: as both 'a museum and a market',[41] the Crystal Palace exhibited a 'phylogeny of manufacture'.[42] The abundance and variety of goods in the Crystal Palace, moreover, 'advanced a prescient vision of the evolutionary development of commodities':[43] in the same way as Darwin brought to light the fecundity of the natural world and the role played by domestication, which increased the rhythm of species reproduction, the commodities in the Crystal Palace seemed to multiply and transgress taxonomies as they entered 'a vast space of association'.[44]

The classical fairy tale's magical metamorphoses with the crossing of boundaries between the organic and the inorganic or the vegetable, animal and human, explains why it became a suitable material to express anxieties related to species interrelationship. Ritchie's play on the glass motif in her 'Cinderella' not only brings together the issue of manufacture and reproduction but also hints at fears related to female reproduction. The motif of the sea anemones kept in glass, for instance, with their medusa-like tentacles ensuring their feeding power and their capacity to multiply through binary fission, together with the collection of eggs, conjures up images of predation and frightening female reproduction. As a result, the hint at the amateur naturalist collecting and categorizing species paves the way for the young woman's visit to the giant glass building (which hosted an aquarium containing over five thousand species of anemones in 1854) in the midst of a 'dense vegetation of things'.[45] Woman herself becomes, indeed, a taxonomical challenge, her mystery encapsulated by the glass palace, which refracts male anxieties of control. Thus, the fairy-tale revision enables Ritchie to compare and contrast nature and culture, the natural and the artificial, positioning woman at the heart of anxieties related to humans' place in nature. By playing on the ambivalent meanings of glass Ritchie modernizes – or remythologizes – 'Cinderella', using glass to allegorize the heroine's soaring desire and hint at woman's nature, thereby mirroring female sexuality through the lens of Victorian glass culture. The issues raised by Ritchie in her 'Cinderella' are very similar to those highlighted in Andersen's 'The Dryad', a fairy tale which uses the Paris Great Exhibition as a significant place to illustrate a young woman's uncontrolled desire. The female character, a wood nymph, closely related to the natural world, finds herself transported to the French capital where she will experience the modern 'glass culture'.

Behind glass panels: framing desire, taming nature

In Hans Christian Andersen's fairy tale, 'The Dryad', the 1867 Paris Exhibition introduces the reader to 'the great and wonderful time of Fairy-Tale'.[46] The tale contrasts the natural world, represented by the Dryad, with the modern urban world marked by steam power and technology. The narrative relates the coming of a Dryad to Paris as a fine young chestnut tree to replace one of the 'dead uprooted tree[s], killed by gas-smoke and kitchen smoke and all the vapours of a town so fatal to plants' (p. 244). But the tale's ecological discourse on nineteenth-century polluted cities camouflages a moral discourse on desire and femininity, using glass buildings, once again, to deal with woman's growth/maturation. Paris – 'the most brilliant and the most wealthy' (p. 238) – lures (female) visitors, such as the poor little girl Marie, who becomes magically changed into a fine lady once she sets off for the capital: 'Everything was splendid about her – horses, servants – everything!' (p. 239). The 'city of enchantment' (p. 239) turns poor young girls into wealthy and elegant duchesses. Andersen's choice of a Dryad who wants to go to Paris, like Marie, the poor girl turned duchess, associates his concern with progress with a young woman's transformation, as Marie's social rise from rags to riches and her transformation into a lady recalls Cinderella. But the issue of 'enchantment' is above all embodied by the Great Exhibition, which epitomizes progress and is ironically described through natural metaphors. The Palace – a 'gigantic sunflower', the 'fairest blossom of art and industry [which has] sprung up upon the barren soil of the Champ de Mars' (pp. 240–2) – comes with the spring and vanishes with the arrival of autumn: short-lived, the Exhibition vanishes as quickly as it appears and leaves no trace of its presence.

The comparison of the Palace of Art and Industry to a gigantic sunflower, a 'fairy-blossom' or lotus plant calls to mind the relationship between the world's Great Exhibitions and hothouses, as mentioned above. It also foreshadows how the tale is going to combine the issue of humans' control of nature's growth with femininity, highlighting in so doing the contradictory readings of the glasshouse, 'both emancipatory and exploitative', in Isobel Armstrong's terms, which explains why '[g]lass culture instigated a kind of taxonomical panic and a struggle for power among taxonomies',[47] as seen in Ritchie's fairy tale. Moreover, because the glass structure collapsed boundaries of space and time – 'flatten[ing] out the diachronic and assimilat[ing] it with the synchronic'[48] – the world, miniaturized in the Palace, literally became a fairy land: every country was downsized to a single room – 'condensed and reduced to a plaything, that it may be represented', as Andersen's narrator suggests (p. 241) – giving the visitors the impression that they could travel the world in a day. The place itself undoubtedly reflected the modern changes of rhythm and the hectic pace of urban culture – miles away from the slow cycles of nature. In Andersen's tale, however, the price the Dryad has to pay to go to see the Paris Exhibition is dear. She must become as short lived as the Exhibition, as transient as the modern world; simultaneously, her desire will increase:

> [T]hy life-time will then be shortened; the number of seasons awaiting thee here in free nature will there wane into a scanty sum of years... Thy longing will grow, thy coveting and craving will wax stronger. The tree itself will be a prison to thee; thou wilt leave thy dwelling, forsake thy nature, fly out and mix with human beings; and then thy years will have dwindled down to half the lifetime of the ephemeral – only one night, and thy life shall be extinguished; the leaves of the tree shall wither and be scattered to the winds, to return no more. (p. 242)

The thematics of desire and the ephemeral are, of course, linked to the glass construction hosting the Exhibition and all 'the glazed urban phantasmagoria'[49] which marked the Victorian period. The proliferation of glass surfaces in the second half of the nineteenth century transformed society into a virtual realm, the real becoming as transient as a short-lived reflection in a mirror or an advertising image promoting the latest fashion. As Isobel Armstrong argues, because '[g]lass and scopic desire are bound up with one another',[50] glass buildings shaped an 'iconography of desire'[51] – 'an ethereal fantasy space'.[52] The dialectic of longing associated with glass has been seen as related to the rise of capitalism. For Thomas Richards, the Great Exhibition of 1851 'fashioned a mythology of consumerism' which illustrated the new capitalist economy.[53] Indeed, glass, which was used massively in constructions after 1845, especially by retailers for their display windows, evokes the exhibition of enticing commodities and the whole world of images on which Victorian visual culture thrived. As Ritchie's 'Cinderella' makes explicit, Paxton's Crystal Palace was a giant glass illustration of Victorian consumer culture, refracting a period marked by the advent of the commodity as, to quote Richards's formulation, 'the master fiction around which society organized and condensed its cultural life and political ideology'.[54] But as Andersen's fairy tale points out, since dazzling images replaced objects, the turning of commodities into so many ideal images behind the glass panels altered the meaning of the real.

Like Paxton's building, designed to make 'ordinary glass look like crystal' with 'the shape of a greenhouse look[ing] like the outline of a palace',[55] the real suddenly appeared as potentially illusory – a deceptive fairy land designed to entice buyers.

In 'The Dryad', the city is a place of temptations; as desire increases, life – and by implication nature – wane. In Paris, houses proliferate, just like chimneys on the roofs and advertisements on the walls, glaring with painted pictures and large letters. Engines whizzing, snorting or puffing clouds of smoke, crowds of people, 'shop upon shop, music, singing, screaming, and talking' (p. 244) welcome the Dryad. But the wood nymph is confined by the tall houses 'as within a cage' (p. 286). The houses, 'pasted over with posters and placards' do not 'flit away, or change shape... and glide aside' (p. 247), increasing the Dryad's 'unsatisfied longing' (p. 286). The connection between urban culture, transformation, evanescence and feminine desire climaxes when the Dryad gives her life to be taken from her 'prison' as a punishment for her 'daring desire' (p. 286) to see the city. The Dryad is freed from her tree, experiencing physical transformation like Marie, the poor young girl turned lady. Compared to the 'goddess of spring' (p. 287), she oscillates between child and woman, taking new forms as she walks through the city. This city is a realm of transformation, manufacture and reproduction. Interestingly, its association with a young woman's (or Dryad's) transformation binds feminine sexuality and reproduction to urban modernity. For the frantic pace of the Dryad's metamorphoses mirrors the continuous transformation of the city and its ever-changing aspect. Seasons vanish; the streams are but the 'tide of rolling carriages, cabriolets, coaches, omnibuses, and cabs' (p. 287).

When she reaches the Wonder of the World – '[t]he Aladdin's castle of the present age' (p. 241) – young women are dancing in the gaslight, as if mechanically reproduced, and the whirling of the female dancers echoes the whirling of carriages and omnibuses outside. But as the Dryad starts dancing, her young partner's arms only embrace 'the transparent, gas-filled air' (p. 292). The Dryad becomes as dematerialized as her environment is derealized: modernity is illusory – and deadly. The Dryad then continues her visit of the palace, but she grows wearier and wearier, and when she tries to drink from a fountain the water is no 'living well'; it 'flows by machinery'.

Similarly, the flowers she sees 'die when [they] are broken off' and the splendour around is bound to 'vanish ere the year is gone' (p. 295). The Dryad finally vanishes too, like a 'soap-bubble' which becomes a drop – a 'tear' (p. 296). The chestnut tree, with drooping branches and withered leaves, dies on the small square and is 'trampled...down into the dust' by humans (p. 296).

Andersen's tale, therefore, contrasts the world of nature with that of capitalism, its marvellous technology and its ephemereal dreams, showing how the world of nature and the world of industry are at odds. Though seen through the prism of the fairy tale, the marvels of technology and progress are in the end disenchanting, recalling the bleak presentation of the Crystal Palace published in *Household Words* seen through the ironic prism of the fairy tale at the beginning of this chapter. By trying to tame and control nature, Andersen tells his readers, humans have eventually constructed an ethereal and lethal world. Interestingly, images of humans' potential degeneration appear at the end of the fairy tale, as the Dryad is visiting the Paris Exhibition. Indeed, the description of the public aquarium in the Palace recalls the craze for aquaria in the late 1850s, as exemplified by William Alford Lloyd's (1826–80) Aquarium Warehouse in Portland Road in London, for instance, which sold seawater alongside glass jars containing colourful marine creatures, from anemones to sea snails and sea squirts.[56] The presence of the motif of the aquarium recalls how Great Exhibitions contributed to the popularization of science and helped disseminate knowledge. In London, the fad for aquaria, for example, led whole families to gaze at marine species feeding, fighting or reproducing themselves, behind the glass and in the safe domestic haven, as the reviewer highlights here:[57]

> A singular class of marine animals have recently attracted much attention, and are now to be met with in most drawing-rooms...The sea anemones and polyps generally consist of a cylindrical cavity opening above in a wide mouth, round which are arranged numerous feelers which the animal extends in search of food. Some of them secrete no hard stony matter, but others form those constructions known in all seas to a greater or lesser extent and recognised as corals. Their variety is endless, and the mass of solid matter thus accumulated almost beyond belief.[58]

Although the craze ended in 1868,[59] aquaria offered an uncensored spectacle of the reproductive modes of single-celled organisms and marine invertebrates. But marine life also involved the question of evolution: the idea that life had originated in a primal ocean from single-celled aquatic life, transmuting into terrestrial forms, suggested that the sea bed hosted evolutionary mysteries which needed but to be deciphered.[60] In Andersen's narrative, the motif of the aquarium conveys a different lesson – a moral one which the dryad, just like the readers, can decipher through the glass. The description of the aquarium collapses species categories and turns progress – epitomized by glass technology – into regression, illustrated here by the turning of humans into natives on display:

> A great flounder lay thoughtfully close by, stretched itself out in confort and ease: the crab crawled like an enormous spider over it, whilst shrimps darted about with a haste, a swiftness, as if they were the moths and butterflies of the sea.
>
> In the fresh water grew water-lilies, sedges, and rushes. The goldfish had placed themselves in ranks, like red cows in a field, all with their heads in the same direction to receive the current with gaping mouths. Thick fat tench stared with stupid eyes at the glass walls; they knew they were at the Paris Exhibition; they knew also that they had made the somewhat difficult journey hither, in casks filled with water, and had been land-sick on the railway as men are sea-sick on the water. They had come to see the Exhibition, and viewed it from their own fluid – brine or fresh water – and stared at the throng of men, moving past them from morning till evening. Each country in the world had exhibited its natives, in order that the old tench and bream, the brisk perch, and the moss-grown carp might see these creatures and give their deliberate opinion upon the species. (p. 293)

The reversal of the point of view is telling, illustrating the extent to which glass walls could refract anxieties related to humans' place in nature. Indeed, the balanced aquarium, which aimed at simulating nature, was seen by naturalists as a civilized microcosm and often read in moral terms or used to illustrate moral standards.[61] The reversed perspective, here, as the inhabitants of the aquarium look at the species/natives on the other side of the glass, ironically points out the excesses of the study of natural history since the marine creatures observe humans' degeneration into more primitive species. As science and technology are turned back on themselves and as Andersen's dryad is killed by the modern urban world, the fairy tale closes on a highly pessimistic note, inviting the readers to reevaluate the 'wonders' of modernity.

As illustrated by Andersen's 'The Dryad' or Ritchie's 'Cinderella', mid-Victorian rewritings of fairy tales used the technologies related to the development and diffusion of natural history to trace fears linked to young women's growth and transformation and frequently hinted at evolutionary anxieties. Although Ritchie's departure from the magic of classical fairy tales may have been intended to illustrate her own point of view on ideologies of domesticity and marriage, it also highlights how the tale served to foreground tensions underlying the modern world of mass transparency and the ambiguities, uncertainties and fears related to humans' control of nature. The role of the fairy tale to question not only the divide between nature and culture but also how such categories of the real resonate with current representations of nature and contemporary scientific theories is fundamental. The fairy tale and fairy-tale motifs, in particular the motifs that play a key part in 'Cinderella', such as the glass slipper or the pumpkin and the images related to metamorphosis, do not solely aim to emphasize the wonders of science and technology. They also, and perhaps more significantly, serve to discuss the categories of the real shaped by science, its discourse, theories and methods. Because of its play with images and metaphors, therefore, the fairy tale mediates natural historical knowledge, bringing to light the meanings of nature, the magical technologies linked with such knowledge as well as nature's magical transformations, epitomized here by glass, helping readers seize the very processes that are involved in the shaping of new definitions of nature. In other words, by providing an access to the cultural practices that are at stake when representations evolve and develop, the fairy tale and its realm of wonders takes us through the looking-glass. We may suggest, to close this chapter, that glass buildings, and most particularly Paxton's Crystal Palace, were perhaps also *loci* of wonder precisely because they could let their visitors have a glimpse of the laws of evolution and visualize laws which were yet as invisible as the Palace's structural frame. For Kingsley, an advocate of evolutionary theory, the marvels of the Great Exhibition could, indeed, serve as a very good illustration of the wonders of nature's invisible power:

> [I]f the changes of the lower animals are so wonderful, and so difficult to discover, why should not there be changes in the higher animals far more wonderful and far more difficult to discover? And may not man, the crown and flower of all things, undergo some change as much more wonderful than all the rest, as the Great Exhibition is more wonderful than a rabbit-burrow.[62]

5
Nature Exposed: Charting the Wild Body in 'Little Red Riding Hood'

Jane Loudon's *The Young Naturalist's Journey; or, the travels of Agnes Merton and her Mamma* (1840) relates a little girl and her mother's expedition by train to visit menageries. Mrs Merton and her daughter see monkeys, mangoustes, lemurs, Virginian partridges and various sorts of other birds; they learn about flying squirrels, hawks, falcons and chameleons. The species they encounter have been brought to England from all parts of the world – Africa, America, the East Indies, Madagascar, Italy and Spain. The book, inspired by the *Magazine of Natural History* and aiming to adapt some of the papers published in the magazine, provides descriptions of the creatures the two women encounter, accompanied by illustrations, with mentions of the creatures' origins and their eating habits. But what seems to interest the two women most is whether the creatures may be tamed. For most of the exotic animals kept in captivity the two women are shown illustrate how wild species may be domesticated. The issue of humans' power over nature is thus at the heart of the narrative, domestication even becoming a means of saving endangered species, as one of the characters tells the women at the end of the journey: 'as no attempt is made to tame [kangaroos], or breed them in confinement, in time the race must become extinct'.[1] From the education of hawks for falconry, with its risks of relapse, to that of rats, used as pets, the 'collection of animals'[2] presented to the readers illustrates humans' capacity to control the natural world, epitomized by the last chapter which concludes the book with a visit of Mr Trelawney's museum, proudly exhibiting stuffed birds. As seen in Chapter 1, fanciful journeys by train were often imagined by Victorian science writers popularizing natural history. However, Loudon's aim here is not limited to providing the little girl and young readers with natural historical knowledge. As Barbara Gates contends, the narrative shows a prototypical middle-class family who 'approved of the domestication of exotic species but then liked to imagine that their wildness might reemerge'.[3] But as rats and monkeys are being made pets of, the little girl's education is interestingly and uncannily paralleled with the animals' adaptation, even more so as she is rewarded with a tame-looking and long-domesticated marmoset which, she knows, is likely to grow fierce with strangers. The discovery of the taming of the creatures' inner nature through domestication aligns the little girl's education with domestication, suggesting thereby that she must tame her own nature – if only superficially – in order to adapt successfully to an adult world. Moreover, together with references to debates over classification, to the arguments between scientists and to the evolution of classification from Linnaeus to Cuvier and later naturalists, the species' wildness is systematically gauged according to the creatures' appetite. Indeed, although most of the species may appear wild and docile, they always become fierce and ravenous when they see food, acting stealthily and cunningly, and revealing the beast that slumbers in them. The wild creatures' hunger epitomizes their instinct – instinctual behaviour becoming the ultimate sign of bestiality, as the mother tells her daughter, hoping that the natural historical lesson will ensure that her little girl will not in her turn be 'rightly punished for [her] gluttony'.[4]

If natural history books aimed at young female readers conveyed discourses on the nature of women, so did Victorian fairy tales, as already seen. Fairy tales dealing with woman's relationship with beasts, however, illustrated perhaps more strikingly the ways in which representations of nature and the natural world were informed by scientific knowledge about nature and current scientific discourses and theories. Like the preceding Victorian fairy tales, the following revisions of 'Little Red Riding Hood' are typically rooted in a modern world, the heroines constructed as fashionable commodities, while the tales bring into play the conflict between nature and culture. We have seen the role played by the motif of glass to encapsulate images of humans' desire to control nature and the issue of woman's nature or sexuality. This time the riding hood marks the divide between nature and culture. Once again, poised between the realm of classical fairy tales and contemporary constructions of nature/civilization, the motif serves to question categories of the real. As shall be seen, by turning the heroines into trendy artefacts, both narratives remorph the body into a series of images. But the visual rhetoric which frames the heroines' and their aggressors' identity may be seen, I argue, as reflecting the Victorians' obsession with classification. As a result, like Loudon's young naturalist's journey, Victorian Little Red Riding Hoods' journey through woods and their encounter with wild species aim to teach them about their own wildness.

We have seen so far that motifs associated with modernity, such as glass, hinted as much to the phantasmagorias of modern culture and the construction of individuals as images as to nature. Likewise, in the following Victorian revisions of 'Little Red Riding Hood', the categories the tales map out (such as the distinction between humans and animals, domestic and wild) reveal changing representations of nature and the relationship between the urge to classify and order nature and the self. In doing so, I contend, they intimate that the language that developed in scientific writing to shape new representations of nature was part of a wider visual culture and was, as a result, also used to define gender differences and modes of behaviour. 'Little Red Riding Hood', which features a little girl plucking flowers in order to emblematize her defloration, may not have much in common with the metaphors that were helping botany emerge as a scientific discipline.[5] However, the ways in which Victorian revisions of the tale rewrote the tale's gender constructions and sexual attitudes by revamping the forest or denouncing the visual codes that transformed humans into deceitful images may well reflect how scientific language and research, notably concerning wildness, influenced people's conceptions of themselves and others. The visual standards the narratives play on reveal how the constructions of the real derive from contemporary constructions, definitions and representations of nature. As the following literary examples suggest, therefore, it may be significant to examine narratives beyond genre categories in order to understand the roots of representation, especially when these representations contrast nature and culture.

Fairy tales, women and nature

In one of Walter Crane's 1874 plates for 'Beauty and the Beast', Beauty and the Beast are having tea in a bourgeois environment.

The picture has frequently been read by feminist criticism as high-lighting the link between woman and creature. The symmetry of the picture, as Beauty and the Beast face each other on the sofa, is broken by the hem of Beauty's dress, which seems attracted to the Beast and conceals feet shaped in stark contrast to the Beast's cloven hooves. In her study of Victorian representations of women, Nina Auerbach develops this idea further by highlighting the role played by complementary colours in the illustration: the red slashes in Beauty's dress, hair and fan mirror the Beast's red waistcoat and hooves.[6] The picture is also striking, however, in the way that the Beast vanishes under fashionable clothes while the garish bourgeois surroundings, with hints at Japanese decoration, Greek and Renais-sance art – revealing, of course, Crane's involvement with the arts and crafts movement – recalls the heavy decoration of mid-Victorian middle-class homes. As Hearne suggests, '[t]here is no wildness in either the setting or the Beast':[7] the Beast's monocle and eighteenth-century French court costume, or Beauty's profiled face, hinting at Greek pottery, turn Beauty and the Beast into fashionable and colour-ful curios that cancel the tale's potential fierceness. By playing upon conventional postures and decorative clichés, Crane's illustration hence becomes a gaudy surface with little depth. As the characters become flat surfaces, the illustration erases the tale's concerns with sex and marriage to stress decoration instead. In doing so, it fore-grounds much more modern concerns, such as the importance of appearance and class, the visual signs that make the lady and the gentleman. Consequently, Crane's modern transposition ironically changes a tale advising readers to read through appearances into a lesson about fashion and decoration, visually encoding woman's role as housekeeper and elegant lady.

The ambiguous reading that the illustration offers, simultaneously suggesting, on the one hand, Beauty's wild nature and her rela-tionship with the Beast and, on the other, the construction of the Victorian lady, fated to be objectified and sold in marriage, under-girded many a Victorian fairy tale dealing with the nature of woman. As already argued, the nature of woman intrigued both scientists and professionals trying to understand and control the forces of nature. 'Little Red Riding Hood' is, perhaps, the classical fairy tale that most enhances the issue of woman's nature: it not only deals with the relationship between woman and nature – the wild nature of woman – but also highlights the artificiality of woman through the red riding hood which frames and defines the heroine. We have seen that fashion often used nature to devise new patterns and trends. In the case of 'Little Red Riding Hood', however, the riding hood was rewritten in the Victorian period as an emblem of mechanical reproduction and artificiality, not only metaphorizing the commodification of the heroine but also setting parallels between the taming of the nature of woman and the transformation of rural scenery through industrialization. Nature, in all its various aspects, thus lies at the heart of Victorian rewritings of the tale. Moreover, as this chapter will show, Victorian revisions of 'Little Red Riding Hood', in their rewriting of the wolf and the heroine, probed the relation between humans and animals. In so doing, the tales show how the image of the beast changed throughout the nineteenth century. Indeed, scientific development and progress gradually transformed definitions of bestiality, as humans no longer saw themselves at the mercy of natural forces and began to 'make much of nature more vulnerable to human control'.[8] For Harriet Ritvo, '[b]y means of either synecdoche or metaphor animals could represent the power of nature, and thus as it became less threatening, so did they'.[9] If the role played by metaphors in scientific language is highly significant, it becomes crucial in literary fairy tales, which often hinge upon tropes to figure magical metamorphoses. It is this play with metaphors which, I argue, the following fairy tales deal with, as they disrupt Victorian means of classification by revising the tropes of classical fairy tales and associating them with contemporary constructions of nature and definitions of animality.

Many fairy tales bring to the fore the issue of woman's relationship with nature. As the heroines' initiatory journeys map out young girls' growth and transformation into women, the tales question the passage from nature to culture. This is particularly the case in 'Little Red Riding Hood', which deals with a little girl who trusts her own nature and indulges in sensual pleasures. The rewritings of 'Little Red Riding Hood' over the ages throw into high relief how the shaping of little girls into women undoubtedly worked in tandem with women's acculturation and control of their natural bodies. The little girl's acculturation is symbolized by the most salient motif of the classical fairy tale: the red riding hood. The *chaperon*, a stylish cap worn by the women of the aristocracy and middle classes in the sixteenth and seventeenth century, encapsulates how Perrault stylized the folktale in order to match the social and aesthetic standards of an upper-class audience.[10] As an upper-class marker, the red riding hood motif codifies the heroine and constructs her as an object. The appearance of the red riding hood motif is an obvious indication of the evolution of the construction of the body in Western society. Jack Zipes contends that the historical evolution of the tale 'parallels a development of sexual socialization in Western society'.[11] The tale highlights the taming of the body and the restraining of natural instincts, since a little girl is punished for indulging in sensuality and must learn to discipline herself and to keep her instincts in check. As the tale stresses the need for the little girl to control her inner nature, it also underscores the importance of physical appearance. The riding hood acts as evidence that the more the little girl's outer appearance is in keeping with the fashion standards of the day, the more the young girl should be able to regulate her nature – or, at least, to cloak it beneath gaudy material.

Many rewritings of the tale especially stress Little Red Riding Hood's vanity,[12] illustrating how the red riding hood sheds light on the contrast between the heroine's inner nature and outer appearance. Bringing into play as it does the clash between the natural body and civilized mores and manners, the tale defines the fashionable cap as an indicator of the little girl's unruly sexuality. The construction of the ideal body not as 'natural' but as 'manufacturable'[13] enhances even more the organic urges that the civilizing process aims to discipline and curb. The transformation of the young girl into a commodified woman luring man and provoking her own violation is a patent illustration of the standards of comportment that Perrault sought to instill into his fairy tales so as to limit the nature of children.[14] In addition, the clash between the natural body and the construction of the self as image gained in significance in the Victorian period, which saw the advent of mass visual culture. Victorian rewritings of fairy tales often bring to the fore images of the body curbed, supervised, regulated – using the fairy tale's widespread emphasis on the body (from metamorphosis to corporal punishment) to convey new meanings regarding the construction of gender. Indeed, the rewriting of fairy tales was frequently a means for Victorian writers to explore the evolution of the construction of

the Western bourgeois body, surveyed and controlled. Many heroines of Victorian fairy tales are taught to turn themselves into images
and to efface their bodies.[15] In so doing, they inevitably construct
themselves into cultural objects ready to be sold to the highest bidder.

Throughout the centuries, the heroines of fairy tales have always
been shaped as ideally beautiful princesses, their beauty not only
guaranteeing their morality but also enabling them to win a prince,
hence securing their wealth. In the Victorian period, fairy tales lay
even more stress on their heroines' beauty. In Christina Rossetti's fantasy, *Speaking Likenesses* (1874) (a rewriting of Lewis Carroll's *Alice's
Adventures in Wonderland* (1865)), for instance, the little girls' bodies are obsessionally reflected in mirrors which rob them of their
corporeality. The title of Lewis Carroll's sequel to *Alice's Adventures
in Wonderland, Through the Looking-Glass and What Alice Found There*
(1871), clearly posits the importance of the relationship between the
little girl's educational journey and the looking-glass that reflects her
image. In fact, Nancy Armstrong has shown the extent to which
the little girl's encounter with tantalizing bottles and cakes luring
her to consume them is related to Alice's regulation of her appetite
(nibbling at one side of the mushroom or the other) and control of
her image. As I have argued elsewhere, Alice's journey in Wonderland could well be regarded as a journey through consumer culture
until she finally becomes commodified as fragile ware as 'lass, [han-
dle] with care' in *Through the Looking-Glass*.[16] Alice is, indeed, a good
example of the way in which the curbing of Victorian little girls'
or princesses' nature and their disembodiment were often shown
to result from their commodification. The case of 'Little Red Riding
Hood' is even more telling, since the little girl's identity merges with
and depends upon the clothes she is wearing, enhancing all the better the heroine's commodification. This may be the reason why many
nineteenth-century rewritings emphasized the importance of Little
Red Riding Hood's appearance.

In America, Alfred Mills's 1872 Red Riding Hood is a vain little girl
who tries to model her body:

> Once upon a time there lived a little girl who had such a sweet
> temper that she seemed to be made of sugar and spice, like the
> little girl in the nursery rhyme. Her mother was very fond of her,

and, in order to set off her beauty, made her a hood out of an old
red flannel petticoat, in which she looked very pretty, and all the
neighbors, in admiration, called her Little Red Riding-Hood. Now,
although she was a very good girl, her school-fellows said that
Little Red Riding-Hood had one very naughty little fault, which no
girl, little or big, ever had before in any age of the world: she was
vain – just a little vain. They even whispered that she had been
known to tie two brass ear-rings to her ears with bits of cotton,
pretending that her ears had been *really* pierced; and that more
than once she had made up her dress into an unseemly bunch
behind, pretending to have a Grecian bend![17]

The transformation of the petticoat into a hood is symbolic of the
way in which the most significant motif of the fairy tale underscores the transformation of the natural body and the repression
of sexuality – turning the little girl into a civilized individual subject to surveillance and discipline. But more revealingly perhaps,
Mills's emphasis on his Little Red Riding Hood's obsession with fashion works in tandem with his transposition of the tale into modern
society. The fairy realm of the classical fairy tale is rewritten as the
chimerical or *unreal* appearance of reality: the modern world is a place
where illusions and delusions prevail, as women use beauty aids to
deceive beholders.

Alfred Mills's transposition of Little Red Riding Hood into modern
society illustrates how, throughout the Victorian period, the rewriting of Perrault's classical fairy tale as a modern tale anchored in
nineteenth-century society enabled writers to deal with the artificial
construction of the female body induced by mass visual culture. Both
Anne Isabella Thackeray Ritchie's 'Little Red Riding Hood' (1868)
and Harriet Louisa Childe-Pemberton's 'All My Doing; or Red Riding-
Hood Over Again' (1882) set their stories in Victorian England and
particularly stress the links between their rewritings of the tale and
the illusory nature of reality. In both tales, the impact of mass
visual culture on the construction of the fairy-tale heroines is of primary importance: the commodified Little Red Riding Hoods convey
Ritchie's and Childe-Pemberton's discourse on the construction of
modern femininity. In so doing, the rewritings foreground the conflict between nature and culture undergirding many a fairy tale. But
their tales also reflect the ambiguous meanings attributed to nature at

a time when technology and scientific knowledge seemed to ensure its control.

Consumption and defloration in Anne Isabella Thackeray Ritchie's rewriting

In Ritchie's 'Little Red Riding Hood' (1868)[18] the narrator, Miss Williamson, and H., her sister-in-law, are in Paris. At the end of the day, they long for a little quiet and silence 'after the noise of the machines thundering all day in the Great Exhibition of the Champ de Mars'.[19] Ritchie's revisiting of 'Little Red Riding Hood' overtly aims to revamp Perrault's tale (a reference to Perrault appears at the beginning). She launches her tale with a description of Rémy de la Louvière – her wolf – and Little Red Riding Hood in her 'fairy palace...lovely to look upon, enchanted; a palace of art, with galleries, and terraces, and belvederes, and orange-flowers scenting the air, and fragrant blossoms falling in snow-showers, and fountains of life murmuring and turning marble to gold as they flowed' (p. 155), while Miss Williamson and H. are just coming back from the Great Exhibition. Compared to the Palace of Art and Industry, Little Red Riding Hood's house (a hotel in which she is staying for a month) already points to the themes of the marvellous and fairy like in a modern culture grounded in illusion and the deceptive nature of reality. However, Ritchie revisits 'Little Red Riding Hood' in order to reveal her heroine's nature rather than to efface it, the heroine contrasting, therefore, with modern society. Ritchie thus counteracts the potential transformation of her heroines into images, thereby subverting the conservative discourse underlying classical fairy tales, advising upper-middle class women to efface their bodies and curb their 'nature'.

In Ritchie's 'Little Red Riding Hood', Rémy de la Louvière has lost his money at gambling and wants to marry his cousin, Patty, who is to inherit their grandmother's fortune. But Rémy falls in love with his cousin, forgetting 'all about his speculation' and forgetting 'his part of wolf altogether' (p. 186). Patty's parents separate the lovers. As a consequence, the revision of the fairy tale becomes a means of mapping out the young girl's passion. Ritchie's play on the tale's motifs serves to foreground the gap between Patty's instincts for pleasure (often rendered through allusions to food) and society's demands that she control her body. In the first part of the story, Patty is depicted as a young woman giving way to her appetite:

> Patty sulked like her father, and ate her bread and jam without speaking a word. There was no great harm done, Mrs. Maynard thought, as she kept her daughter supplied. She herself had been so disturbed and overcome by the stormy events of the day that she could not eat. She made the mistake that many elders have made before her: they mistake physical for mental disturbance; poor well-hacked bodies that have been jolted, shaken, patched and mended, and strained in half-a-dozen places, are easily affected by the passing jars of the moment: they suffer and lose their appetite, and get aches directly which take away much sense of the mental inquietude which brought the disturbance about. Young healthy creatures like Patty can eat a good dinner and feel keen pain and hide it, and chatter on scarcely conscious of their own heroism. (p. 195)

Ritchie's description of female heroism is far removed from women's prescribed repression and silent suffering. On the contrary, Ritchie seems to use the fairy tale in order to show the need for women not to deny their instincts for pleasure, as the reference to food exemplifies here, and other twists to the fairy tale further this argument. Patty is 'heedless,' 'impulsive' (p. 198), an 'Undine-like' creature (p. 195). The focus on her hunger and instinctual behaviour, as well as Patty's description, in particular the reference to Undine, resonate with current (scientific and/or medical) constructions of womanhood[20] and hint at her proximity to the natural world. The fact that she is guided by instinct must therefore be controlled and bridled. Significantly, the transformation of the young girl and her acculturation is performed through clothes, as in the classical fairy tale. When the time comes for her annual visit to her grandmother's, Patty is artificially transformed by her grandmother who firmly believes marriage to be vital to women: 'All manner of relics were produced out of the old lady's ancient stores to adorn Miss Patty's crisp locks and little round white throat and wrists; small medallions were hung round her neck, brooches and laces pinned on, ribbons tied and muslins measured' (p. 196). The grandmother's conflation of her granddaughter's body with wealth both heightens Patty's commodification and ominously hints at the theft of her jewel – her rape – as metaphorized in the classical fairy tale. Her commodification is furthered when her grandmother sends for the best modiste in the town and orders 'a scarlet "capeline" – such as ladies wear by the sea-side – a pretty frilled, quilted, laced, and braided scarlet hood, close round the cheeks and tied up to the chin' (p. 197). The red bonnet which, according to her father, makes Patty 'too conspicuous' (p. 199), marks her transformation into a commodity: Ritchie's Red Riding Hood is transported to the capital to be seen.

In the classical fairy tale, the transformation of the little girl into an object of the gaze through the riding hood testifies to the need to regulate her nature. In Ritchie's rewriting, Patty's appetite is heightened as she travels to the capital and 'dine[s] off delicious little dishes with sauces, with white bread and butter to eat between the courses' (p. 199). The significance of food is developed throughout the tale, as Patty's mother and her attached attendant imagine dishes to carry by train to the 'starving' grandmother (p. 201). One may deduce that Patty's physical transformation and the stress on her appetite mark her sexual maturation, foreshadowing her meeting – and mating – with the wolf. It is at the theatre, where she sees a play, 'a grand fairy piece – where a fustian peasant maiden was turned into a satin princess in a flash of music and electric light' (p. 199), that she notices Rémy again, just as the satin princess is re-transformed. The site Ritchie chooses for the scene (a theatre) illuminates the heroine's (sexual) maturation: the heroine, commodified as a Little Red Riding Hood, is now ripe enough to be displayed on a stage and constructed as an object of male desire. The transformation staged in the embedded fairy play mirrors Patty's, while Rémy metamorphoses into a wolf 'ready to eat [Patty] up' (p. 200).

The wolf has schemed to seduce and abandon Patty to avenge himself. Rémy's trap enables Ritchie nevertheless to debunk romantic meetings. Her hero is 'smiling, handsome, irresistible, trying to make a sentimental scene out of a chance meeting' (p. 206). Though Patty 'set[s] her teeth and look[s] quite fierce at Rémy' (pp. 207–8), her brief wildness only serves to hint at her lack of restraint and foreshadows the confession of her love for her cousin. Ironically, her openness transforms Rémy, who is 'only half a wolf after all – a sheep in wolf's clothing' (p. 208). Rémy takes off his wolf's 'skin' (p. 208) and confesses his love too. They then decide to ask their grandmother to help them get married, taking two different paths to reach Madame Capuchon's house for fear that people may recognize Patty's red hood. Ritchie completely rewrites the meeting between the little girl and the wolf whose part is played by the grandmother: the latter speaks 'hoarsely' (p. 219) because of her cold, smells butter in Patty's basket, asks for her spectacles 'the better to see' Patty (p. 220), while her ivory teeth, kept in a box, fall on the floor. As an embodiment of the conservative ideology that literally eats up little girls by demanding that they suppress their desires and appetites, Ritchie's 'wolf' effectively revamps Perrault's. Ironically, Patty's nervousness is not due to her fear of the wolf but to Rémy's absence, as she waits for him to tell Madame Capuchon the truth. Rémy, meanwhile is devouring the remains of a pie in the dining room.

Ritchie's rewriting thus disrupts expectations: her heroine's spontaneous behaviour wins her a prince whose 'good appetite should imply a good conscience' (p. 225). Passionate reactions and uncontrolled emotions replace the classical fairy tale's physical violence. Patty does not 'want to hide *anything*' (p. 220) and bursts into tears which causes her to knock over a box on the table containing her grandmother's teeth. Though farcical, the detail is nonetheless revelatory. Not only does it reshuffle roles, bestowing the part of the villain on the grandmother, but it tips the tale's socializing discourse on its head. Though Patty eventually loses her money (Rémy finally becomes heir for 'a girl does not want money like a man' (p. 224)) – and her virginity – the displacement of the rape motif and the effacement of sexuality do not cancel the revision's subversive potential. Ritchie's fairy tales often foreground the importance of appearances and modern fashion,[21] but here, trusting nature pays more than decking oneself in fashionable red clothes, and Patty's innocence, though it may cost her her inheritance, enables her to marry the wolf.

By making explicit how the classical fairy tale deals with woman's nature, Ritchie thus highlights the motifs and tropes used to define her heroine's 'beastly' nature and which partake of the tale's civilizing discourse. Her play on the tension between wildness and domestication is continually informed by Victorian constructions of animality, as her heroine is dressed up and exhibited, and the acculturated young woman is compared to a seemingly domesticated animal whose wildness is free to re-emerge at any time. But by constructing wildness through tropes, Ritchie inevitably renders the metaphors – as that of the 'wolf', for instance – less dangerous, toning down the power of nature in the process. The realm of the literary fairy tale and its motifs thus enable readers once more to see through the looking-glass and look at constructions of nature from a different perspective. Like Ritchie, Childe-Pemberton revises Perrault's classical fairy tale by transposing the narrative into Victorian reality. Rewriting the fairy tale as a realistic narrative, Childe-Pemberton engages with the deceptive appearance of everyday reality, at a time when smooth appearances and visual codes defined individual identity, effacing the body as the basis of truth.

Pussy and the Wolf: the case of Harriet Louisa Childe-Pemberton

Harriet Louisa Childe-Pemberton was a late Victorian writer whose tales for children were regarded as didactic and in line with Christian principles. Her revamping of fairy tales, as exemplified by *The Fairy Tales of Every Day* (1882), further emphasizes the moral purport of classical fairy tales by cancelling magic from the narrative. Childe-Pemberton's 'All My Doing; or Red Riding-Hood Over Again' opens in a nursery, where bourgeois little girls are educated. The narrator's niece, Margery, denounces 'Little Red Riding Hood' for being 'too unlikely',[22] leading the narrative to explore the relationship between fairy tales and reality: 'We don't meet with wolves now, you see, and if we did, we couldn't talk to them' (p. 211). However, as the narrator makes explicit, reading and decoding meaning in fairy tales trains little girls to read and decode reality. The fairy-tale motifs serve to reflect upon the codes defining reality. The laying bare of the fairy-tale discourse suggests that the world is legible, but, as the narrator implies throughout the tale, if reality is a series of images, these images may be deceptive. Of course, the transposition of the tale into Victorian reality uncovers the moralistic discourse of the fairy tale: the narrator starts telling her story so that Margery may 'read the meaning of the tale of Red Riding-Hood' – the 'true story' (p. 213). The narrative aims less at revealing the discourse hidden beneath the fairy tale, however, than at disclosing the way reality itself is encoded and needs to be deciphered.

The narrator tells her niece her own story, in fact. Her misfortune, probably resulting from her parents' chaotic way of educating her, is very much connected with the modern world. The prevailing disorder in the household (everybody is 'always in a hurry' (p. 215)) mirrors the hectic rhythm of modern urban society and paves the way for the tale's introduction of the train as the first motif related to Little Red Riding Hood's fall. As a matter of fact, the fairy tale hints at the development of means of transport (the train, the underground, the tramway), which shifted people faster and faster from place to place, as if by magic. But the marvels of technology lead to the heroine's fall: the train conveys Childe-Pemberton's moral message, fusing the tale's lesson on the taming of woman's nature with technological progress and the control of nature.

The train, as the epitome of modern technology, emphasized humans' conquest of nature. In *The Young Naturalist's Journey*, the motif of the train enables Loudon to merge 'the thrills of natural history [with] the thrills of railway travel',[23] allowing the little girl both to gain knowledge and to conquer fear. Indeed, at the beginning, the little girl, who has never travelled by a railroad before, is 'very much struck with, and almost frightened at, the number of carriages; and still more so at the crowd of people who bustled about, all eager to secure their places, and all seeming in the greatest hurry and confusion'.[24] The book uses the train therefore as more than a narrative technique common to many popular science works: it symbolizes the characters' encounter with the wild and the exotic, foretelling the girl's combat against her own wildness. Moreover, as Michael Freeman contends, the train had 'profound implications for Christian belief'.[25] The train was associated not only with the transformation of England's rural landscapes but also with the scientific theories that had challenged biblical truths. As mentioned in Chapter 1, railway expansion throughout the country exposed rock sections that constantly reminded travellers of new theories about the evolution of the earth, as expounded for instance by Charles Lyell's uniformitarianism, a new way of thinking which paved the way for evolutionary theory through the development of stratigraphic palæontology. Thus, train journeys confronted passengers with vivid and sometimes sensational images related to the evolution of life on earth and that of humankind.[26] In Childe-Pemberton's tale the train conveys the narrative's moral message. The thematics of speed connoted by the machine symbolize Little Red Riding Hood's growth, all the more so as the heroine is described 'steaming out' of the station (p. 219), her body fusing with the engine. The modern rewriting of Little Red Riding Hood's journey through the forest thus suggests that young girls should not wander off the tracks of proper femininity – literally. The association of the train with transgression was very frequently used in the Victorian period.[27] Indeed, as a symbol of British modernity and progress, not only did the train illustrate the disruption of temporal and spatial boundaries (it shrinks distances and reduces time by transporting passengers far away at full speed) but it was also used as a metaphor for the breaking down of moral boundaries.

In the case of Childe-Pemberton's 'Little Red Riding Hood' understanding the rules of civilization lies at the heart of the young woman's education. When the heroine describes her father, who has no time to sit but has his tea standing, 'like the Hatter in "Alice in Wonderland"' (p. 214), the intertextual vignette constructs the modern world as a Wonderland ruled by arbitrary laws, which the narrator cannot grasp. Carroll's *Alice's Adventures in Wonderland*, as already argued, may easily be seen as a humorous rewriting of a travel narrative, featuring a young naturalist entering a wild territory whose codes of conduct and signs of civilization have become useless or turned upside down. The clash between the natural world that Alice encounters – where nature has full sway, as creatures speak and turn themselves into other species untamed and uncontrolled – and the civilizing lessons the little girl has improperly learnt positions the conflict between nature and culture at the heart of the narrative. Likewise, the arbitrary conventions that Childe-Pemberton alludes to are the bourgeois mores and manners by which Lewis Carroll's fantasy, as well as her own rewriting, are meant to teach their heroines to abide. In this way, both the frame-narrative and the beginning of the narrator's tale emphasize the idea that reality is legible. This implies that the world is made up of codes, which little girls must learn to crack. The fairy-tale genre is, therefore, a very efficient way of representing reality: for Perrault and his followers the classical fairy tale was a means of internalizing social norms and naturalizing bourgeois mores and manners, framing the world as a set of codes and rules that defined the upper and middle classes. Transposed into Victorian reality, these codes become visual codes and may be deceptive, as Childe-Pemberton's Red Riding Hood is about to learn: they are, in fact, empty codes, easily appropriated by wolves in gentlemen's clothing.

'Little Red Riding Hood' defines bourgeois femininity by fusing the little girl with her riding hood, and the tale is marked by upper-middle-class preoccupations. From the beginning of her story, Childe-Pemberton's narrator underlines the extent to which the rhythm of the world is linked to industrialization and mass production: she uses fashion and taste to define the middle classes and to illustrate the tempo of society – its frantic rhythm being paralleled with the evanescence of fashion:

> My story, said I, is of more than twenty years ago, at a time when the fashions in dress were just the reverse of what they are now, when crinolines could hardly be worn large enough, when the pork-pie hat was the rage, and when, instead of sage-greens, the peacock-blues, and rhubarb-reds of the present day, bright scarlet, crude violet, and two new colours called mauve and magenta, found favour in the eyes of those who pretended to taste in the matter of dress.
>
> Amongst these I, who had just grown up, took my place, of course. I wore red stockings, and a violet dress, and a scarlet cloak, and nobody ever thought, as they would now, of calling my taste vulgar. What I must have looked like you can very well imagine... (p. 213)

Time is here measured through fashion. The heroine, whose identity hinges upon an accumulation of accessories, is shown to belong to the middle class through her commodification: she takes her place, as if on display among other objects. More significantly still, the allusion to taste and the suggestion that we could very well imagine what she looked like constructs her as an aesthetic representation of the Victorian ideal – as an image that matches the visual stereotypes of the period. The description of her cloak further highlights the significance of mass reproduction in the construction of the feminine ideal:

> That scarlet cloak in particular was my great pride. Cloaks at that time were made in a particular shape, a sort of double cloak, the upper one being shorter than the under, and drawn in at the waist with a rosette – Connemara cloaks I think they were called; and though I am quite ready to admit that the fashions of that

date were for the most part hideous and tasteless, the Connemara cloaks were by no means ugly or unbecoming.

They were made in all colours… Trotting about in this cloak, with a pair of red stockings, just showing above laced boots, the smallest of small black hats on my head, and my hair drawn back into a chenille net – such was the monstrous fashion of the moment – I must have looked not very unlike Red Riding-Hood herself. (p. 214)

The beautiful results from mass reproduction. As her identity depends upon mass-produced accessories that function as so many visual codes, the narrator becomes an artifact – that is, a reproduction of Little Red Riding Hood. Moreover, she is eager to visit her grandmother, who will make her presents of new dresses and hats, and prepares her journey to her grandmother's through many shopping expeditions. Her mother's advice before she leaves home, therefore, is to care less about her dresses and amusements, and not to talk to strangers. The two recommendations subtly set side-by-side the theme of appearances with the motif of the wolf, making explicit that the little girl's rape is related to her excessive commodification. When she arrives at the station, furthermore, she is wearing her Connemara cloak. The use of passive forms reinforces her objectification, paving the way for her 'violation': 'I was hurried from platform to platform, hustled into a carriage' (p. 219). Thus, the appearance of Childe-Pemberton's 'wolf' on the train is not coincidental. Indeed, concealing his real nature under the appearance of the gentleman, the wolf caricatures the taming of nature, a theme which underlies the whole fairy tale.

The narrator, tired of reading her book and of looking out of the window, wants 'to vary the monotony of the journey' and welcomes the 'new fellow-traveller as a variety' (p. 220). The term *variety* calls to mind Victorian taxonomies and the era's obsession with classifying beings and species according to particular body signs, which scientists claimed they could read so as to range beings on the evolutionary scale. This idea is developed further when the narrator attempts to read the stranger:

He was a small man, rather unusually small, and of an age that it was impossible to guess at; he might have been anything from thirty to five-and-forty, or even fifty, for he had a sort of fair hair that, if it has any gray in it, blends both together till the gray becomes indistinguishable, and he had light invisible eyebrows and a very light moustache and 'imperial,' that imparted a certain indefiniteness to his whole physiognomy. Then he had a habit of screwing up his eyes till it was impossible to guess whether the lines at their corners were due to advancing age or were merely the result of trick... He was a very dapper little man, too; he was dressed in a neat grey overcoat, and carried a plaid rug, which he spread over his knees when he had settled himself in the carriage. Altogether, I rather liked his looks, and certainly I have had many companions since sitting on the seat opposite me whose aspect was not nearly so pleasant nor their manners so good. I was particularly struck by his manners. (p. 220)

The reference to physiognomy[28] and the narrator's endeavour to read the stranger's face foregrounds Victorian mechanistic science, which turned humans into machines whose pieces could be understood and controlled, highlighting the 'natural historical way of knowing'[29] that typified the nineteenth century, as described in Chapter 3. The allusion to the pseudo-science of physiognomy, the popularity of which soared with the development of photography, and the belief that the external signs of the body could reflect the soul, brings into play the transformation of individuals into sets of shared codes with 'images [usurping] the position of the individual body as the basis of legibility'.[30] But in so doing, it also stresses the delusive appearance of reality. For the narrator cannot successfully analyse the stranger. The colour of his hair is 'indistinguishable', his eyebrows 'invisible'; the man's identity is 'impossible to guess' as his face has 'a certain indefiniteness'. Childe-Pemberton's choice of a wolf whose outward features conceal his wildness is significant; it points to the development of sexual socialization in Western society, as argued above, and the effacement of the natural body through repression and discipline. Simultaneously, it shows how the urge towards disembodiment worked in tandem with the transformation of individuals into sets of visual codes – in other words, images. Classification ultimately effaces wildness and suppresses depth; Childe-Pemberton's wolf remains dangerous precisely because he cannot be read. The narrator can only trust the stranger as a gentleman because of his manners, which mark his belonging to the upper middle classes (he cannot be a 'low ruffian' as she believes thieves to be (p. 237)), his manners standing for another set of codes shared by a particular social class. Childe-Pemberton's concealment of the wild nature of the wolf in her rewriting of 'Little Red Riding Hood' is hence highly modern. The rewriting of the fairy tale enables her to bring to light the dangers of consumer culture, where anybody can pass for anybody and where bodies vanish beneath visual codes. Interestingly, the wolf, concealed behind the aspect of a gentleman, may thus be seen as a reflection of the young woman, who artificially constructs herself through fashion accessories. Both are artifacts – products of mass reproduction.[31]

Moreover, the story reworks 'Little Red Riding Hood' by exchanging physical violence for theft, thereby emphasizing the importance of wealth in the construction of the Victorian bourgeoisie. The narrator later naively lets the wolf into her grandmother's house to have a look at and to reproduce the carving over the chimney piece and the moulded ceiling. It is interesting to notice that the works of art the stranger wants to see are carvings and mouldings – three-dimensional artworks that he wants to paint, thereby turning them into two-dimensional images. More significantly, perhaps, when the narrator finds him outside the shrubbery, the wolf is sketching 'a picturesque bit of land' (p. 229). The idea of landscaping and reproducing nature links the wolf once again to the transformation of nature into an artificial image, a copy of the real. The picturesque site is not just meant to stage erotic desire and to act as a foil to the domesticated nature of the gardens or the civilized realm of the home. The term *picturesque* also implies its capacity to be reproduced as an image: for Nancy Armstrong, the 'guarantee of picturesqueness was the reproducibility inherent in that information rather than the sensitivity and talent of the individual who observed and copied it'.[32] As it turned natural beauty into semiotic codes, the picturesque aesthetic shifted the value from objects to images. Hence, Nancy Armstrong argues, it paved the way for realism, whose main principle lies in the recognition of visual standards and is defined as a series of images, 'the conventional images that make the world deceptively familiar'.[33] The allusion to the picturesque and the way it entailed aesthetic responses to nature is highly significant in Childe-Pemberton's rewriting of 'Little Red Riding Hood', since the classical fairy tale revolves around responses to the natural body. By turning the wolf into an artist and setting the encounter on a picturesque piece of land, Childe-Pemberton's meeting between Little Red Riding Hood and the wolf is rendered as a visual experience – the visual pleasure displacing erotic desire. Thus, the rewriting aestheticizes sensations, making the wolf respond not to the young girl's erotic power but to the picturesque landscape's roughness and aesthetic value. By effacing Little Red Riding Hood's body (the narrator never fears physical danger, though she meets the stranger three times) and staging the metamorphosis of British culture into a realm of images where truth resides on the surface (note how the narrator's family loathes secrets), the tale thus exchanges the sexual for the visual.

Ironically, the narrator also visits the picturesque grounds with her suitor, Herbert, wearing her red cloak and picking some flowers. Herbert then tells her that the stranger's choice of mid-day to sketch suggests he is not a true artist: 'at mid-day the sun is just over one's head ... and there are no lights or shadows. No true artist would ever choose such a time for making a picture' (p. 234). Herbert's remark emphasizes even more the idea that the setting functions as an image, flattened by the lack of light or shadow. The wolf appears as 'a genuine lover of artistic beauties' (p. 230) – that is, of reproducible objects whose value resides in their image, hence his turning his interest on the house – 'a perfect specimen of its style' (p. 230). The house exemplifies bourgeois taste, once again, based upon reproducibility, not uniqueness. Pictures, mirrors, and china are collected as 'pleasant things to look at' (p. 226), and the house attracts many visitors for its 'artistic beauties' (p. 227) – more than for its inhabitants. When the grandmother leaves Little Red Riding Hood alone at home, the narrator, 'presiding over the teapot' (p. 228) and embodying the Victorian ideal, is just another commodity. In the house, the wolf's big eyes are wide open, staring at the costly commodities from several points of view. Childe-Pemberton's symbolic play upon the open house displaying its precious jewels foreshadows the ultimate theft, the responsibility for which lies 'at her door' (p. 239). The merging of the female body with the house, however, is not so much a displacement as an effacement of sexuality that is thoroughly in keeping with British capitalist culture: the value of Little Red Riding Hood is economic, just as the loss will be monetary – propriety has become property.

As suggested, Childe-Pemberton's rewriting of 'Little Red Riding Hood' hinges on the dangers of appearances and is anchored in consumer culture. Just like the heroine, who fashions herself artificially, the wolf conceals his wildness beneath manners and clothes – visual codes typifying the gentleman. Likewise, the revision reduces the tale's physical violence (the devouring of Little Red Riding Hood) to a set of metaphors – empty figures of speech that enhance the effacement of the body and sexuality all the more. Indeed, though the narrator has only slight physical contact with the wolf on the train (a 'very slight jolt' (p. 222) when the stranger stands behind her and helps her lift her things down), the heroine's violation of her mother's prohibition is represented through metaphors: she goes off the tracks by speaking to the stranger on the train; she does not realize that he should have put his bag in the net over his head (and not hers) on the train, thereby walking into his net; she experiences the cost of disobedience literally (her purse is stolen at the station on market day; his trespassing on her private grounds is a violation of property; the final theft replaces the rape). Thus, not only is Little Red Riding Hood disembodied and turned into a commodity, she is further effaced by figures of speech – such as her being a 'madcap' and being 'hoodwinked' (p. 236) by a thief – which emphasize her construction as an image.

What is interesting to note, however, is that the narrator never really wears her red cloak. The most significant moment when she wears it is when she visits the 'gorsty piece' (p. 228) with Herbert (the 'real' gentleman) and picks some flowers. Her cloak is laid aside on the train and left in her grandmother's sitting room on the night of the theft, leading her to catch her foot in it and fall when she hears her grandmother scream. Paradoxically, the scarlet cloak is associated with her disorderly nature ('I often left my things in grandmamma's sitting-room, and she was much too indulgent and good-natured ever to rebuke me for untidiness or forgetfulness' (p. 235)) and finally linked to the crime: unlike the classical fairy tale, in which the wolf puts on the grandmother's clothes, here, the grandmother sees the wolf with Pussy's scarlet cloak on his head and mistakes the thief for her granddaughter. The conflation of Little Red Riding Hood and the wolf is a means of staging the young girl's participation in the crime – her self-induced rape and murder, to follow Zipes's analysis of Perrault's version: the narrator is 'the accomplice of [the wolf's] crimes' (p. 242). But the changes in the scenario may also be read as ambiguous. The hunter (the narrator's suitor) does not kill the wolf, as in the Brothers Grimm's version, for instance, but is shot in the leg and remains a cripple, abandoning his career in the army. Moreover, the awareness of her guilt liberates Pussy's 'fierceness' ('I felt almost fierce'; 'such a very decided fierceness to my feelings against this man' (p. 242)), turning the pussy into a wild beast: the innocent maiden becomes an amateur detective, bent on incriminating the man who 'traded on' her heedlessness.

In this way, though Little Red Riding Hood's punishment is rendered through a public trial and a judgment, she is not the guilty party. Furthermore, the violated body is, in a way, male, since her suitor has been shot in the leg and compelled to stay at home. Little Red Riding Hood's punishment is ambiguous too: the heroine is not rewarded by marriage, but marrying a lame husband would have sounded much more like a punishment. Moreover, she has hardly learned to discipline herself: she becomes, on the contrary, as wild as the wolf so that he may be sentenced to penal servitude for life. Zipes's contention that Childe-Pemberton's rewriting, just like Anne Isabella Thackeray Ritchie's, are 'examples of the manner in which women writers of the nineteenth century contributed to their own oppression and circumscription' is, hence, disputable.[34] Childe-Pemberton's writing for an evangelical publishing house may have compelled her to stress the moral discourse of the tale through her realistic revision of 'Little Red Riding Hood,' but subversive aspects remain, perhaps suggesting that modern Little Red Riding Hoods may have a dash of wildness in them.

Thus, Ritchie's and Childe-Pemberton's rewritings of 'Little Red Riding Hood' offer modern heroines whose 'nature' has not been tamed nor effaced by layers of clothes. In spite of being identified as Victorian 'Little Red Riding Hoods', Ritchie's and Childe-Pemberton's heroines exemplify how women may cloak their nature under riding hoods without completely surrendering to the demands of culture. More significantly still, by anchoring their rewritings at the heart of industrial England, both Ritchie and Childe-Pemberton suggest that human control of bestiality – and of nature – will always remain uncertain. Thus, the visual rhetoric that seems to define individual identity in both tales, the tropes and images that aim at taming nature and which underline nature's commodification and economic value, are ultimately debunked by Ritchie and Childe-Pemberton, suggesting their potential to be reactivated at any time. If such revisions of the classical tale's meaning(s) may unsettle Victorian constructions of gender and of the real, they also undermine the control of nature that the visual rhetoric encoded: as scientific language attempted to distinguish between humans and beasts or to shape portraits of the savage or of the criminal, literary culture, it seems, sometimes counteracted the mapping of nature and of individuals, bringing to light the pervasive influence of the scientific rhetoric and turning it on its head. This idea intimates that literary narratives, by mediating constructions of the real informed by contemporary representations of nature, participated in the debates that concerned the re-evaluation of the self, especially as new conceptions of nature redefined humans, the self and the Other.

6
Nature and the Natural World in Mary Louisa Molesworth's *Christmas-Tree Land*

Robins were one of the themes chosen by the fairy painter John Anster Christian Fizgerald (1819?–1906) for a series of works on Cock Robin, including *The Captive Robin* (*c*.1864), *Who Killed Cock Robin?*, *Cock Robin Defending his Nest* and *Fairies Sleeping in a Bird's Nest*. In *Who Killed Cock Robin?*, the death of the robin illustrates how Fitzgerald's paintings, often dark and permeated by a dream-like or nightmarish atmosphere suggestive of his familiarity with drugs, connect the world of fairies not only with the natural world but also with that of spirits and ghosts. Of course, the series reproduces natural ecosystems and the deaths of animals depict the struggle for life in the natural world. As Nicola Bown suggests, Fitzgerald's *Who Killed Cock Robin?* may have been influenced by Victorian taxidermic displays, in particular Walter Potter's *The Death of Cock Robin* (1861) which was widely advertised.[1] As both decorative art and scientific arrangement, aimed at helping naturalists or amateurs wishing to learn about natural history, taxidermic displays represented ecosystems safely encased in glass. But the fad for anthropomorphic taxidermy also drew attention to the links between humans and animals and anxieties related to humans' place in the natural world.

Both Fitzgerald's paintings and Potter's taxidermic display underscore, moreover, the powerful connections between robins and death. Robins were, indeed, believed to cover up or bury the bodies of people who died in the woods,[2] a belief on which Mary Louisa Molesworth capitalizes in one of her fairy tales. In 'Ask the Robin', Molesworth plays upon identical themes to connect birds both to the world of fairies and to the realm of death. The fairy tale relates the story of two sisters, one of whom (Linde) is visited in her dream by a strange woman telling her to go into the enchanted forest, dig up a robin which is buried but not dead (lying entranced, as in sensational cases of live burial and catalepsy) and resuscitate the bird. The tale's play on the tension between life and death and the life-in-death condition of the robin may recall as well taxidermic displays. Moreover, the narrative stresses humans' impact on natural ecosystems, presenting both animals and fairies as victims of humans' disrespect for nature and nature's creatures. As the legend has it, the fairies once haunted the forest, until one day a cruel man killed a robin. The act of digging up the bird by the pure and innocent maiden will put an end to a spell on the forest which led to the disappearance of the fairies. Because it induced the vanishing of both fairies and birds, the murder points to the closeness of fairies to the natural world. The lesson underlying Molesworth's fairy tale enhances the educational role that children's fiction played at the time, teaching children how to protect nature. Indeed, while controlling nature was at the heart of Victorian preoccupations, more and more women attempted to raise children's interest in and concern for 'nonhuman nature',[3] underlining the need for the conservation and the preservation of species threatened by industrial societies in both popular science works and fiction. In addition, Molesworth's fairy tale, just like Fitzgerald's 'Cock Robin' series, aligns nature and human nature, capitalizing on the association of fairies with the world of dreams and the unconscious. As we shall see, Mrs Molesworth's tales often foreground women's relationship with nature the better to valorize feminine intellectual faculties. 'Ask the Robin' highlights women's high sensitivity and preternatural powers, as illustrated by Linde's premonitory dream, which stem from women's closeness with nature and nature's inhabitants, be they fairies or birds. The maiden's 'fairy perceptions' and her association with the dead are strongly reminiscent of occult experiments,[4] and Molesworth's narrative, though aimed at children, seems to contain a latent discourse related to women's mental powers that reaches beyond the fairy tale. Similarly, in *Christmas-Tree Land* (1884), women's power to communicate with nature enables them not only to teach children how to protect the natural world and become well versed in natural history but also to invent fairy stories – a form of knowledge buried in individuals' minds and which the civilizing process has repressed.

Fairy stories, animal stories and children's literature

Molesworth's *Christmas-Tree Land* (1884) is a late Victorian fantasy which merges fairy stories and animal stories in a complex narrative and in which children are told stories about characters protecting the natural world and find themselves miniaturized in order to live with animals and learn about their habitats, as if the magic spell made it possible for them to step into a taxidermic glasscase. Throughout her literary career, Mary Louisa Stewart Molesworth (1839–1921) published no less than a hundred works, ranging from realistic stories to fantasies. Her most famous fantasies are undoubtedly *The Cuckoo Clock* (1877) and *The Tapestry Room* (1879). *Christmas-Tree Land*, as the title suggests, is overtly rooted in the natural world and reveals Molesworth's passion for woods – especially pine woods, which also appear in *She Was Young and He Was Old: A Novel* (1872), *Nurse Heatherdale's Story* (1891) and *Christmas-Tree Land*. Combining as it does fairy stories and animal stories, *Christmas-Tree Land* foregrounds the theme of nature both to convey anti-cruelty messages and hint at natural historical information and to explore the children's fancy and teach them how to control it.

From the beginnings of children's literature, the issue of the treatment of animals was a familiar theme. Many books addressed to children were meant to teach them to behave with Christian benevolence towards animals. The most significant example is, perhaps, Mrs Trimmer's *Fabulous Histories: Designed for the Instruction of Children Respecting Their Treatment of Animals* (1786) (which appeared from 1820 as *The History of the Robins*). As Trimmer's book and many others contended, humans' position and power over all living beings at the head of creation should not give them the right to kill or be cruel to inferior creatures. Trimmer's *Fabulous Histories* placed side by side a family of humans and a family of robins, the robins representing proper human behaviour – a construction which Molesworth also uses in *Christmas-Tree Land*, when she sends the children to visit squirrels, birds or eagles. Little by little, animal stories became more entertaining than didactic, as exemplified by John Newbery's publications for children, and those of his successors, Benjamin Tabart and John Harris, which, though still retaining some reference to the naturalistic, combined amusement and instruction.[5] But in the Victorian period, many fantasies condemned the exploitation and mistreatment of animals, such as Jean Ingelow's *Mopsa the Fairy* (1869), in which horses are overworked and die – a theme which gained even more significance with the rise of anti-vivisectionism in the last decades of the century, and paved the way for Anna Sewell's *Black Beauty* (1877).

Molesworth's fiction is very much in line with older moral and didactic tales for children. Her knowledge of late eighteenth-century books for children such as those of Mrs (Barbara) Hofland (1770–1844) and Maria Edgeworth (1767–1849), Aikin and Barbauld's *Evenings at Home*, Mrs Sherwood's *The Fairchild Family* or Charlotte Yonge's later publications,[6] suggests that she was familiar with such evangelical publications for children. Her fiction does not praise religious teaching, however, and – though informed by romantic constructions of nature – is more in keeping with late Victorian perceptions of non-human creatures in relation to humankind, and more particularly women. Indeed, in *Christmas-Tree Land*, the merging of the fairy story and the animal story enables Molesworth to go a step further: for the tale investigates nature, its mysteries and its meaning, the term standing both for the natural world and human nature.

Christmas-Tree Land relates the story of two children, Rollo and Maia, who are sent to stay with their cousin, Lady Venelra, while their father is away. Lady Venelra lives in the White Castle, encircled by hills and fir-trees. For the children, the place becomes 'a land of Christmas trees',[7] giving an instant spur to their imagination. The austere atmosphere of the White Castle, where they must study all day long, is soon counterbalanced by journeys into the forest where they find a cottage inhabited by two children of about the same age, Silva and Waldo. Silva and Waldo's godmother sometimes visits them and tells them stories or offers them fantastic journeys in the woods. Little by little, the fantasy takes us more and more into the natural world, changing fairy stories into animal stories. The world of the castle and the world of the cottage function as inverted reflections of one another. In the White Castle, where the two children undergo a strict education, 'sit straight up in [their] chairs like dolls, and only speak when … spoken to' (p. 57), nature has been reduced to mere objects of social use: in the hall 'branches of trees [have been] rudely twisted into chairs and feet [are] the horns of several kinds of deer … to please their ancestors' whimsical taste in furniture' (pp. 12–13). Likewise, the tapestry in Lady Venelra's boudoir represents a hunting scene with creatures chased by cruel dogs and riders lashing their horses, while the couch is 'antlered' (p. 20). For the children the effect is 'strange and barbaric' (p. 12), constructing the civilized place as a realm marked by cruelty to nature. The woods, in contrast, are linked to the past and to Lady Venelra's ancestors – 'a sort of shrine dedicated to the memory of her race' (p. 23) – an original link in the chain:

> Now, if Lady Venelra had a weakness, it was for these same woods. They were to her a sort of shrine dedicated to the memory of her race, for the pine forests of that country had been celebrated as far back as there was any record of its existence.
> 'They are indeed beautiful, my child. Beautiful and wonderful. There have they stood in their solemn majesty for century after century, seeing generation after generation of our race pass away while yet they remain. They and I alone, my children. I, the last left of a long line! (p. 23)

As obvious here, though the fantasy (or 'semi-fairy story')[8] draws attention to natural details, it has no real scientific pretensions. The aim is rather to draw links between the woods and Lady Venelra's 'race' so as to teach the children how close they are to the natural world and discover what 'nature' means. Still, as the children are invited to journey through the forest instead of merely listen to fairy tales, they are led to experience nature from 'within' through living with animals: they visit squirrels in their nests and learn what squirrels eat and how they preserve their food through eating acorn cake and chestnut pasties out of season; they encounter sparrows, blackbirds and robins; find themselves dressed in feathers, get acquainted with eagles' modes of living and learn about their piercing sight. Their various experiences with the animals teach them how to live in an ecosystem, the children being part of it and often compared with the animals. If providing little natural historical information, the narrative thus nonetheless dispenses much practical advice regarding how to protect nature. As suggested, however, Molesworth's merging of fairy stories and animal stories (both naturalistic and fabular) and her constant comparison of children to animals ultimately aims to teach children how to deal with their own 'nature'. Indeed, the natural world is recurrently aligned with the wild territory of the children's imagination, offering a post-Darwinian narrative which goes much beyond traditional eighteenth-century tales for children featuring animals endangered by humans.

As a late Victorian example, Molesworth's fiction illustrates, in Tess Cosslett's words, how fairy tales and animal stories 'migrated down the hierarchy of literary genres from adults to children, in consequence of an increasing polarization between adults and children'.[9] In fact, the association of children with imagination and primitive creatures while adults were seen as rational and civilized beings was partly due to the publication of Charles Darwin's *On the Origin of Species* in 1859 and the view (expressed as well by Rousseau and the Romantics before) that 'children are somewhat "nearer" to nature and to animals than adults', as Cosslett puts it.[10] Darwin compared the child to animals or primitive peoples, a link which was confirmed by recapitulation theory (which posited that the development of each individual mirrored the development of the race as a whole).

Molesworth's complex fantasy plays on the divide between adult and child, the human and the animal, culture and nature, through her reconstruction of fancy as a wild territory (potentially inhabited by beasts) which humans repress too much. The structure of her fantasy – that of gradually taking the children away from fairy tales and into the natural world – suggests that the repression of fancy prevents humans from seeing the beauty of nature. As suggested by Molesworth's title, her fantasy foregrounds nature and constructs the wood as a place which hosts stories which must be told and deciphered. As a consequence, though the title of the fantasy hints at the ideals of Christianity, Molesworth invites us to interpret the stories of nature rather than the meaning of God, so as to redefine nature and human nature simultaneously.

Framing fairy stories: fancy as a dangerous territory

As we have seen in the introduction to this chapter, the example of Molesworth's 'Ask the Robin' shows that the connection between fairies and nature (whether the natural world or human nature) was not infrequently exploited by women artists who drew upon the definitions of woman as an irrational and sensitive being in order to emphasize the power of the feminine unconscious. As already argued, Victorian popularizers of science recurrently grouped together fairies and the imagination, the scientific frame ensuring that readers might make a distinction between imagination and fancy and learn to develop their intellectual faculties in concordance with new scientific methods. In the case of fairy tales that take their readers into a completely imaginary world, however, imagination (or fancy, as the terms are sometimes undistinguishable, as we shall see) is often defined as feminine territory. Yet, far from constructing women as superstitious creatures, women's proximity with the natural world emphasizes their mental capacity to weave plots and create stories – their '*natural*' artistic creativity. In the world of art, paintings showed fairies exemplifying the fashion for séances, as in Adelaide Claxton's paintings, Atkinson Grimshaw's (1836–93) *Iris, Spirit of the Rainbow* (1876) or Edward Robert Hughes's (1851–1914) pictures of fairies and the spirit world. Claxton's *Wonderland* (1859–79) features a fair-haired little girl dressed in white – a likeness of Carroll's Alice – reading the Grimms' *Fairy Tales* and surrounded by ghostly shapes, as though her reading of fairy tales had empowered her to conjure spectres. The scene recalls the era's fascination with apparitions and spectral phenomena, fashioning the little girl, avidly reading fairy tales, into a miniature version of adult (female) spiritualists. In the last decades of the nineteenth century women's imaginative creativity and mental faculties were not infrequently re-evaluated by pseudo-sciences like spiritualism which recuperated evolutionary theories and defined women's extra-sensitive capacities as intellectual power. Attempts to connect the elementals with the fairies and Little People of folklore were, in fact, a means of maintaining a spiritual view of the world and must be read in the context of a deep religious crisis that followed the advent of evolutionary theory. Occultists used fairies to bridge the gap between the supernatural and the natural. The rise of Theosophy in the late 1870s, headed by Madame Helena Blavatsky (1831–91), saw fairies as elementals or nature spirits, and connected them with the departed, as in spiritualism. Similarly, in *The Science of Fairy Tales: An Inquiry into Fairy Mythology* (1891), Edwin Sidney Hartland posited the close resemblance between fairies and ghosts.[11] As such experiments tried to bridge the gap between the supernatural and the natural, bringing together fairy tales and romances of natural history, fairy lore revealed the Victorians' interest in primitivism at a time when scientists were probing the prehistoric past and exploring exotic countries. The world was replete with invisible life forms awaiting 'scientific' interpretations: naturalist approaches to fairies were not rare[12] and certainly revealed the way in which Darwin's transformation of the perception of the natural world opened up new possibilities and marched hand in hand with scientific, artistic and even amateur attempts to materialize invisible natural forces, as suggested by the boom in spirit photography in London in the 1870s and 1880s or the many experiments in 'natural magic'.[13]

In *Chrismas-Tree Land*, the highly civilized Lady Venelra (as the decoration of the castle suggests) can no longer have access to the cottage nested at the heart of the forest in which a fairy godmother tells fairy tales. Stressing the view of fairy tales as examples of primitive culture (the cottage of the Three Bears is believed to have existed 'hundreds of years [before]' (p. 37)), the fantasy appears to hint at late Victorian research carried out by folklorists, ethnologists and anthropologists (such as Sabine Baring-Gould (1834–1924), Andrew Lang (1844–1912), Joseph Jacobs (1854–1916) and Sir John Rhys (1840–1915)) which defined fairies as examples of inferior races of mankind.[14] Indeed, as soon as they approach the White Castle, the children notice the cottage in the forest, and Maia believes that gnomes or wood spirits live in the place. Though her brother asserts that gnomes and wood-spirits do not live in cottages, Maia opts 'for a change' (p. 7). The cottage encompasses change and variation – evolution. Constructed as a realm where fancy is set free from the constraints of the civilized world, it aligns storytelling with endless imaginative possibilities. As a result, the variants of stories told there map out the children's fancy, as shall be seen. The pervading presence of Lady Venelra's ancestors (represented as well by the unaltered decoration in the castle) is far removed from the old storyteller who inhabits the forest and whose stories are not rigid and frozen but varied and changeable.

Silva and Waldo's godmother, whom the villagers believe to be a witch, both old and young, is not just a puzzling fairy-tale character. She acts simultaneously as a repository of ancestral stories and as a personification of fancy – youthful and always capable of being remodelled. Her dark green cloak, 'almost the colour of the darkest of the foliage of the fir-trees' (p. 69), which makes her hard to distinguish from the woods, and her dress, which feels like feathers and makes Maia wonder whether she is a bird as well as a fairy, illustrate how Molesworth uses fairy-tale motifs and stereotypical characters in order to explore the natural world and human nature. The god-mother is associated with the spring flowers she gives to the children so that their scent may help them revive Fairyland ('How much they bring back! Cherish them, my child' (p. 121)), just as the aromatic odours of the woods make people sleep and dream. Fairy tales and fairy lands – as expressions of the children's *nature* – are buried trea-sures which can be dug up when summoned. Hence, as the natural site encapsulates the power of fancy, the children are taught not so much to hold their imagination in check but to make good use of it. As the doctor says, 'Fancy isn't a bad thing sometimes' (p. 47), but '[i]t would not be good for [the children] to go *too* often' (p. 49).

The use of a medical authority to control the children's fantastic ventures and prescribe them a day out into the forest when they have worked long enough is revealing of Molesworth's modern conception of the fairy tale. As a matter of fact, one of the gateways to Fairyland is through a bookcase in the doctor's study:

> He led them some way along a rather narrow passage, where they had never been before, then, opening a door, signed to them to pass in in front of him, and when they had done so, he too came in, and shut the door behind him. It was a queer little room – the doctor's study evidently, for one end was completely filled with books, and at one side, through the glass doors of high cupboards in the wall, all kinds of mysterious instruments, chemical tubes and globes, high bottles filled with different coloured liquids, and ever so many things the children had but time to glance at, were to be perceived. But the doctor had evidently not brought them there to pay him a visit. He touched a spring at the side of the book-shelves, and a small door opened.
>
> 'Come, children', he said, speaking at last, 'this is another short cut. Have no fear, but follow me.'
>
> … They had perfect trust in the old doctor, and all they had seen and heard since they came to the white castle had increased their love of adventure, without lessening their courage. (pp. 125–6)

The passage through the laboratory frames the children's imaginary journey, ensuring that their fancy is kept under medical supervision.

The fairy adventures they experience, the fairy tales they hear, aim to better their minds, albeit not in traditional ways. Through the figure of the doctor, who has no name and functions as an embodiment of order and authority, Molesworth revises more traditional fairy tales which foreground Christian values and God's omniscience. Here, the doctor becomes the modern authority which purveys a moral – though much more materialistic – discourse.[15] The telling and hearing of stories are never envisaged as a means of escaping reality but as a means of developing the children's intellect. This idea is emphasized by Maia, who wonders whether their first adventure in the forest, when they discover the mysterious cottage, was a dream, as the doctor suggests, induced by the aromatic odours of the woods. Similarly, the nurse, Nanni, whenever she is knitting in the woods, systematically starts dreaming. Maia replies that 'People don't dream together of exactly the same things at exactly the same moment, as if they were reading a story-book' (p. 43). The parallel between the world of dreams and storytelling (also symbolized here by the nurse's knitting activity, recalling the stereotypical image of the spinning of tales) underlines the narrative's almost 'scientific' exploration of imagination. The cottage at the heart of the forest becomes a representation of the children's minds, a little house in which they store and recreate fairy tales which may evolve and change.

Indeed, the children try to decode the cottage through the fairy tales they know, from 'Snow White', suggested by the little beds and chairs, small enough for dwarves, to 'The Three Bears', when they see three cups and three plates on the table. They also fear being changed into frogs or devoured by a witch, as in 'Hansel and Gretel'. The references to classical fairy tales point to the tales' social discourse, aimed at teaching girls (and boys) obedience so that they may fit in the prescribed order. Yet, Maia and Rollo are neither turned into frogs nor punished for their greed.[16] The embedded literary encodings, rather than being intended to mould the children into social roles (such as by turning the heroine into a perfectly contented housekeeper), mirror the children's minds: fairy tales, like children's literature, epitomize a mental world which will grow up and evolve with them: as the godmother has it, 'fairyland is one little part of that other country. You will find that out as you get older' (p. 73). Hence, the little house must be neat and tidy, as the godmother has taught Silva, and gets even neater and tidier on each of their adventures: to be cherished and developed, it is suggested, the imagination must be controlled.[17]

The use of fairy tales as embodiments of children's fancy is enhanced by the figure of the godmother, as argued above. The godmother oscillates between the benevolent godmother and the witch (fancy being good *and* evil), and is defined by three main features – her age, her eyes and her close relationship to nature:

> She was old – of that there was no doubt, at least so it seemed at the first glance. Her hair was perfectly white, her face was very pale. But her eyes were the most wonderful thing about her. Maia could not tell what colour they were. They seemed to change with every word she said, with every new look that came over her face. Old as she was they were very bright and beautiful, very soft and sweet too, though not the sort of eyes – Maia said afterwards to Rollo – 'that I would like to look at me if I had been naughty'. (p. 69)

The power of penetration of her eyes indicates as much her imaginative power (her capacity to invent ever new stories) as her capacity to read the children's minds. Discipline and surveillance, as illustrated by the godmother's field of perception, are no enemies to fancy, here represented by her transformations. The godmother's power is tied to her capacity to maintain order and to educate children to restrain their desires while indulging in the fantasy world she creates for them.[18] Hence her secret relationship with the doctor, who contacts her whenever the children need mental relief. Likewise, her closeness to nature is no hint at disorder. When she starts telling 'The Story of a King's Daughter', her eyes frame the story-telling experience:

> *Her* eyes looked very kind and gentle, and yet very 'seeing', as she caught their gaze.
>
> 'I believe,' thought Maia, 'that she can tell all we are thinking'; and Rollo had something of the same idea, yet neither of them felt the least afraid of her. (p. 70)

As a tale-teller, a seer or a prophetess, associated with transformation and metamorphosis, the godmother illustrates the occult powers of women who, like fairies, can foretell the future. Storytelling was often linked to 'heterodox forms of knowledge'.[19] As Marina Warner contends, at the time it was thought that woman's knowledge of illicit science revealed woman's relationship with the devil. Even the origins of the word 'fairy', from the Latin *fatum* – the thing spoken – and *fata* – the fates who speak it, hinted at the fairies' power to foretell the future (like the Three Fates spinning the thread of the past, the present and the future on a spindle with their fingers). The figure of the female tale-teller – transformed by male collectors or writers of fairy tales (from Charles Perrault to the Brothers Grimm) and rewritten into a domesticated old crone devising fairy tales for children – may have evolved in order to tame the female teller, eradicating the beast in woman to contain her potential occult powers. This idea was often illustrated in Victorian fairy tales by women writers which highlighted women's occult powers as a sign of their limited potency. In Ingelow's *Mopsa the Fairy*, for instance, women's capacity to tell stories and foretell the future only illustrates their preshaped destiny.[20] Molesworth's late Victorian fantasy suggests, on the contrary, that children may use their mental powers if they learn to control their fancy. What is noteworthy here is that the godmother's powers and relationship with the natural world help Molesworth merge contemporary constructions of nature and female nature, thereby showing how the two were often conflated in the Victorian period. This association is emphasized even more by the embedded story which the two children are told and which links Molesworth's discourse to the urge to protect the environment with late Victorian preoccupations with woman's physiology and the dangers of fancy.

At the end of the Victorian period, the prevalence of Darwinian theories and the development of mental physiology aligned women with children, idiots and animals and positioned woman at the bottom of the evolutionary scale. But despite the fact that women were associated with the weak-minded, woman's mental powers were seen as potentially dangerous. Illustrations of men trying to cut off women's heads, exemplified by Lustucru, the seventeenth-century Skull Doctor or 'Le Médecin Céphalique', who hammered out women's heads on his anvil to shape them into better-behaved wives,[21] typified the dangers that women's intellect could represent. This may be the reason why in many classical fairy tales women's heads are severed, and in 'Bluebeard', for example, since the almighty patriarch rewards the heroine's curiosity and intellectual powers (which enable her to discover his secret) by threatening to chop off her head. Moreover, just as women's intellectual powers were subjected to scientific scrutiny in the last decades of the nineteenth century, women's spiritual sensibility and extrasensory capacity became a topical theme. The development of spiritualism from 1848 with the Fox sisters in New York and the multiplication of séances featuring clairvoyance, telepathy or automatic writing enabled women to achieve positions of power.[22] As mediums – or seers – women could remain innocently 'possessed' of fragile and passive ideals, yet gain ascendency over men. The significance of inner vision, increasingly underlining the subjectivity of vision,[23] testified to the Victorians' obsession with seeing the invisible – an obsession stirred up by evolutionary theory which allowed the use of the imagination as a scientific method, as argued in the previous chapters.

Reconnecting with nature

Hence, fairy tales, centred on the powers of the imagination, opened onto 'the country of the mind'.[24] As a significant instance, Molesworth believed throughout her life that she had second sight, and her belief strongly anchors her in a society in which séances, mediums and mesmerism were highly popular.[25] In *The Tapestry Room*[26] and *Christmas-Tree Land*, and in most – if not all – of her fairy tales, the children align Fairyland with the world of dreams. More significantly still, her embedded tales lead her a step further in her investigation of fancy and the (female) mind. In 'The Story of a King's Daughter', the embedded fairy tale which the godmother tells Rollo and Maia, the narrative hinges upon the heroine's prophetic dreams and her close relationship to nature.[27] 'The Story of a King's Daughter' relates the story of Princess Auréole, who saves and protects animals, and Prince Halbert, whose cruelty to animals condemns him to be turned into a beast and remain prisoner of the enchanted forest until twelve dumb animals mount on his back and let him carry them out of the forest. Though depicted by Halbert as 'fanciful and unreasonable' (p. 85), Auréole judges by 'instinct' but truly. Thus, her closeness to nature is represented by her intuitive behaviour, her relationship to animals and her desire to live in the woods with her animals. Moreover, Auréole has prophetic dreams. These start on the very night of her father's death the better to mark the end of male power. As the king dies, male authority vanishes and the country is threatened with war and invasion. Auréole dreams of a frightening monster which is transformed into Prince Halbert. In fact, Halbert has disappeared in the enchanted forest, in the very centre of which a magician is said to live in a castle and to cast spells on people so as to get them in his power. Communicating with Auréole through her dreams, Halbert begs her to rescue him in the forest with her 'dumb friends'. The animals only agree to mount on Halbert's back once Auréole has climbed on the beast's back as well. Instinctively trusting her own nature (her imagination), like nature more generally (represented by the animals she saves and protects),[28] the king's daughter is able to transform reality and to save the prince who has been turned into a wild beast and is held captive in the forest. Consequently, the embedded tale reflects significant issues of the frame-narrative in order to teach Maia and Rollo how to trust their imagination. Furthermore, the embedded tale contains other embedded tales, which turn the whole narrative into a series of Chinese boxes. These different fairy-tale layers, as I will show, map out the children's minds.

'The Story of a King's Daughter' comprises Chapters 5 and 6 in the fantasy. It is significant that Chapter 6 is introduced by a quotation from the Brothers Grimm's 'The Raven': 'I have been enchanted, and thou only canst set me free.'[29] However, Molesworth's rewriting is a complete reversal of the Brothers Grimm's fairy tale: Molesworth bestows the role of the saviour on her heroine, while endowing her with typically feminine qualities – most significantly her sympathy for suffering. Yet Auréole is not meant to endure suffering herself; she protects the defenceless inferior creatures. Furthermore, if the Brothers Grimm's tales generally emphasize their heroines' lack of independence and subjection to male rule, Molesworth's king's daughter, even though her identity may be subordinated to that of the king, is wilful. Auréole refuses to accept the cruel Prince Halbert as her 'king and master' (p. 82), but her independence is no sign of unruliness. She reveres rules yet refuses to become queen after her father's death and Prince Halbert's disappearance: 'A king's daughter am I, but no queen. I feel no fitness for the task of ruling ... and I could never rest satisfied that I was where I had a right to be' (p. 96). In addition, the tale proceeds in reverse when compared with traditional animal bridegroom tales in which the heroines must accept their beastly partners and learn to see through their furry appearance. Prince Halbert first appears 'manly and handsome' and has 'winning manners' (p. 82), until his cruelty comes to the surface and is literally illustrated by his transformation into a wild beast. The fairy tale, if it advises not to trust appearances, also suggests that women should not submissively and blindly accept prescribed partners.

It is to be noted that the motifs of dumbness, male transformation, the twelve animals and the heroine's journey into the forest to save the male character resonate with other fairy tales by the Brothers Grimm, such as 'The Twelve Brothers' and other variants, playing upon identical motifs, such as 'The Seven Ravens' and 'The Six Swans'.[30] The possible intertextuality here evokes multiple meanings,[31] because the Brothers Grimm's three variants of the same narrative increasingly weaken the woman's power: the heroine manages to transform fewer and fewer brothers. Furthermore, the three variants are significant through their treatment of the relationship of women with nature. Generally, in the Brothers Grimm's tales women's relationship with nature is ambiguous. Women sometimes rule over the natural world, or are subjected to natural forces. For Bottigheimer, 'women's power over nature is more than balanced by nature's and society's power over nature'.[32] In these three variants, particularly, Bottigheimer underlines, the forest and the trees on which the heroines have to stay 'invert[-] the ancient belief in women's control over nature and attempt[-] to eradicate it, for the tree isolation in *Grimms' Tales* poses far greater danger than tower isolation'.[33]

In Molesworth's fantasy, in contrast, both Auréole in the embedded tale and the godmother in the frame-narrative are prescient characters whose power derives from their close relationship with nature. Like the godmother, who can take the children anywhere, change their clothes at will and reshape the world (the carriage she drives through the forest is small enough for a baby and yet the children all fit into it, their size adapting to that of the vehicle as they enter it), Auréole can change the beast back into a prince. Thus, it could be suggested that the revision of the classical model foregrounds not only the female characters' control over nature and supernatural powers but also the narrator's power to revise the tale. As already noted, the cottage in the forest is, from the very beginning, a place linked to change and variation. Similarly, at the opening of the embedded fairy tale, the children underline the issue of retelling and revising. They fear the godmother may alter the tale and its motifs:

> 'Once – '
> 'Once upon a time; do say "once upon a time" ', interrupted Silva.
> 'Well, well, once upon a time', repeated godmother, 'though, by the by, how do you know I was *not* going to say it? ... ' (p. 78)

Auréole's natural power to reshape reality finds a parallel with the godmother's power to retell ancient stories. Furthermore, Auréole's trust in her own dreams, just like her instinctive concern for nature, encapsulate the fantasy's conflation of nature and human nature. As a result, the embedded vignette creates a *mise-en-abyme*. On the one hand, it leads children to question animal protection in contemporary society, as suggested by Maia after their adventure among birds:

> [T]he birds overhead twittered and trilled in their perfect happiness.
> 'How can one be so cruel as to shoot them?' said Maia one afternoon about a week after the visit to the squirrels.
> 'I don't think any one would shoot these tiny birds,' said Rollo.
> 'I am afraid they do in some countries,' said Maia. (p. 159)

On the other, it drifts away from mere natural historical information or ecological understanding – such as when the children are told that eagles are not fed with 'poor little lambs, all raw' as told in 'the natural history books' (p. 192) and that the creatures which the children encounter would not easily be classed in 'tribes' or 'genus' by the 'learned men of that country' (p. 215) – in order to underline how listening to nature will enable humans to counteract the discourse of unimaginative scientists and experience the joys of the imagination:

> [C]hildren who come to our woods and amuse themselves without ever robbing a nest, catching a butterfly, or causing the slightest alarm to even a hare – such children *deserve* to be rewarded. (p. 166)

The reward is a narrative combining fairy tales and animal stories where species never struggle ('As if any creature that lives in
Chistmas-Tree Land would kill any other!' (p. 193)) and humans
respect the environment in the same way as they respect their own
nature. One may conclude that mechanical attitudes, based on the
domination of nature, have destroyed the natural world. The conse-
quent loss of the capacity of humans to communicate with nature has
alienated them, Molesworth seems to argue, from their own nature.
The depiction of characters living in harmony with nature together
with the fir trees as symbols of fairy tales in *Christmas-Tree Land* suggest, therefore, that fairy lore is a knowledge, and that this knowledge
must form an integral part of human nature. Moreover, what this late
Victorian example illuminates by placing side by side nature's varieties and varieties of stories, stored in humans' minds or in a cottage
in the forest, is once again how fantasies borrow from contemporary knowledge structures. As underlined, Molesworth's definition of
nature, her stress on women's mental powers and her construction of
humans' 'beastly' nature, more and more located in the brain, highlights the impact of evolutionary thought on Molesworth's fantasy.
The narrative is therefore a good instance of the ways in which scientific thought shapes literary culture and how literary culture in turn
reflects upon its society's definitions of nature. This idea will be further illustrated by Edith Nesbit's children's fiction, which particularly
reflects the popularization of evolutionary theory and its implications, especially at a time of imperial expansion. This time, nature
and nature's specimens, framed by scientific discourse or exhibited
in museums and shows, seem to hint at humans' doomed ecological
future.

7
Edith Nesbit's Fairies and Freaks of Nature: Environmental Consciousness in *Five Children and It*

My name is Know-a-Bit...I was once a fairy, living under the greenwood tree, dancing my rounds on the soft green turf, to the light of the glow-worm's lamp and the sound of the nightingale's song. Then I drank honey-dew from the blossoms, and decked myself out in the petals of flowers, or spoils from the butterfly's wing. But times have changed – and so have I. A railway now runs right through the valley which was our favourite haunt – there are engine-lights instead of the glow-worm's, and the scream of the whistle drowns the song of the bird! Education is now all the fashions, and fairies, like bigger people, are sent to learn lessons at school. As for me, I was the first of my race to give up a rural life. For more than four hundred years, ever since printing was invented, I have taken to books; and I now make my home within the leaves of this volume... [1]

In C. M. Tucker's *Fairy Know-A-Bit; or, a nutshell of knowledge*, fairy Know-a-Bit is an instructor to children, giving them lessons that merge didacticism with entertainment. By becoming an urban creature, fairy Know-a-Bit has gained an education, and her transformation traces the evolution of civilization. The scholarly fairy is much more evolved than her rural ancestors, and as such she becomes a suitable instructor to children – primitive creatures in need of an education. Tucker's fairy Know-a-Bit is a good introduction to Edith Nesbit's treatment of fairies in *Five Children and It* because evolutionary allusions inform Nesbit's supernatural being who reluctantly acts as a teacher to children. Both writer and poetess,[2] Edith Nesbit remains famous today for her children's books, notably *The Story of the Treasure Seekers* (1899), *The Wouldbegoods* (1901), the Psammead series (*Five Children and It* (1902), *The Phoenix and the Carpet* (1904), *The Story of the Amulet* (1906)), *The Railway Children* (1906), *The Enchanted Castle* (1907) and *The Magic City* (1910). Her fiction often interweaves children's reality with fantasy, using magical objects to spur the children's adventures. Nesbit also wrote literary fairy tales (collected in *The Book of Dragons* (1900) and *Nine Unlikely Tales* (1901)), written for *The Strand* in 1899 and 1900, which merge the fairy-tale world with contemporary reality and recurrently highlight moral or cultural issues.[3]

Five children and It is a fantasy which features a fairy and borrows conventions from classical fairy tales: the fairy the children encounter grants them wishes which enable them to experience magical adventures in their contemporary reality. 'It' is the last of the fairies, however, and is thus another of the extinct creatures that Nesbit features in her children's fiction. Indeed, dinosaurs and prehistoric creatures punctuate Nesbit's work, from the dragons that haunt her fairy tales, as in *The Book of Dragons* or 'The Last of the Dragons', which are presented as scientific specimens and whose necks and tails often recall more sauropods than mythic creatures, to the dinosaurs brought to life in *The Enchanted Castle* through the magic of imagination and the giant sloth in *The Magic City* (inspired by the Megatherium of the Crystal Palace Park). As in most popular science works and events of the second half of the nineteenth century, Nesbit interweaves scientific objects, specimens or models and fairy-tale motifs: 'Beauty and the Beast' and 'Sleeping Beauty' are central to *The Enchanted Castle*, for instance, sealing the union of antediluvian monsters with the beasts and time-frame of fairy tales. This may be explained by the fact that Nesbit believed that

> children should be taught no facts unless they asked for them ... They should just be taught the old wonder-stories, and learn their facts through these. Who wants to know about pumpkins until he has heard of Cinderella? Why not tell the miracle of Jonah first, and let the child ask about the natural history of the whale afterwards, if he cares to hear it?[4]

Combining instruction and entertainment through using the fairy-tale mode, Nesbit's views of education are thoroughly in keeping with Victorian pedagogical methods.[5] For Nesbit, education should ban materialistic science and dry lessons. Because knowledge implies belief, she believes, education involves imagination. Hence her setting side by side of physical phenomena and imaginary beings, so as to present knowledge as fairy tales are told:

> You show the child many things, all strange, all entrancing... You tell it that the stars, which look like pin-holes in the floor of heaven, are really great lonely worlds, millions of miles away; that the earth, which the child can see for itself to be flat, is really round; that nuts fall from the trees because of the force of gravitation, and not, as reason would suggest, merely because there is nothing to hold them up. And the child believes; it believes all the seeming miracles.
>
> Then you tell it of other things no more miraculous and no less; of fairies, and dragons, and enchantments, of spells and magic, of flying carpets and invisible swords. The child believes in these wonders likewise. Why not? If very big men live in Patagonia, why should not very little men live in flower-bells? If electricity can move unseen through the air, why not carpets? The child's memory becomes a storehouse of beautiful and wonderful things which are or have been in the visible universe, or in that greater universe, the mind of man. Life will teach the child, soon enough, to distinguish between the two.
>
> But there are those who are not as you and I. These say that all the enchanting fairy romances are lies, that nothing is real that cannot be measured or weighed, seen or heard or handled. Such make their idols of stocks and stones, and are blind and deaf to the things of the spirit. These hard-fingered materialists crush the beautiful butterfly wings of imagination, insisting that pork and pews and public-houses are more real than poetry; that a looking-glass is more real than love, a viper than valour. These Gradgrinds give to the children the stones which they call facts, and deny to the little ones the daily bread of dreams.[6]

Thus, even if Nesbit was quite ambivalent concerning the nature of the imagination (many of her books deal with the dangers of books and of the imagination, such as 'The Book of Beasts' (first story published in the *Strand Magazine* in March 1899)), her narratives combine fantasy with reality, often by foregrounding the imaginative potential of science, from geology and palæontology to mathematics and physics, her narratives turning technological advances into wonders.[7] As this chapter will show, Edith Nesbit's children's literature draws upon geology and palæontology both to offer an imaginative world away from industrial society and to propose science lessons to her readers. Her merging of fact and fiction, of reality and fantasy is telling, for her construction of fairies as species contemporary with prehistoric creatures, from pterodactyls and plesiosaurs to megatheria purveys an ecological discourse on extinction which reaches beyond fantasy and is strongly reminiscent of mid-Victorian popular science books.

Extinct creatures and natural wonders: mediating the science lesson

Nesbit's *The Psammead, or The Gifts* was serialized in the *Strand Magazine* in April 1902 in nine instalments. *The Strand* did not merely publish fiction but a mix of fictional and non-fictional essays not primarily intended for child readers, touching on science and nature's wonders. The theme of wishes directly alludes to 'The Three Wishes' ('I daresay you have often thought what you would do if you had three wishes given to you, and have despised the old man and his wife in the black-pudding story'),[8] which was one of the tales collected and published by Joseph Jacobs in *More English Fairy Tales* (1893).[9] Recurrent hints of this type intimate that Nesbit was familiar with contemporary anthropological approaches to folk and fairy tales and reveals that her narrative reaches beyond mere fantasy. Moreover, the fantasy is reminiscent of educational children's literature because geological and palæontological information undergirds the narrative. As in popular science books for children, fairy tales and motifs mediate the science lesson. As the children leave London for the countryside, the trip from an urban to a rural environment is equated with an entry into Fairyland. The house seems 'a sort of Fairy Palace', while the limekilns and oasthouses look like 'an enchanted city out of the *Arabian Nights*' (p. 10). The use of fairy-tale allusions brings out the wonders of the rural scenery, recalling popular science books offering children imaginary excursions. Moreover, when the children imagine that the gravel-pit in which they discover the Psammead is 'seaside', Anthea adds that this was actually the case thousands of years before, as their father has taught them. The allusion to marine regression underlines the narrative's interest in geological processes and paves the way for the apparition of the fairy. Indeed, marine regressions (just like transgressions, which implied the flooding of exposed land) were linked with mass extinctions, whether they involved them or were correlated to them (by causing the extinction of marine organisms and leading to the extinction of land animals as well through chain effects). Marine regressions were one of the causes of the Cretaceous-Tertiary extinction (65 Ma) which led to the end of dinosaurs. The children rehearse science lessons, arguing that the sea vanished when 'the earth got too hot underneath' (p. 17), and the comparison of Anthea kneeling to 'scratch like a dog does when he has suddenly remembered where it was that he buried his bone' (p. 18) equates the children's metaphorical regression into animals with a palæontological search for fossilized bones. The quest will be a quest for origins, as the fairy dating back to prehistoric times is soon to suggest. The lesson is furthered as the children dig a hole, believing, like Carroll's Alice, they will reach Australia, recalling that the earth is round, and so hoping to see exotic creatures, from kangaroos and opossums to blue-gums and Emu Brand birds. The biological diversity which the children imagine, together with the idea that the place was once covered in water and inhabited by fishes, corals or mermaids, launches a narrative mid-way between a natural history narrative and a fantasy. The Psammead seems to be an imaginary compound of five different species (symbolizing the five children), recalling that, in Australia, 'unusual composites, like the appositively primitive duck-billed platypus, a mixture of duck and mammal that also lays eggs' could be found.[10] By hinging her tale on a natural creature likely to be collected by the children as an unknown specimen, Nesbit launches her narrative with hints at amateur naturalists and collectors, going on excursions in search of shells, ferns or other collectibles.

Moreover, Nesbit's fantasy constantly draws parallels between the children's wishes and sense of wonderment and her scientific culture. The fairy recalls the wonder associated with exotic specimens brought back to England, and the children's holiday to the countryside is redolent of the fictional journeys popularizers of natural history offered their young readers as previously seen, all the more so as the children seek to know more about the several-thousand-year old creature whose history is not 'in books' (p. 21). If the fairy dug out of the sand will not be the children's instructor, refusing to be anthropomorphized as in popular science books for children, however, the story nonetheless deals with the evolution of the earth, its changes, and points to the possibility of extinction:

> 'Oh, don't go!' they all cried; 'tell us more about it when it was Megatheriums for breakfast! Was the world like this then?'
> ... 'Not a bit,' it said; 'it was nearly all sand where I lived, and coal grew on trees, and the periwinkle were as big as tea-trays. We sand-fairies used to live on the sea-shore ... That's thousands of years ago, but ... as soon as a sand-fairy got wet it caught cold, and generally died. And so there got to be fewer and fewer ... (p. 23)

As if digging up their own past, the children are invited to participate in the story of life and of humans' and the earth's evolution. Rat or snake, the 'brown and furry and fat' (p. 18) fairy as an endangered species may be the last of its race, its disappearance wiping fairyland off the map:

> It was worth looking at. Its eyes were on long horns like a snail's eyes, and it could move them in and out like telescopes; it had ears like a bat's ears, and its tubby body was shaped like a spider's and covered with thick soft fur; its legs and arms were furry too, and it had hands and feet like a monkey's. (p. 19)

The description of the creature hints at comparative anatomy and functionalist deductions. The association of several species, from land and flying mammals to gastropods and arachnids, mixing vertebrates and invertebrates, recalls analyses of fossil finds, often seen as *collages* of different species too. That the creature should be a sand-fairy is not coincidental either, recalling how geologists and palæontologists themselves stressed the almost supernatural powers of the palæontologist, able to 'call forth from their rocky sepulchres, the beings of past ages, and like the fabled sorcerer, give form and animation to the inhabitants of the tomb'.[11] As research in geology and palæontology developed in the nineteenth century, the interrelations between science and imagination partook of modern scientific methods – albeit rational and materialistic – radically transforming the real and images of the environment. Georges Cuvier (1769–1832), the leading exponent of comparative anatomy, had already made explicit that species could and must be reconstructed even when they no longer existed, and palæontologists after him (who were often also geologists as well), drawing on his work, capitalized on the narrative potential of the new scientific discipline and invited their audiences to imagine the world inhabited by monstrous creatures from fragmentary fossilized remains. Thus, the furry and simian fairy highlights the evolution of new scientific methods which relied upon speculation and imagination, climaxing with evolutionary theory which suggested the possibility of ever-new, even grotesque, creations.

Nesbit's fantasy, playing upon magic wishes and enchantments and fairy creatures, simultaneously draws upon the magic powers of the natural world and the enchantment of evolutionary theory, which had enabled scientists to imagine the unimaginable and the most extraordinary transformations and creations. Here, although it was not possible to visualize evolutionary theory and only comparative anatomy could help scientists reconstruct extinct species, the Psammead teaches children how to visualize the invisible, as if providing empirical evidence. Consequently, the encounter with the Psammead makes explicit the extent to which the popularization of extinction often led to a merging of fact and fantasy, most especially in children's literature. Seeing is knowing, the Psammead seems to suggest, just as seeing is also believing – linking the wonders of nature and naturalists' discoveries to the world of fairies, wishes and beliefs:

> 'Well,' said Anthea ... Who are you? And don't get angry because we really don't know.'
>
> 'You don't know?' it said. 'Well, I knew the world had changed – but – well, really – do you mean to tell me seriously you don't know a Psammead when you see one?'

'A Sammyadd? That's Greek to me.'

'So it is to everyone,' said the creature sharply. 'Well, in plain English, then, a *Sand-fairy*. Don't you know a Sand-fairy when you see one?'

It looked so grieved and hurt that Jane hastened to say, 'Of course I see you are, *now*. It's quite plain now one comes to look at you.'

'You came to look at me several sentences ago,' it said crossly, beginning to curl up again in the sand.

'Oh – don't go away again! Do talk some more,' Robert cried. 'I didn't know you were a Sand-fairy, but I knew directly I saw you that you were much the wonderfullest thing I'd ever seen. (pp. 19–20)

The dialogue recalls Lewis Carroll's nonsense and the way in which his fantasies shift from the literal to the metaphorical.[12] In addition, it underlines the importance of the visual in the children's educa-tion. In the middle of the nineteenth century, new theories of visual education, such as those of the Swiss educationalist Johann Heinrich Pestalozzi (1746–1827), for whom knowledge had to be conveyed directly through the senses, appeared. They were, revealingly, at the root of the Crystal Palace dinosaur park project which was to be a powerful source of inspiration for Nesbit.[13] For Benjamin Waterhouse Hawkins (1807–94), the sculptor who reconstructed the prehistoric creatures, the visualization of extinct species was essential to edu-cation, 'revers[ing] that order of teaching' by presenting 'the things with their names' to the people and not simply their names.[14] This is why, when the children first become introduced to the Psammead and merely focus on the name, the sand-fairy's ironic remark on their lack of observation alludes to the type of visual education that underlay mid-Victorian popularization of geology and palæontology at Sydenham.

This idea explains why Nesbit's fairy does not share much with the ethereal fairies that haunt Victorian culture. Although Nesbit's fairy tales feature lovely, light and winged fairies,[15] the striking materiality of the sand-fairy in *Five Children and It* launches a narrative grounded in extinction and in which magical transformations reverberate with evolutionary principles. The visualization of the fairy also enables the narrator to convey Nesbit's views on education and make an ironical comment on positivism, contrasting adults' beliefs in facts with children's trust in imagination:

> Grown-up people find it very difficult to believe really wonderful things, unless they have what they call proofs. But children will believe almost anything, and grown-ups know this. That is why they tell you that the earth is round like an orange, when you can see perfectly well that it is flat and lumpy; and why they say that the earth goes round the sun, when you can see for yourself any day that the sun gets up in the morning and goes to bed at night like a good sun as it is, and the earth knows its place, and lies as still as a mouse. Yet I daresay you believe all that about the earth and the sun, and if so you will find it quite easy to believe that before Anthea and Cyril and the others had been a week in the country they had found a fairy. (p. 14)

The fairy creature is thus embedded within a narrative whose aim is to raise the child reader's awareness as to the threat of extinction. Though entertaining above all and not designed as a purely didactic text, *Five Children and It* functions, however, like many a popular science book for children of the second half of the nineteenth century. The hints at various interpretations of physical phenomena contrast different scientific methods, validating the role of imagination in science. Such knowledge structures underlying the narrative is another example which typifies how science and technology informed Victorian literary culture. Furthermore, that the fairy should be related to the issue of interpretation and the significance of imagination in science links the creature all the more to evolutionary science, as it evokes the way in which fossils were inextricably related to mental reconstructions even before the advent of evolutionary theory. For instance, in his writings Georges Cuvier deplored empiricism,[16] and even invited scientists to scrape the surface of fictional accounts and to find in literary texts a confirmation of natural evidence, suggesting thereby that reality was concealed behind fantasy and myth.[17] For him, fictional accounts recorded humans' struggle in the environment, giants and monsters often appearing as the products of humans' allegorization of nature to metaphorize predators and magnify his battle against nature. Inevitably, because scientific theory increasingly combined reason and imagination, it also contained within itself, as Tess Cosslett contends, 'inevitable contradictions and tensions, which provid[ed] loop-holes for complexity, ambiguity and even "supernaturalism" to creep back in'.[18]

Extinction in nineteenth-century children's literature

Such tensions were most to be noted in discourses on and representations of extinction, which may explain why Nesbit's creature belongs to the Little People. Extinct creatures and the reasons for their extinction permeated nineteenth-century culture as a whole as scientists attempted more and more to popularize palæontology and geology so as to present to the people the latest scientific discoveries and, perhaps, to warn people about the potential threat of extinction awaiting humans as well. Throughout the nineteenth century, humans' place in nature and the authority of God were constant bones of contention as new fossil discoveries were made, more often than not undermining the theory of the Flood. The idea of competition as necessary for survival, for instance, often associated with natural selection (though Darwin foregrounded much the ideal of altruism as well), obsessively recurs in palæontological accounts of the latest fossil discoveries, as scientists were trying to imagine the modes of living and habits of the extinct species they unearthed. Fossils of extinct creatures were positioned at the heart of heated debates because palæontology both struggled with creation theory and used new scientific methods, namely, comparative anatomy, which demanded imagination and redefined the real.[19] The issue of extinction raised questions for naturalists, more especially so for natural theologians whose literal readings of the Bible made extinction impossible. While Cuvier argued as early as in 1796[20] for the reality of species extinction, believing that species had disappeared through environmental changes – catastrophes, or *revolutions* – the preservation of each species on Noah's Ark hardly squared with Cuvier's late eighteenth-century conclusions.

Following Cuvier's systematic description of mammalian remains in his *Ossemens fossiles* and his affirmation that 'it is quite impossible to conceive that the enormous *mastodontes* and gigantic *megatheria*... can still exist alive in that quarter of the world',[21] fewer and fewer British geologists dared refute the reality of extinction from the newly found fossils of quadrupedal remains in North and South America (the mastodon and mammoth (members of the elephant family) and of the Megalonyx and Megatherium), though some opponents contended that the monstrous shape of some fossils resulted from environmental influences such as climate, or others compared the mammoth with other fabulous monsters, like the centaur, or even believed that the mammoth might still inhabit unexplored regions.[22] Of course, the issue of extinction undermined the ideal chain of being posited by natural theology in which each species formed a link in the history of creation: a gap in the harmonious and perfect whole would endanger the whole system since the story of the Noachian Flood posited the permanence of species, claiming that representatives of all species had been preserved. Throughout the eighteenth century, however, the argument was revised to fit in with new geological discoveries, perhaps, as Nicolaas Rupke argues, as studies related to the annihilation of the dodo of the Mascarene Islands around 1690 (which became extinct due to the development of commerce between Europe and the East Indies) evidenced that extinction could occur without entailing 'a domino effect of species annihilation'.[23] Thus, extinction gradually became reconciled with the language of natural theology: seen through a temporal lens, 'the chain of being would have no deficiencies if considered as a chain of history. All past life should be intercalated in the sequence of current species.'[24]

Consequently, the advent of evolutionary theory and natural selection did not radically change cultural representations of extinction. This was mostly reflected in Victorian children's literature. In *Peter Parley's Wonders of the Earth, Sea, and Sky* the extinction of the dodo is explained as the result of some finality – a well-deserved end for a creature whose appearance certainly betrayed, he claims, its silliness and greed:

> If we may judge of what his character was, from his appearance, he must have been a silly, voracious creature, with hardly any power of resistance or flight. But like all the rest of God's works, he was no doubt adapted for the circumstances in which he was placed, and had enough means of enjoyment, to make it well worth his while to live as long as he could.[25]

Likewise, as suggested in Chapter 1, even if Charles Kingsley advocated evolutionary theory, in *The Water-Babies* extinction signals lack of evolution and regression to some more primitive stage. Although Nesbit's tale does not intend to advocate natural theology, Nesbit seems to follow in the footsteps of such popularizers, even featuring a performance of *The Water-Babies* at the end of *The Phoenix and the Carpet*. The children's encounter with the antediluvian creature enables Nesbit to relate the issue of evolution to the threat of regression in order to purvey a discourse of morality. In fact, as Nesbit's Psammead recalls contemporary efforts to understand the evolution of the earth and the processes of extinction and constantly points to humans' doomed future on earth, the narrative's moralistic stance teaches the children about evolution – the earth's as well as their own. More grotesque than Carroll's Dodo, Nesbit's Psammead nevertheless signals how close Nesbit's and Carroll's fantasies are, both using extinct creatures and hinting at evolutionary theory, and playing on children experiencing physical changes and metamorphoses. As shall now be seen, however, Nesbit's connection of extinction to Britain's exploitation of natural resources at the turn of the century anchors her narrative much more in late Victorian debates related to imperialism.

Nesbit's hairy fairy: extinction and imperialism

In 1824 Caroline Crachami, the 'Sicilian fairy', was taken to London for exhibition. The nine-year old nineteen-and-a-half-inch dwarf was the alleged daughter of Dr Gilligan, a showman, who rented an exhibition hall in Bond Street to welcome up to two hundred paying visitors daily. After her death, the corpse of the 'Sicilian fairy' was sold for dissection, her skeleton mounted and exhibited in the Hunterian Museum, standing between those of the giants Charles Freeman and Charles Byrne.[26] Miss Crachami is a good instance of the kind of entertainments that were most popular in the Victorian period. Exhibitions of freaks of nature, whether in travelling exhibitions, museums or circuses, or even on stage, as in fairy plays, thrilled the Victorians. The merging of supernatural creatures and scientific specimens was probably epitomized when models of dwarfs, believed to be members of a lost race, were made for the ethnological department of the Crystal Palace.[27]

That dwarfs may have influenced folk and fairy tales featuring goblins, gnomes, leprechauns and other species of Little People is one thing. But anthropologists and scientists were also studying creatures believed to belong to the Little People and trying to provide natural explanations for the supernatural, reading freaks through evolutionary theory as atavistic and primitive creatures, their 'otherness' being seen as 'a metonym for the savage and animal nature of people who were not white'.[28] Carole G. Silver argues that such scientific constructions of freaks of nature resulted in the rise of a 'new racial myth', the *de*mythification of dwarfs leading to their *re*mythification.[29] As good illustrations, indeed, travellers and explorers (such as George August Schweinfurth (1836–1925) or Henry Morton Stanley (1841–1904)) described the Pygmies of the Ituri forest in the 1870s as survivals of an extinct aboriginal population of the African Continent – or even an earlier Palæolithic dwarf population.[30] Such scientific measurements and examinations of a foreign population and the alignment of their otherness with fairy creatures typifies the way in which evolutionary theory permeated culture as a whole. In George MacDonald's *The Princess and the Goblin* (1872), the goblins are grotesque misshapen dwarfs, a 'strange race of beings'[31] who connect contemporary anthropological research with fairy tales. This also brings to light the connections that were drawn between the Little People, now viewed as less evolved creatures with childlike characteristics, and children – a parallel which brought home the way in which ontology was then believed to recapitulate phylogeny (meaning that the development of an individual from an embryo maps out the evolution of the species).

Moreover, fairy tales were regarded at mid-century as 'relics that offered insights into cultural origins – insights into the "childhood" of the race'.[32] For instance, in the children's magazine *Good Words for the Young*, Hugh Macmillan paralleled 'the earth's story book' to 'the fairy-story books of childhood', comparing the geological evolution of the earth with the evolution of humans from childhood to adulthood.[33] As shown by the example of Kingsley's *Water-Babies*, children could be used to represent evolutionary processes and illustrate humans' pre-human past. Though Kingsley adapts his moral teleology to recapitulation theory, his fairy tale makes explicit how Victorian children's literature revisited the wonders of nature to propose new forms of instruction in line with current scientific theories.

For Jessica Straley, the influence of recapitulation theory on Victorian child psychology and on pedagogical programmes intended for Victorian children explains the stress on the child's proximity to animals and his evolution from beast to boy or girl. Herbert Spencer's recapitulative psychology in *Education: Intellectual, Moral, and Physical* (1861) is a case in point: the way in which nature taught species how to evolve, effacing the species which failed to adapt to their environment, could be used as a pedagogical message for children. Kingsley's hint at Spencer's pedagogical programme is manifest in *The Water-Babies*. His theory of moral development is grafted onto recapitulation and the need for the child to evolve into a good boy as the species evolved in the natural world to avoid extinction. This type of instruction by nature[34] in mid-century fantasies was strongly related to contemporary scientific debates and the new sciences of mankind, such as anthropology, which emerged in the 1860s and aimed to explore mankind's origin and progress. The Anthropological Society was founded in London in 1863,[35] and many of the scholars who researched folklore also researched early humankind and contemporary savages. Edward Tylor's *Researches into the Early History of Mankind and the Development of Civilization* (1865) and *Primitive Culture* (1871), which defines 'civilized humankind against both savage and beast',[36] are relevant cases in point.

The capturing of folk and fairy tales by Victorian anthropologists and folklorists eager to classify them, as illustrated by the anthologies of fairy tales of Andrew Lang, to which *Five Children and It* alludes, is particularly revealing of the way in which folk and fairy tales merged fiction with concerns typically linked to scientific development and research. As a matter of fact, if often compared to Mary Louisa Molesworth's cuckoo in *The Cuckoo Clock* (1877) or even Carroll's caterpillar or Humpty-Dumpty,[37] Nesbit's (rude) fairy mentor is nonetheless marked by its hairiness, an index of its bestiality, and its rudeness. Because the children's encounter with the monkey-like Psammead whose ancestors have all become extinct evokes mankind's ancestry, the creature draws links between the children and animals which will be furthered throughout the fantasy and even in sequels to *Five Children and It*, as in *The Story of the Amulet*, where the antediluvian creature is a 'mangy old monkey'.[38] Consequently, Nesbit's fantasy draws upon the association between fairies and 'savage or barbarous peoples, [creatures who] lacked the civilized virtues, behaving like children (the Victorian "little savages")'.[39] As we shall see, the connection between the supernatural creature and contemporary visions of African tribes as remnants of extinct aboriginal populations filters through the description of the Psammead.

In fact, the children's wishes, which spur their adventures, symbolically take them into the past. They successively wish to be beautiful, rich, have wings, be tall, grow up quickly, meet Indians or medieval soldiers. If their battles with soldiers may be equated with time travel, the other adventures also enable them to visit past times and ancient peoples. Gaby Wood, drawing on the cultural historian Leslie Fielder's study of 'scale freaks', contends that 'Midgets, Giants, Fat Ladies and Human Skeletons all function as perspectival trick: like the magic potion that made Alice in Wonderland "shut up like a telescope" or the cake that made her stretch to more than nine feet high, these freaks skew their viewers' sense of scale'.[40] In Nesbit's narrative the prehistoric fairy, the giant, the medieval soldiers or the Indians all play upon the stretching of time and space. Furthermore, because the body is, in Susan Stewart's terms, 'our mode of perceiving scale',[41] Nesbit uses physical metamorphoses to help the children experience current definitions of civilization: the characters do not explore the exotic Empire but physically experience rather the disempowering effect of colonization. Indeed, their adventures through time and space recurrently equate them with the Other, making them experience how it feels to look foreign, monstrous or poor. No longer at the heart of the system – Britain – the characters in *Five Children and It* pave the way for Kipling's later imperialist warning in *Puck of Pook's Hill* (1906).[42] Robert's transformation into a giant is highly relevant, for example, because it underlines the extent to which Nesbit's fantasy draws upon natural history specimens to purvey her moralistic discourse. As Stewart contends, 'the gigantic [is] at the origin of public and natural history [and] becomes an explanation for the environment, a figure on the interface between the natural and the human':[43] the giant is 'linked to the earth in its more primitive, or natural, state. Giants, like dinosaurs, in their anonymous singularity always seem to be the last of their race.'[44] Because Robert, as a giant, is turned into a fair specimen and exhibited, his commodification shows how the fantasy aims to rewrite colonization by taming the Western Other, disrupting the boundary between the animal and the human, and highlighting difference and identity as mere constructs. Indeed, the metamorphosis of the child into a freak, if hinting at a child's growth, also points to the issue of identity and selfhood, positioning the freak as a 'frame of reference'.[45]

Thus, Nesbit uses freaks and extinct fairies – figures oscillating between reality and fantasy – to undermine modern constructions of the Western self and to underline the position and role of humans on earth. Her narrative constantly borrows from scientific knowledge, leading her fairy to sensationalize 'Otherness': the antediluvian creature symbolizes the century's imperial expansion and its fears related to the collections of specimens regarded as uncivilized and primitive. But through the figure of the fairy, the narrative relates scientific exploration to the plundering of the earth's riches, illustrated, for instance, by Robert's plan to make money as an explorer in Africa. So, the fairy seems to warn, humans' excessive consumption – of pterodactyls, ichthyosauria or plesiosaurs – may condemn them to extinction, just as the antediluvian creature is condemned. Nesbit's fantasy featuring extinct species of sorts and drawing upon modern geology is therefore not just meant as an escape from reality. If fictional, her narrative aims to educate children to the wonders of the world, humans' impact upon the natural world and the dangers of consumption. As the sand-fairy has become an endangered species because of lack of care, as people have consumed megatheria and ichthyosauria thoughtlessly and without fearing the future, the Psammead teaches the children that excess may lead to want. Indeed, as Monica Flegel analyses, some of the children's wishes – 'for unlimited wealth and unlimited freedom – leads to hunger and a longing for the comfort of the world they have temporarily left behind, as well as a frightening experience of being outside the law'.[46]

However, humans' uncontrolled consumption of natural resources is given an ironic twist through the children's wishes. In fact, each wish leads them to flirt with degeneration – and therefore potentially with extinction as well. The fantasy teaches children how to grow up responsibly and avoid regression, and the five children, whose nicknames associate most of them with animals (Lamb, Panther, Pussy, Squirrel), are constantly equated with animals. After her first wish, Anthea, who wishes them all to be 'beautiful as the day', dreams that she is walking in the Zoological Gardens and hears animals growling. The growling is, in fact, her sister's breathing, but the dream suggests that their physical transformation has symbolically revealed their own bestiality, perhaps because the girls were 'donkeys enough to ask for [them] all to be beautiful as the day' (p. 32). Moreover, as nobody recognizes them, they look like strangers, as though their wish had in fact led them to experience foreignness. Furthermore, as Robert has difficulty controlling himself with the baker's boy, he becomes 'a perfect savage' (p. 145) and is ultimately turned into a freak – a giant – exhibited in a fair, who feels like '*kill*[ing]' the baker's boy (p. 145) and appears 'soft' or 'dotty' (pp. 151, 152). His abnormal size, murderous urges or his idiocy aligns him with degenerate creatures subjected to scientific inquiry and exhibited in fairs. Likewise, Cyril and Anthea believe they are 'beast[s]' (pp. 166, 167) and have to face 'untutored savages' (p. 191) – Indians – who want to scalp and roast them. Cyril becomes chief Squirrell of the Moning Congo tribe, while Anthea is the 'Black Panther', chief of the Mazawattee tribe, and Jane Wild Cat, leader of the Phiteezi tribe. The same fate is reserved for Lamb, who appears 'hungry as a lion', scratches 'like a cat' and bellows 'like a bull' (p. 27) or roars, and ultimately grows too fast, becoming a dandy in no time. Their wishes constantly bring out their animality, making them eat like 'dogs' (p. 128), feel thirsty like 'dogs [which] put their tongues out when they're hot' (p. 42), resemble pigs, draw pony-carriages like horses, or turn them into changelings, as when the 'dear duck of a babe' (p. 70) is stolen by gipsies.

Nevertheless, their transformations never empower them but, on the contrary, make them understand how the Other is constructed and reduced to a set of conventions and objectified. Consequently, their physical changes help them experience difference and Otherness, teaching them to face Otherness. For Mavis Reimer, having been turned 'into exotic and strange creatures, with bodies out of their control', the children 'manage their imperial adventures in part by taking the role of the objectified other'.[47] Aligned with criminals, insane or inferior 'races', or uncivilized soldiers, the children are taught to control their desires and their consumption in order to protect the environment and ensure their own survival. Thus, the narrative's ultimate moral message is that humans' protection of their environment is crucial, and the children's understanding of their difference from or proximity to animals makes them aware of the role they can play to protect the weakest. In fact, it might be interesting to return here to the displays at the Crystal Palace at Sydenham which have so informed Nesbit's fiction. While the dinosaur park exhibited Waterhouse Hawkins's prehistoric reconstructions in the gardens, the Palace showed various sorts of 'savages' from around the world alongside animals in the Natural History Department. Nesbit recalls the experience of visiting the Palace as a place where identity was unstable and difference vanished:

> There were groves or shrubberies; you entered them a-tremble with a fearful joy. You knew that round the next corner or the next would be black and brown and yellow men; savages, with their huts and their wives and their weapons, their looking-glass pools and their reed tunics, so near you that it was only a step across a little barrier and you could pretend that you also were a black, a brown, or a yellow person, and not a little English child in a tunic, belt, and peaked cap. You never took the step, but none the less those savages were your foes and your friends, and when you met them in your geography you thrilled to the encounter.[48]

A visit to Sydenham thus collapsed time and space, blurred the self and the Other. Moreover, in contemporary articles reviewing the palace and gardens, the 'savages' were often compared to Hawkins's dinosaurs and extinct creatures, as if the ethnological collection of natives paved the way for the visitors' discovery of extinct species at the end of the gardens, the journey through the whole site tracing the evolution of the earth and of civilization.[49] For Nesbit, however, as suggested by both her fictional and non-fictional works,[50] civilization had progressed to the detriment of the natural world:

> The chariot wheels of advancing civilisation must always furrow some green fields, grind some fair flowers in the dust. But the chariot wheels in which civilisation to-day advances grow less and less like a chariot and more and more like a steam-roller, and unless we steer better there will very soon be few flowers left to us.[51]

Thus, Nesbit's condemnation of the modern world's ugliness, nature being blighted and polluted by urban development, suggests the extent to which her endangered prehistoric fairy in *Five Children and It* ultimately functions as an epitome of the threat underlying the exploitation of the earth's riches. Following in the footsteps of such writers as Jane Barlow whose fairies had, indeed, left England,

Nesbit, drawing upon such Victorian landmarks of the progress of science and civilization as the Crystal Palace, nonetheless offered a disenchanted vision of the future lying in wait.

> For this holds true – too true, alas! –
> The sky that eve was clear as glass,
> Yet no man saw the Fairies pass
> Where azure pathways glisten;
> And true it is – too true, ay me –
> That never more on lawn or lea
> Shall mortal man a Faery see,
> Tho' long he look and listen.[52]

Epilogue

'It's some time since I heard that sung, but there's no good beating about the bush: it's true. The People of the Hills have all left. I saw them come into Old England and I saw them go. Giants, trolls, kelpies, brownies, goblins, imps; wood, tree, mound, and water spirits; heath-people, hill-watchers, treasure-guards, good people, little people, pishogues, leprechauns, night-riders, pixies, nixies, gnomes, and the rest—gone, all gone!...

'...what made the People of the Hills go away?' Una asked.

'Different things. I'll tell you one of them some day – the thing that made the biggest flit of any', said Puck. 'But they didn't all flit at once. They dropped off, one by one, through the centuries. Most of them were foreigners who couldn't stand our climate. *They* flitted early'.

'How early?' said Dan

'A couple of thousand years or more'.[1]

As Rudyard Kipling's nature spirit Puck points out, at the end of the nineteenth century the fairies had left England. Kipling's construction of fairies as a species likely to become extinct is not original. We have seen how Nesbit presented the issue of extinction through her prehistoric fairy, and how nineteenth-century writers in general used fairies to point out the dangers of massive industrialization, from Hugh Miller's *The Old Red Sandstone* (1841) to May Kendall and Andrew Lang's *That Very Mab* (1885) at the end of the century. Whether the fairies were used to support a discourse on geology or to express concern about the latest scientific discoveries and the implications of scientific materialism, fairies appeared in many different kinds of publications to give a voice to the natural world, its history and the importance of its conservation.

The recurrent use of fairies and fairy tales in discourses about nature went beyond the commercial demands of publishers eager to attract readers in search of sensations. Remorphed from the Romantic to the Victorian era, fairies vigorously emblematized the transformations of the meanings of nature. They helped scientists push the limits of the real and disrupted the boundaries between the possible and the impossible, blurring the frontiers between different types of discourses and illustrating a science that could hardly be conceived or experienced merely rationally. They helped popularizers deal with contradictions and make room for the spirituality and Christian belief that science seemed to have banished from its laboratories and universities. They reflected the wonder associated with new discoveries and displays, as when the huge fossils exhibited in museums triggered the imaginative fancy of visitors. As miniaturized humans, they helped the Victorians come to terms with their changing environment. From the fairies that inhabited natural theological narratives, whose ever changing shapes invited scientists to find the truth concealed by nature's many guises to later fairies which heralded the extinction of excessively urban humans, fairies forced humans to reflect on their deeds and examine their souls.

Whether literary or scientific, Victorian fairies showed how a range of different understandings of nature could be derived from material exhibits, not least those in the great new public venues – from museums of natural history to Great Exhibitions. By thus illustrating the material culture of natural history, the narratives we have analysed throughout this book all helped bridge the gap between objects and knowledge. They played a highly significant part not simply in the diffusion of natural history but also in its formation; their metaphors or linguistic figures encoded both scientific and cultural discourses, as when women are aligned with the mysterious forces of nature and its sudden metamorphoses. In his historical study of varieties of knowledge, John Pickstone not only sees a 'natural historical way of knowing'[2] as a key element of nineteenth-century science but also stresses the concurrent dynamics of cultural understandings. Fairies suggest one way of construing the relationship between the two – and not merely as popularization of science, or the cultural influence of natural history as a form of collecting, describing and identifying. We have seen in this study that Victorian fairyland had its own natural history – extending and reflecting that of more prosaic realms, both mundane and exotic. A whole catalogue of fairies illuminated the more material creatures and habitats that included men and women, integrating in so doing concomitant definitions of nature that were all constitutive of the human, whether as beasts or as machines – from the wolves of Ritchie and Childe-Pemberton to the automata of de Morgan.

By the end of the century, however, fairies lightly regressed to become the almost exclusive entertainers of the nursery, their old connections with childrens' tales sticking to their wings. The worlds of wonder they carried with them seemed increasingly at odds with an age of reason and of professionalized scientific disciplines. Bound to the realm of childhood, *fin-de-siècle* fairies now seemed to brand people who refused to grow up, as J. M. Barrie suggested in his 1904 play. Still, fairies regularly come back, and with a vengeance. In a rational age, they may no longer help people believe in wonders. But they often point out the complexity of the modern world, suggesting how difficult it is to integrate various approaches, data or fields of knowledge as we try to understand our endangered ecosystems. Thus, from being mediators of knowledge, it seems, fairies may well become metaphors of ignorance.

Notes

Introduction

1. See Lyn Barber, *The Heyday of Natural History: 1820–1870* (Garden City, NY: Doubleday and Company, 1980), pp. 13–14.
2. Nicola Bown, *Fairies in Nineteenth-Century Art and Literature* (Cambridge: Cambridge University Press, 2001), p. 1.
3. Bown, *Fairies in Nineteenth-Century Art and Literature*, p. 2.
4. Andrew Lang, 'Introduction', *The Lilac Fairy Book* (1910), qtd in Carole G. Silver, *Strange and Secret Peoples: Fairies and Victorian Consciousness* (Oxford: Oxford University Press, 1999), p. 186.
5. There are three main anthologies of Victorian fairy tales: Jack Zipes (ed.), *Victorian Fairy Tales: The Revolt of the Fairies and Elves* (London: Routledge, 1987); Michael Patrick Hearn (ed.), *The Victorian Fairy Tale Book* (New York: Pantheon Books, 1988); and Nina Auerbach and U. C. Knoepflmacher (eds), *Forbidden Journeys: Fairy Tales and Fantasies by Victorian Women Writers* (Chicago and London: University of Chicago Press, 1992).
6. Criticisms of industrialism and the mechanical age were often conveyed through the fairy-tale language. Examples might be Thomas Carlyle (Thomas Carlyle, 'Signs of the Times', *Edinburgh Review* 49 (1829), pp. 439–59), Charles Dickens's articles and novels, as well as essays that were published in *Household Words* in the 1850s, such as [W. H. Wills and George A. Sala], 'Fairyland in 'fifty-four', *Household Words* 193 (3 Dec. 1853), pp. 313–17. Bown also connects winged fairies with modern inventions, such as the air balloon; Bown, *Fairies in Nineteenth-Century Art and Literature*, p. 48.
7. John V. Pickstone, *Ways of Knowing: A New History of Science, Technology and Medicine* (Chicago: University of Chicago Press, 2001), p. 11.
8. Lynn L. Merrill, *The Romance of Victorian Natural History* (Oxford, NY: Oxford University Press, 1989), p. 6.
9. Barbara T. Gates, *Kindred Nature: Victorian and Edwardian Women Embrace the Living World* (Chicago and London: University of Chicago Press, 1998), p. 3.
10. Though Victorian fairy painting was not a movement in itself, its golden age was between 1840 and 1870; after 1870, fairies mainly appeared in children's literature and illustrations, in particular those of Arthur Rackham and Edmund Dulac. Christopher Wood, *Fairies in Victorian Art* (Woodbridge: Antique Collectors' Club, 2000), p. 11.
11. Most popular science books were aimed at women and children as I argue in Chapter 1. The issue of readership is more complex for the fairy tales and fantasies I analyse which were published in the *Cornhill Magazine* and the *Strand Magazine*.

12. George Levine, *Darwin Loves You: Natural Selection and the Re-Enchantment of the World* (Princeton: Princeton University Press, 2006), p. 22; Gillian Beer, *Darwin's Plots: Evolutionary Narrative in Darwin, George Eliot and Nineteenth-Century Fiction* (Cambridge: Cambridge University Press, (1983) 2000); George Levine, *Darwin and the Novelists: Patterns of Science in Victorian Fiction* (Chicago: University of Chicago Press, (1988) 1991).

13. U. C. Knoepflmacher and G. B. Tennyson (eds), *Nature and the Victorian Imagination* (Berkeley: University of California Press, 1977), p. xix. Although Knoepflmacher and Tennyson argue that the imagination of Victorian artists and men of science never fully coalesced, artists using science yet expressing their ambivalence, particularly regarding Darwin's theory of evolution, their collection hardly looks at nature seen through the prism of natural history. Knoepflmacher and Tennyson mention Alfred Tennyson (who, in *In Memoriam* (1850), uses Charles Lyell's geology, but expresses doubts in 1868 regarding the implications of the theory of evolution as regards Christianity) and George Eliot's portrait of Lydgate in *Middlemarch* (1871–2).

14. Bown, *Fairies in Nineteenth-Century Art and Literature*, p. 135.

15. Merrill, *Romance of Victorian Natural History*, p. 95.

16. Barber, *Heyday of Natural History*, p. 19.

17. David Elliston Allen, *The Naturalist in Britain: A Social History* (Princeton: Princeton University Press, (1976) 1994), p. 65.

18. Bernard Lightman, ' "The Voices of Nature": Popularizing Victorian Science', in Bernard Lightman (ed.), *Victorian Science in Context* (Chicago and London: University of Chicago Press, 1997), pp. 187–211 (198).

19. See, for instance, Juliana Horatia Ewing's 'old-fashioned' fairy tales, such as 'The Neck', 'Kind William and the Water Sprite' or 'The Fiddler and the Fairy Ring'; Juliana Horatia Ewing, *Old-Fashioned Fairy Tales* (London: Society for Promoting Christian Knowledge, (1882) 1894). I will argue later on that Ewing's fairy tales are closer to folktales, hence their natural setting.

20. See Jack Zipes's introduction to *Victorian Fairy Tales.*

21. See Nicola Bown's analysis of Edward Hopley's *Puck and a Moth (Pre-Raffaelite Version)* (1854); Bown, *Fairies in Nineteenth-Century Art and Literature*, pp. 41–3.

22. Isobel Armstrong, *Victorian Glassworlds: Glass Culture and the Imagination, 1830–1880* (Oxford and New York: Oxford University Press, 2008).

23. Hugh Miller, *The Old Red Sandstone; or, new walks in an old field* (Edinburgh: John Johnston, 1841), pp. 222–3, qtd in Silver, *Strange and Secret Peoples*, p. 34.

24. Bown, *Fairies in Nineteenth-Century Art and Literature*, p. 85.

25. Silver, *Strange and Secret Peoples*, p. 209.

1   From the Wonders of Nature to the Wonders of Evolution: Charles Kingsley's Nursery Fairies

1. Philip Henry Gosse, *The Romance of Natural History* (London: James Nisbet & Co., 1860), pp. 271–2.

2. Lynn L. Merrill, *The Romance of Victorian Natural History* (Oxford, NY: Oxford University Press, 1989), p. 13. Gosse's book was originally entitled *The Poetry of Natural History*.
3. Gosse, *Romance of Natural History*, p. v.
4. Gosse, *Romance of Natural History*, p. 9.
5. Gosse, *Romance of Natural History*, p. 5.
6. Gosse, *Romance of Natural History*, p. 6.
7. *Zoologist*, p. 3650, qtd in Gosse, *Romance of Natural History*, pp. 24–5.
8. *Zoologist*, p. 6621, qtd in Gosse, *Romance of Natural History*, p. 190.
9. Merrill, *Romance of Victorian Natural History*, p. 15.
10. Gosse, *Romance of Natural History*, p. 42.
11. Gosse, *Romance of Natural History*, p. 187.
12. Fairy painting drew heavily upon Shakespeare's *A Midsummer Night's Dream* and *The Tempest*, two plays which particularly emphasized the way fairies were related to nature and the forces of nature (Christopher Wood, *Fairies in Victorian Art* (Woodbridge: Antique Collectors' Club, 2000), p. 13). In addition to Fuseli and Blake, Carole G. Silver mentions David Scott's *Puck Fleeing Before the Dawn* (1837), Richard Dadd's *Puck*, Robert Huskisson's *The Midsummer Night's Fairies*, Sir Joseph Noel Paton's *Oberon Watching a Mermaid* (1883), Edwin Landseer's *Titania and Bottom* and John Simmons's oil paintings and watercolours of Titania as major fairy paintings derived from *A Midsummer Night's Dream*. John Stothard, Francis Danby, Henry Thomason or Joseph Severn contributed Shakespearian fairy paintings as well (Carole G. Silver, *Strange and Secret Peoples: Fairies and Victorian Consciousness* (Oxford: Oxford University Press, 1999), pp. 19–20, 215). Victorian fairy painting changed after 1850, freeing itself from literary influences.
13. Gosse, *Romance of Natural History*, p. 9.
14. Fairies peopled the 'fairy' poetry of Samuel Taylor Coleridge, John Keats or Percy Bysshe Shelley, or darker and more supernatural tales by Sir Walter Scott or James Hogg. Blake even claimed he had witnessed a fairy's funeral. Far more than proposing an expedition to discover the mysteries of the natural world, however, Blake's work suggests rather 'traditional associations of fairies, sexuality, and the fertile earth' (Silver, *Strange and Secret Peoples*, p. 26).
15. The microscopic quality of Victorian fairy painting is most exemplified by Richard Dadd's *The Fairy Feller's Master Stroke* (1855–64). The painting presents an unknown territory, and its variations on the fairies' size construct the little people as a new species to be catalogued. Moreover, the fairies merge with the natural world, the grass in the foreground giving the viewers the impression that the painter's brush has provided them access to an invisible universe, as if seen through a microscope: among fairies, elves and gnomes of different sizes, a dragonfly plays the trumpet, a gnat acts as coachman. Aligned with insects, the little people's diversity is evaluated as if by a naturalist. Though many will argue that Victorian fairy paintings, like Dadd's *The Fairy Feller's Master Stroke* and its play with various sizes, entail a dream-like atmosphere,

their sometimes disorientating effect is nevertheless in keeping with the politics of observation of the time. As Merrill argues, the use of the microscope in Victorian England was likely to produce 'a disoriented sense of fragmentation . . . a loss of unity . . . Too many details signal a failure of meaning, a collapse of unity, the death of hope' (Merrill, *Romance of Victorian Natural History*, p. 123). This dark aspect of the Victorians' obsession with microscopic vision permeates Dadd's fairy paintings, perhaps to suggest the tensions brought about by scientific development and its dangers, while simultaneously playing upon the nostalgia for a lost natural world threatened by extinction because of pollution and massive urbanization. Indeed, it is significant to note here that Victorian fairy painting illustrates how Victorian art in general could mediate between scientific and popular culture. Natural history illustrations in popular science books and paintings uncannily echoed one another, and undoubtedly showed the interchange between science and art throughout the period: the painters linked to fairy painting looked at nature not so much with an artistic eye but with a scientific eye, offering a microscopic realism and scientific accuracy in their depiction of fairy lands. Natural historians' highly visual prose appealed to Victorian artists eager to experiment with perspective and to take their viewers into invisible realms beyond the reach of human perception. The journeys to some unknown worlds that Victorian fairy painting offers look like expeditions to worlds invisible to the naked eye and which only the artist's paintbrush can reveal, recalling the period's attempt at giving shape (and reality) to an invisible world which science and technology were daily revealing to the public. The precise and minute realism of Victorian fairy painters (or 'microscopic optics' (W. F. Axton, 'Victorian Landscape Painting: A Change in Outlook', in U. C. Knoepflmacher and G. B. Tennyson (eds), *Nature and the Victorian Imagination* (Berkeley: University of California Press, 1977), pp. 281–308 (288)), directly spurred by the pre-Raphaelite movement, committed to the faithful description of the natural world, capitalized on the vision of nature as a source of wonder and astonishment: their fairies' resemblance to insects and animals allegorizes the Victorians' vision of nature, its secrets, mysteries and wonders. Furthermore, Victorian fairy painters' insights into more folkloric and rural lands, especially Fitzgerald's fairy banquets and funerals, for instance, cannot fail to recall both scientific and anthropological studies of the time. The (sometimes random) cruelty at stake in many Victorian fairy paintings, though enabling the artists to evade censorship and add sadomasochistic and erotic elements on the canvasses, could be read as revelatory of anxieties related to life's competitiveness and the struggle for life, or even the way in which savage elements of folktales seen after 1859 were deemed examples of primitivism and less evolved cultures, primitive races of mankind. These are aspects developed in Nicola Bown, *Fairies in Nineteenth-Century Art and Literature* (Cambridge: Cambridge University Press, 2001).

16. Bown, *Fairies in Nineteenth-Century Art and Literature*, p. 102.

17. A typical example might be Michael Aislabie Benham's pamphlet, *A Few Fragments of Fairyology, Shewing its Connection with Natural History* (Dunhelm: Will, Duncan and Son, 1859), which tries to connect fairy slippers, stones (Encrinites and Entrochi), butter *(Tremella mesenterica)*, pipes (smoking pipes), cups, cauldrons, elf locks, elf shots (flint), fairy children (changelings – in fact often idiots) with nature.

18. Bown traces the rise of fairies in popular science works as early as in Hugh Miller's *The Old Red Sandstone; or, new walks in an old field* (Edinburgh: John Johnston, 1841); Bown, *Fairies in Nineteenth-Century Art and Literature*, p. 106.

19. For example: 'I will presently tell you how you can try a simple experiment, that will go a great way towards accounting for these idle Will-o'-the-Wisps. The inflammable gas called Hydrogen, is copiously produced by the decomposition of animal and vegetable bodies. The substance called Phosphorus, is contained in animal bodies, and is set at liberty in small quantities by their decomposition. When phosphorus and hydrogen come together under certain cercumstances [*sic*], they mix, and a gas called Phosphuretted hydrogen is the result. There is, therefore, no difficulty in supposing that most marshy grounds may produce this gas; and this experiment will show that it is very likely that the Will-o'-the-Wisp is nothing more'; Peter Parley [Samuel Clark], *Peter Parley's Wonders of the Earth, Sea, and Sky* (London: Darton & Clark, n.d.), pp. 268–9.

20. Parley, *Peter Parley's Wonders of the Earth, Sea, and Sky*, p. 302.

21. Parley, *Peter Parley's Wonders of the Earth, Sea, and Sky*, p. 5.

22. See Silver, *Strange and Secret Peoples*. As ideas of cultural evolution developed and fairies and fairy tales were increasingly associated with primitive civilizations, the symbolic value of fairies was used in a multitude of contexts. See Caroline Sumpter, 'Making Socialists or Murdering to Dissect? Natural History and Child Socialization in the *Labour Prophet* and *Labour Leader*', in Louise Henson, Geoffrey Cantor, Gowan Dawson et al. (eds), *Culture and Science in the Nineteenth-Century Media* (Aldershot: Ashgate, 2004), pp. 29–55, for an analysis of how science and politics were allied.

23. Rev. J. G. Wood, *Common Objects of the Country* (London: Routledge, 1858), pp. 1–2, qtd in Bernard Lightman, *Victorian Popularizers of Science: Designing Nature for New Audiences* (Chicago and London: University of Chicago Press, 2007), p. 189.

24. Aileen K. Fyfe, *Science and Salvation: Evanglical Popular Science Publishing in Victorian Britain* (Chicago and London: University of Chicago Press, 2004), p. 2.

25. Susan Stewart, *On Longing: Narratives of the Miniature, the Gigantic, the Souvenir, the Collection* (Durham,North Carolina, and London: Duke University Press, 1993), p. 44.

26. John Cargill Brough, *The Fairy Tales of Science: A Book for Youth* (London: Griffith and Farran, 1859), p. iii.

27. Charles Kingsley, 'How to Study Natural History', *Scientific Lectures and Essays* (London, Macmillan & Co., 1880), pp. 287–310 (291).

28. John Henry Pepper, *The Boys' Playbook of Science* (London: George Routledge & Sons, (1860) 1881), p. 2

29. Charles Kingsley, 'Address to Boys and Girls', *The Boys' and Girls' Book of Science* (London: Strahan & Co. Limited, 1881), p. vii.

30. Lyn Barber, *The Heyday of Natural History: 1820–1870* (Garden City, NY: Doubleday and Company, 1980), p. 15.

31. See Peter Hunt et al. (eds), *Children's Literature: An Illustrated History* (Oxford: Oxford University Press, 1995), p. 13.

32. Hunt et al. (eds), *Children's Literature*, p. 26.

33. Maria Edgeworth (1767–1849) was regarded as a classic writer for children. She was very much involved in educational issues. Her children's stories were very close to children's experience but hardly allowed any room to the imagination.

34. Sarah Fielding's *The Governess, or Little Female Academy* (1749) was a novel meant to instruct and entertain little girls. Mrs Teachum, the governess, has established a school for nine girls. The novel contains embedded fairy tales, which are told by the children and which the governess systematically rephrases in moral terms. She warns her pupils against fairy tales and dismisses the magical elements of the story.

35. Hunt et al. (eds), *Children's Literature*, pp. 35–7.

36. Sarah Trimmer (1741–1810) was an author of children's books who launched *Family Magazine* (1788–9), which contained moral tales and sermons. She also wrote on education; her *Guardian of Education* (1802–6) directly addressed parents and governesses and warned them about the qualities or dangers of newly published children's literature. Likewise, Mary Sherwood (1775–1851) disliked fairy tales. When she re-edited Sarah Fielding's *The Governess* in 1820, she deleted the two fairy tales. What is highly significant, as Hunt explains, is that the 'women writers who dominated the children's market at this time were themselves heavily involved in education' (Hunt et al. (eds), *Children's Literature*, pp. 54–5). Hannah Moore, Anna Barbauld, Mary Sherwood, Sarah Trimmer or Mary Pilkington either managed schools or were governesses. See also Aileen K. Fyfe, 'Reading Children's Books in Late Eighteenth-Century Dissenting Families', *Historical Journal* 43.2 (2000), pp. 453–73.

37. Charles Kingsley, *Madam How and Lady Why; or, First Lessons in Earth Lore for Children* (New York: Macmillan & Co., (1870) 1888), p. viii. Kingsley also mentions it in his preface to *The Boys' and Girls' Book of Science*, 'Address to Boys and Girls', p. vii. Among Victorian popularizers of science, the story influenced John Ruskin (1819–1900), Jane Loudon (1807–58), Gideon Algernon Mantell (1790–1852) and Phebe Lankaster (1825–1900). See Aileen Fyfe, 'Tracts, Classics and Brands: Science for Children in the Nineteenth Century', in Julia Briggs, Dennis Butts and M. O. Grenby (eds), *Popular Children's Literature in Britain* (Aldershot: Ashgate, 2008), pp. 209–28 (209). Fyfe also adds that *Evenings at Home*

was one of the very few science books for children which did not only use science as a means of teaching religious lessons.

38. Kingsley, 'How to Study Natural History'.
39. Kingsley, 'How to Study Natural History', pp. 300–1.
40. Kingsley, 'How to Study Natural History', p. 310.
41. Kingsley, 'How to Study Natural History', p. 303.
42. Kingsley, 'How to Study Natural History', p. 299.
43. Kingsley, 'How to Study Natural History', p. 299.
44. This paves the way for Kingsley's later definition of the fairy tale as a primitive way of framing knowledge about humans and their environment, as shall be seen.
45. David Elliston Allen, *The Naturalist in Britain: A Social History* (Princeton: Princeton University Press, (1976) 1994), p. 123.
46. Richard Noakes, 'The *Boy's Own Paper* and Late-Victorian Juvenile Magazines', in Geoffrey Canton, Gowan Dawson, Graeme Gooday et al. (eds), *Science in the Nineteenth-Century Periodical: Reading the Magazine of Nature* (Cambridge: Cambridge University Press, 2004), pp. 151–71 (155).
47. Merrill, *Romance of Victorian Natural History*, p. 10.
48. *Madam How and Lady Why* appeared in serial form in *Good Words for the Young* in 1869, and was dedicated to Kingsley's son Grenville Arthur and to his schoolfellows at Winton House. See Charles Kingsley, *Words of Advice to School-Boys by Charles Kingsley, Collected from Hitherto Unpublished Notes and Letters of the Late Charles Kingsley*, ed. E. F. Johns (London: Simpkin & Co., 1912).
49. Kingsley, *Madam How and Lady Why*, p. 24.
50. Lightman, *Victorian Popularizers of Science*, p. 75.
51. Charles Kingsley, *Glaucus; or, the wonders of the shore* (London: Macmillan & Co., (1855) 1890), p. 1.
52. The rise of the microscope was linked to the discovery of the cell nucleus by Robert Brown in 1831, leading to an increase in the discovery of the number of species of fungi (Allen, *Naturalist in Britain*, pp. 113–14). In the early 1850s, marine aquaria invaded middle-class homes. The principle of the marine aquarium, accidentally invented in the early 1830s by the surgeon Nathaniel Bagshaw Ward (1791–1868), whose name became associated with glazed cases, enabled people to preserve marine collections, especially when the chemist Robert Warington understood that adding plants to the water would give off enough oxygen to support animal life. Anna Thynne (1806–66) later managed to aerate her tank by having the water poured backward and forward. The vivarium, designed to keep snakes and amphibians, just like the aqua-vivarium, followed in the 1850s, and Ward publicized the principle of his case in the catalogue of the 1851 Great Exhibition. Other names were also associated with the principle such as Philip Henry Gosse who described the marine aquarium in *A Naturalist's Rambles on the Devonshire Coast* (1853); Allen, *Naturalist in Britain*, pp. 117–21; Barber, *Heyday of Natural History*, pp. 115–16.

53. Francis O'Gorman, 'Victorian Natural History and the Discourses of Nature in Charles Kingsley's *Glaucus*', *Worldviews: Environment, Culture, Religion* 2.1 (April 1998), pp. 21–35 (22).
54. Kingsley, *Glaucus*, pp. 54–5.
55. Kingsley, *Madam How and Lady Why*, p. 185.
56. Kingsley, *Glaucus*, p. 73.
57. Merrill, *Romance of Victorian Natural History*, p. 228.
58. Kingsley, *Glaucus*, p. 32.
59. Kingsley, *Glaucus*, p. 77.
60. Kingsley, *Madam How and Lady Why*, p. 134.
61. Kingsley, *Glaucus*, p. 155.
62. Kingsley, *Madam How and Lady Why*, pp. 164–5.
63. Kingsley, *Glaucus*, pp. 43–6.
64. Jonathan Smith, *Charles Darwin and Victorian Visual Culture* (Cambridge: Cambridge University Press, 2006), p. 61.
65. O'Gorman, 'Victorian Natural History', p. 24.
66. O'Gorman, 'Victorian Natural History', p. 24.
67. Kingsley, *Glaucus*, p. 3.
68. Kingsley, *Glaucus*, p. 224.
69. Kingsley, *Glaucus*, p. 238, emphasis in original; this example is cited by O'Gorman, 'Victorian Natural History', p. 24.
70. Kingsley, *Madam How and Lady Why*, p. x.
71. Kingsley, *Madam How and Lady Why*, p. xii.
72. Kingsley, *Madam How and Lady Why*, p. 2.
73. Kingsley, *Madam How and Lady Why*, p. 3.
74. Kingsley, *Madam How and Lady Why*, p. 38.
75. Kingsley, *Glaucus*, pp. 94–5.
76. Kingsley, *Glaucus*, p. 39.
77. Carlo Ginsburg, *Clues, Myth, and the Historical Method* (Baltimore: Johns Hopkins University Press, 1992), p. 103.
78. Jonathan Smith, *Fact and Feeling: Baconian Science and the Nineteenth-Century Literary Imagination* (Madison and London: University of Wisconsin Press, 1994), p. 4.
79. Smith, *Fact and Feeling*, p. 9.
80. George Henry Lewes, *The Foundations of a Creed*, 2 vols (London: Trübner, 1874–5), vol. 1, sections 14, 61, 62; qtd in Smith, *Fact and Feeling*, p. 20.
81. James Krasner, *The Entangled Eye: Visual Perception and the Representation of Nature in Post-Darwinian Narrative* (New York and Oxford: Oxford University Press, 1992), p. 5.
82. Krasner, *Entangled Eye*, p. 46.
83. Krasner, *Entangled Eye*, p. 43.
84. Amanda Hodgson, 'Defining the Species: Apes, Savages and Humans in Scientific and Literary Writing of the 1860s', *Journal of Victorian Culture* 4.2 (Autumn 1999), pp. 228–51 (242).
85. Krasner, *Entangled Eye*, p. 46.

86. Daniel Wilson, *Caliban: The Missing Link* (London: Macmillan & Co., 1873), p. 8, qtd in Hodgson, 'Defining the Species', p. 242.
87. Hodgson, 'Defining the Species', p. 243.
88. Hodgson, 'Defining the Species', p. 245.
89. T. H. Huxley, 'Science and Morals' (1886), *Collected Essays*, vol. IX: *Evolution and Ethics and other essays* (Bristol: Thoemmes, (1886) 2001), p. 146, qtd in Tess Cosslett, *The 'Scientific Movement' and Victorian Literature* (Brighton: Harvester Press; New York: St. Martin's Press, 1982), p. 32.
90. Kingsley, *Madam How and Lady Why*, p. 30.
91. Kingsley, *Madam How and Lady Why*, p. 133–4.
92. Kingsley, *Madam How and Lady Why*, p. 93.
93. Kingsley, *Madam How and Lady Why*, pp. 119–20.
94. Kingsley, *Madam How and Lady Why*, p. 125.
95. Kingsley, *Madam How and Lady Why*, p. 129.
96. Silver, *Strange and Secret Peoples*, p. 32.
97. This essay was included in the third volume of Thomas Crofton Croker's *Fairy Legends and Traditions of the South of Ireland* (London: John Murray, Thomas Tegg & Son, (1825–6) 1838).
98. Silver, *Strange and Secret Peoples*, p. 29.
99. Silver, *Strange and Secret Peoples*, p. 31.
100. Kingsley, *Madam How and Lady Why*, pp. 130–1.
101. Lewis Carroll, *Through the Looking-Glass and What Alice Found There*, *The Annotated Alice*, ed. Martin Gardner (London: Penguin (1871), 2001), p. 251.
102. Charles Kingsley, *The Water-Babies, a Fairy Tale for a Land Baby* (London: Penguin, (1863) 1995), p. 74. All further references are to this edition and will be given in the text.
103. The engraver Thomas Bewick (1753–1828) was most famous for his life-like illustrations and descriptions of rural English life, notably in *A General History of Quadrupeds* (1790) and *A History of British Birds* (1797–1804). See Jenny Uglow, *Nature's Engraver: A Life of Thomas Bewick* (London: Faber and Faber; New York: Farrar, Straus & Giroux, 2006).
104. Wilberforce had asked Huxley if he was descended from a monkey on his grandmother's or his grandfather's side.
105. The book was reviewed in *The Athenaeum* (11 May 1861), pp. 621–3, see Hodgson, 'Defining the Species', p. 231.
106. The Hippocampus controversy began in Oxford in 1860 with the Wilberforce–Huxley debate over humankind's relationship to monkeys. This was followed by more and more dissections of primate brains by British surgeons and anatomists in search of the hippocampus minor. Huxley's opponent was in fact Owen more than Wilberforce: both men published their attacks in the *Natural History Review* (Huxley) and the more conventional *Annals and Magazine of Natural History* (Owen), their fight being furthered during the 1861 BAAS meeting, when a paper on du Chaillu's collection was discussed. The controversy climaxed during the 1862 BAAS meeting in Cambridge. See Nicolaas Rupke, *Richard*

Owen: Biology Without Darwin, a Revised Edition (Chicago and London: The University of Chicago Press, (1994), 2009), pp. 192–208.

107. Rupke, *Richard Owen*, pp. 201–4.
108. Charles Kingsley, 'Speech of Lord Dundreary in Section D, on Friday Last, on the Great Hippocampus Question', *Charles Kingsley: His Letter and Memories of His Life; Edited by His Wife*, vol. 3, pp. 145–8 (London: Macmillan, 1901), qtd in Rupke, *Richard Owen*, p. 221.
109. Even Tenniel's illustrations, featuring the head of an ape in some of them, contributed to the satire of contemporary debates and disputes over evolution.
110. Let us add here, however, that some reviews particularly warned parents that Carroll's fairy tale was no popular science book on natural history. In a review published in *Aunt Judy's Magazine* in 1866, the reviewer, ironically describing the 'exquisitely wild, fantastic, impossible, yet most natural history of "Alice in Wonderland" ', adds, however, that 'parents and guardians . . . must not look to "Alice's Adventures" for knowledge in disguise'; *Aunt Judy's Magazine, The Christmas Volume for 1866* (London: Bell and Daldy, 1866), p. 123.
111. Kingsley, *Madam How and Lady Why*, p. 40.

2   'How Are You to Enter the Fairy-Land of Science?': The Wonders of the Natural World in Arabella Buckley's Popular Science Works for Children

1. Arabella Burton Buckley, *Life and Her Children* (New York: D. Appleton & Co., (1880) 1881), p. 77.
2. Philip Henry Gosse, *The Romance of Natural History* (London: James Nisbet & Co., 1860), p. 225.
3. [Anon], 'Fairy Tales', *Monthly Packet* 25 (Jan. 1878), pp. 80–94 (93). See also Rev. S. Goldney, 'Fables and Fairy Tales', *Aunt Judy's Annual Volume* (London: Hatchards, 1885), pp. 20–32.
4. Bernard Lightman, *Victorian Popularizers of Science: Designing Nature for New Audiences* (Chicago and London: University of Chicago Press, 2007), p. viii.
5. Secord coined the term 'commercial science' to define Victorian popular science as it partook of the commercial culture of exhibition in the early nineteenth century. James A. Secord, *Victorian Sensation: The Extraordinary Publication, Deception and Secret Authorship of* Vestiges of the Natural History of Creation (Chicago: University of Chicago Press, 2000), p. 437, qtd in Lightman, *Victorian Popularizers of Science*, p. 10.
6. Alan Rauch, 'Mentoria: Women, Children, and the Structures of Science', *Nineteenth-Century Contexts* 27.4 (Dec. 2005), pp. 335–51 (335–6).
7. Mitzi Myers, 'Impeccable Governesses, Rational Dames, and Moral Mothers: Mary Wollstonecraft and the Female Tradition in Georgian Children's Books', *Children's Literature* 14 (1986), pp. 31–59 (33).

8. Rauch, 'Mentoria: Women, Children, and the Structures of Science', p. 341.
9. Bernard Lightman, 'Depicting Nature, Defining Roles: The Gender Politics of Victorian Illustration', in Ann B. Shteir and Bernard Lightman (eds), *Figuring It Out: Science, Gender, and Visual Culture* (Hanover and London: University Press of New England, 2006), pp. 214–39 (219).
10. Lightman, 'Depicting Nature, Defining Roles', p. 219.
11. Barbara T. Gates, 'Those Who Drew and Those Who Wrote: Women and Victorian Popular Science Illustration', in Shteir and Lightman (eds), *Figuring It Out*, pp. 192–213 (211).
12. Arabella Burton Buckley, *The Fairy-Land of Science* (Chapel Hill: Yesterday's Classics, (1879) 2006), pp. 1–5.
13. Kate Flint, *The Victorians and the Visual Imagination* (Cambridge: Cambridge University Press, 2000), pp. 33–4.
14. Buckley, *Fairy-Land of Science*, p. 12.
15. Buckley, *Fairy-Land of Science*, p. 20.
16. Buckley, *Fairy-Land of Science*, p. 1.
17. Buckley, *Fairy-Land of Science*, pp. 5–6.
18. The colour pictures (printed by means of wood engraving by Edmund Evans) were accompanied by a verse text by William Allingham in *In Fairy Land* (1870) and later pre-issued with a new story by Andrew Lang under the title 'The Princess Nobody'.
19. This was not always the case among children's writers. A case in point here might be Juliana Horatia Ewing (1841–85), Mrs Gatty's daughter, both writer and naturalist, whose literary fairy tales drew upon folklore. See, for instance, Juliana Horatia Ewing, *Old-Fashioned Fairy Tales* (London: Society for Promoting Christian Knowledge, (1882) 1894).
20. Buckley, *Fairy-Land of Science*, p. 34.
21. Buckley, *Fairy-Land of Science*, p. 7.
22. Barbara T. Gates, *Kindred Nature: Victorian and Edwardian Women Embrace the Living World* (Chicago and London: University of Chicago Press, 1998), p. 53.
23. Buckley, *Fairy-Land of Science*, p. 55.
24. Gates, *Kindred Nature*, p. 52.
25. Buckley, *Fairy-Land of Science*, pp. 12–13.
26. John Tyndall, 'Scientific Use of the Imagination', *Fragments of Science for Unscientific People* (London: Longmans, Green, & Co., 1871), pp. 125–67 (129).
27. Tyndall, 'Scientific Use of the Imagination', p. 130.
28. Tyndall, 'Scientific Use of the Imagination', p. 131.
29. Tyndall, 'Scientific Use of the Imagination', p. 160.
30. Tyndall, 'Scientific Use of the Imagination', p. 166.
31. [James Hinton], 'The Fairy Land of Science', *Cornhill Magazine* 5 (Jan.–June 1862), pp. 36–42 (37).
32. [Hinton], 'Fairy Land of Science', p. 39.
33. [Hinton], 'Fairy Land of Science', p. 41.

34. Nicola Bown, *Fairies in Nineteenth-Century Art and Literature* (Cambridge: Cambridge University Press, 2001), p. 100. Bown explains how Hinton's definition of mid-Victorian science and its power to open up to higher mysteries resonates with Kantian metaphysics, perhaps linked to his reading of Hans Christian Oersted's *The Soul in Nature* (translated into English in 1852). Oersted's *The Soul in Nature* defined the world as a unity of opposing forces, drawing links between the universe and the human mind.
35. Bown, *Fairies in Nineteenth-Century Art and Literature*, p. 102.
36. Qtd in [Hinton], 'Fairy Land of Science', p. 41.
37. Buckley, *Fairy-Land of Science*, pp. 36–7.
38. Lightman, *Victorian Popularizers of Science*.
39. Buckley, *Life and Her Children*, pp. 22, 46, 50, 56, 93, 134, 177, 167.
40. Buckley, *Life and Her Children*, p. 134.
41. Buckley, *Life and Her Children*, pp. 54, 150, 218.
42. Buckley, *Life and Her Children*, pp. 49, 54, 150, 218.
43. Buckley, *Life and Her Children*, p. 6.
44. Buckley, *Life and Her Children*, p. 6.
45. Lightman, *Victorian Popularizers of Science*, p. 222.
46. Lynn L. Merrill, *The Romance of Victorian Natural History* (Oxford, NY: Oxford University Press, 1989), p. 66.
47. Merrill, *Romance of Victorian Natural History*, p. 66.
48. Buckley, *Life and Her Children*, pp. 81, 104.
49. Lightman, *Victorian Popularizers of Science*, p. 238.
50. Buckley, *Life and Her Children*, p. 4.
51. Lightman, *Victorian Popularizers of Science*, p. 247.
52. Buckley, *Life and Her Children*, p. 301.
53. Buckley, *Life and Her Children*, p. 301.
54. Buckley, *Life and Her Children*, p. v.
55. Arabella Burton Buckley, *Winners in Life's Race or the Great Backboned Family* (London: Edward Stanford, (1883) 1892), pp. 351–3.
56. Arabella Burton Buckley, *Moral Teachings of Science* (London: Edward Stanford, 1891), p. 46.
57. Buckley, *Moral Teachings of Science*, p. 35.
58. Buckley, *Moral Teachings of Science*, pp. 35, 64.
59. Gates, *Kindred Nature*, p. 61.
60. This is highlighted in her essay 'The Soul, and the Theory of Evolution', which was written while Buckley was writing her *Fairy-Land of Science*, and in which she looks at different types of spiritualism through the lens of evolutionary theory; Arabella Burton Buckley, 'The Soul, and the Theory of Evolution', *University Magazine* 3 (1879), pp. 1–10.
61. Lightman, *Victorian Popularizers of Science*, p. 246.
62. Edwin Sidney Hartland, *The Science of Fairy Tales: An Inquiry into Fairy Mythology* (London: Walter Scott, 1891), p. 23.
63. Hartland, *Science of Fairy Tales*, p. 335.
64. Hartland, *Science of Fairy Tales*, p. 347.

65. Srdjan Smajic, *Ghost-Seers, Detectives and Spiritualists: Theories of Vision in Victorian Literature and Science* (Cambridge: Cambridge University Press, 2010), p. 175.

66. Janet Oppenheim, *The Other World: Spiritualism and Psychical Research in England, 1850–1914* (Cambridge: Cambridge University Press, 1985), p. 326, qtd in Carole G. Silver, *Strange and Secret Peoples: Fairies and Victorian Consciousness* (Oxford: Oxford University Press, 1999), p. 51.

67. Silver, *Strange and Secret Peoples*, p. 51.

68. Lightman, *Victorian Popularizers of Science*, p. 239.

69. Gates, *Kindred Nature*, p. 61. Ecology was, historically, closely related to Darwinism: the word, coined by the zoologist Ernst Haeckel (1834–1919) in his *Generelle Morphologie* in 1866, aimed to forward the cause of Darwinism. Indeed, Haeckel defined the new science as 'the investigation of the total relations of the animal both to its inorganic and to its organic environment; including above all, its friendly and inimical relations with those animals and plants with which it comes directly or indirectly into contact', and foregrounded 'the complex interrelations referred to by Darwin as the conditions for the struggle for existence'. Translation by W. C. Allee et al., *Principles of Animal Ecology*, qtd by Robert C. Stauffer, 'Haeckel, Darwin, and Ecology', *Quarterly Review of Biology* 32 (1957), pp. 138–44 (141). For more on the links between ecology and Darwinian evolutionary theory see Karl Kroeber, *Ecological Literary Criticism: Romantic Imaging and the Biology of Mind* (New York: Columbia University Press, 1994), p. 22.

70. Buckley, *Moral Teachings of Science*, p. 80.

71. Edmund Gosse, *The Naturalist of the Sea-shore, The Life of Philip Henry Gosse* (London, (1890) 1896), pp. 264–96, qtd in William H. Brock, *Science for All: Studies in the History of Victorian Science and Education* (Aldershot: Varorium, 1996), p. 29.

72. See, for instance, Juliana Horatia Ewing, 'Our Field' (1870), *A Great Emergency and Other Tales* (London: George Bell & Sons, 1877), pp. 225–43; Laurence Talairach-Vielmas, 'Victorian Children's Literature and the Natural World: Parables, Fairy Tales and the Construction of "Moral Ecology"', in Jennifer Harding, Elizabeth Thiel and Alison Waller (eds), *Deep into Nature: Ecology, Environment and Children's Literature* (Lichfield: Pied Piper Publishing, 2009), pp. 222–47.

3   The Mechanization of Feelings: Mary de Morgan's 'A Toy Princess'

1. Thomas Carlyle, 'Signs of the Times', *The Works of Thomas Carlyle* (London: G. Routledge & Sons, 1896–99), XXVII, p. 59.

2. Mary Louisa Molesworth, 'The Weather Maiden', *Fairies Afield* (London: Macmillan, 1911), pp. 121–75 (174).

3. John V. Pickstone, *Ways of Knowing: A New History of Science, Technology and Medicine* (Chicago: University of Chicago Press, 2001), p. 102.

4. Carolyn Merchant, *The Death of Nature: Women, Ecology and the Scientific Revolution* (San Francisco: Harper, (1980) 1989), p. 193.
5. Lorraine J. Daston and Katharine Park, *Wonders and the Order of Nature, 1150–1750* (New York: Zone, 1998), p. 95.
6. Daston and Park, *Wonders and the Order of Nature*, p. 281.
7. Katherine Inglis, 'Becoming Automatous: Automata in *The Old Curiosity Shop* and *Our Mutual Friend'*, *19: Interdisciplinary Studies in the Long Nineteenth Century* 6 (2008), p. 3 <www.19.bbk.ac.uk> (accessed 3 Jan. 2014). See also Richard D. Altick, *The Shows of London* (Cambridge, MA, and London: Belknap, 1978), p. 65; Annie Amartin-Serin, *La Création défiée : L'Homme fabriqué dans la littérature* (Paris : PUF, 1996), p. 26; Jacques Vaucanson, *Account of the Mechanism of an Automaton, or Image Playing on the German-Flute: As it was presented in a Memoire, to the Gentlemen of the Royal Academy of Sciences at Paris*, trans. J. T. Desaguliers (London: T. Parker, 1742), p. 23; Gaby Wood, *Living Dolls: A Magical History of the Quest for Mechanical Life* (London: Faber & Faber, 2002), p. 23.
8. [Anon], 'Talking Machines', *All the Year Round* (24 September 1870), pp. 393–6 (393).
9. William Gaunt and M. D. E. Clayton-Stamm, *William de Morgan* (London: Studio Vista, 1971), p. 12.
10. Roger Lancelyn Green, 'Introduction', in Mary de Morgan, *The Necklace of Princess Florimonde and Other Stories Being the Complete Fairy Tales of Mary de Morgan, with Original Illustrations by William de Morgan, Walter Crane, Olive Cockerell* (London: Victor Gollancz, 1963), pp. 7–13.
11. Mary Augusta de Morgan, 'A Toy Princess', *On a Pincushion and Other Fairy Tales* (London: Seeley, Jackson & Halliday, 1877), pp. 153–76.
12. Mary Augusta de Morgan, 'Vain Kesta', *The Windfairies and Other Tales* (London: Seeley & Co., 1900), pp. 35–52.
13. Mary Augusta de Morgan, 'The Story of Vain Lamorna', *On a Pincushion and Other Fairy Tales* (London: Seeley, Jackson & Halliday, 1877), pp. 4–26.
14. Mary Augusta de Morgan, 'The Ploughman and the Gnome', *Windfairies and Other Tales*, pp. 209–36.
15. Mary Augusta de Morgan, 'The Hair Tree', *On a Pincushion and Other Fairy Tales*, pp. 100–52.
16. Mary Ann Kilner, *The Adventures of the Pincushion designed chiefly for the use of young ladies* (London: Thomas Hughes, (1788) 1824).
17. ' "Do not suppose, my young friend," he said blandly, "that people have more than one reflection. It is a common mistake to suppose so, but in reality there is only one reflection to each object; only, as the object moves before a glass, the reflection moves too, so that all sides of it are shown. If we can steal this vain girl's image as she leans over the brook, she will not be able to see herself in any glass" ' (de Morgan, 'Story of Vain Lamorna', p. 9).
18. 'All the Sun-beams are in reality tiny Sun-fairies, who run down to earth on golden ladders, which look to mortals like rays of the Sun. When they see a cloud coming they climb their ladders in an instant, and draw them up after them into the Sun. The Sun is ruled by a mighty fairy, who tells

his tiny servants (the beams) every morning where they are to shine, and every evening counts them on their return, to see he has the right number' (Mary Augusta de Morgan, 'The Story of the Opal', *On a Pincushion and Other Fairy Tales*, pp. 57–73 (57).

19. The characters from the frame narrative emphasize its instructive aspect: ' "I like that kind of story", said the Brooch; "it is instructive as well as amusing. Now we know why the Opal has changing colours" ' (de Morgan, 'Story of the Opal', p. 73).

20. de Morgan, 'Hair Tree'.

21. A little ill boy, Jack embarks upon a journey to ask the old man who sits on the North Pole for advice; the old man's answer recalls the narrative techniques of popular science books: 'Oh, the stupidity of people! And all this time they are afraid of doing the very thing they ought to do. Of course it's impossible for them to marry till he is dried up, or she is put out. What puts out fire but water? and what dries up water but fire? Princess Pyra has been educated at a good school. I should think she might have known better' (Mary Augusta de Morgan, 'Through the Fire', *On a Pincushion and Other Fairy Tales*, pp. 177–228 (218–19)).

22. Mary Augusta de Morgan, 'The Wise Princess', *The Necklace of Princess Fiorimonde and other Stories* (London: Macmillan & Co., 1880), pp. 175–84.

23. Mary de Morgan, 'A Toy Princess', in Jack Zipes (ed.), *Victorian Fairy Tales: The Revolt of the Fairies and Elves* (New York and London: Methuen, 1987), pp. 165–74 (172). All further references to this edition will be given in the text.

24. Examples might be the Grimm Brothers' 'The Twelve Brothers', 'The Seven Ravens' and 'The Six Swans'. As Ruth Bottigheimer notes, mute women do not appear in Perrault's tales while they are recurrent in the Brothers Grimm's fairy tales. Beautiful women are necessarily silent and silence is 'almost exclusively female'. Silent heroines help their brothers through their dumbness or are punished through voicelessness as in 'The Glass Coffin' (Ruth B. Bottigheimer, *Grimms' Bad Girls and Bold Boys: The Moral and Social Vision of the Tales* (New Haven and London: Yale University Press, 1987), p. 74).

25. Later on, allusions to female neurasthenia and hysteria even appear when the fishermen wonder whether Ursula is 'mad' (p. 169).

26. Term borrowed from Donna J. Haraway, *Simians, Cyborgs, and Women: The Reinvention of Nature* (London: Free Association Books, 1991).

27. David Brewster, *Letters on Natural Magic, Addressed to Sir Walter Scott, Bart.* (London: John Murray, 1834), qtd in Wood, *Living Dolls*, p. 104.

28. Kempelen's chess player also inspired another of E. T. A. Hoffmann's short stories, 'The Automata'. Hoffmann had read about the chess player in Johann Christian Wiegleb's *Instruction in Natural Magic* (Unterricht in der natürlichen Magie (Berlin, 1779)); see Wood, *Living Dolls*, p. 59.

29. Amartin-Serin, *La Création défiée*, p. 89.

30. Douglas Nickel argues that the recurrent invocations of the marvellous and the supernatural to describe new technologies in the scientific writings of the first decades of the nineteenth century must be seen as

metaphysical tropes emerging in reaction to the Enlightenment project and as attempts at reinscribing irrationality and mythology in explanations of the world and of nature (Douglas Nickel, 'Talbot's Natural Magic', *History of Photography* 26.2 (Summer 2002), pp. 132–40). By implication, his use of metaphors related to the marvellous to describe the technology of automata underlines the idea that automata, by imitating humans, were aligned with the hidden forces of nature.

31. Inglis, 'Becoming Automatous', p. 1.
32. Pete Orford, 'Dickens and Science Fiction: A Study of Artificial Intelligence in *Great Expectations*', *19: Interdisciplinary Studies in the Long Nineteenth Century* 10 (2010), p. 9 <www.19.bbc.ac.uk> (accessed 3 Jan. 2014).
33. Orford, 'Dickens and Science Fiction', p. 10.
34. Derek de Solla Price, 'Automata and the Origins of Mechanism and Mechanistic Philosophy', *Technology and Culture* 5.1 (Winter 1964), pp. 9–23 (10).
35. Simon Schaffer, 'Babbage's Dancer and the Impresarios of Mechanism', in Francis Spufford and Jenny Uglow (eds), *Cultural Babbage: Technology, Time and Invention* (London, Boston: Faber & Faber, 1996), pp. 52–80 (68).
36. Sally Shuttleworth, 'Female Circulation: Medical Discourse and Popular Advertising in the Mid-Victorian Era', in Mary Jacobus, Evelyn Fox Keller and Sally Shuttleworth (eds), *Body Politics: Women and the Discourses of Science* (New York, London: Routledge, 1990), pp. 47–68 (55).
37. Shuttleworth, 'Female Circulation', p. 53.
38. Shuttleworth, 'Female Circulation', p. 53.
39. Mary Ann Doane, 'Technophilia: Technology, Representation, and the Feminine', in Mary Jacobus, Evelyn Fox Keller and Sally Shuttleworth (eds), *Body Politics: Women and the Discourses of Science* (New York and London: Routledge, 1990), pp. 163–76 (163).
40. [George Dodd], 'Dolls', *Household Words* 7.168 (11 June 1853), pp. 352–6 (353).
41. [Dodd], 'Dolls', p. 353.
42. [Dodd], 'Dolls', p. 353.
43. [Dodd], 'Dolls', p. 354.
44. [Dodd], 'Dolls', p. 355.
45. [Dodd], 'Dolls', p. 355.
46. [Dodd], 'Dolls', p. 355.
47. As early as in 1824, a speaking doll that could say 'Maman' and 'Papa' was patented by Johann Maelzel. Inglis, 'Becoming Automatous', p. 3.
48. [Anon], 'The Euphonia, or Speaking Automaton', *Illustrated London News* (25 July 1846), p. 59.
49. [Dodd], 'Dolls', p. 352.
50. Schaffer, 'Babbage's Dancer and the Impresarios of Mechanism', p. 56.
51. Schaffer, 'Babbage's Dancer and the Impresarios of Mechanism', p. 56.
52. See Inglis, 'Becoming Automatous'. Dickens's use of automata must of course be read as an illustration of his criticism of the mechanization of humanity and the utilitarian condemnation of fancy, as in *Hard Times*, for instance.

53. Hal Foster, *Compulsive Beauty* (Cambridge, MA, and London: MIT Press, 1993), p. 131, qtd in Inglis, 'Becoming Automatous', p. 5.
54. Inglis, 'Becoming Automatous', p. 5.
55. Shuttleworth, 'Female Circulation', p. 54.
56. Merchant, *Death of Nature*, p. 205. Emma Spary also mentions that revolutionary political writers warned their audiences of the dangers of becoming automata through sacrificing their autonomy to despotic rulers; Emma Spary, 'Political, Natural, and Bodily Economies', in N. Jardine, J. Secord and E. Spary (eds), *The Cultures of Natural History* (Cambridge: Cambridge University Press, 1996), pp. 178–96 (192).
57. Mary de Morgan, 'The Windfairies', *Windfairies and Other Tales*, pp. 1–34.
58. Mary de Morgan, 'The Rain Maiden', *Windfairies and Other Tales*, pp. 192–208.
59. Ironically, the year that followed the publication of 'The Toy Princess', Edison's doll was awarded the Grand Prize at the 1878 Paris Exhibition – his android inspiring Villiers de l'Isle-Adam (Wood, *Living Dolls*, p. 113).

4   Nature under Glass: Victorian Cinderellas, Magic and Metamorphosis

1. Charles Kingsley, *Glaucus; or, the wonders of the shore* (London: Macmillan & Co., (1855) 1890), p. 128.
2. Lionel Lambourne, 'Fairies and the Stage', in Jane Martineau (ed.), *Victorian Fairy Painting* (London: Royal Academy of Arts, 1997), pp. 46–53 (53).
3. Charlotte Gere, 'In Fairyland', in Martineau (ed.), *Victorian Fairy Painting*, pp. 62–73 (64).
4. Lambourne, 'Fairies and the Stage', pp. 51–2.
5. [W. H. Wills and George A. Sala], 'Fairyland in 'fifty-four', *Household Words* 193 (3 Dec. 1853), pp. 313–17 (313).
6. Nicola Bown, *Fairies in Nineteenth-Century Art and Literature* (Cambridge: Cambridge University Press, 2001), p. 96.
7. Bown, *Fairies in Nineteenth-Century Art and Literature*, p. 136. See also David Elliston Allen, 'Tastes and Crazes', in N. Jardine, J. Secord and E. Spary (eds), *The Cultures of Natural History* (Cambridge: Cambridge University Press, 1996), pp. 394–407; and Anne Larsen, 'Equipment for the Field', in Jardine, Secord and Spary (eds), *Cultures of Natural History*, pp. 358–77. The connections between glass and the scientific world displaying specimens in glass cases or preserved in glass jars were not strictly limited to natural history. It is noteworthy that the naturalist Eliza Brightwen refers to a fairy tale to depict late Victorian museum experience: '[The student of nature] must pass alone, from chamber to chamber, down corridor after corridor, until he discovers that sleeping princess, Knowledge, who is never found until we industriously seek for her. All I can do is point out the difference between languidly strolling with vacant face between the glass walls of our great museums, and passing

eagerly with intelligent interest from one cabinet of recognised treasures to another' (Eliza Brightwen, *More About Wild Nature* (London: Unwin, 1892), p. 222, qtd in Samuel J. M. M. Alberti, 'The Museum Affect: Visiting Collections of Anatomy and Natural History', in Aileen Fyfe and Bernard Lightman (eds), *Science in the Marketplace: Nineteenth-Century Sites and Experiences* (Chicago and London: University of Chicago Press, 2007), pp. 371–403 (382). The reference to Sleeping Beauty enhances the process of distanciation (of the museum exhibits from the public, just as of the female body crystallized in its glass and solely to be gazed upon and thus objectified) that characterized nineteenth-century museology. We will see further on how Anne Isabella Thackeray Ritchie undermines this construction through her Cinderella whose bodily desires and inner nature are, on the contrary, reflected by the glass motif.

8. '[A]s the place is so much visited by Londoners, it may be worth while to give a few hints as to what might be done, by anyone whose curiosity has been excited by the salt-water tanks of the Zoological Gardens and the Crystal Palace' (Kingsley, *Glaucus*, p. 163).

9. Juliana Horatia Ewing, 'Among the Merrows. A Sketch of a Great Aquarium', *Aunt Judy's Christmas Volume* (London: Bell and Daldy, 1873), pp. 44–57.

10. Philip Henry Gosse, *The Romance of Natural History* (New York: A. L. Burt Company, Publishers, (1860) 1902), p. 183. The exclamation is, in fact, that of Robert Schomburgk, discoverer of the giant water lily.

11. Isobel Armstrong, *Victorian Glassworlds: Glass Culture and the Imagination, 1830–1880* (Oxford and New York: Oxford University Press, 2008), p. 151.

12. Armstrong, *Victorian Glassworlds*, p. 151.

13. Margaret Flanders Darby, 'Joseph Paxton's Water Lily', in Michel Conan (ed.), *Bourgeois and Aristocratic Cultural Encounters in Garden Art, 1550–1850* (Washington DC: Dumbarton Oaks Research Library and Collection, 2002), pp. 255–83 (266).

14. Darby, 'Joseph Paxton's Water Lily', p. 266.

15. [Anon.], 'Good Friday, and a Better Friday', *All the Year Round* 13 (13 May 1865), pp. 373–6 (374–5).

16. The Crystal Palace was often seen as a place teeming with women's fantasies and unregulated desires; see Andrew H. Miller, *Novels behind Glass: Commodity Culture and Victorian Narrative* (Cambridge: Cambridge University Press, 1995), pp. 66–8.

17. Ritchie was particularly interested in the female literary tradition, as her essays, such as *A Book of Sybils: Mrs. Barbauld, Mrs. Opie, Miss Edgeworth, Miss Austen* (1882), suggest. Most importantly, as underlined in *Toilers and Spinsters, and Other Essays* (1874), Ritchie was much concerned with the social condition of Victorian women and the few choices offered to women outside marriage.

18. William Makepeace Thackeray, *The Letters and Private Papers of William Makepeace Thackeray*, 4 vols, ed. Gordon N. Ray (London: Oxford University Press, 1946), iv, p. 161, qtd in Gowan Dawson, 'The *Cornhill Magazine* and the Shilling Monthlies in Mid-Victorian Britain', in Geoffrey Canton,

Gowan Dawson, Graeme Gooday et al. (eds), *Science in the Nineteenth-Century Periodical: Reading the Magazine of Nature* (Cambridge: Cambridge University Press, 2004), pp. 123–50 (124).

19. Armstrong, *Victorian Glassworlds*, p. 1.
20. Armstrong, *Victorian Glassworlds*, p. 205.
21. The Cinderella revisions Isobel Armstrong examines are: [Anon.], *The History of Cinderella and her Glass Slipper* (London: Orlando Hodgson, 1830(?)); [Anon.], *The Amusing History of Cinderella; or, the Little Glass Slipper* (London, 1850(?)); George Cruikshank, *Cinderella and the Glass Slipper* (London: D. Bogue, 1854); [Anon.], *Cinderella and the Glass Slipper* (London: J. Bysh, 1861); [Anon.], *Cinderella; or, the Little Glass Slipper* (London: Dean & Son, 1870); [Anon.], *Cinderella; or the little glass slipper* (London: Dean & Son, 1876).
22. Iona Opie and Peter Opie, *Classic Fairy Tales* (Oxford: Oxford University Press, 1974), p. 121; qtd in Armstrong, *Victorian Glassworlds*, p. 205. Valerie Paradiz argues that the motif of the glass slipper dates further back and already appears in Giambattista Basile's *Pentamerone* (1637) (Valerie Paradiz, *Clever Maids: The Secret History of the Grimm Fairy Tales* (New York: Perseus Books, (2004) 2005), p. 154.
23. Jack Zipes, *Fairy Tales and the Art of Subversion: The Classical Genre for Children and the Process of Civilization* (London: Heinemann, 1983), p. 30.
24. See Zipes, *Fairy Tales and the Art of Subversion*.
25. Charles Dickens, 'Fraud on the Fairies', *Household Words* 184 (1 Oct. 1853), p. 99.
26. Armstrong, *Victorian Glassworlds*, p. 6.
27. As a significant instance of the period's obsessional fear related to the blurring of human and vegetative worlds, Isobel Armstrong analyses an illustration of Paxton's gigantic *Victoria regia* at Chatsworth which figures a little girl – a 'fairy' child – standing on the water lily, typifying fears related to the collapse of boundaries between plants and humans (Armstrong, *Victorian Glassworlds*, p. 174).
28. Anne Isabella Thackeray Ritchie, 'Cinderella' (1868), reprinted in Jack Zipes, *Victorian Fairy Tales: The Revolt of the Fairies and Elves* (New York and London: Routledge, 1987), pp. 101–26 (111). Subsequent references to this edition will be given in the text.
29. Caroline Sumpter, *The Victorian Press and the Fairy Tale* (Basingstoke: Palgrave Macmillan, 2008), p. 81. Sumpter also examines Ritchie's 'Beauty and the Beast': 'we have but to ring an invisible bell (which is even less trouble), and a smiling genius in a white cap and apron brings in anything we happen to fancy' (Anne Thackeray Ritchie, 'Beauty and the Beast' (1867), in Nina Auerbach and U. C. Knoepflmacher (eds), *Forbidden Journeys: Fairy Tales and Fantasies by Victorian Women Writers* (Chicago and London: University of Chicago Press, 1992), pp. 35–74 (36). Likewise, in 'Maids-of-All-Work and Blue Books', Ritchie compares the exploited maid-of-all-work to the 'benevolent race of little pixies who live underground in subterranean passages and galleries' (Anne Isabella Thackeray

Ritchie, 'Maids-of-All-Work and Blue Books', *Cornhill Magazine* 30 (1874), pp. 281–96.

30. Rebecca Stott, *Theatres of Glass: The Woman who Brought the Sea to the City* (London: Short Books, 2003), p. 25. As Rebecca Stott has shown, women were also involved with glass culture from a more scientific perspective: the marine aquarium, for instance, was invented by Anna Thynne in 1849 (*Theatres of Glass*, p. 126). As mentioned in Chapter 1, the chemist Robert Warington was the first to enunciate the aquarium principles in a paper delivered to the Chemical Society in 1850 by adding plants to the water to give off enough oxygen to support animal life, but Anna Thynne managed to aerate her tank by having the water poured backward and forward. Warington's invention owned his aquaria the name of the 'Warington Case', advertised as an 'Aquatic Plant Case or Parlour Aquarium' (Lyn Barber, *The Heyday of Natural History: 1820–1870* (Garden City, NY: Doubleday and Company, 1980), pp. 115–16.

31. In 'A Vision of Animal Existences' the depiction of a lady holding a copy of John Murray's first edition of *The Origin of Species* and allegorizing natural selection sets a parallel between the lady's appearance and Buffon's and Cuvier's classifications of the natural world; [E. S. Dixon], 'A Vision of Animal Existences', *Cornhill Magazine* 5 (March 1862), pp. 311–18.

32. Susan David Bernstein, 'Designs after Nature: Evolutionary Fashions, Animals, and Gender', in Deborah Denenholz Morse and Martin A. Danahay (eds), *Victorian Animal Dreams: Representations of Animals in Victorian Literature and Culture* (Aldershot: Ashgate, 2007), pp. 66–79 (66).

33. Bernstein, 'Designs after Nature', p. 67.

34. Bernstein, 'Designs after Nature', p. 68.

35. Bernstein, 'Designs after Nature', p. 68.

36. Isobel Armstrong mentions an article published in the *Illustrated London News* of 5 July 1851, 'A Lady's Glance at the Great Exhibition', in which the reviewer notes the profusion of items designed to adorn the female form and hinting at miscegenated metamorphosis, such as artificial flowers made from the tusks of elephants (Armstrong, *Victorian Glassworlds*, p. 217). In an article published in *All The Year Round*, this association between make-up and waste is brought to light in order to deter women from using make-up: it denounces blush, made with alloxan, a chemical substance derived from the fœtal membranes of animals, together with other examples of recycled refuse that fashionable women use; [Anon.], 'Paint, and No Paint', *All the Year Round* 7 (9 August 1862), p. 521.

37. Armstrong, *Victorian Glassworlds*, p. 117.

38. Armstrong, *Victorian Glassworlds*, p. 165.

39. Armstrong, *Victorian Glassworlds*, p. 206.

40. Armstrong, *Victorian Glassworlds*, pp. 206–7.

41. Thomas Richards, *The Commodity Culture of Victorian England: Advertising and Spectacle, 1851–1914* (Stanford: Stanford University Press, 1990), p. 18.

42. Richards, *Commodity Culture of Victorian England*, p. 27.

43. Richards, *Commodity Culture of Victorian England*, p. 27.
44. Richards, *Commodity Culture of Victorian England*, p. 31.
45. Richards, *Commodity Culture of Victorian England*, p. 25.
46. Hans Christian Andersen, 'The Dryad', trans. A. M. Plesner and Augusta Plesner, *Aunt Judy's Magazine* 6.34 (1 February 1869) and 6.35 (1 March 1869), reprinted in *Aunt Judy's May-Day Volume for Young People* (London: Bell and Daldy, 1869), pp. 237–47 and 286–96 (296). All further references are to this edition and will be given parenthetically in the text.
47. Armstrong, *Victorian Glassworlds*, p. 169.
48. Armstrong, *Victorian Glassworlds*, p. 147.
49. Armstrong, *Victorian Glassworlds*, p. 8.
50. Armstrong, *Victorian Glassworlds*, p. 121.
51. Armstrong, *Victorian Glassworlds*, p. 126.
52. Armstrong, *Victorian Glassworlds*, p. 142.
53. Richards, *Commodity Culture of Victorian England*, p. 18.
54. Richards, *Commodity Culture of Victorian England*, p. 53.
55. Richards, *Commodity Culture of Victorian England*, p. 3.
56. Stott, *Theatres of Glass*, p. 126.
57. Stott, *Theatres of Glass*, p. 21.
58. [Anon.], 'Wonders of the Sea', *All The Year Round* 4 (5 January 1861), pp. 294–9 (298).
59. The Rev. J. G. Wood notes the end of the craze for aquaria in such terms: 'Some years ago, a complete aquarium mania ran through the country. Every one must needs have an aquarium, either of sea or fresh water, the former being preferred ... The fashionable lady had magnificent plate-glass aquaria in her drawing-room, and the schoolboy managed to keep an aquarium of lesser pretensions in his study. The odd corners of newspapers were filled with notes on aquaria, and a multitude of shops were opened for the simple purpose of supplying aquaria and their contents. The feeling, however, was like a hothouse plant, very luxuriant under artificial conditions, but failing when deprived of external assistance ... So, in due course of time, nine out of every ten aquaria were abandoned; many of the shops were given up, because there was no longer any custom; and to all appearance the aquarium fever had run its course, never again to appear, like hundreds of similar epidemics' (Rev. J. G. Wood, *The Fresh and Salt-Water Aquarium* (London, 1868), pp. 3–6, qtd in Barber, *Heyday of Natural History*, pp. 121–2).
60. See Stott, *Theatres of Glass*, p. 92.
61. In the Victorian period, the habits of aquarium animals were often read in moral terms as human moral standards tended to be projected upon aquarium creatures. See Christopher Hamlin, 'Robert Warington and the Moral Economy of the Aquarium', *Journal of the History of Biology* 19 (1986), pp. 131–53.
62. Charles Kingsley, *The Water-Babies: A Fairy Tale for a Land Baby* (London: Penguin, (1863) 1995), p. 75.

5 Nature Exposed: Charting the Wild Body in 'Little Red Riding Hood'

1. Jane Loudon, *The Young Naturalist; or, the travels of Agnes Merton and her mamma*, 3rd edn (London: Routledge, Warne, and Routledge, (1840) 1860), p. 177. The case is similar with the Dodo whose extinction results from the creature's failure to become domesticated.
2. Loudon, *Young Naturalist*, p. 80.
3. Barbara T. Gates, *Kindred Nature: Victorian and Edwardian Women Embrace the Living World* (Chicago and London: University of Chicago Press, 1998), p. 46.
4. Loudon, *Young Naturalist*, p. 70.
5. Carl Linnaeus's system of metaphors expressed plant sexuality by modelling it on human society.
6. Nina Auerbach, *Woman and the Demon: The Life of a Victorian Myth* (Cambridge, MA: Harvard University Press, 1982), p. 65.
7. Betsy Hearne, *Beauty and the Beast: Visions and Revisions of an Old Tale* (Chicago and London: University of Chicago Press, 1989), p. 43.
8. Harriet Ritvo, *The Animal Estate: The English and Other Creatures in the Victorian Age* (Cambridge, Massachusetts, and London: Harvard University Press, 1987), p. 3.
9. Ritvo, *Animal Estate*, p. 3.
10. Jack Zipes (ed.), *The Trials and Tribulations of Little Red Riding Hood*, 2nd edn (New York and London: Routledge, 1993), pp. 75–6.
11. Zipes (ed.), *Trials and Tribulations*, p. 43.
12. Walter de la Mare's 'Little Red Riding Hood' (1927) is a case in point. His Red Riding Hood is 'happy for hours together with nothing but a comb and a glass' and, when she comes out of the wolf's stomach, the first thing she does is 'to run off to the looking-glass and comb out her yellow curls and uncrumple her hood'; Walter de la Mare, 'Little Red Riding Hood' (1927), in Zipes (ed.), *Trials and Tribulations*, pp. 208–14 (214).
13. Zipes (ed.), *Trials and Tribulations*, p. 63.
14. Though there are many versions of 'Little Red Riding Hood', belonging both to the oral and the literary tradition, once Perrault had appropriated the story and adapted it for an upper-class audience at the end of the seventeenth century, 'it became practically impossible for either oral storytellers or writers not to take into account his version, and thus storytellers and writers became the conveyors of both the oral and literary tradition of this particular tale' (Zipes (ed.), *Trials and Tribulations*, p. 7).
15. Laurence Talairach-Vielmas, *Moulding the Female Body in Victorian Fairy Tales and Sensation Novels* (Aldershot: Ashgate, 2007), pp. 33–87.
16. Talairach-Vielmas, *Moulding the Female Body*, pp. 49–65.
17. Alfred Mills, 'Ye True Hystorie of Little Red Riding Hood or The Lamb in Wolf's Clothing' (1872), in Zipes (ed.), *Trials and Tribulations*, pp. 188–92 (188).
18. Ritchie's 'Little Red Riding Hood' was first published in the *Cornhill Magazine* 16 (Oct. 1867), pp. 440–73, then reprinted in Anne Isabella Thackeray

Ritchie, *Five Old Friends and a Young Prince* (London: Smith, Elder, 1868), pp. 151–225.

19. Ritchie, 'Little Red Riding Hood', *Five Old Friends and a Young Prince*, p. 155. All further references to this edition will be given parenthetically in the text.
20. Many Victorian alienists, such as Henry Maudsley (1835–1918), under-lined women's nervousness, lack of control and predisposition to hysteria. To give one mid-century example here, let us mention Dr Millingen, arguing that woman is 'less under the influence of the brain than the uterine system, the plexi of abdominal nerves, and irritation of the spinal chord; in her, a hysteric predisposition is incessantly predominating from the dawn of puberty' (Dr Millingen, *The Passions, or Mind and Matter* (London: John & Daniel A. Darling, 1848), p. 157).
21. In 'Bluebeard's Keys,' Mrs De Travers believes it is her duty to remain 'in the fashionable whirlpool' for her two daughters. Anne Isabella Thackeray Ritchie, 'Bluebeard's Keys', *Bluebeard's Keys and Other Stories* (London: Smith, Elder, 1874), pp. 1–118.
22. Harriet Louisa Childe-Pemberton, 'All My Doing; or Red Riding-Hood Over Again', *The Fairy Tales of Every Day* (1882), reprinted in Jack Zipes (ed.) *Victorian Fairy Tales: The Revolt of the Fairies and Elves* (New York and London: Routledge, 1987), pp. 209–48 (211). All further references to this edition will be given parenthetically in the text.
23. Gates, *Kindred Nature*, p. 46.
24. Loudon, *Young Naturalist*, pp. 1–2.
25. Michael Freeman, *Railways and the Victorian Imagination* (New Haven and London: Yale University Press, 1999), p. 49.
26. As Freeman notes, early railway guides, such as Wyld's *Great Western Railway Guide* of 1839, capitalized on their passengers' potential interest in geology (Freeman, *Railways and the Victorian Imagination*, p. 55).
27. To mention but two significant examples, it appears in the sensation novels of the 1860s, for instance in Rhoda Broughton's *Not Wisely but Too Well* (1867), in which the heroine twice attempts to elope with her lover (a married man) by train, or in Mrs Henry Wood's *East Lynne* (1861), in which the adulterous heroine is disfigured in a train crash and loses her illegitimate baby, which enables her to return to England and work unrecognized as a governess to her own children.
28. The pseudo-science of physiognomy was grounded on the premise that the human and animal kingdoms shared features whereby animals' temperamental features could exemplify humans' (see Lucy Hartley, *Physiognomy and the Meaning of Expression in Nineteenth-Century Culture* (Cambridge: Cambridge University Press, 2001). In the 1850s, the technological innovation of photography clearly marked the era of physiognomy and other (pseudo) sciences focused on reading and categorizing the human body: attempts to trace the close links between humans and animals underpinned scientific explorations of human character traits.

29. John V. Pickstone, *Ways of Knowing. A New History of Science, Technology and Medicine* (Chicago: University of Chicago Press, 2001).
30. Nancy Armstrong, *Fiction in the Age of Photography* (London; Cambridge, Massachusetts: Harvard University Press, (1999) 2002), p. 19. Armstrong deals here with Alphonse Bertillon and Francis Galton's attempts to read the criminal body.
31. The comparison is also prolonged through the narrator's name 'Pussy': as Childe-Pemberton compares her heroine with a cat, thereby enhancing woman's 'nature', her tamed version of the wolf fuses girl and wolf even more.
32. Armstrong, *Fiction in the Age of Photography*, p. 44.
33. Armstrong, *Fiction in the Age of Photography*, p. 71.
34. Zipes (ed.), *Trials and Tribulations*, p. 48.

6 Nature and the Natural World in Mary Louisa Molesworth's *Christmas-Tree Land*

1. The stress on the theme of death in both Fitzgerald's 'Cock Robin' pictures and taxidermic cases, Bown argues, reinforces the idea that the painter may have seen Potter's case. Nicola Bown, *Fairies in Nineteenth-Century Art and Literature* (Cambridge: Cambridge University Press, 2001), pp. 139–40.
2. Jane Cooper, *Mrs Molesworth: A Biography* (Crowborough: Pratts Folly Press, 2002), p. 109.
3. Barbara T. Gates, *Kindred Nature: Victorian and Edwardian Women Embrace the Living World* (Chicago and London: University of Chicago Press, 1998), p. 113.
4. Mrs Molesworth, 'Ask the Robin', *Fairies Afield* (London: Macmillan, 1911), pp. 1–59 (56).
5. Examples might be Sarah Catherine Martin's *The Comic Adventures of Old Mother Hubbard and Her Dog* (1805), William Roscoe's *The Butterfly's Ball* (1807) or Catherine Dorset's *The Peacock 'At Home', and Other Poems* (1807) – a few of them collected in John Harris's *Harris's Cabinet of Amusement and Instruction* (1807–9), as mentioned in Chapter 1; Peter Hunt et al. (eds), *Children's Literature: An Illustrated History* (Oxford: Oxford University Press, 1995), pp. 35–7.
6. Cooper, *Mrs Molesworth*, pp. 45–6.
7. Mary Louisa Molesworth, *Christmas-Tree Land* (London: Macmillan, 1884), p. 2. All references to this edition will be given in the text.
8. Letter to George Lillie Craik, 21 Jan. 1883, qtd in Cooper, *Mrs Molesworth*, p. 228.
9. Tess Cosslett, *Talking Animals in British Children's Fiction, 1786–1914* (Aldershot: Ashgate, 2006), p. 1.
10. Cosslett, *Talking Animals in British Children's Fiction*, p. 2.
11. Carole G. Silver, *Strange and Secret Peoples: Fairies and Victorian Consciousness* (Oxford: Oxford University Press, 1999), p. 42.
12. Carole G. Silver mentions how the occultist Charles W. Leadbeater placed fairies on an evolutionary tree to 'classify them in scientific fashion ... like

Cuvier or…Linnaeus' (Charles W. Leadbeater, *The Hidden Side of Things* (Adjar, India: Theosophical Publishing House, (1913) 1974), p. 123; and Edward Gardner (secretary of the Theosophical Society) believed fairies were '[a]llied to the lepidoptera, or butterfly genus' (Edward L. Gardner, *Fairies: The Cottingley Photographs and Their Sequels* (London: Theosophical Publishing House, 1945), p. 122); Silver, *Strange and Secret Peoples*, p. 54.

13. See Jennifer Tucker, *Nature Exposed: Photography as Eyewitness in Victorian Science* (Baltimore: Johns Hopkins University Press, 2005), pp. 65–125.

14. George Laurence Gomme's *English Traditional Lore* (1885), David MacRitchie's *The Testimony of Tradition* (1890) and *Fians, Fairies and Picts* (1895) compared fairies and pygmies. Similarly, Sir Edward Burnet Tylor in *Primitive Culture* (1871) contended that fairies were not highly developed beings, while Canon J. A. MacCulloch saw kings as primitive tribal chieftains and interpreted princesses' sleep as early tribal experiments with hypnosis in *The Childhood of Fiction* (1905) (Silver, *Strange and Secret Peoples*, pp. 44–8).

15. As Anita Moss contends, Molesworth 'enlists the dream vision to subvert the constraints of the moral tale so prevalent in Victorian children's literature'. Moss also argues that the dream vision, which Molesworth often uses as a central structural feature, may have been influenced by Chaucer's medieval dream visions *The Parlement of Foules* and *The Pearl* (Anita Moss, 'Mrs Molesworth: Victorian Visionary', *Lion and the Unicorn* 12.1 (1988), pp. 105–10 (106).

16. A citation from Christina Rossetti's 'Goblin Market' opens Chapter 4 as well, suggesting that women cannot resist the lure of the goblins' fruits.

17. Silva is a younger version of the godmother. They look strangely alike and differ only in their eyes. The tidy little house is thus a metaphor for the 'house of stories' that the godmother embodies.

18. Indeed, the godmother lays stress on the importance of the imagination: 'If you knew all about everything, and could see through everything, there wouldn't be much interest left. Nothing to find out or fancy. Oh, what a dull world!' (p. 71).

19. Marina Warner, *From the Beast to the Blonde: On Fairy Tales and Their Tellers* (London: Vintage, (1994) 1995), p. xx.

20. Victorian fiction often features women's premonitory dreams. In Charlotte Brontë's *Jane Eyre* (1847), the eponymous heroine has premonitory dreams foreshadowing the failure of her mariage. In Wilkie Collins's *The Woman in White* (1859–60), Anne Catherick's dreams on the eve of the heroine's marriage are also premonitory. In Mrs Henry Wood's *East Lynne* (1861), Mrs Hare experiences premonitory dreams as well which help the detectives find out who the real murderer is. What is interesting is that the women who have prophetic dreams often match the stereotype of the feminine ideal. Anne Catherick is an obedient asylum inmate who so much corresponds to the model patient that she fails to arouse the suspicion of the asylum guardians and manages to escape. Constructed as a victim, dressed in white, she is a modern Cinderella, as Barbara Fass Leavy has argued; Barbara Fass Leavy, 'Wilkie Collins' Cinderella: The History of

Psychology and *The Woman in White'*, *Dickens Studies Annual* 10 (1982), pp. 91–141. Likewise, Mrs Hare is a prototypical invalid. She stays by the fireplace all day long but she escapes the domestic boundaries of home at night through her dreams and plays the part of the detective without technically transgressing gendered roles and spheres.

21. Warner, *From the Beast to the Blonde*, p. 28.
22. See Alex Owen, *The Darkened Room: Women, Power, and Spiritualism in Late Victorian England* (Chicago: University of Chicago Press, 2004). It is interesting to note, moreover, that several women writers involved in spiritualism also wrote children's stories, such as Camilla Toulmin Crosland; see Sarah A. Willburn, *Possessed Victorians: Extra Spheres in Nineteenth-Century Mystical Writings* (Aldershot: Ashgate, 2006), p. 56.
23. Vision was more and more perceived as subjective throughout the nineteenth century, becoming 'physiological'. Numerous experiments with visual experience testify to the Victorians' concern with human vision and its defects. As Jonathan Crary contends, the visible 'escape[d] from the timeless order of the camera obscura and [became] lodged in another apparatus, within the unstable physiology and temporality of the human body'; Jonathan Crary, *Techniques of the Observer: On Vision and Modernity in the Nineteenth Century* (Cambridge, Massachusetts, and London: MIT Press, 1992), p. 70.
24. Marina Warner, *Phantasmagoria: Spirit Visions, Metaphors, and Media into the Twenty-First Century* (Oxford: Oxford University Press, 2006), p. 208.
25. Though Molesworth claimed such strange mysteries were often fraudulent attempts at fooling gullible ladies, she constantly noted coincidences and her fiction resonated with occult practices: 'I am far too sound and healthy to medle over much with those strange mysteries which no doubt we shall understand by & by...but which just now are so desecrated by fools and jugglers', qtd in Cooper, *Mrs Molesworth*, p. 102. Moreover, her ghost stories, such as 'Lady Farquhar's Old Lady', as Cooper surmises, may have been directly linked to her interest in coincidences and occult phenomena. Her belief in her own second sight would have encouraged her both to hear and to write ghost stories. A footnote in a publication of the Society for Psychical Research mentions one of Louisa Molesworth's stories as though it were a literal account of a personal experience (Cooper, *Mrs Molesworth*, p. 173). Similarly, 'The Story of the Rippling Train' follows so closely a case recounted in a book published in 1886 by the Society for Psychical Research that it is virtually certain Molesworth drew her story from this source (Cooper, *Mrs Molesworth*, p. 269). In 'Old Gervais. A Curious Experience' a female character communicates with a ghost; her dreamy voice recalls seance practices; Mary Louisa Molesworth, 'Old Gervais. A Curious Experience', *Studies and Stories* (London: A. D. Innes & Co., (1892) 1893), pp. 95–129. Peter, the owner of the magic table in 'A Magic Table', has also 'wandered some little way into the regions where few mortals are allowed to tread' and has had 'some dealings with beings of another kind of life than ours' (Molesworth, 'A Magic Table', *Fairies Afield* (London: Macmillan, 1911), pp. 60–120 (85)). 'The Weather Maiden

depicts a young girl who, with the help of fairy gifts, can predict the weather; her relationship with the fairy gifts – her 'extra sense' – depends on her sensitivity and receptivity (Molesworth, 'The Weather Maiden', *Fairies Afield*, pp. 121–75, p. 169).

26. See Laurence Talairach-Vielmas, 'Weaving the Threads of the Tapestry: Storyspinning in Mrs Molesworth's *The Tapestry Room* (1877)', *Women's Writing* 20.1 (2013), pp. 518–36.

27. Some of Molesworth's male characters could also have prophetic dreams, such as the Prince in 'Fairy Godmothers', the embedded tale in 'The Groaning Clock' (in Molesworth, *Fairies of Sorts*, pp. 3–137).

28. It may be worth mentioning again here the animal bridegroom tale in Mary de Morgan's 'The Hair Tree', which also uses an embedded story to underline the need to protect the environment: 'The Story of Trevina' relates the adventure of Trevina, an amateur naturalist who entertains herself by collecting animals and seaweed and who is punished by being captured by the king of the tortoises. In 'The Hair Tree' the queen is uncivil to a bird and starts losing her hair as a punishment; Mary Augusta de Morgan, 'The Hair Tree', *On a Pincushion and Other Fairy Tales* (London: Seeley, Jackson & Halliday, 1877), pp. 100–52.

29. 'The Raven' relates the story of a king's daughter turned into a raven and locked up in the castle of Stromberg. The king's daughter has premonitions which are proven true (she knows beforehand that the man who comes to rescue her will, in fact, be asleep and dreaming). To save her the man enters a dark forest and is led by a howling and crying. There he meets a giant who shows him the way to the castle of Stromberg. The castle stands on an inaccessible glass mountain. The man then hears three robbers who have a stick which strikes doors open, a mantle which makes one invisible and a horse which can ride up a glass mountain. He takes the magical objects and frees the king's daughter who agrees to marry him.

30. In 'The Twelve Brothers', a king wants to increase his daughter's wealth by killing her twelve brothers. The latter escape into the forest. The king's daughter enters the forest and finds her brothers, lives with them and keeps the house tidy until she plucks twelve flowers which change her brothers into ravens. She must remain dumb for seven years to set them free. A king finds the king's daughter and marries her; but she is suspected by her mother-in-law of being a common beggar girl and sentenced to death. The seven years expire just as she is being burnt and she is saved by her brothers. In 'The Seven Ravens', the daughter saves her brothers in the glass mountain by cutting off one of her fingers to use as a key. In 'The Six Swans', the six brothers are turned into swans by their stepmother and can only regain their human appearance for a quarter of an hour each evening; the sister saves them by remaining dumb, even when sentenced to death for being a cannibal.

31. It is significant that the tales were also individually revised throughout the various editions. As Maria Tatar explains, in the first edition of *Nursery and Household Tales* (*Kinder- und Hausmärchen*), 'The Twelve Brothers' showed a king who did not want to have a daughter and threatened his

wife with killing their twelve sons as a punishment; in the second edition, the king is so keen upon increasing his daughter's fortune that he is ready to sacrifice his twelve sons. See Maria Tatar, *The Hard Facts of the Grimms' Fairy Tales* (Princeton: Princeton University Press, 1987), p. 31.

32. Ruth B. Bottigheimer, *Grimms' Bad Girls and Bold Boys: The Moral and Social Vision of the Tales* (New Haven and London: Yale University Press, 1987), p. 168.

33. Bottigheimer, *Grimms' Bad Girls and Bold Boys*, p. 105.

7   Edith Nesbit's Fairies and Freaks of Nature: Environmental Consciousness in *Five Children and It*

1. A.L.O.E. [Charlotte Maria Tucker], *Fairy Know-A-Bit; or, a nutshell of knowledge* (London: T. Nelson & Sons, 1868), pp. 12–13.

2. Julia Briggs, *Edith Nesbit: A Woman of Passion* (Stroud: Tempus, (1987) 2007); Doris Langley Moore, *E. Nesbit: A Biography*, rev. edn (London: Ernest Benn, 1967).

3. Teya Rosenberg, 'Generic Manipulation and Mutation: E. Nesbit's Psammead Series as Early Magical Realism', in Raymond E. Jones (ed.), *E. Nesbit's Psammead Trilogy: A Children's Classic at 100* (Lanham, Toronto: Children's Literature Association; Oxford: Scarecrow Press, 2006), pp. 63–88 (69).

4. Edith Nesbit, *Wings and the Child; or the Building of Magic Cities* (London: Hodder and Stoughton, 1913), p. 27.

5. W. W. Robson believes, on the contrary, that Nesbit's fiction is not designed to be educational, as he argues in W. W. Robson, 'E. Nesbit and *The Book of Dragons*', in Gillian Avery and Julia Briggs (eds), *Children and Their Books: A Celebration of the Work of Iona and Peter Opie* (Oxford: Clarendon Press, 1989), pp. 251–70 (261).

6. Nesbit, *Wings and the Child*, pp. 24–6. A very similar remark appears in *The Enchanted Castle*: 'When you are young so many things are difficult to believe, and yet the dullest people will tell you that they are true – such things, for instance, as that the earth goes round the sun, and that it is not flat but round. But the things that seem really likely, like fairy-tales and magic, are, so say the grown-ups, not true at all' (Edith Nesbit, *The Enchanted Castle* (London: Puffin Classics, (1907) 1994), p. 27).

7. Science is also subject to irony: for instance, the Psammead's explanation for fossils (wished-for objects turned into stone) may be read as a potential ironical reversal of contemporary 'far-fetched "explanations" for fossils, such as that of the fundamentalist Philip Henry Gosse' (Briggs, *Edith Nesbit*, p. 233).

8. Edith Nesbit, *Five Children and It* (London: Penguin, (1902) 1995), p. 24. All further references are to this edition and will be given parenthetically in the text.

9. Rosenberg, 'Generic Manipulation and Mutation', p. 72.

10. David Rudd, 'Where It Was, There Shall Five Children Be: Staging Desire in *Five Children and It'*, in Jones (ed.), *E. Nesbit's Psammead Trilogy*, pp. 135–49 (140).

11. Gideon Algernon Mantell, *The Wonders of Geology; or, A Familiar Exposition of Geological Phenomena; Being the Substance of a Course of Lectures Delivered at Brighton*, 3rd edn, 2 vols (London: Relfe and Fletcher, (1838) 1839), I, p. 181, qtd in Lawrence Frank, *Victorian Detective Fiction and the Nature of Evidence: The Scientific Investigations of Poe, Dickens, and Doyle* (London now Basingstoke: Palgrave Macmillan, (2003) 2009), p. 25.

12. Nesbit's fiction often alludes to Carroll's Alice's books. In 'Melisande or Long and Short Division', the princess Melisande cannot stop growing and starts crying, before she remembers the scene in Carroll's *Alice's Adventures in Wonderland* ('Melisande or Long and Short Division', in Nina Auerbach and U. C. Knoepflmacher (eds) *Forbidden Journeys: Fairy Tales and Fantasies by Victorian Women Writers* (Chicago and London: University of Chicago Press, 1992), pp. 177–91 (185–6); the tale was originally published in *Nine Unlikely Tales*).

13. Education was for Nesbit shaped like a Palace: 'In the Palace of Education ... many stones will be needed – and so I bring the little stone I have hewn out and tried to shape, in the hope that it may fit into a corner of that great edifice' (Nesbit, *Wings and the Child*, p. 16). Moreover, for Nesbit the Crystal Palace epitomized the conflation of beauty and knowledge now vanished: 'Think of the imagination, the feeling for romance that went to the furnishing of the old Crystal Palace. There was a lake in the grounds of Penge Park ... How did these despised mid-Victorians deal with it? They set up, amid the rocks and reeds and trees of the island in that lake, life-sized images of the wonders of a dead world. On a great stone crouched a Pterodactyl, his vast wings spread for flight. A mammoth sloth embraced a tree, and I give you my word that when you came on him from behind, you, in your six years, could hardly believe that he was not real, that he would not presently leave the tree and turn his attention to your bloused and belted self ... There was an Ichthyosaurus too, and another chap whose name I forget, but he had a scalloped crest all down his back to the end of his tail. And the Dinosaurus ... he had a round hole in his antediluvian stomach: and, with a brother ... to give you a leg-up, you could explore the roomy interior of the Dinosaur with feelings hardly surpassed by those of bandits in a cave. It is almost impossible to overestimate the dinosaurus as an educational influence' (Nesbit, *Wings and the Child*, p. 48). The Crystal Palace is referred to in many of her works (at the beginning of 'The Ice Dragon' (in Edith Nesbit, *The Book of Dragons* (Mineola, New York: Dover Publications, [1900] 2004), in which the protagonists go to the North Pole (see Rosenberg, 'Generic Manipulation and Mutation', p. 70), in 'Whereyouwantogoto' (Edith Nesbit, 'Whereyouwantogoto', *Nine Unlikely Tales* (London: T. Fisher Unwin, 1901), pp. 49–84), *The Magic City* and *The Phoenix and the Carpet*), and underlies *The Enchanted Castle* in a particularly striking way.

14. Reprinted from the *Journal of the Society of Arts*, 78, reproduced as a leaflet by James Tennant, qtd in Steve MacCarthy, *The Crystal Palace Dinosaurs: The Story of the World's First Prehistoric Sculptures* (London: Crystal Palace Foundation, 1994), p. 89.

15. See, for instance, her description of fairies in *Nine Unlikely Tales* (1901).

16. '[I]nstead of imagining causes, one has collected facts' (Georges Cuvier, 'Espèces de quadrupèdes' (1801), trans. Martin J. S. Rudwick, in Martin J. S. Rudwick, *Georges Cuvier, Fossil Bones and Geological Catastrophes: New Translations and Interpretations of the Primary Texts* (Chicago and London: University of Chicago Press, 1997), pp. 45–58 (47).

17. Cuvier did not believe, however, that legends or ancient texts (including the Bible) should be read literally as revealing truths about natural history and the history of the earth; rather, he believed in the rigorous use of fictional accounts.

18. Tess Cosslett, *The 'Scientific Movement' and Victorian Literature* (Brighton: Harvester Press; New York: St. Martins Press, 1982), p. 30.

19. Cuvier's geology, which did not privilege the story of creation, was not only very often a first introduction to geology for many but also positioned the question of species extinction at the heart of studies of the earth and its inhabitants, perhaps for the first time. It was in 1813 that Cuvier's 'Preliminary Discourse' was published in English as *Essay on the Theory of the Earth* (trans. Robert Jameson, 3rd edn (Edinburgh and London: William Blackwood, 1817), over a decade after the first publication of *Recherche sur les ossemens fossiles* (1799). Cuvier's inclusion of ecological scenarios to explain extinction seemed thus to go against all biblical interpretation of natural history and the idea of God's creation as perfect. Still, Cuvier's catastrophism ensured his favourable reception in British scientific circles. See Ralph O'Connor, *The Earth on Show: Fossils and the Poetics of Popular Science, 1802–1856* (Chicago and London: University of Chicago Press, 2007), p. 61.

20. See his paper on living and fossil elephants : Georges Cuvier, 'Mémoire sur les espèces d'éléphans tant vivantes que fossiles, lu à la séance publique de l'Institut National le 15 germinal, an IV', *Magasin encyclopédique*, 2ème année, 3 (1796), pp. 440–5.

21. Cuvier, *Essay on the Theory of the Earth*, p. 86.

22. Nicolaas A. Rupke, *The Great Chain of History: William Buckland and the English School of Geology (1814–1849)* (Oxford: Clarendon Press, 1983), p. 132.

23. Rupke, *Great Chain of History*, p. 171.

24. Rupke, *Great Chain of History*, pp. 172–3.

25. Peter Parley [Samuel Clark], *Peter Parley's Wonders of the Earth, Sea, and Sky* (London: Darton and Clark, n.d.), p. 47.

26. Jan Bondeson, *A Cabinet of Medical Curiosities* (New York and London: Norton, (1997) 1999), pp. 203–14.

27. Carole G. Silver, *Strange and Secret Peoples: Fairies and Victorian Consciousness* (Oxford: Oxford University Press, 1999), pp. 118–19.

28. Silver, *Strange and Secret Peoples*, p. 129.

29. Silver, *Strange and Secret Peoples*, p. 129.

30. Silver, *Strange and Secret Peoples*, pp. 129–30.

31. George MacDonald, *The Princess and the Goblin* (1872), *The Princess and the Goblin and The Princess and Curdie*, ed. Roderick McGillis (Oxford and New York: Oxford University Press, 1990), p. 6.

32. Caroline Sumpter, *The Victorian Press and the Fairy Tale* (Basingstoke: Palgrave Macmillan, 2008), p. 39.

33. [Anon], 'A Lump of Coal', *Good Words for the Young* 1 (Dec. 1868), pp. 102–5 (102), qtd in Sumpter, *Victorian Press and the Fairy Tale*, p. 41.

34. Jessica Straley, 'Of Beasts and Boys: Kingsley, Spencer and the Theory of Recapitulation', *Victorian Studies* 49.3 (Summer 2007), pp. 583–609.

35. Amanda Hodgson, 'Defining the Species: Apes, Savages and Humans in Scientific and Literary Writing of the 1860s', *Journal of Victorian Culture* 4.2 (Autumn 1999), pp. 228–51 (230).

36. Hodgson, 'Defining the Species', p. 240.

37. Briggs, *Edith Nesbit*, p. 233.

38. Edith Nesbit, *The Story of the Amulet* (London: T. Fisher Unwin, 1906), p. 24. *The Story of the Amulet* even makes explicit that because the Psammead is a prehistoric creature, it may not be as mentally developed as the children: 'For a creature that had in its time associated with Megatheriums and Pterodactyls, its quickness was really wonderful.'

39. Silver, *Strange and Secret Peoples*, p. 150.

40. Gaby Wood, *Living Dolls: A Magical History of the Quest for Mechanical Life* (London: Faber & Faber, 2002), p. 228.

41. Susan Stewart, *On Longing: Narratives of the Miniature, the Gigantic, the Souvenir, the Collection* (Durham, North Carolina, and London: Duke University Press, 1993), p. xii.

42. Hunt and Sands underline 'the positive role of the other' in Kipling's *Puck of Pook's Hill*; Peter Hunt and Karen Sands, 'The View from the Center: British Empire and Post-Empire Children's Literature', in Roderick McGillis (ed.), *Voices of the Other: Children's Literature and the Postcolonial Context* (New York and London: Garland Publishing, 2000), pp. 39–53 (45).

43. Stewart, *On Longing*, p. 71.

44. Stewart, *On Longing*, p. 74.

45. Erin O'Connor, *Raw Material: Producing Pathology in Victorian Culture* (Durham, North Carolina, and London: Duke University Press, 2000), p. 180. Erin O'Connor argues that the display and frequent fictionalization of freaks in Victorian shows lifted them 'into a symbolic structure whose ultimate thrust was to depict the monstrous body as pure representation' (O'Connor, *Raw Material*, p. 180). His study also foregrounds the extent to which freaks were linked to Victorian economy, highlighting the 'vexed status of the human body under capitalism' (O'Connor, *Raw Material*, p. 167). His idea that 'monstrosity was the fairy tale of modern embodiment', equating the monstrous body with a wonderful machine well adapted to industrial society (except for freaks which were defined as throwbacks, of course, as is more the case in *Five Children and It* since

Nesbit uses the giant to parody growth and denounce capitalism and its commodification and exploitation of bodies), underlines once again the close links between natural wonders, science and the fairy tale.

46. Monica Flegel, 'A Momentary Hunger: Fabianism and Didacticism in E. Nesbit's Fiction', in Jones (ed.), *E. Nesbit's Psammead Trilogy*, pp. 17–38 (30).

47. Mavis Reimer, 'The Beginning of the End: Writing Empire in E. Nesbit's Psammead Books', in Jones (ed.), *E. Nesbit's Psammead Trilogy*, pp. 39–62 (44).

48. Nesbit, *Wings and the Child*, pp. 49–50.

49. See: [Elizabeth Eastlake], 'The Crystal Palace', *Quarterly Review* CXCII (March 1855), pp. 303–55; [Harriet Martineau], 'The Crystal Palace', *Westminster Review* 6 (1854), pp. 534–50; and [John Lindley], 'The Crystal Palace Gardens', *The Athenaeum* (1854), p. 780. For Lindley, 'Savages under a glass roof are neither more or less absurd than Saurian monsters in Penge Wood. The difficulty of a proper exhibition of these curiosities is one which exists in the nature of things, and which no artistic arrangement could remove. The juxtaposition is ridiculous: – but if the public will have savages and Saurians in their palace and park, they must reconcile their minds to the incongruity.'

50. This is similar in 'Fortunatus Rex & Co.' as well as in *The Story of the Amulet*, which features extinct species such as mammoths.

51. Nesbit, *Wings and the Child*, pp. 43–4.

52. Jane Barlow, *The End of Elfintown* (London: Macmillan & Co., 1894).

Epilogue

1. Rudyard Kipling, *Puck of Pook's Hill* (Ware: Wordsworth Editions, (1906) 1994).

2. John V. Pickstone, *Ways of Knowing: A New History of Science, Technology and Medicine* (Chicago: University of Chicago Press, 2001), p. 11.

Bibliography

Aikin, John, and Barbauld, Anna Lætitia, *Evenings at Home; or, the juvenile budget opened: consisting of a variety of miscellaneous pieces, for the instruction and amusement of young persons* (London: John Johnson, 1802–).

Alberti, Samuel J. M. M., 'The Museum Affect: Visiting Collections of Anatomy and Natural History', in Fyfe and Lightman (eds), *Science in the Marketplace*, pp. 371–403.

Allee, W. C., et al., *Principles of Animal Ecology* (Philadelphia and London: W. B. Saunders Co., 1949).

Allen, David Elliston, *The Naturalist in Britain: A Social History* (Princeton: Princeton University Press, (1976) 1994).

Allen, David Elliston, 'Tastes and Crazes', in Jardine, Secord and Spary (eds), *Cultures of Natural History*, pp. 394–407.

Allingham, William, *In Fairy Land. A series of pictures from the elf-world by Richard Doyle. With a poem by W. Allingham* (London: Longmans & Co., (1869) 1870).

A.L.O.E. [Charlotte Maria Tucker], *Fairy Know-A-Bit; or, a nutshell of knowledge* (London: T. Nelson & Sons, 1868).

Altick, Richard D., *The Shows of London* (Cambridge, Massachusetts, and London: Belknap, 1978).

Amartin-Serin, Annie, *La Création défiée : L'Homme fabriqué dans la littérature* (Paris : PUF, 1996).

Andersen, Hans Christian, 'The Dryad', trans. A. M. and Augusta Plesner, in *Aunt Judy's May-Day Volume for Young People* (London: Bell and Daldy, 1869), pp. 237–47 and 286–96.

[Anon.], *The Amusing History of Cinderella; or, the Little Glass Slipper* (London, 1850(?)).

[Anon.], *Cinderella; or, the Little Glass Slipper* (London: Dean & Son, 1870).

[Anon.], *Cinderella; or the little glass slipper* (London: Dean & Son, 1876).

[Anon.], *Cinderella and the Glass Slipper* (London: J. Bysh, 1861).

[Anon.], 'The Euphonia, or Speaking Automaton', *Illustrated London News* (25 July 1846), p. 59.

[Anon.], 'Fairy Tales', *Monthly Packet* 25 (Jan. 1878), pp. 80–94.

[Anon.], 'Good Friday, and a Better Friday', *All the Year Round* 13 (13 May 1865), pp. 373–6.

[Anon.], *The History of Cinderella and her Glass Slipper* (London: Orlando Hodgson, 1830(?)).

[Anon.], 'A Lump of Coal', *Good Words for the Young* 1 (Dec. 1868), pp. 102–5.

[Anon.], 'Paint, and No Paint', *All the Year Round* 7 (9 August 1862), p. 521.

[Anon.], 'Talking Machines', *All the Year Round* (24 September 1870), pp. 393–6.

[Anon.], 'Wonders of the Sea', *All the Year Round* 4 (5 January 1861), pp. 294–9.

Armstrong, Isobel, *Victorian Glassworlds: Glass Culture and the Imagination, 1830–1880* (Oxford and New York: Oxford University Press, 2008).

Armstrong, Nancy, *Fiction in the Age of Photography* (London and Cambridge, Massachusetts: Harvard University Press, (1999) 2002).

Auerbach, Nina, *Woman and the Demon: The Life of a Victorian Myth* (Cambridge, Massachusetts: Harvard University Press, 1982).

Auerbach, Nina, and Knoepflmacher, U. C. (eds), *Forbidden Journeys: Fairy Tales and Fantasies by Victorian Women Writers* (Chicago and London: University of Chicago Press, 1992).

Axton, W. F., 'Victorian Landscape Painting: A Change in Outlook', in Knoepflmacher and Tennyson (eds), *Nature and the Victorian Imagination*, pp. 281–308.

Barbauld, Anna Lætitia, *Lessons for Children* (London: Johnston & Co., (1778–9) 1812).

Barber, Lyn, *The Heyday of Natural History: 1820–1870* (Garden City, NY: Doubleday and Company, 1980).

Barlow, Jane, *The End of Elfintown* (London: Macmillan & Co., 1894).

Barrie, J. M., *Peter Pan* (Ware: Wordsworth Classics, (1904) 1993).

Beer, Gillian, *Darwin's Plots: Evolutionary Narrative in Darwin, George Eliot and Nineteenth-Century Fiction* (Cambridge: Cambridge University Press, (1983) 2000).

Benham, Michael Aislabie, *A Few Fragments of Fairyology, Shewing its Connection with Natural History* (Dunhelm: Will, Duncan & Son, 1859).

Bernstein, Susan David, 'Designs after Nature: Evolutionary Fashions, Animals, and Gender', in Deborah Denenholz Morse and Martin A. Danahay (eds), *Victorian Animal Dreams: Representations of Animals in Victorian Literature and Culture* (Aldershot: Ashgate, 2007), pp. 66–79.

Bondeson, Jan, *A Cabinet of Medical Curiosities* (New York and London: Norton, (1997) 1999).

Bottigheimer, Ruth B., *Grimms' Bad Girls and Bold Boys: The Moral and Social Vision of the Tales* (New Haven and London: Yale University Press, 1987).

Bown, Nicola, *Fairies in Nineteenth-Century Art and Literature* (Cambridge: Cambridge University Press, 2001).

Brewster, David, *Letters on Natural Magic, Addressed to Sir Walter Scott, Bart.* (London: John Murray, 1834).

Briggs, Julia, *Edith Nesbit: A Woman of Passion* (Stroud: Tempus, (1987) 2007).

Brightwen, Eliza, *More About Wild Nature* (London: Unwin, 1892).

Brock, William H., *Science for All: Studies in the History of Victorian Science and Education* (Aldershot: Varorium, 1996).

Brontë, Charlotte, *Jane Eyre* (Oxford: Oxford University Press, (1847) 1989).

Brough, John Cargill, *The Fairy Tales of Science: A Book for Youth* (London: Griffith and Farran, 1859).

Broughton, Rhoda, *Not Wisely But Too Well* (Dover: Alan Sutton, (1867) 1993).

Buckley, Arabella Burton, *The Fairy-Land of Science* (Chapel Hill: Yesterday's Classics, (1879) 2006).

Buckley, Arabella Burton, *Life and Her Children* (New York: D. Appleton & Co., (1880) 1881).

Buckley, Arabella Burton, *Moral Teachings of Science* (London: Edward Stanford, 1891).

Buckley, Arabella Burton, 'The Soul, and the Theory of Evolution', *University Magazine* 3 (1879), pp. 1–10.

Buckley, Arabella Burton, *Winners in Life's Race or the Great Backboned Family* (London: Edward Stanford, (1883) 1892).

Canton, Geoffrey, Dawson, Gowan, Gooday, Graeme, et al. (eds), *Science in the Nineteenth-Century Periodical: Reading the Magazine of Nature* (Cambridge: Cambridge University Press, 2004).

Carey, Annie, *The Wonders of Common Things* (London: Cassell, Peter, Galpin & Co., 1880).

Carlyle, Thomas, 'Signs of the Times', *Edinburgh Review* 49 (1829), pp. 439–59.

Carlyle, Thomas, *The Works of Thomas Carlyle* (London: G. Routledge & Sons, (1896–9) 1905–7).

Carroll, Lewis, *Through the Looking-Glass and What Alice Found There, The Annotated Alice*, ed. Martin Gardner (London: Penguin, (1871) 2001).

Childe-Pemberton, Harriet Louisa, 'All My Doing; or Red Riding-Hood Over Again' (1882), in Zipes (ed.), *Victorian Fairy Tales*, pp. 209–48.

Childe-Pemberton, Harriet Louisa, *The Fairy Tales of Every Day* (London: Christian Knowledge Society, 1882).

Collins, Wilkie, *The Woman in White* (Dover: Alan Sutton, (1860) 1992).

Cooper, Jane, *Mrs Molesworth: A Biography* (Crowborough: Pratts Folly Press, 2002).

Cooter, Roger, and Pumfrey, Stephen, 'Separate Spheres and Public Places: Reflections on the History of Science Popularisation and Science in Popular Culture', *History of Science* 32 (1994), pp. 237–67.

Cosslett, Tess, '"Animals under Man?" Margaret Gatty's *Parables from Nature*', *Women's Writing* 10.1 (2003), pp. 137–52.

Cosslett, Tess, 'Child's Place in Nature: Talking Animals in Victorian Children's Fiction', *Nineteenth-Century Contexts* 23 (2002), pp. 475–95.

Cosslett, Tess, *The 'Scientific Movement' and Victorian Literature* (Brighton: Harvester Press; New York : St. Martin's Press, 1982).

Cosslett, Tess, *Talking Animals in British Children's Fiction, 1786–1914* (Aldershot: Ashgate, 2006).

Crary, Jonathan, *Techniques of the Observer: On Vision and Modernity in the Nineteenth Century* (Cambridge, Massachusetts, and London: MIT Press, 1992).

Croker, Thomas Crofton, *Fairy Legends and Traditions of the South of Ireland* (London: John Murray, Thomas Tegg & Son, (1825–6) 1838).

Cruikshank, George, *Cinderella and the Glass Slipper* (London: D. Bogue, 1854).

Cuvier, Georges, 'Espèces de quadrupèdes' (1801), trans. Martin J. S. Rudwick, in Martin J. S. Rudwick, *Georges Cuvier, Fossil Bones and Geological*

Catastrophes: New Translations and Interpretations of the Primary Texts (Chicago and London: University of Chicago Press, 1997), pp. 45–58.

Cuvier, Georges, *Essay on the Theory of the Earth*, trans. Robert Jameson, 3rd edn (Edinburgh and London: William Blackwood, 1817).

Cuvier, Georges, 'Mémoire sur les espèces d'éléphans tant vivantes que fossiles, lu à la séance publique de l'Institut National le 15 germinal, an IV', *Magasin encyclopédique*, 2ème année, 3 (1796), pp. 440–5.

Darby, Margaret Flanders, 'Joseph Paxton's Water Lily', in Michel Conan (ed.), *Bourgeois and Aristocratic Cultural Encounters in Garden Art, 1550–1850* (Washington DC: Dumbarton Oaks Research Library and Collection, 2002), pp. 255–83.

Darwin, Charles, *The Origin of Species by Means of Natural Selection or the Preservation of Favoured Races in the Struggle for Life* (Oxford: Oxford University Press, (1859) 1998).

Daston, Lorraine J., and Park, Katharine, *Wonders and the Order of Nature, 1150–1750* (New York: Zone, 1998).

Dawson, Gowan, 'The *Cornhill Magazine* and the Shilling Monthlies in Mid-Victorian Britain', in Canton, Dawson, Gooday et al. (eds), *Science in the Nineteenth-Century Periodical*, pp. 123–50.

de la Mare, Walter, 'Little Red Riding Hood' (1927), in Zipes (ed.), *Trials and Tribulations*, pp. 208–14.

de Morgan, Mary Augusta, 'The Hair Tree', *On a Pincushion and Other Fairy Tales* (London: Seeley, Jackson & Halliday, 1877), pp. 100–52.

de Morgan, Mary Augusta, *The Necklace of Princess Fiorimonde and other Stories* (London: Macmillan & Co., 1880).

de Morgan, Mary Augusta, *The Necklace of Princess Florimonde and other stories being the Complete Fairy Tales of Mary de Morgan, with original illustrations by William de Morgan, Walter Crane, Olive Cockerell*, intr. Roger Lancelyn Green (London: Victor Gollancz, 1963).

de Morgan, Mary Augusta, *On a Pincushion and Other Fairy Tales* (London: Seeley, Jackson & Halliday, 1877).

de Morgan, Mary Augusta, (ed.), *Threescore Years and Ten: Reminiscences of the Late Sophia Elizabeth de Morgan* (London: Richard Bentley & Son, 1895).

de Morgan, Mary Augusta, 'A Toy Princess', in Zipes (ed.), *Victorian Fairy Tales*, pp. 165–74.

de Morgan, Mary Augusta, *The Windfairies and Other Tales* (London: Seeley & Co., 1900).

[de Morgan, Sophia E.], *From Matter to Spirit. The result of ten years' experience in spirit manifestations. Intended as a guide to enquirers* (London: Longman, Green, Longman, Roberts & Green, 1863).

Dickens, Charles, 'Fraud on the Fairies', *Household Words* 184 (1 Oct. 1853), p. 99.

[Dixon, E. S.], 'A Vision of Animal Existences', *Cornhill Magazine* 5 (March 1862), pp. 311–18.

Doane, Mary Ann, 'Technophilia: Technology, Representation, and the Feminine', in Jacobus, Keller and Shuttleworth (eds), *Body Politics*, pp. 163–76.

[Dodd, George], 'Dolls', *Household Words* 7.168 (11 June 1853), pp. 352–6.

Dorset, Catherine Ann Turner, *The Peacock 'At Home'* (London: John Harris, (1807) 1822).

du Chaillu, P. B., *Explorations and Adventures in Equatorial Africa, 1856–9* (London: John Murray, 1861).

[Eastlake, Elizabeth], 'The Crystal Palace', *Quarterly Review* CXCII (March 1855), pp. 303–55.

Eliot, George, *Middlemarch* (London: Penguin, (1871–2) 1989).

Ellegård, Alvar, *Darwin and the General Reader: The Reception of Darwin's Theory of Evolution in the British Periodical Press, 1859–72* (Chicago: University of Chicago Press, 1990).

Ewing, Juliana Horatia, 'Among the Merrows. A Sketch of a Great Aquarium', *Aunt Judy's Christmas Volume* (London: Bell and Daldy, 1873), pp. 44–57.

Ewing, Juliana Horatia, *A Great Emergency and Other Tales* (London: George Bell & Sons, 1877).

Ewing, Juliana Horatia, *Old-Fashioned Fairy Tales* (London: Society for Promoting Christian Knowledge, (1882) 1894).

Fielding, Sarah, *The Governess, or Little Female Academy* (London: Pandora, (1749) 1987).

Flegel, Monica, 'A Momentary Hunger: Fabianism and Didacticism in E. Nesbit's Fiction', in Jones (ed.), *E. Nesbit's Psammead Trilogy*, pp. 17–38.

Flint, Kate, *The Victorians and the Visual Imagination* (Cambridge: Cambridge University Press, 2000).

Foster, Hal, *Compulsive Beauty* (Cambridge, Massachusetts, and London: MIT Press, 1993).

Frank, Lawrence, *Victorian Detective Fiction and the Nature of Evidence: The Scientific Investigations of Poe, Dickens, and Doyle* (London, now Basingstoke: Palgrave Macmillan, (2003) 2009).

Freeman, Michael, *Railways and the Victorian Imagination* (New Haven and London: Yale University Press, 1999).

Fyfe, Aileen K., 'Copyrights and Competition: Producing and Protecting Children's Books in the Nineteenth Century', *Publishing History* 45 (1999), pp. 35–59.

Fyfe, Aileen K., ' "How the Squirrel Became a Squgg": The Long History of a Children's Book', *Paradigm* 27 (1999), pp. 25–37.

Fyfe, Aileen K., 'Reading Children's Books in Late Eighteenth-Century Dissenting Families', *Historical Journal* 43.2 (2000), pp. 453–73.

Fyfe, Aileen K., *Science and Salvation: Evanglical Popular Science Publishing in Victorian Britain* (Chicago and London: University of Chicago Press, 2004).

Fyfe, Aileen K. (ed.), *Science for Children*, 7 vols (Thoemmes Press, 2003).

Fyfe, Aileen, 'Tracts, Classics and Brands: Science for Children in the Nineteenth Century', in Julia Briggs, Dennis Butts and M. O. Grenby (eds), *Popular Children's Literature in Britain* (Aldershot: Ashgate, 2008), pp. 209–28.

Fyfe, Aileen K., 'Young Readers and the Sciences', in Marina Frasca-Spada and Nicholas Jardine (eds), *Books and the Sciences in History* (Cambridge: Cambridge University Press, 2000), pp. 276–90.

Fyfe, Aileen, and Lightman, Bernard (eds), *Science in the Marketplace: Nineteenth-Century Sites and Experiences* (Chicago and London: University of Chicago Press, 2007).

Gardner, Edward L., *Fairies: The Cottingley Photographs and Their Sequels* (London: Theosophical Publishing House, 1945).

Gates, Barbara T., *Kindred Nature: Victorian and Edwardian Women Embrace the Living World* (Chicago and London: University of Chicago Press, 1998).

Gates, Barbara T., 'Those Who Drew and Those Who Wrote: Women and Victorian Popular Science Illustration', in Shteir and Lightman (eds), *Figuring It Out*, pp. 192–213.

Gatty, Margaret, *British Sea-Weeds: Drawn from Professor Harvey's 'Phycologia Britannica'* (London: Bell & Daldy, 1863).

Gatty, Margaret, *Parables from Nature* (Chapel Hill: Yesterday's Classics, (1855–71) 2006).

Gaunt, William, and Clayton-Stamm, M. D. E., *William de Morgan* (London: Studio Vista, 1971).

Gere, Charlotte, 'In Fairyland', in Martineau (ed.), *Victorian Fairy Painting*, pp. 62–73.

Gifford, Isabella *The Marine Botanist: An Introduction to the Study of Algology* (London: Darton & Co., (1840) 1853).

Ginsburg, Carlo, *Clues, Myth, and the Historical Method* (Baltimore: Johns Hopkins University Press, 1992).

Goldney, Rev. S., 'Fables and Fairy Tales', *Aunt Judy's Annual Volume* (London: Hatchards, 1885), pp. 20–32.

Gomme, George Laurence, *English Traditional Lore* (London: Stock, 1885).

Gosse, Edmund, *The Naturalist of the Sea-shore, The Life of Philip Henry Gosse* (London, (1890) 1896).

Gosse, Philip Henry, *The Aquarium; an unveiling of the wonders of the deep sea* (London and Bath, 1854).

Gosse, Philip Henry, *Evenings at the Microscope; or, researches among the minuter organs and forms of animal life* (London: SPCK, 1859).

Gosse, Philip Henry, *A Naturalist's Rambles on the Devonshire Coast* (sn: sl, 1853).

Gosse, Philip Henry, *The Romance of Natural History* (New York: A. L. Burt Company, Publishers, (1860) 1902).

Green, Roger Lancelyn, 'Introduction', in de Morgan, *Necklace of Princess Florimonde and Other Stories Being the Complete Fairy Tales of Mary de Morgan*, pp. 7–13.

Greville, Robert Kaye, *Algae Britannicae; or, descriptions of the marine and other inarticulated plants of the British Islands, belonging to the order Algæ: with plates, illustrative of the genera* (Edinburgh, 1830).

Hamlin, Christopher, 'Robert Warington and the Moral Economy of the Aquarium', *Journal of the History of Biology* 19 (1986), pp. 131–53.

Haraway, Donna J., *Simians, Cyborgs, and Women: The Reinvention of Nature* (London: Free Association Books, 1991).

Hartland, Edwin Sidney, *The Science of Fairy Tales: An Inquiry into Fairy Mythology* (London: Walter Scott, 1891).

Hartley, Lucy, *Physiognomy and the Meaning of Expression in Nineteenth-Century Culture* (Cambridge: Cambridge University Press, 2001).

Harvey, W. H., *Manual of British Algae* (London, 1841).

Hearn, Michael Patrick (ed.), *The Victorian Fairy Tale Book* (New York: Pantheon Books, 1988).

Hearne, Betsy, *Beauty and the Beast: Visions and Revisions of an Old Tale* (Chicago and London: University of Chicago Press, 1989).

Hilgartner, Stephen, 'The Dominant View of Popularization: Conceptual Problems, Political Uses', *Social Studies of Science* 20 (1990), pp. 519–39.

Hilton, Mary, *Women and the Shaping of the Nation's Young: Education and Public Doctrine in Britain 1750–1850* (Aldershot: Ashgate, 2007).

[Hinton, James], 'The Fairy Land of Science', *Cornhill Magazine* 5 (Jan.–June 1862), pp. 36–42.

Hodgson, Amanda, 'Defining the Species: Apes, Savages and Humans in Scientific and Literary Writing of the 1860s', *Journal of Victorian Culture* 4.2 (Autumn 1999), pp. 228–51.

Hoffmann, E. T. A., *Tales* (New York: Continuum, 1982).

Hunt, Peter, et al. (eds), *Children's Literature: An Illustrated History* (Oxford: Oxford University Press, 1995).

Hunt, Peter, and Sands, Karen, 'The View from the Center: British Empire and Post-Empire Children's Literature', in Roderick McGillis (ed.), *Voices of the Other: Children's Literature and the Postcolonial Context* (New York and London: Garland Publishing, 2000), pp. 39–53.

Hutchinson, H. N., *The Autobiography of the Earth: A Popular Account of Geological History* (London: Edward Stanford, 1890).

Hutchinson, H. N., *Extinct Monsters: A Popular Account of Some of the Larger Forms of Ancient Animal Life* (London: Chapman & Hall, 1892).

Huxley, T. H., *Collected Essays*, vol. IX: *Evolution and Ethics and other essays* (Bristol: Thoemmes, (1886) 2001).

Ingelow, Jean, *Mopsa the Fairy* (1869), in Auerbach and Knoepflmacher (eds), *Forbidden Journeys*, pp. 215–316.

Inglis, Katherine, 'Becoming Automatous: Automata in *The Old Curiosity Shop* and *Our Mutual Friend*', *19: Interdisciplinary Studies in the Long Nineteenth Century* 6 (2008) <www.19.bbc.ac.uk> (accessed 3 Jan. 2014).

Jackson, Mary V., *Engines of Instruction, Mischief and Magic: Children's Literature in England from Its Beginnings to 1839* (Lincoln: University of Nebraska Press, 1989).

Jacobs, Joseph, *More English Fairy Tales* (London: D. Nutt, (1893) 1894).

Jacobus, Mary, Keller, Evelyn Fox, and Shuttleworth, Sally (eds), *Body Politics: Women and the Discourses of Science* (New York and London: Routledge, 1990)

Jardine, N., Secord, J., and Spary, E. (eds), *The Cultures of Natural History* (Cambridge: Cambridge University Press, 1996).

Jones, Raymond E. (ed.), *E. Nesbit's Psammead Trilogy: A Children's Classic at 100* (Lanham, Toronto: Children's Literature Association; Oxford: Scarecrow Press, 2006).

Katz, Wendy R., *The Emblems of Margaret Gatty: A Study of Allegory in Nineteenth-Century Children's Literature* (New York: AMS Press Inc., 1987).

Keightley, Thomas, *The Fairy Mythology: Illustrative of the Romance and Superstition of Various Countries* (London: George Bell & Son, (1828) 1892).

Kendall, May, Andrew Lang, *That Very Mab* (London: Longmans, Green & Co., 1885).

Kilner, Dorothy, *The Life and Perambulation of a Mouse* (London: John Marshall, (1783) 1815).

Kilner, Mary Ann, *The Adventures of the Pincushion designed chiefly for the use of young ladies* (London: Thomas Hughes, (1788) 1824).

Kingsley, Charles, *The Boys' and Girls' Book of Science* (London: Strahan & Co. Limited, 1881).

Kingsley, Charles, *Glaucus; or, the wonders of the shore* (London: Macmillan & Co., (1855) 1890).

Kingsley, Charles, 'How to Study Natural History', *Scientific Lectures and Essays* (London, Macmillan & Co., 1880), pp. 287–310.

Kingsley, Charles, *Madam How and Lady Why; or, First Lessons in Earth Lore for Children* (New York: Macmillan & Co., (1870) 1888).

Kingsley, Charles, 'Speech of Lord Dundreary in Section D, on Friday Last, on the Great Hippocampus Question', in *Charles Kingsley: His Letter and Memories of His Life; Edited by His Wife*, vol. 3, pp. 145–8 (London: Macmillan, 1901).

Kingsley, Charles, *The Water-Babies, a Fairy Tale for a Land Baby* (London: Penguin, (1863) 1995).

Kingsley, Charles, *Words of Advice to School-Boys by Charles Kingsley, Collected from Hitherto Unpublished Notes and Letters of the Late Charles Kingsley*, ed. E. F. Johns (London: Simpkin & Co., 1912).

Kipling, Rudyard, *Puck of Pook's Hill* (Harmondsworth: Penguin, (1906) 1987).

Kirby, Mary, and Kirby, Elizabeth, *The Sea and Its Wonders: A Companion Volume to 'The World at Home'* (London: T. Nelson & Sons, 1871).

Knoepflmacher, U. C., and Tennyson, G. B. (eds), *Nature and the Victorian Imagination* (Berkeley: University of California Press, 1977).

Krasner, James, *The Entangled Eye: Visual Perception and the Representation of Nature in Post-Darwinian Narrative* (New York and Oxford: Oxford University Press, 1992).

Kroeber, Karl, *Ecological Literary Criticism: Romantic Imaging and the Biology of Mind* (New York: Columbia University Press, 1994).

Lambourne, Lionel, 'Fairies and the Stage', in Martineau (ed.), *Victorian Fairy Painting*, pp. 46–53.

Larsen, Anne, 'Equipment for the Field', in Jardine, Secord and Spary (eds), *Cultures of Natural History*, pp. 358–77.

Leadbeater, Charles W., *The Hidden Side of Things* (Adjar, India: Theosophical Publishing House, (1913) 1974).

Leavy, Barbara Fass, 'Wilkie Collins' Cinderella: The History of Psychology and *The Woman in White'*, *Dickens Studies Annual* 10 (1982), pp. 91–141.

Levine, George, *Darwin and the Novelists: Patterns of Science in Victorian Fiction* (Chicago: University of Chicago Press, (1988) 1991).

Levine, George, *Darwin Loves You: Natural Selection and the Re-Enchantment of the World* (Princeton: Princeton University Press, 2006).

Lewes, George Henry, *The Foundations of a Creed*, 2 vols (London: Trübner, 1874–5).

Lightman, Bernard, 'Depicting Nature, Defining Roles: The Gender Politics of Victorian Illustration', in Shteir and Lightman (eds), *Figuring It Out*, pp. 214–39.

Lightman, Bernard, *Victorian Popularizers of Science: Designing Nature for New Audiences* (Chicago and London: University of Chicago Press, 2007).

Lightman, Bernard, ' "The Voices of Nature": Popularizing Victorian Science', in Bernard Lightman (ed.), *Victorian Science in Context* (Chicago and London: University of Chicago Press, 1997), pp. 187–211.

[Lindley, John], 'The Crystal Palace Gardens', *The Athenaeum* (1854), p. 780.

Locke, John, *Elements of Natural Philosophy . . . to which are added some thoughts concerning reading and study for a gentleman* (London, ?1750).

Locke, John, *Essay Concerning Human Understanding* (Brighton: Harvester Press, (1689) 1978).

Loudon, Jane, *Botany for Ladies; or, a popular introduction to the natural system of plants, according to the classification of De Candolle* (London: John Murray, 1842).

Loudon, Jane, *The First Book of Botany: being a plain and brief introduction to that science, for students and young persons* (London: George Bell, 1841).

Loudon, Jane, *The Young Naturalist; or, the travels of Agnes Merton and her mamma*, 3rd edn (London: Routledge, Warne, & Routledge, (1840) 1860).

Lyell, Charles, *Principles of Geology* (London: John Murray, (1830–3) 1834–5).

MacCarthy, Steve, *The Crystal Palace Dinosaurs: The Story of the World's First Prehistoric Sculptures* (London: Crystal Palace Foundation, 1994).

MacCullock, J. A. Canon, *The Childhood of Fiction: A Study of Folk Tales and Primitive Thought* (London: John Murray, 1905).

MacDonald, George, *The Princess and the Goblin and The Princess and Curdie*, ed. Roderick McGillis (Oxford and New York: Oxford University press, 1990).

MacRitchie, David, *Fians, Fairies, and Picts* (London: Kegan Paul, 1890).

MacRitchie, David, *The Testimony of Tradition* (London: Kegan Paul, 1890).

Mantell, Gideon Algernon, *The Wonders of Geology; or, A Familiar Exposition of Geological Phenomena; Being the Substance of a Course of Lectures Delivered at Brighton*, 3rd edn, 2 vols (London: Relfe and Fletcher, (1838) 1839).

Martin, Sarah Catherine, *The Comic Adventures of Old Mother Hubbard and Her Dog* (London: J. Harris, 1805).

[Martineau, Harriet], 'The Crystal Palace', *Westminster Review* 6 (1854), pp. 534–50.

Martineau, Jane (ed.), *Victorian Fairy Painting* (London: Royal Academy of Arts, 1997).

Merchant, Carolyn, *The Death of Nature: Women, Ecology and the Scientific Revolution* (San Francisco: Harper, (1980) 1989).

Merrill, Lynn L., *The Romance of Victorian Natural History* (Oxford, NY: Oxford University Press, 1989).

Miller, Andrew H., *Novels behind Glass: Commodity Culture and Victorian Narrative* (Cambridge: Cambridge University Press, 1995).

Miller, Hugh, *The Old Red Sandstone; or, new walks in an old field* (Edinburgh: John Johnston, 1841).

Millingen, Dr, *The Passions, or Mind and Matter* (London: John & Daniel A. Darling, 1848).

Mills, Alfred, 'Ye True Hystorie of Little Red Riding Hood or The Lamb in Wolf's Clothing' (1872), in Zipes (ed.), *Trials and Tribulations of Little Red Riding Hood*, pp. 188–92.

Molesworth, Mary Louisa, *Christmas-Tree Land* (London: Macmillan, 1884).

Molesworth, Mary Louisa, *Fairies Afield* (London: Macmillan, 1911).

Molesworth, Mary Louisa, *Fairies of Sorts* (London: Macmillan, 1908).

Molesworth, Mary Louisa, *Nurse Heatherdale's Story* (London: Macmillan, 1891).

Molesworth, Mary Louisa, *She Was Young and He Was Old: A Novel* (London, 1872).

Molesworth, Mary Louisa, *Studies and Stories* (London: A. D. Innes & Co., (1892) 1893).

Moon, Marjorie, *John Harris's Books for Youth, 1801–1843* (Cambridge: Five Owls Press, 1976).

Moon, Marjorie, *A Supplement to John Harris's Books for Youth* (Richmond: Five Owns Press, 1983).

Moore, Doris Langley, *E. Nesbit: A Biography*, rev. edn (London: Ernest Benn, 1967).

Moss, Anita, 'Mrs Molesworth: Victorian Visionary', *Lion and the Unicorn* 12.1 (1988), pp. 105–10.

Myers, Greg, 'Science for Women and Children: The Dialogue of Popular Science in the Nineteenth Century', in John Christie and Sally Shuttleworth (eds), *Nature Transfigured: Science and Literature, 1700–1900* (Manchester: Manchester University Press, 1989), pp. 171–200.

Myers, Mitzi, 'Impeccable Governesses, Rational Dames, and Moral Mothers: Mary Wollstonecraft and the Female Tradition in Georgian Children's Books', *Children's Literature* 14 (1986), pp. 31–59.

Nesbit, Edith, *The Book of Dragons* (Mineola, New York: Dover Publications, (1900) 2004).

Nesbit, Edith, *The Enchanted Castle* (London: Puffin Classics, (1907) 1994).

Nesbit, Edith, *Five Children and It* (London: Penguin, (1902) 1995).

Nesbit, Edith, *The Magic City* (Charleston, South Carolina: BiblioBazaar, (1910) 2007).

Nesbit, Edith, 'Melisande or Long and Short Division', in Auerbach and Knoepflmacher (eds), *Forbidden Journeys*, pp. 177–91.

Nesbit, Edith, *Nine Unlikely Tales* (London: T. Fisher Unwin, 1901).

Nesbit, Edith, *The Phoenix and the Carpet* (London: T. Fisher Unwin, (1904) 1908).

Nesbit, Edith, *The Story of the Amulet* (London: T. Fisher Unwin, 1906).

Nesbit, Edith, *The Story of the Treasure Seekers* (Ware: Wordsworth Classics, (1899) 1995).

Nesbit, Edith, *Wings and the Child; or the Building of Magic Cities* (London: Hodder and Stoughton, 1913).

Nesbit, Edith, *The Wouldbegoods* (London: T. Fisher Unwin, 1901).

Newbery, John, *A Little Pretty Pocket-Book, intended for the instruction and amusement of little Master Tommy* (London: John Newbery, (1744) 1760).

Nickel, Douglas, 'Talbot's Natural Magic', *History of Photography* 26.2 (Summer 2002), pp. 132–40.

Noakes, Richard, 'The *Boy's Own Paper* and Late-Victorian Juvenile Magazines', in Canton, Dawson, Gooday et al. (eds), *Science in the Nineteenth-Century Periodical*, pp. 151–71.

O'Connor, Erin, *Raw Material: Producing Pathology in Victorian Culture* (Durham, North Carolina, and London: Duke University Press, 2000).

O'Connor, Ralph, *The Earth on Show: Fossils and the Poetics of Popular Science, 1802–1856* (Chicago and London: University of Chicago Press, 2007).

O'Gorman, Francis, 'Victorian Natural History and the Discourses of Nature in Charles Kingsley's *Glaucus*', *Worldviews: Environment, Culture, Religion* 2.1 (April 1998), pp. 21–35.

Oersted, Hans Christian, *The Soul in Nature: With Supplementary Contributions*, trans. Leonora and Joanna B. Horner (London: H. G. Bohn, 1852).

Opie, Iona, and Opie, Peter, *Classic Fairy Tales* (Oxford: Oxford University Press, 1974).

Oppenheim, Janet, *The Other World: Spiritualism and Psychical Research in England, 1850–1914* (Cambridge: Cambridge University Press, 1985).

Orford, Pete, 'Dickens and Science Fiction: A Study of Artificial Intelligence in *Great Expectations*', *19: Interdisciplinary Studies in the Long Nineteenth Century* 10 (2010) <www.19.bbc.ac.uk> (accessed 3 Jan. 2014).

Ospovat, Dov, *The Development of Darwin's Theory: Natural History, Natural Theology, and Natural Selection, 1838–1859* (Cambridge: Cambridge University Press, 1981).

Owen, Alex, *The Darkened Room: Women, Power, and Spiritualism in Late Victorian England* (Chicago: University of Chicago Press, 2004).

Owen, Richard, 'On the Aye-Aye (*Chiromus*, Cuvier; *Chiromus madagascariensis*, Desm.; *Sciurus madagascariensis*, Gmel., Sonnerat; *Lemur psilodactylus*, Schreber, Shaw)', *Transactions of the Zoological Society* 5, pt 2 (1863), pp. 33–101.

Owen, Richard, 'On the Zoological Significance of the Cerebral and Pedal Characters of Man', *BAAS Report 1862* (1862), pp. 116–18.

Paradiz, Valerie, *Clever Maids: The Secret History of the Grimm Fairy Tales* (New York: Perseus Books, (2004) 2005).

Parley, Peter [Samuel Clark], *Peter Parley's Wonders of the Earth, Sea, and Sky* (London: Darton & Clark, n.d.).

Pepper, John Henry, *The Boys' Playbook of Science* (London: George Routledge & Sons, (1860) 1881).

Pickstone, John V., *Ways of Knowing: A New History of Science, Technology and Medicine* (Chicago: University of Chicago Press, 2001).

Price, Derek de Solla, 'Automata and the Origins of Mechanism and Mechanistic Philosophy', *Technology and Culture* 5.1 (Winter 1964), pp. 9–23.

Rauch, Alan, 'Mentoria: Women, Children, and the Structures of Science', *Nineteenth-Century Contexts* 27.4 (Dec. 2005), pp. 335–51.

Rauch, Alan, 'Parables and Parodies: Mrs. Gatty's Audiences in the *Parables from Nature*', *Children's Literature* 25 (1997), pp. 137–52.

Rauch, Alan, *Useful Knowledge: The Victorians, Morality, and the March of Intellect* (Durham, North Carolina: Duke University Press, 2001).

Reimer, Mavis, 'The Beginning of the End: Writing Empire in E. Nesbit's Psammead Books', in Jones (ed.), *E. Nesbit's Psammead Trilogy*, pp. 39–62.

Richards, Thomas, *The Commodity Culture of Victorian England: Advertising and Spectacle, 1851–1914* (Stanford: Stanford University Press, 1990).

Ritchie, Anne Isabella Thackeray, 'Beauty and the Beast' (1867), in Auerbach and Knoepflmacher (eds), *Forbidden Journeys*, pp. 35–74.

Ritchie, Anne Isabella Thackeray, *Bluebeard's Keys and Other Stories* (London: Smith, Elder, 1874).

Ritchie, Anne Isabella Thackeray, *A Book of Sibyls: Mrs. Barbauld, Miss Edgeworth, Mrs. Opie, Miss Austen* (Leipzig, Bernhard Tauchnitz, 1883).

Ritchie, Anne Isabella Thackeray, 'Cinderella' (1868), in Zipes (ed.), *Victorian Fairy Tales*, pp. 101–26.

Ritchie, Anne Isabella Thackeray, (ed.), *The Fairy Tales of Madame d'Aulnoy* (London: Lawrence & Bullen, 1892).

Ritchie, Anne Isabella Thackeray, *Five Old Friends and a Young Prince* (London: Smith, Elder, 1868).

Ritchie, Anne Isabella Thackeray, 'Little Red Riding Hood', *Five Old Friends and a Young Prince*, pp. 151–225.

Ritchie, Anne Isabella Thackeray, 'Maids-of-All-Work and Blue Books', *Cornhill Magazine* 30 (1874), pp. 281–96.

Ritchie, Anne Isabella Thackeray, *Miss Williamson's Divagations* (London: Smith, Elder, 1881).

Ritchie, Anne Isabella Thackeray, *To Esther and Other Sketches* (London: Smith, Elder, 1869).

Ritchie, Anne Isabella Thackeray, *Toilers and Spinsters, and Other Essays* (London: Smith, Elder, 1874).

Ritvo, Harriet, *The Animal Estate: The English and Other Creatures in the Victorian Age* (Cambridge, Massachusetts, and London: Harvard University Press, 1987).

Ritvo, Harriet, 'Learning from Animals: Natural History for Children in the Eighteenth and Nineteenth Centuries', *Children's Literature* 13 (1985), pp. 72–93.

Robson, W. W., 'E. Nesbit and *The Book of Dragons*', in Gillian Avery and Julia Briggs (eds), *Children and Their Books: A Celebration of the Work of Iona and Peter Opie* (Oxford: Clarendon Press, 1989), pp. 251–70.

Roscoe, Sidney, *John Newbery and His Successors, 1740–1814: A Bibliography* (Wormsley: Five Owls Press, 1973).

Roscoe, William, *The Butterfly's Ball, and the Grasshopper's Feast* (London, (1807) 1855).

Rosenberg, Teya, 'Generic Manipulation and Mutation: E. Nesbit's Psammead Series as Early Magical Realism', in Jones (ed.), *E. Nesbit's Psammead Trilogy*, pp. 63–88.

Rossetti, Christina, *Poems and Prose*, ed. Jan Marsh (London: Everyman, (1994) 2001).

Rudd, David, 'Where It Was, There Shall Five Children Be: Staging Desire in *Five Children and It*', in Jones (ed.), *E. Nesbit's Psammead Trilogy*, pp. 135–49.

Rupke, Nicolaas A., *The Great Chain of History: William Buckland and the English School of Geology (1814–1849)* (Oxford: Clarendon Press, 1983).

Rupke, Nicolaas A., *Richard Owen: Biology without Darwin, a Revised Edition* (Chicago and London: University of Chicago Press, (1994) 2009).

Saintine, X. B. [Joseph Xavier Boniface], *The Fairy Tales of Science: Being the Adventures of the Three Sisters, Animalia, Vegetalia, and Mineralia* (London: Ward, Lock & Co., 1886).

Schaffer, Simon, 'Babbage's Dancer and the Impresarios of Mechanism', in Francis Spufford and Jenny Uglow (eds), *Cultural Babbage: Technology, Time and Invention* (London, Boston: Faber & Faber, 1996), pp. 52–80.

Secord, James A., *Victorian Sensation: The Extraordinary Publication, Deception and Secret Authorship of* Vestiges of the Natural History of Creation (Chicago: University of Chicago Press, 2000).

Sewell, Anna, *Black Beauty* (Oxford: Oxford University Press, (1877) 1931).

Sherwood, Mary Martha, *The History of the Fairchild Family; or the Child's Manual* (London: T. Hatchard, (1818) 1853–4).

Shteir, Ann B., *Cultivating Women, Cultivating Science: Flora's Daughters and Botany in England 1760–1860* (Baltimore and London: Johns Hopkins University Press, 1996).

Shteir, Ann B., and Lightman, Bernard (eds), *Figuring It Out: Science, Gender, and Visual Culture* (Hanover and London: University Press of New England, 2006).

Shuttleworth, Sally, 'Female Circulation: Medical Discourse and Popular Advertising in the Mid-Victorian Era', in Jacobus, Keller and Shuttleworth (eds), *Body Politics*, pp. 47–68.

Silver, Carole G., *Strange and Secret Peoples: Fairies and Victorian Consciousness* (Oxford: Oxford University Press, 1999).

Slack, Henry James, *Marvels of Pond-Life; or, a Year's Microscopic Recreations among the Polyps, Infusoria, etc.* (London, 1861).

Smajic, Srdjan, *Ghost-Seers, Detectives and Spiritualists: Theories of Vision in Victorian Literature and Science* (Cambridge: Cambridge University Press, 2010).

Smith, Jonathan, *Charles Darwin and Victorian Visual Culture* (Cambridge: Cambridge University Press, 2006).

Smith, Jonathan, *Fact and Feeling: Baconian Science and the Nineteenth-Century Literary Imagination* (Madison and London: University of Wisconsin Press, 1994).

Spary, Emma, 'Political, Natural, and Bodily Economies', in Jardine, Secord and Spary (eds), *Cultures of Natural History*, pp. 178–96.

Spencer, Herbert, *Education: Intellectual, Moral, and Physical* (London: Williams & Norgate, (1861) 1888).

Stauffer, Robert C., 'Haeckel, Darwin, and Ecology', *Quarterly Review of Biology* 32 (1957), pp. 138–44.

Stewart, Susan, *On Longing: Narratives of the Miniature, the Gigantic, the Souvenir, the Collection* (Durham, North Carolina, and London: Duke University Press, 1993).

Stott, Rebecca, *Theatres of Glass: The Woman who Brought the Sea to the City* (London: Short Books, 2003).

Straley, Jessica, 'Of Beasts and Boys: Kingsley, Spencer and the Theory of Recapitulation', *Victorian Studies* 49.3 (Summer 2007), pp. 583–609.

Sumpter, Caroline, 'Making Socialists or Murdering to Dissect? Natural History and Child Socialization in the *Labour Prophet* and *Labour Leader*', in Louise Henson, Geoffrey Cantor, Gowan Dawson et al. (eds), *Culture and Science in the Nineteenth-Century Media* (Aldershot: Ashgate, 2004), pp. 29–55.

Sumpter, Caroline, *The Victorian Press and the Fairy Tale* (Basingstoke: Palgrave Macmillan, 2008).

Talairach-Vielmas, Laurence, *Moulding the Female Body in Victorian Fairy Tales and Sensation Novels* (Aldershot: Ashgate, 2007).

Talairach-Vielmas, Laurence, 'Rewriting *Little Red Riding-Hood*: Victorian Fairy Tales and Mass Visual Culture', *Lion and the Unicorn* 33.3 (2009), pp. 259–81.

Talairach-Vielmas (ed.), *Science in the Nursery: The Popularisation of Science in Britain and France, 1761–1901* (Newcastle: Cambridge Scholars Publishing, 2011).

Talairach-Vielmas, Laurence, 'Victorian Children's Literature and the Natural World: Parables, Fairy Tales and the Construction of "Moral Ecology"', in Jennifer Harding, Elizabeth Thiel and Alison Waller (eds), *Deep into Nature: Ecology, Environment and Children's Literature* (Lichfield: Pied Piper Publishing, 2009), pp. 222–47.

Talairach-Vielmas, Laurence, 'Weaving the Threads of the Tapestry: Storyspinning in Mrs. Molesworth's *The Tapestry Room* (1877)', *Women's Writing* 20.1 (2013), pp. 518–36.

Tatar, Maria, *The Hard Facts of the Grimms' Fairy Tales* (Princeton: Princeton University Press, 1987).

Tennyson, Alfred Lord, *In Memoriam*, ed. Michael Davis (London: Macmillan, (1850) 1956).

Thackeray, William Makepeace, *The Letters and Private Papers of William Makepeace Thackeray*, 4 vols, ed. Gordon N. Ray (London: Oxford University Press, 1946).

Topman, Jonathan, 'Science, Natural Theology, and the Practice of Christian Piety in Early Nineteenth-Century Religious Magazines', in Geoffrey Canto and Sally Shuttleworth (eds), *Science Serialized, Representations of the Sciences in Nineteenth-Century Periodicals* (Cambridge, Massachusetts: MIT Press, 2003), pp. 37–66.

Trimmer, Mrs Sarah, *An Easy Introduction to the Knowledge of Nature, and reading the holy scriptures, adapted to the capacities of children* (London: T. Longman and G. Robinson, (1780) 1787).

Trimmer, Mrs Sarah, *Fabulous Histories: Designed for the Instruction of Children Respecting Their Treatment of Animals* (London: J. G. & F. Rivington, (1786) 1838).

Tucker, Jennifer, *Nature Exposed: Photography as Eyewitness in Victorian Science* (Baltimore: Johns Hopkins University Press, 2005).

Tylor, Sir Edward Burnett, *Primitive Culture: Researches into the Development of Mythology, Philosophy, Religion, Art and Custom* (London: John Murray, 1871).

Tylor, Sir Edward Burnett, *Researches into the Early History of Mankind and the Development of Civilization* (London: John Murray, 1865).

Tyndall, John, *Essays on the Use and Limit of the Imagination in Science*, 2nd edn (London: Longmans, 1870).

Tyndall, John, 'Scientific Use of the Imagination', *Fragments of Science for Unscientific People* (London: Longmans, Green, & Co., 1871), pp. 125–67.

Uglow, Jenny, *Nature's Engraver: A Life of Thomas Bewick* (London: Faber and Faber; New York: Farrar, Straus & Giroux, 2006).

Vaucanson, Jacques, *Account of the Mechanism of an Automaton, or Image Playing on the German-Flute: As it was presented in a Memoire, to the Gentlemen of the Royal Academy of Sciences at Paris*, trans. J. T. Desaguliers (London: T. Parker, 1742).

Villiers de L'Isle-Adam, Auguste, *L'Eve future*, éd. Alan Raitt (Paris : Gallimard, (1886) 1993).

Warner, Marina, *From the Beast to the Blonde: On Fairy Tales and Their Tellers* (London: Vintage, (1994) 1995).

Warner, Marina, *Phantasmagoria: Spirit Visions, Metaphors, and Media into the Twenty-First Century* (Oxford: Oxford University Press, 2006).

Watts, Isaac, *Divine Songs, Attempted in Easie Language for the Use of Children* (Coventry: M. Luckman, (1715) 1800).

Whitley, Richard, 'Knowledge Producers and Knowledge Acquirers: Popularisation as a Relation between Scientific Fields and Their Publics', in Terry Shinn and Richard Whitley (eds), *Expository Science: Forms and Functions of Popularisation* (Dordrecht: D. Reidel Publishing Company, 1985), pp. 3–28.

Wiegleb, Johann Christian, *Unterricht in der natürlichen Magie* (Berlin, 1779).

Willburn, Sarah A., *Possessed Victorians: Extra Spheres in Nineteenth-Century Mystical Writings* (Aldershot: Ashgate, 2006).

[Wills, W. H., and Sala, George A.], 'Fairyland in 'fifty-four', *Household Words* 193 (3 Dec. 1853), pp. 313–17.

Wilson, Daniel, *Caliban: The Missing Link* (London: Macmillan & Co., 1873).

Wood, Christopher, *Fairies in Victorian Art* (Woodbridge: Antique Collectors' Club, 2000).

Wood, Gaby, *Living Dolls: A Magical History of the Quest for Mechanical Life* (London: Faber & Faber, 2002).

Wood, Mrs Henry, *East Lynne* (London: Everyman's Library, (1861) 1988).

Wood, Rev. J. G., *Common Objects of the Country* (London: Routledge, 1858).

Wood, Rev. J. G., *The Fresh and Salt-Water Aquarium* (London, 1868).

Wood, Rev. J. G., *Insects at Home: being a popular account of British insects, their structure, habits, and transformations* (London: Longmans, Green, 1872).

Wood, Rev. J. G., 'On Killing, Setting, and Preserving Insects. I–Killing', *Boy's Own Paper* 1 (1879), pp. 431–2.

Wyatt, Mary, *Algae Danmonienses; Or, dried specimens of marine plants, principally collected in Devonshire; Carefully named according to Dr Hooker's British Flora* (Torquay: Cockrem, 1833).

Zipes, Jack, *Fairy Tales and the Art of Subversion: The Classical Genre for Children and the Process of Civilization* (London: Heinemann, 1983).

Zipes, Jack (ed.), *The Trials and Tribulations of Little Red Riding Hood*, 2nd edn (New York and London: Routledge, 1993).

Zipes, Jack (ed.), *Victorian Fairy Tales: The Revolt of the Fairies and Elves* (London: Routledge, 1987).

Index

Printed and bound by CPI Group (UK) Ltd, Croydon, CR0 4YY